Every Woman's Dream

Also by Mary Monroe

The Neighbors Series
One House Over

The Lonely Heart, Deadly Heart Series
Every Woman's Dream
Can You Keep a Secret?
Never Trust a Stranger
The Devil You Know

Mama Ruby Series
Mama Ruby
The Upper Room
Lost Daughters

The God Series
God Don't Like Ugly
God Still Don't Like Ugly
God Don't Play
God Ain't Blind
God Ain't Through Yet
God Don't Make No Mistakes

Gonna Lay Down My Burdens
Red Light Wives
In Sheep's Clothing
"Nightmare in Paradise" in *Borrow Trouble*
Deliver Me From Evil
She Had It Coming
The Company We Keep
Family of Lies
Bad Blood
Remembrance

Published by Kensington Publishing Corp.

Every Woman's Dream

MARY MONROE

Dafina Books

KENSINGTON BOOKS
http://www.kensingtonbooks.com

To the extent that the image or images on the cover of this book depict a person or persons, such person or persons are merely models, and are not intended to portray any character or characters featured in the book.

DAFINA BOOKS are published by

Kensington Publishing Corp.
119 West 40th Street
New York, NY 10018

London Borough of Barking & Dagenham	
90600000151416	
Askews & Holts	13-Aug-2018
AF GNR	£6.99
BDBAR	

All _____ts, and distributed ____ __e available
at _____ es promo-
tio_____l use.

Sp__ _____rpts or cu_____d _____ ___ ____ be created
to ____ _____s. For de_____ __le or phone the ___fice of the
Ke_____r S_____ _____ _____es Depart-
me__ _____ __op Publishing Corp., 119 West 40th _____treet, New
Yo_____

Dafina and the Dafina logo Reg. U.S. Pat. & TM Off.

ISBN-13: 978-1-61773-802-9
ISBN-10: 1-61773-802-6
First Kensington Hardcover Edition: June 2016
First Kensington Trade Edition: January 2017
First Kensington Mass Market Edition: August 2018

eISBN-13: 978-1-61773-799-2
eISBN-10: 1-61773-799-2

10 9 8 7 6 5 4 3 2 1

Printed in the United States of America

This book is dedicated to my fans. You are all #1 to me!

Acknowledgments

My acknowledgments would be longer than this book if I thanked each person individually for my success. I'm taking the easy way out this time. Thanks to EVERY-ONE who helped me make it this far!

This is book #1 in my Lonely Heart, Deadly Heart Series.

Chapter 1

Lola

September 1999

TWO WEEKS AFTER LABOR DAY, SOMEBODY RANG OUR doorbell. It was a Saturday, about an hour before noon. When I opened the door without looking through the peephole or asking who it was, I was surprised to see a woman—I had never seen her before—standing on our porch. She was almost as wide as she was tall, and she had to be at least six feet. She was a light-skinned, middle-aged black woman with a scary scowl on her face and one hand on her hip. She wore a dark green pantsuit that looked like it was at least two sizes too small. There were a few strands of gray hair on her two chins and several black moles dotted her thick neck. I could tell she had been crying because her eyes were red and swollen.

"I'm sorry, ma'am. No solicitors," I said, pointing to

the NO SOLICITORS sign that my stepmother had made me tack on the wall outside next to the doorbell. It was not my nature to be mean to strangers, so I smiled.

The woman didn't smile back and the scowl on her face was even scarier now. She narrowed her eyes and gave me a skeptical look. Her short, reddish brown wig sat at such a crooked angle on her head, the bangs that should have been above her eyes were on the side of her face. There was bright red lipstick smeared on her teeth and she had on two different earrings. On top of everything else that was off, this creature had dressed in such a hurry, she had buttoned only the three top buttons on her blouse.

"Fuck that damn shit! I didn't come to this goddamn place to sell a motherfucking thing, so you can forget about that 'no solicitors' bullshit!" she screeched with spit flying out both sides of her mouth. I knew a lot of people who cussed, myself included. But this woman had used more profanity in just a few seconds than everybody else I knew used in an hour. Whoever she was, she obviously had a bone to pick with somebody, but I couldn't imagine *who*.

The smile was no longer on my face and I was ready to do some cussing myself, but I chose not to. This woman was already hot enough. The last thing I needed to do was add fuel to a flame when I didn't even know what had caused it.

I stood up straighter and folded my arms. "Lady, you need to chill," I began, speaking in the most civil tone of voice I could manage under the circumstances. "I don't know what your problem is and why you're here."

What I heard next made my jaw drop. "I'M HERE TO KICK SOME ASS!" she roared, wagging her finger in my face.

I was so taken aback; it was a couple of seconds before I could speak again. "You—you're w-what?" I stuttered. If this woman had shot me with a stun gun, I could not have been more stunned and frightened. My chest tightened and my heart rate felt like it had doubled. I thought hard and tried to recall if my stepmother, Bertha, had mentioned anything about her being involved in a dispute that would explain this angry woman's presence. If that had been the case, Bertha would have been talking about it nonstop every day. "Ma'am, I don't even know who the hell you are! You've come to the wrong address!" I said bluntly.

"No, I did not come to the wrong address, so don't you stand here with your mealy mouth and tell me that shit! I'm looking for Joan Proctor, the whore who has been fooling around with my husband!"

My head felt like it was swimming in a mud puddle and my stomach was churning. "Oh," I said in a small voice. So many thoughts suddenly formed in my head, it was hard to decide which one to deal with first. Only one made any sense to me. And that was for me to slam the door shut and lock it. *But if I do that, what will I do next?* I asked myself. I gulped when I noticed a pink envelope with a red rose above the return address in the woman's hand. I recognized it immediately. I had purchased a hundred of the same envelopes with matching stationery from Office Depot. Because of that, I couldn't call the cops on this ferocious woman without digging a hole for myself. She waved the envelope at me in a threatening manner.

"So . . . uh, you're looking for Joan Proctor?" I asked with my lips quivering.

"Tell that bitch to come out here and settle this shit with me right now!"

"Uh . . . well . . . um . . ." For a streetwise girl like me, who always had a lot to say, this was one time when I didn't know what to say next. Here I was spewing gibberish.

"Where is she?" the woman hollered as she looked over my shoulder. "I want that no-good slut to know that I found the letters she sent to my husband! And I found the canceled checks he sent to her gold-digging ass! I am not leaving here until I set that wench straight! The man she's in love with and wants to marry already has a wife! Me! We've been married thirty-five years and we have five children and nine grandchildren! I don't care what he told her. He still loves me and I will never give him a divorce. Shit. We just paid off our mortgage and I'm not about to let another woman replace me after all I've done and been through with that man of mine. Least of all some bitch he met through a magazine ad! *A magazine ad!* I never in my life heard of black folks getting caught up in foolishness like a lonely hearts club! For goodness' sake! I even found, hidden in his sock drawer, the issue of the magazine with his name, picture, and all them lies about him being a widower! He ain't no widower, but I might end up being a widow if he don't stop this mess! Before I left my house, I beat the tar out of that cheating motherfucker and I'm going to do the same thing again when I get back home! Him and Joan are crazy if they think I'm going to sit back and let them ruin my life so they can live happily ever after, like she said in her last letter. That bitch!"

I sucked in some air and bit my bottom lip. "Ma'am, uh, Joan doesn't live here," I managed, looking around to make sure none of our neighbors were out and about. We lived in a quiet, low-crime area, but we had some of the nosiest, most meddlesome neighbors in South Bay City, California. If they knew that a strange woman had come to our house to attack somebody, they would gossip about it for weeks.

"I ain't playing with you, girl! I can see you ain't nothing but a teenager, but do I look like a fool, *fool*? I was going to write a letter to that Joan Proctor bitch myself, but I thought it'd be better for me to straighten her out in person. From all that shit she wrote in her letters, she sounds like the type of die-hard skank who needs a hands-on approach!" The woman waved the envelope at me again. Her fat fingers covered the name of the man the letter had been sent to, but I could see Joan's name and my address in the sender's section.

"Honest to God, lady. Joan Proctor does not live here."

"This letter with this house address was postmarked last week! It's full of every sex word in the book and then some! That sex-crazed hoochie-coochie woman mentioned things in her letters that she's going to do to my husband—tongue baths and dick milking and whatnot— that I ain't never even heard of! Now, if you think I don't believe Joan lives here, you just as crazy as she is! I drove a long way and I am not about to get back in my car and turn around and leave until I straighten out her nasty self!"

I had to say something that made sense and it had to be convincing. "Joan Proctor *used* to live here!" I said quickly, clutching the doorknob. This huge woman could easily overpower me and force her way in and crucify me. "She moved last Saturday. Just me and my stepmother live here now."

My confused thoughts were bouncing from one side of my head to the other. It was hard for me to hide the fact that I was scared. I was shaking like a leaf and sweat had already formed on my forehead. I didn't care how scared I was and what I had to say, I had to get rid of this woman before my stepmother returned. If she blabbed to Bertha, not only would Joan Proctor's goose be cooked, mine would be too.

"I don't want to stand here talking to a young child like you. I want to talk to your stepmother."

"Huh? Oh, s-see—she's not here," I stammered. "She just left to go shopping and then she's going to have lunch with a friend. After that, they're going to the beauty shop, so she'll be gone for several hours. Uh, look, ma'am, I feel bad about this Joan woman chasing after your husband and taking his money and talking about doing nasty stuff with him, but I can't help you. Check with the post office and see if she turned in a change-of-address form." I managed to smile again. "I hope you can track her down and straighten out this mess. . . ."

The irate stranger's scowl disappeared, but she still looked mean. She let out a heavy sigh and blinked. "What's your name?"

"Lola," I said with a sniff. "Lola Poole."

"Well, can I use your telephone, Lola? I left my cell phone in my hotel room."

"Uh, I'm not allowed to let strangers in the house when I'm here by myself." I paused and swallowed the dry lump that had suddenly formed in my throat. "This is a high-crime area and I'll get a whupping if I let somebody I don't know in the house."

"I don't know why my husband did this to me. I'm a good wife," the woman said, choking on a sob. A tear rolled down the side of her face. "He's driving me crazy."

"I know just how you feel, ma'am. Some husbands don't know how to behave. My dead daddy was so buck wild when it came to women, he had the nerve to move his girlfriend into our house to live with him, my mother, and me! But I really am sorry that I can't help you. If you don't mind, I have to go so I can finish my chores before

my stepmother gets back. Now, you have a blessed day."
The woman looked so hurt and sad, I felt awful when I
abruptly closed the door before she could say anything
else. I immediately secured the chain lock and the dead
bolt. I put my eye up to the peephole and watched as she
stumbled off the porch and down the walkway to a shiny
black Ford parked in front of our house. She slowly
opened the door on the driver's side. Before she got in,
she looked at my house and shook her head. Right after
the car drove away, I ran to the telephone on the stand by
the living-room couch and called up Joan Proctor, my
best friend. I prayed she was home and wouldn't freak
out too much when I told her about the angry visitor. We
were in our last year of high school and I wanted it to be
as pleasant as possible for us, especially since she was
pregnant.

I tried to reach Joan on her cell phone first, but she
didn't answer. I didn't leave a voice mail or send her a
text because if she didn't answer her phone, there was no
telling when she'd hear my voice mail or see my text
message.

I had no choice but to call the landline.

Joan's mother, Pearline, another scary woman, answered the telephone. "Lola, didn't you just talk to Joan
last night?" she growled.

"Uh-huh, I did. But I forgot to tell her something about
our biology class assignment," I muttered. "May I please
speak to her? It'll only take a few minutes."

"Don't y'all tie up this line too long. Joan's got a lot of
things to do around this house today and I'm sure you
have things to do yourself."

"Yes, ma'am." I started tapping my foot on the floor
while I waited for Pearline to call Joan to the telephone.
"I'm so glad you're home!" I yelled when she came on
the line a few seconds later. "Can you talk?"

"Yeah, I can talk. What's up?"

"Girl, we are so busted!" I hollered.

"Busted how?" she asked, speaking in a casual manner. "Talk fast. I'm drying my nails so I can go to the mall with Mama."

"Listen up. A real mean, fat old woman just left here! She was looking for you!"

"Huh? Why would a 'real mean, fat old woman' be looking for me?" Joan didn't sound so casual now. She sounded frightened. "What did she say?"

"She said she came here to kick your ass for fooling around with her husband!"

"WHAT?"

"She's one of the wives of the old men we've been writing to in that damn lonely hearts club!"

Chapter 2

Joan

*L*OLA WAS THE ONLY PERSON WHO KNEW I WAS PREG-nant. But The way I had been running to the bathroom almost every morning for the past two weeks to throw up, I knew I'd have to tell my family and my baby daddy soon. In the meantime, I planned to act as normal as possible.

I had been up since before dawn and I had the living room all to myself that morning. I was standing in front of the opened front window, waving and blowing on my just-polished nails to help them dry faster when Mama yelled from the kitchen for me to pick up the telephone on the end table next to the couch.

As soon as Lola mentioned some old man's wife looking for me and threatening to kick my ass, I forgot about my wet nails and raked my fingers through my hair, smudging all five nails on my right hand. I plopped down onto the couch and everything on my body, except my mouth, froze. "What wife? The men I'm writing to aren't married," I said with a gulp.

"Well, one of them is! Matter of fact, all of mine and all of yours could be married or shacking up with some woman, for all we know. We lie to all of them in our letters, so more than likely they are writing a bunch of lies to us too!" Lola screamed. "I don't understand why so many older people don't want to communicate by e-mail like the rest of the world! If our pen pals did, we wouldn't have to use a street address and nobody could come after us in person like that woman did!"

"Lola, will you stop screaming like a banshee? I'm not deaf." With my parents, my old maid cousin, and three of my six siblings living under the same roof with me, there was not much privacy in our house. I kept my eyes on the door and began to whisper. "Which one's wife was it?"

"How the hell should I know, Joan? The woman didn't tell me her name. She said she drove a long way to kick your ass. From the size of her, you would have looked like a wet noodle by the time she got through with you. She said she found the canceled checks her husband sent to you. She had the letter you sent to him last week. The way she was holding it, I couldn't see who you had addressed it to. And she went on and on about how they have a bunch of kids and grandkids and how she'd never give him a divorce so he could be with you."

"It's Mr. Blake in Reno! He was the only one I wrote to last week. He always sent me three or four letters *every* week—until last week."

"What if it's not Mr. Blake?"

"Oh, it's him, all right. My other men friends live on the East Coast and in foreign countries or thousands of miles away in other directions. Only somebody close enough would actually get in a car and come here—like his wife did! I should have known better than to get involved with somebody who lives only a few hours away!"

"Why did you write to Mr. Blake in the first place? He looked like a bulldog in his picture."

"Because he sounded so sweet and generous in his profile. When I received that first letter from him, with that three-hundred-dollar check made out to me, he sounded even sweeter."

"Every single one of them sounded sweet and generous in their profiles and letters. You were the one who said we should only write to men who lived so far away that we would never have to worry about them sneaking up on us!"

"None of the *men* did! It was only that one woman!"

"It's only that one woman, so far. Do you have a telephone number for Mr. Blake? If you do, call him up and see if it's his wife. And if it is, can you come up with a story to tell him so he can call off that pit bull wife of his?"

"I don't have his telephone number, but I do believe he's the one. Some of the stuff he told me in his first letters didn't jibe with some of the stuff he told me later. First he said that he was a retired army captain collecting a fat pension check every month from Uncle Sam. A few weeks later, he told me he was a retired navy man."

"Army, navy, so what? What difference does it make what those old men are really doing to get the money they send to us? We need to be worried about the woman who came to my house! Bertha will have a cow if she ever finds out what we've been up to, using her address and all. And her kids—oh, God, Bertha's kids! They will shit bricks and do God knows what to me!"

For a stepmother, Bertha was a nice enough woman. Lola never said anything bad about her except that she whined a lot and kept her on a real short leash. She liked her stepmother and they got along well. But I could totally understand her being scared of her stepmother's children. Libby and her twin brother, Marshall, were twelve years older than Lola. They were the stepsiblings from hell: "mean," "self-centered," and "greedy" were just a few ways to describe those two. There was just no telling what they would do to Lola if they found out what we'd done.

"You're right," I agreed. "Those two miserable jack-asses would make your life even more of a living hell. I feel sorry for you if they ever find out."

"You feel sorry for *me*? You're the one who dragged me into this lonely hearts club mess! What do you think your mother and your stepfather would say if they found out about our scheme—that *you* came up with?"

"They wouldn't be happy about it. But goddamn, somebody's wife coming to beat me up? I never expected something like that to jump off!"

"Neither did I. If I had, I wouldn't have let you use my address. Now I'm afraid that the wife of one of the geezers I'm writing to might come here looking for me while I'm at school! We need to figure out a way to get out of this mess before anybody finds out about it."

It had been my idea for us to write pen pal letters to a bunch of lonely, love-struck old men. I'll address this issue in more detail later, but I'd like to reveal my side of the basics of this bizarre story now. Anyway, joining a lonely hearts club was originally supposed to be something to do to keep us from getting bored, and a way to kill time between boyfriends. Especially since we had already participated in a previous pen pal project last year in Mr. Maynard's social studies class.

Writing to teenagers in foreign countries had fizzled out real quick. They had badgered us to send them expensive gifts and forward letters from them to American celebrities, like Will Smith, Denzel Washington, and Madonna. A girl in Uganda had the nerve to ask me to send her a plane ticket so she could come and stay with me for two weeks.

Lola got tired of her pen pals asking her for gifts and favors, so she stopped writing to them after only six weeks. I continued to write to a few—only dudes, though. They were much more interesting than girls—and never asked me to send them gifts or to hook them up with celebrities. I enjoyed corresponding with boys all over the world. Learning about their cultures was good practice for me because one of the things that I thought I wanted to be when I grew up was a journalist for a cool publication like *National Geographic*.

I had sent my male pen pals some real cute pictures of myself, so they had all fallen in love with me. Writing "love letters" to dudes I had never met, and probably never would, had been a lot of fun, until today.

Chapter 3

Joan

I HAD WRITTEN TO THOSE YOUNG BOYS FOR ABOUT SIX months until I got bored. I decided that older people would be much more interesting pen pals for me and Lola to write to, this year.

We joined Aunt Martha's Friendship Association, which was a fancy way of describing one of those lonely hearts clubs where desperate people hooked up by mail. It was featured in a cheesy confession magazine that came in the mail every month addressed to my unmarried, plain, heavyset, middle-aged cousin. Her name was Flossie, but everybody called her "Too Sweet." We shared the same bedroom, and in addition to her being a nuisance, she was a slob. She left her magazines all over the place, so I didn't have to look far to find what I needed. As far as I knew, Too Sweet had no interest in corresponding with strangers. For one thing, she was too cheap to spend money on stamps. When I had my teenage pen pals, she told me one time that she thought it was stupid for me to write letters to strangers telling them my business.

Too Sweet had been reading her magazines for as long as I could remember. Every month, in addition to several lurid confession stories with outrageous titles and provocative illustrations, the last four or five pages in back of the magazines were devoted to mature people looking for love. Their names, profiles, and pictures of them in color were featured in the section called "Let's Become Friends." And, boy, did they sound desperate! Some bragged about how "fine" they were and what great personalities they had. Most of the people on the list were women. But there were a lot of men looking for "new friends" too. A few were honest enough to admit that they were not "exactly easy on the eyes" or were "a little on the heavy side," but that they made up for those flaws in other ways.

The majority of the men and almost half of the women came right out and said they were people of means and didn't have a problem being generous. That grabbed my attention right away, of course. With that in mind, our original notion—we'd only be writing to a bunch of older dudes for the heck of it—took on a whole new meaning. Once it dawned on me that we could kill two birds with one stone, I decided we could say things in our letters that would make our pen pals send us gifts. But even if they turned out to be stingy and didn't want to be nice to us, I still thought that communicating with them would be something fun to do. Who wouldn't want to correspond with people who were all but telling the world that they were willing to practically *pay* for some attention? Those were the ones we focused on, and the older the better. There were only a few people under the age of fifty. But as far as I was concerned, they were "too young" for what I had in mind. I was acquainted with a lot of people in their fifties, so I knew that their brains were still somewhat fresh and sharp so they'd be too much trouble to get over on.

And we only selected the lonely hearts who lived out of state. Some were as far away as Canada, the Caribbean, Europe, and several Latin American countries. The reason I used Lola's address was because I couldn't take a chance on one of my meddlesome family members opening my mail. I'd already had one bad experience in that area and didn't want to have another one. One of my former teenage pen pals, a gorgeous redhead named Pierre, lived in France. He liked to write sexually explicit letters. I looked forward to reading about the things he would do to my body if we ever met. One day one of my nosy sisters opened one of my letters from Pierre "by accident" and read it. She ratted me out. My whole family was horrified when they found out what I'd been up to. At that point, they all still thought I was a virgin and decided that even "sex by mail" was not acceptable for the "baby of the family."

Mama told me I could no longer write to Pierre or any other pen pals. I had always been rebellious, so I continued to write to Pierre. The only difference was I had him send his letters to me in care of my "cousin Lola" at her address.

Lola didn't have to worry about some busybody opening any mail that came addressed to her. Her biological parents were deceased and her stepsiblings had their own homes, so she and her stepmother lived in the big house on Evelyn Circle alone. Bertha was way too lazy to get off her fat ass and go out to their curbside mailbox to get the mail every day. Lola picked it up when she got home from school during the week and on weekends so we didn't have to worry about Bertha intercepting any of my correspondence. There was no way I could have let my new pen pals send letters to my address, so that was the reason I had used Lola's again.

Lola's loud voice interrupted my thoughts. "What if that lady comes back one day and Bertha answers the door and blows the whistle on you?" she asked. "What in the world would we do then? What would *you* do if I was forced to tell that lady the truth and where you live? I was lucky enough to get rid of her this morning without too much trouble, but she didn't look like the kind of woman who would give up on anything too easily. You know how black women are when it comes to men and money."

"Tell me about it. I hope that lady doesn't come back and cause a ruckus in front of Bertha. She's already got one foot in the grave. Something like that would probably make her have a fatal heart attack!"

"Or what if that woman is driving around right now, looking for you, and runs into you on the street when you leave the house? She might even come back to my street and knock on one of my neighbor's door and ask a bunch of questions about the people at this address. The first thing they'll tell her is that nobody named Joan lives here, but that I have a best friend with the same name! You know how Mr. Fernandez next door likes to run his mouth."

"Let's pray that Mr. Fernandez is not home *if* and *when* she returns to the neighborhood. In the meantime, that old battle-axe can cruise around this town all she wants looking for me. She's never seen me, so she wouldn't know me from the Queen of Sheba. We didn't send pictures of ourselves to anybody, remember?"

"Oh, yeah. I forgot."

* * *

Most of the men had requested friendships with women in their twenties and thirties. We had sent each one a recent photograph of my twenty-seven-year-old divorced sister, Elaine. My sister—bitch that she was—got on my last nerve, but I couldn't deny her beauty. Before she moved back in with us last year, she had lived in L.A. and worked as a swimsuit model for four months. With her big brown eyes, high cheekbones, curly brown hair, and butterscotch-colored skin, she practically had to beat the men off with a stick. Using Elaine's picture without her permission or knowledge was real deceitful, but we didn't let that stop us. That was not the only deceitful thing going on, though. I had another scheme in the works that Lola didn't know about. One of the lonely people I'd been writing to and receiving money orders and checks from was a childless, sixty-five-year-old woman in Miami named Lee Lawson. With a name that could also belong to a man in the return address on the envelopes, Lola had no reason to suspect that I was corresponding with a woman.

In the first sentence of her profile, Lee stated that she was not interested in men in her own age group. She wanted one who was young enough to be the son she never had so she could "mother" him, as well as enjoy his "manly favors." She bragged about the mansion she owned, the real estate business she ran, and how much money her late husband had left her. Now that she was alone again, she stated, all she was interested in was having a good time with the right person. I couldn't believe it! A woman that desperate had no business advertising for a young lover in the first place. Couldn't she find a son/lover in Miami? Didn't she realize how she was setting herself up to be taken advantage of? I wrote a letter to her five minutes after I finished reading her profile, hoping I'd get to her before somebody else did. Lee looked like a typical woman her age, moon-faced and grandmotherly. The ex-

pensive-looking earrings and diamond necklace she wore
in her profile picture looked good on her. But the Tina
Turner–style wig made her look ridiculous. I sent Lee a
picture of a thirty-five-year-old man from my church
named Leroy Puckett. I told her that my father had recently left my mother after being married for forty years
and she had had a nervous breakdown. I had to work
three jobs to help support her. She was so attached to me,
her only child, that she couldn't stand the thought of me
leaving her, not even for a woman. Therefore, until my
mother got well, all mail to me needed to be addressed to
my cousin Joan Proctor. I doubted that Lee would buy
such a cock-and-bull story, but the following week I received a three-page letter from her. She told me in the
first paragraph that she was so impressed with my letter
and good looks, she decided not to write to any of the
other men who had responded to her ad. She also said
that since I was so good to my own mother, she knew I'd
be good to her. In the meantime, she wanted to help me
out as much as she could until we could be together. I received a check for a thousand dollars from her the following week so I could buy myself "something nice."

Maybe it was a good thing that that angry woman
came looking for me today because the Lee woman had
become real demanding. Last week I received three letters from her on the same day, saying almost the same
thing: I had to come to Miami, or return the five thousand
dollars she had sent to help me get my car fixed and pay
off some bills, so I wouldn't have to keep working three
jobs. I stalled her by claiming some new issues related to
my mother had suddenly come up, so I couldn't come
until I resolved them. My plan was to give her enough
time to cool off. Then I'd send her a letter telling her that
I was going to take my mother to Mexico to live with my
uncle Alex. I would explain that I'd be gone for at least

three weeks and would write to her again as soon as I could. I actually did have an uncle Alex, my stepfather Elmo's older brother. And he had moved to Mexico last year. Elmo and some of his friends drove down there a couple of times a month to visit him and do some deep-sea fishing. I planned to accompany them on a future trip and mail a letter from there to Lee so it'd have a Mexico postmark. In the last letter I planned to write to her, I'd tell her that I had to stay down there indefinitely, because I'd been in an accident. I had sustained a broken back and I had no idea how long it would be before I recovered. If she was stupid enough to travel to Mexico to look for me, she'd never find me. The letter I planned to send would have a bogus address. Before I could even write that letter, Lee suggested something I didn't like and had refused to do with any of my other pen pals: she *demanded* that I include a phone number in my next letter so she could talk to me.

So far, Lola and I had been able to avoid giving out our phone numbers. We told everybody that first we wanted to get to know them really well. When some of them got too pushy on that subject, we stopped writing to them, and replaced them with new friends. Our lives were complicated enough. The last thing we needed was for some love-struck old person to start pestering us on the phone. The letters were bad enough. One of my pen pals had suffered a stroke a few months ago, so his handwritten letters looked like chicken scratch now and took me twice as long to read as the others.

After what happened today, going to Mexico to send my final letter to Lee was out of the question. I had to send her that letter *today*.

In the meantime, I was more concerned about the woman who came snooping around today and how we had dragged my innocent sister into our mess.

* * *

"Oh, shit! What if that old woman cruises around and sees Elaine swishing down the street?" I wailed.

"'Oh, shit' is right. There is just no telling what she might do to her if that happens. She'd probably shoot first and ask questions later. Your poor sister could get beaten up or killed and not even know why!"

"If it comes to that, I'd never be able to forgive myself!"

"Neither would I. You'd better hope it doesn't come to that," Lola told me.

Chapter 4
Lola

THE THOUGHT THAT JOAN AND I WERE PLAYING A DAN-
gerous game never crossed my mind, but it should have.
She and I knew better! We watched a lot of the true crime
TV shows, the daily six o'clock news, and we read the
newspapers and tabloids regularly. We knew that there
were a lot of stalkers and serial killers running around
loose. Like a lot of teenagers, we didn't think anything
bad could happen to us. The truth of the matter was, it
was not a stretch for one of our desperate pen pals—or
the mate they'd been "cheating" on with me or Joan—to
become a stalker or something worse.

"Joan, what have we gotten ourselves into?" I asked,
sounding more and more like a scared rabbit as the seconds rolled by. "And your sister!"

"We may have gotten ourselves into a fine mess for
sure," Joan admitted.

"You're damn right. That lady made it clear that she

didn't come all this way from wherever she came from for nothing. She might run into somebody who knows you! If she comes to your house and sees Elaine, all hell could break loose. That woman had a big purse and there could be weapons in it. I knew this scam was going too good. Why did I ever let you talk me into this shit? What was I thinking? I've never done anything this crazy before in my life!"

"Calm down, Lola."

"Calm down, my ass. We could be in a lot of trouble, so how do you expect me to calm down? If that woman comes back and beats you up, you being pregnant and all, it'll be all over the newspaper."

"Let's not even discuss me being pregnant. That has nothing to do with this new problem we have. And don't worry, because I'll figure out something."

"Well, you'd better figure out something quick. Since that woman is from out of town, she probably won't hang around here too long. She might decide to try and catch up with Bertha and come back here today or tomorrow."

"Listen, the very first thing we need to do is stop writing letters to all those men immediately. I had been thinking for a long time, anyway, about stopping this shit. I guess we don't have a choice now."

"Oh, really? As if I hadn't already come to that conclusion," I sneered.

"Did any new letters come today?"

"All the mailman delivered this morning was a bunch of bills."

"Good. I'm glad to hear that. Now I *know* it was Mr. Blake's wife who came looking for me. He would never let a whole week go by without sending me his usual two or three rambling letters on the same day. Look here . . ." Joan paused and sucked on her teeth for a few seconds. "When the mailman brings some new letters, shred them.

Uh, but open the envelopes first and make sure they don't have any money or checks in them."

I agreed with Joan, but I didn't agree when she suggested we write Dear John letters to all of our pen pals and tell them we're in love with somebody else and couldn't write to them anymore. "I don't think we should write any more letters, period," I argued.

"Look, we have to write to them one last time. We've been writing to some of them so long, if we stop without giving them an explanation, they will probably keep writing for God knows how long. And if that one woman had the nerve to come to your house, some of the men or some of the other wives or girlfriends might do the same thing. Now we need to write to them all *today*—except for that lying-ass Mr. Blake—and tell them we're going off with another man to, uh, someplace far away, where they won't come looking for us."

"All right, then," I muttered.

"How do you spell 'Cairo,' one *r* or two?"

"*Cairo, Egypt?* Be serious. Those old men are not stupid enough to believe some crap like that. American women who fall in love and run off with men do not go to a dangerous place like the Middle East, where Americans are so unpopular. Mexico would make more sense."

"Yeah, you're right about that. Mexico sounds more believable, I guess. So does Canada," Joan said. "As long as we pick a foreign country. Nobody would be fool enough to look for us if they think we've left the States."

"What if they don't believe us and come here to look for us, anyway? We used our real names and sooner or later they'll run into somebody who knows us."

"You're not making this easy, Lola."

"This was never 'easy.' It was wrong from the get-go, and you knew it."

"You knew it was wrong from the get-go too! Don't

you put all of the blame for this shit on me! I didn't twist your arm to get you involved. You came into this with your eyes wide open, so don't you dare go there with me!"

"I'm sorry." I sucked in a mouth full of air and rubbed the back of my neck, which had begun to ache. So had other parts of my body. My head was still throbbing and my stomach felt like it had turned upside down. "I'm just as guilty as you are, I guess."

"Is 'Bertha Butt' home?"

"Joan, I wish you wouldn't call my stepmother that. Her butt is not even as big as your mama's. . . ."

"I'm sorry. I keep forgetting. Anyway, I need to come over there so we can get busy writing those letters so we can mail them all today."

"Bertha's having lunch with Reverend Bailey's wife. You'd better get over here real quick so we can get as many letters written as possible before she comes home and starts breathing down my neck."

"It shouldn't take long to write 'breakup' letters with a few sentences telling each man basically the same thing. Cool?"

"Cool," I agreed with a heavy sigh. Even though I had just apologized to Joan for putting most of the blame on her shoulders, I was still mad because most of the blame did belong on her shoulders. "Let me tell you one thing right now, Miss Proctor, don't you ever suggest something like this to me again! We should have stopped this nonsense a long time ago. That angry woman coming to my house could be just the tip of a very big iceberg. Some of these old fossils have gotten so pushy there's no telling what they're cooking up. That retired banker I've been writing to in Spokane has been badgering me to move up there and marry him. That's all he's been talking about in his letters for the past three weeks. He even suggested coming down here so we could drive over to Reno and get married! I had to make up some more bogus stories real quick. He backed off when I told him about my mean stepfather, who is also a cop, and my violent ex, who is still trying to get me back. But from the way that old goat's been whining about how lonely he is without me, and how anxious he is to be with me in person, my stories about a mean stepfather and a violent ex are not enough to hold him off too much longer."

"After today we won't have to worry about any of them anymore, I hope. *All* of mine have gotten pushy! They were all so nice and sweet and easygoing in the beginning. 'Honey' this and 'honey' that. I don't know what this world is coming to. Have people gone completely crazy?"

"*We* must have gone completely crazy, Joan. Other than cheating on a few tests in school, gobbling up a few swiped grapes in the supermarket, and shoplifting a few items from the department stores, I had never done anything *too* dishonest before this lonely hearts thing. We need to get back on the right track."

"Yeah, yeah, yeah. Okay, we are so done with this lonely hearts thing. By doing so, we are back on the right track already. I'm going to read the Bible before I go to bed tonight so God will know we are seriously repenting."

"I will too, but I don't feel so good right now. My stomach and my head have been hurting since that woman left."

"Take an aspirin with a glass of warm milk. Now, let me get off this phone. Mama's going to have a fit when I tell her I don't want to go to the mall with her after all the fuss I made about going. I'd better come over to your house right now so we can get started on those letters. I'm not even going to take the time to put on my makeup. And, uh, I'm sorry I got you involved in this. I didn't mean any harm. I was bored, and I needed a little spending money. Other than us getting money from those horny, silly old men, nobody got hurt."

"Those old men got hurt, Joan. We lied so they'd feel sorry for us and send us money," I reminded. "I feel like shit about it now and you should too."

"Um . . . I guess you're right. I do feel like shit too. My parents raised me right so I can't blame my foolishness on anybody but myself." Joan snorted and remained silent so long it made me wonder if she really felt the way she just said she did. Before I could speak again, she took a deep breath and continued. "I'll go by the post office before it closes and pick up some stamps."

"We don't need to bother with the men who never sent us any money or the ones who stopped writing to us on their own. So we'll need a whole pack of stamps, right? That's twenty."

Joan didn't respond right away and that made me even more nervous. "Well, it's like this . . . ," she started, then paused. I didn't care what she decided to do; I was done! If she wanted to continue this scheme, or start up a new one, I was not about to let her continue using my address. It took her a few moments to tell me, "Not exactly."

"Not exactly what, Joan? We don't need exactly that many stamps?"

"Uh, no. Thirty would be more like it. . . ."

Chapter 5

Joan

"JOAN, WHY DO WE NEED THIRTY STAMPS? I HAVE only ten men on my list. And I thought that's how many you had? One less now because Mr. Blake is on your shit list so you don't need to send him a breakup letter. Please tell me you're kidding." Lola was talking so fast she almost lost her breath.

"I'm not kidding. I was writing to a few more guys that I didn't tell you about. I was going to tell you, but I kept forgetting."

"I thought I was your best friend. How come you're keeping stuff from me?" I hated it when Lola pouted because of something I'd said or done. It made me feel guilty.

"I didn't mean to," I eased in. "And yeah, you are still my best friend. . . ."

I had a lot of friends, but Lola had been my number one girl since second grade. That was when she'd helped me beat up the Baker sisters, Patty and Jean, two of the meanest human grizzly bears ever born.

One day during recess, Patty lunged at me because I had refused to pay her a dollar each week to "protect" me from other bullies. She pummeled me with her fists until I hit the ground. Then Jean kicked me a few times while I was down. I had endured the wrath of those two bitches since kindergarten and I'd finally had enough. I leaped up like a frog and lit into Patty. She went down in no time. Before Jean realized what was going on, I sucker punched her in the stomach and knocked her to the ground. I knew that once they got up, they'd beat the crap out of me, but I didn't care. None of the other kids jumped in to help me. That was the day I found out who my real friends were. Lola was the only one who came to my defense. She used her shoe to beat the Bakers. By the time the fight was over, blood was spurting from their noses and lips, and they were bawling like babies. Lola and I had no injuries at all. The Bakers never bothered me or Lola again.

I knew then that she and I would be best friends forever. I'd take a bullet for my BFF and I knew she would do the same for me. Even so, there were things I didn't tell Lola. One thing I did know was that it was not smart to let everybody know everything about yourself. My own mother, who was always telling me she knew me better than I knew myself, didn't even know the real me. As far as I was concerned, what she didn't know wouldn't hurt her. I felt the same way about Lola. For one thing, I didn't want her to know just how greedy I really was. But since things had begun to fall apart, I saw no reason to keep certain information from her now.

"Why were you writing to so many?" Lola asked. "The way some of them were sending two or three letters at the same time, it was hard enough for us to keep up with the ones we had! Last Saturday it took me two hours to answer all the mail I had received in just three days."

"A couple of mine were getting stingy and there were a lot of things I wanted to buy. When it comes to money, you know how stingy some black men can get after a while. That's why I went after some of those lonely white dudes."

"Oh, my God! And you thought I'd never find out?"

"You told me yourself you didn't pay any attention to the names and the return addresses on the letters that came for me. Since some of them started sending several letters in the same week, I didn't think you'd notice me getting a little more mail than before."

"You should have told me before now. I thought we were in this together, and I've always told you every-thing," Lola pouted.

"I didn't want you to know I was so greedy," I admit-ted with a pout of my own.

"You've always been greedy, so I don't know why you had a problem with me knowing you had added more men to your list. When we first got involved in this stupid shit, we agreed not to get too carried away in case some-thing happened to me one day and somebody else had to go to the mailbox to pick up the mail. It would be just our luck that that would happen on a day when ten or more letters came in!"

"You've got a point there. From now on, I promise I'll let you know every move I make, no matter what we do." Despite my promise, I didn't plan to ever tell Lola about the Lee woman in Miami and that I'd been posing as a man. We had several gay classmates that we liked and re-spected, but I didn't want her to think I had a lesbian thing going on.

"Joan, if you want me to continue having your back, you need to let me know everything you're up to."

Chapter 6

Lola

I LIVED IN A NICE QUIET NEIGHBORHOOD WITH MY STEP-mother, Bertha. Our house was about half an hour's drive from San Jose, California, in a Silicon Valley suburb called South Bay City, which had about forty thousand residents. Both of my parents had passed years ago and I had no other relatives to speak of.

When I was growing up, my father had cheated on my mother with other women, left and right, but the only one I'd ever cared about was a former hairdresser named Shirelle Odom. Daddy had moved her in with us and she had been very nice to me and Mama. I referred to her as "my other mother," because she'd treated me like her own daughter and she helped take care of my mother when Mama had contracted terminal cancer. Shirelle had even bathed and fed my mother every day. But after a few months, that backbreaking responsibility and Daddy cheating on Shirelle with other women, got to be too much for

Shirelle. She moved out and didn't tell us where she was going. A few weeks later, Bertha Mays moved in with us. She was a retired elementary-school teacher and one of Mama's best friends. Mama and Bertha had taught at the same elementary school I had attended.

Bertha took care of Mama until she died; and when Daddy got sick, she took care of him until he died. He'd made me promise him on his deathbed that I would "be nice" to Bertha and take care of her as long as she lived. I was only fourteen at the time, but I didn't have a problem making that promise because I cared about Bertha. Her adult children, twins named Libby and Marshall, were not only selfish and greedy, but they were also mean to me and Bertha. Living with my stepmother was a real challenge. Sometimes I felt like I was in prison because she was so attached to me and I had so little freedom. It didn't do me any good to complain. When I did, I only felt worse, because Bertha constantly reminded me about the promise I'd made to Daddy.

Next to Bertha, Joan Proctor was the most important person in my life. Her friendship meant the world to me. A visit to the big house three blocks from ours that she shared with her large, rowdy family was always interesting. For one thing, her bedroom was so much cooler than mine. She had posters of all the best rappers and other big stars on her wall, a brass bed, and a bookcase that contained some of the best street lit that had ever been published.

When I knocked on Joan's front door the first Saturday in March, around six months ago, her grumpy mother greeted me with a puzzled look on her plain, high-yellow face. "How did you manage to escape? I thought Bertha was sick with gout. She must be doing better," Pearline snarled, waving me into the house. There was nothing ladylike or dainty about Joan's mother. She was so big and scary that when she'd applied for a job as a prison guard ten years ago, they'd hired her right away.

"Uh, no, she's about the same. My stepsister's husband offered to stay with her so I could take a break," I replied. "Joan is expecting me."

Pearline rolled her tight black eyes and let out a heavy sigh. "She's in her room. Go on up there and don't y'all make a lot of noise. Too Sweet's on a new diabetes medication, so she's been real cranky all day and I just got her calmed down enough to take a nap before dinner. Do you hear me?"

"Uh-huh," I mumbled.

When I got to the room Joan shared with Too Sweet, I was glad to see she was alone. She occupied a chair at the small desk next to her window, humped over the laptop computer that her real father had sent to her for her birthday.

"Get in here and come look at this," she said in a low voice. "Lock the door first. You're not going to believe what I'm going to show you."

I locked the door and sprinted across the floor. I was so curious I could barely contain myself. "Joan, what are you up to?" I asked, stopping next to her. There was a pile of magazines on the desk. She had one in her hand and was waving it like it was a winning lottery ticket. "What's up with that magazine?"

"I'm really going to have some fun now," she announced. "Wait until you see some of the people I'm going to write to."

"Are you talking about that pen pal thing you were babbling about the other day?" I asked. Last week Joan had mentioned something in passing about pen pals. I hadn't shown any interest in the subject then, so I was surprised she was bringing it up again now.

She stopped waving the magazine and held it up to my face. I frowned when I read the name of this publication: *Modern Love*. Yeah, right. I was tempted to laugh. The cover featured a beautiful, young, voluptuous blonde in a skimpy white dress sitting alone at a table, with candles and flowers on top, in a fancy restaurant. There was a menu in her hand and a huge smile on her face. Standing behind her, peeping over her shoulder, were several well-dressed men with mysterious expressions on their faces. The headline above the woman's head screamed in bold capital letters: IS LOVE ON YOUR MENU TONIGHT? It may as well have been a Pandora's Box because, in a way, that's exactly what it turned out to be. The unspeakable event that happened down the road years later, which would change my life forever, started with this magazine and a bunch of lonely old people seeking new friends. . . .

"This magazine has tons of dudes in the pen pal section and all of them are dying to correspond with women." Joan waved the magazine again. There was an anxious, wild-eyed look on her face. Whenever I saw that expression, I knew she was up to some mischief.

"What dudes?" I asked.

Instead of answering, she waved the magazine in my face some more, but harder this time. "The men in Aunt Martha's Friendship Association."

"Who the heck is 'Aunt Martha'?" I mouthed. I was still tempted to laugh. For one thing, Joan was way too cool and fly to be reading love story magazines! One day I leafed through a few at the newsstand, where I purchased some of the hip-hop and hair and makeup magazines every month. I couldn't believe how corny the "true confessions" and the articles were in rags like the one Joan was waving in my face. Even some of the ads were laughable: outrageous wigs, crotchless girdles, and wrinkle-removing face creams that promised to turn a beast into a beauty. "Girl, have you been sneaking into your step-daddy's liquor cabinet again?"

"I am not drunk. Now, do you want to get in on a good thing or not?"

"Yeah, I guess," I said with a shrug. "So tell me about Aunt Martha."

"She's this old lonely hearts club woman who likes to help people find love. According to her bio in every issue, she's been married six times, so she knows more about love and matchmaking than most people."

"A woman who has been married that many times ought to know a lot about love and matchmaking," I said, my voice dripping with sarcasm. "Does Aunt Martha say why she couldn't hold on to her husbands?" As hard as I tried not to, I couldn't hold in my laugh.

Joan gave me a hot look and waited until I stopped laughing. "That's besides the point. The problem must be with the men she married. She's been with her latest husband for five years, so she must be doing something right this time. She used to live in a trailer park in Bakersfield, but now she lives in a mansion in Pebble Beach, so she must be doing all right by working for this magazine." Joan snorted and gave me a critical look. "Anyway, every month Aunt Martha—and I'm sure that's not her real name—writes a column about how nobody has to be alone anymore, blah, blah, blah. She posts a long list of names of lonely men and women looking for mates. Some of them are fairly young, but the majority of them are senior citizens. You pick out the ones you want to write to and send letters to them in care of the magazine. The magazine forwards the letters to the people to let them choose the ones they want to reply to."

I gave Joan an incredulous look. "You were serious the

other day when you talked about getting some new pen pals?"

"Of course I was serious the other day. I am even more serious today. I'm going to correspond with senior citizens." It was hard to believe that she could tell me something so outlandish and keep a straight face.

"If you want to start writing to pen pals again, why don't you write to people your own age, like we did last year in Mr. Maynard's social studies class? Why would you want to write to some lonely *old* people? And why would some lonely old people want to write to a teenager?"

"The *mature* people in this magazine sound much more interesting than a bunch of kids in foreign countries that Mr. Maynard had us writing to!" Joan stood up and folded the magazine open to a page that contained names, pictures, and profiles of people seeking new friends. "I'll bet some of them have some good stories to share. Look at this dude. Check out his picture." Joan pointed to the man in the first column at the top of the page. "Manfred Ledbetter. He's from Jamaica, but he lives in England now."

I looked at the picture and did a double take. "With those orange dreadlocks, his droopy eyes, and his long face, he looks like the Cowardly Lion from *The Wizard of Oz*," I teased.

"So what? The man worked for the royal family. Read his profile."

"Good God!" I exclaimed after I read that the man claimed he'd worked in Buckingham Palace. "If he's telling the truth, then I'm sure *he* is an interesting character." My eyes went back to the picture. I was impressed, but I didn't want Joan to know that too soon. I didn't care how excited she was; I didn't want her to think that I was even remotely interested in any kind of club that catered to horny senior citizens. "Wow. Can you imagine the stories he can tell about Prince Charles and the queen. I wonder if he was still working there when Lady Diana was alive." I looked at some of the other pictures and profiles. One thing I noticed that a lot of the people on the list had in common was that they all claimed to be very well-off. "I wonder why these folks are bragging about being rich."

"If you were old and lonely, who would want you if you didn't have money? Some of these people in this magazine are in their *eighties*—practically deceased!"

I blinked at Joan and shook my head in amazement. "*Dinosaurs* like them ought to be looking for a mate in Jurassic Park, not some magazine. And another thing, why would somebody that old still be looking for love in the first place? Their body parts must be mummified by now."

"That's not our problem," she clucked.

I placed my hands on my hips and gave Joan a guarded look. "What are you really up to? Have you finally gone off the deep end this time, or are you just trying to get my goat? I know you don't think I'm dumb enough to believe you want to get acquainted with some old men just for the hell of it. What's really in something like this for you?"

"My mama and all three of my sisters told me that the best kind of man for a woman to have is a rich old geezer with a bad heart."

"Are you telling me that you're actually going to write letters to some of these rich old men?" I laughed again. Joan pressed her lips together and gave me a testy look. I gave her an apologetic look as I rubbed my chin and cleared my throat. I decided to humor her. "I'm sure they are some nice old men. And real generous too. They might send you all kinds of nice presents. You know how rich old people like to spend money," I said with a nod. "But there's no telling what you'll have to say to them in your letters for them to start sending you stuff."

Joan gave me a look that was so intense, it made me shudder. "I'll tell them anything I think they might want to hear," she vowed.

Chapter 7

Lola

I SNATCHED THE MAGAZINE OUT OF JOAN'S HAND, FROWN-ing and shaking my head. I had always thought that magazines like the one in my hand now were only for people like Joan's pathetic cousin, Too Sweet, and other sad sacks who didn't care about fashion, makeup tips, and celebrity gossip.

"Damn, girl," I mouthed, gazing at the page I had turned to, the one with the most names. "This sounds like a real serious lonely hearts club. Look at all of the people on this list!" I paused and gave Joan an amused look. I was trying to decide if she really was serious about this thing or if my girl was just punking me. From the tight look on her face, I knew she was into this for real. I decided that the least I could do was act like I was really interested. When Joan sank her teeth into something, she didn't let go until she had gotten as much out of it as she could. And for her to be all hyped up about something this peculiar, I had to go along for the ride. It would be good for a few laughs if nothing else.

"I didn't know organizations like this were still around. I saw a movie that was made thirty or forty years ago about people looking for love in a lonely hearts club that ran ads in magazines. Who is going to look for somebody in a magazine when we have the Internet available now?" I asked.

"Who cares? We're talking about a different generation, girl. People who still like to do things the old way. You know how older people are when it comes to all the new technology available these days. Shoot! Mama doesn't even know how to use a computer." Joan paused and laughed. Then she took a deep breath and lifted another one of the magazines. "I checked out the listings in the last four months' issues. Each edition has all new names, two or three dozen each month. I had no idea there were so many old men out there looking for love or reading magazines like *Modern Love*."

I didn't know what to say next. "Since when did *you* become interested in old men?" I dropped the magazine back onto the desk.

"*Rich* old men. What girl wouldn't want an old man with deep pockets?"

"I wouldn't. The last thing I want is some old goat fumbling all over my body. Or having a heart attack while he's on top of me. The gossipmongers would be talking about that from now on."

"Pfffft!" Joan gave me a dismissive wave and an exasperated look. "It'll never come to that. Even just corresponding with them will be fun. Look at it this way—I'm still thinking about becoming a journalist someday so I can write human-interest-type stories. I could learn a lot from elderly people, especially the oldest ones and the ones who live in foreign countries. They must be like human encyclopedias. This is one way for me to get a leg up in case I do become a journalist, and a way to get some nice gifts. Rich old men can be real generous. I've already written a letter to the first one. He's a retired oil man in Texas in a wheelchair. He has no family, so I won't have to worry about any meddlesome sons or daughters or grandchildren getting all up in his business. If I'm lucky, he could turn out to be a gold mine in knowledge and, uh, everything else."

"Just being pen pals with some of these people and sharing stories with them because you're bored is one thing. There's nothing wrong with that. Taking money and gifts from them is something else. And it's risky business."

"Getting out of bed every day is 'risky business.' Why are you acting so worried about this, anyway?"

"Because I am worried. All kinds of freaky and bizarre shit could happen to you. I don't want to read about you in one of those gory true crime books."

"Get a grip, Lola. I don't understand why you're even going there. All I'm talking about is exchanging a few fun letters with some interesting men and making a little money. How many times have we not been able to go shopping or buy the latest CDs because we were both broke?"

"So?"

"So . . . if we hook a few sugar daddies, we won't have that problem anymore. These old dudes sound so lonely, all they want is some cute young thing to correspond with. And like I told you, it'll be fun to hear some of their stories."

"Joan, can't you find a better hobby?"

"I hate it when you give me a hard time! I knew I should not have told you about this!" Joan hissed, rolling her eyes and shaking her head. She was exasperated with me and I was just as exasperated with her. But this was nothing new. Despite being BFFs, Joan and I still locked horns from time to time.

"Then why did you?"

"Well, uh, I thought you might want to get into it too." Joan rose from her seat and moved toward the door. "Listen, I'm going to go downstairs and get us some soda. Be right back."

As soon as she left the room, I picked up the first magazine again and turned to the listing for the lonely hearts club. This time I looked at some of the pictures and profiles longer and more thoroughly. I put that magazine down and picked up another one and turned to the lonely hearts section. I ignored the women and concentrated on the men.

Joan returned ten minutes later with two Diet Cokes and handed one to me. I remained standing by the side of her desk, still looking at the faces of those lonely people. Some of them looked so sad and I felt so sorry for them.

"So, Lola, what do you think?" she asked with a loud sniff as she sat back down at her desk and took a sip of her drink.

I took a sip of mine before I responded in a stern tone of voice. I knew she didn't like to be scolded, especially by me, but this was one time when I didn't care. "Be serious. You're *seventeen*. Every single one of these men say they'd like to hear from women in their twenties and thirties." I set my drink on the desk and flipped to the last page. "Look at this eighty-four-year-old Julio Mendoza—with his *five* middle names—in Puerto Vallarta, Mexico!" I howled, stabbing the page with my finger. "He says he's only interested in hearing from women in their twenties."

"No problema, chica," Joan rattled on, speaking with an exaggerated fake Spanish accent. She continued in her

regular voice. "I'll send them a picture of a woman in that age range—Elaine." She stared at me and winked.

I squinted my eyes and looked at her as if she'd lost her mind. And I was beginning to think she had. It took me a few seconds to respond. "Your sister? Have you lost your mind, girl? What if she opens your mail like she did when you were pen pals with that sex-starved boy in France who used to write letters to you with all that nasty talk last year?"

"She won't. That's where you come in."

"Me? Oh, now I know you've lost your mind! I'm not getting caught up in this foolishness!" I dropped the magazine back onto the desk. "What way would I 'come in,' anyhow?"

"Relax. Keep your titties in place. I'm just going to use your address. That's where you come in."

I gave Joan the most incredulous look I could manage. "Oh, hell no!" I hollered, waving my hand and shifting my weight from one foot to the other. "If you're going to do this crazy shit, rent a post office box or one of those private mailboxes. I'm not going to get in trouble."

"Look, 'Paranoid Patty.' I'm trying to earn a little extra money, not spend it. Elaine pays over two hundred bucks a year to rent her private mailbox." Joan snorted and gave me a thoughtful look. "Didn't you tell me that you're still the only one who gets the mail out of the box at your house?"

"Yeah. Bertha hasn't gone out to get the mail in years."

"Then, why can't you help me save a few dollars and let my mail come to your house instead of me wasting money on one of those private mailboxes?"

"Because I have a good reputation in school and everywhere else and I want to keep it that way. If I'm going to be a teacher or a nurse, I can't get caught up in a lonely hearts scandal—"

Joan gave me a look that was so hot, I actually felt the heat on my face. "Why would there be any kind of scandal?" she snarled.

"Well, something bad could happen. Remember what happened to Anna Nicole Smith on account of that rich old man she married? The late-night talk show hosts made so many jokes about her, it ruined her career—"

Joan wasted no time interrupting me. "Jay Leno and Letterman make jokes about her because she got fat and lost her shape."

"Whatever, whatever," I chanted. "I just don't want to get myself in trouble over something this off-the-wall. I have enough to worry about already."

"Suit yourself." Joan tilted her head to the side and gave me a look that made me uneasy. "If you're smart, you'll write to some yourself. We have to move on this fast, though, before some other women grab up all the best men. Some of them are probably no longer available, anyway, so I'm going to write to a whole bunch."

"Uh-uh," I said, shaking my head so hard it felt like my brain was rattling. I glanced at the magazine I had just held a few moments ago. "I wouldn't know what to say to an older man that he'd be interested in hearing, anyway. You know how dull my life is." To this day, I don't know what made me pick up that magazine again and turn to that list of names. One in particular caught my eye. "Look what Orin Hillyer, age seventy-five, in Salt Lake City has to say. He claims he'll spend his whole fortune if it means he'll find a suitable companion. Hmmm. He doesn't look too bad for a man his age. He's a retired real estate developer. Isn't that what Donald Trump is?"

"Something like that. I've already drafted a letter to Mr. Hillyer," Joan told me with a hungry look in her eyes.

I read the rest of Mr. Hillyer's profile. He liked to watch old black-and-white movies, take long walks, and read science-fiction novels: three things I enjoyed. I was not having much luck keeping my interest low or my common sense in the front of my mind. Despite me protesting up a storm, laughing, and talking all kinds of other shit, I had to admit to myself that Joan might be onto something real cool. "Dude has a yacht and a beach house in Aruba! Damn," I said, giving her a slack-jawed look. "This one must have a hell of a huge fortune. What I can't figure out is why men with so much to offer can't find a woman the normal way. Could you imagine Donald Trump advertising in a magazine when he was between wives?"

Joan's lips curled up at the ends and she blinked rapidly for a few seconds. I couldn't tell if she was amused or just anxious. "Lola, most rich people are eccentric. Maybe they've all tried to find somebody the normal way and it didn't work out."

"Poor Mr. Hillyer. He hasn't been in a relationship since his wife died five years ago! He must be the loneliest one on the list. I feel so sorry for him. If I were you, I'd write to him just for the heck of it. It could be a lot of fun, I guess. Maybe he'll send you pictures of his beach house. What do you think?"

"I think there's only one way to find out," Joan chimed in, stabbing my chest with her finger. "You can write to him if you want to, since I haven't mailed my letter to him yet. I've picked out enough names already and I don't want you to think I'm too greedy. I'll give you some real hot pictures of Elaine that you can send in your letters claiming it's you."

I narrowed my eyes and glared at Joan. "I don't know about doing *that*. There's another thing I'm sure you didn't consider."

"What?"

"What you're planning to do may not be legal. . . ."

"Girl, it's not legal to jaywalk, but you do it. You cheat on your exams—"

"I only did that twice!" I interrupted.

"Will you hold your tongue and let me finish! You lie to your stepmother, and you sneak into the movies without paying when we go to the mall. And what about that time you swiped that bottle of Versace perfume from Macy's?"

"That was over three years ago when I was too young to know better and I never stole another thing! I had just lost my daddy and I needed something to cheer me up," I pouted.

"The point I'm trying to make is, don't you get all 'holier than thou' on me now. Besides, you keep talking about how bored you are. Well, let me tell you something. Since Lonnie Roberts broke up with me, I'm more bored than you are. And when I'm bored and the boys are not paying me enough attention or even telling me how good I look, I feel homely. Just think of all the compliments you can get from an older man."

I gave Joan a reserved look. I decided to continue being opposed to her plan as long as I could, just to keep myself balanced. But the truth of the matter was, the more she talked about it, the more interesting it sounded. "If, and I do mean *if,* I decide to write a few letters, what would I say to a bunch of old men? I barely know what to say to boys our age."

"Lonesome old men would be happy to hear anything from a beautiful young woman. By the way, not all older men are gross. My stepfather's niece married a real handsome man in his fifties. For all we know, you might find your soul mate this way."

With a weak smile, I gave Joan a submissive look. She was the leader; I was the follower. Unfortunately, I almost always ended up going the distance with her, no matter where she led me. What Joan was proposing this time was serious and something I would never consider on my own. However, I had visions of older, dapper men in the same league with Sidney Poitier, Harry Belafonte, and Donald Trump fawning over me and treating me like a princess. Men like them could introduce me to a life I could only experience in my dreams. When I looked at it from that perspective, it didn't seem so bad. "I don't have anything against older men. But if I get involved with one, I'd rather do it the normal way."

"Look, as long as you're under your stepmother's thumb, you won't be doing much of anything the normal way. Now, hand me that book of stamps off the dresser."

"Do you really think I could connect with somebody real interesting? Somebody who's not too old, sick, and ugly?"

"Like I said, there's only one way to find out. As long as we're careful and don't get too carried away, we have nothing to lose except the few dollars we'd spend on stamps, envelopes, and paper. But we have a lot to gain."

I handed Joan the stamps and lifted another one of the magazines from a previous month. Most of the men on the list for that month sounded even more interesting— and wealthier and more desperate—than the ones I'd already checked out. And they all sounded so cultured and polished.

Even though I was paranoid and apprehensive, I told myself that maybe this was a way I could break up the monotony in my life. . . .

"Uh, I think I'll write a short letter to the dude with the beach house in Aruba and the yacht, just to introduce myself," I said sheepishly.

Chapter 8

Joan

I WAS GLAD I HAD GROWN UP IN A FAMILY THAT HAD A "take no PRISOners" type of attitude. I had a great relationship with Mama and my stepfather, Elmo. Mama was a guard in a women's detention center; Elmo was a mechanic. They worked hard for their money, obeyed the law, paid their taxes on time, and treated everybody with respect. They punished me when I got out of line, but I didn't do that too often. But I was such a free spirit . . . I was still willing to take a few risks to get what I wanted. And now what I wanted was to have some serious fun and make some money at the same time, something I had never done before. When I thought about all the pussy I'd already given away for free, it made me angry. I would never even consider being a prostitute. But I didn't see anything wrong with making money in other ways that were indirectly related to love and sex: write sweet letters to love-struck old men who had indicated in magazine

ads, for anybody in the world to see, that they were looking for a beautiful young woman to be nice to them so
they could be nice to her.

A lot of people told me I was cute because of my round
face, full lips, and big brown eyes. I always wore my jet-
black hair short because it made me look a little like
Halle Berry. Even though I was seventeen and had the ID
to prove it, I looked more like a fourteen-year-old. I
looked even younger in my photographs, so there was no
way I was going to send pictures of myself to my new
pen pals. Lola also looked younger than seventeen. With
her cinnamon-brown skin, almond-shaped brown eyes,
full lips, and shoulder-length black hair, she was even
cuter than I was. (I'd never admit that to her!) We were
both five feet five, with just enough meat in all the right
places.

Bertha was feeling much better, so Lola came back to
my house the following Saturday evening. After Mama
had grilled her for a few minutes about what was happening with Bertha, she sent her up to my room, where I was
about to take some pictures of Elaine.

My sister was happy to pose for a few pictures. She
was the best-looking female in our immediate family and
she knew it. She loved being in front of a camera. It was
no wonder that she had once worked as a swimsuit model.

"Just don't photograph my left side," she advised,
tossing her head back and showing off her pearly white
teeth like she had just been crowned Miss America. She
sat in a chair in the middle of the floor with her legs
crossed. "And head shots only now. If you want some full
body shots, you'll have to wait until I lose a few pounds.
Right now my hips look as wide as Texas. That's why I
can't get me a *Playboy* centerfold deal."

"Elaine, just be still and smile," I said, giving Lola a wink. She stood by the door in my bedroom, looking like a scared mouse. Even though she had agreed to let me use her address and had agreed to write to a few lonely old men herself, she still looked like she wanted to jump out of her skin. She padded across the floor and stretched out on my bed as I fiddled around with the cheap throwaway camera we had purchased at Walgreens an hour ago. It had twenty-seven shots, but I had wasted the first one trying to figure out how to use the damn thing. I took a picture of Lola lying on my bed on her back, pretending to be asleep. A few minutes later, the real photo session began.

"I can't wait to get these developed so I can send some to Daddy," I said, smiling at Elaine as I snapped away. The smile on her face was so obviously forced, it was a shame. But most men wouldn't notice a minor detail like that.

A second after I'd clicked the first photograph, Elaine's fake smile faded, her shoulders drooped, and she held up her hand. "Wait a minute, Joan. I thought you said you wanted some recent pictures of me so you could send them to Lenny."

"Uh, that too," I said quickly. I had become such a frequent and careless liar I couldn't keep up with everything I'd told people. Yes, I had told Elaine that I wanted to send some recent photos of her and other family members to our brother Lenny, who was in the navy. And as far as our daddy was concerned, none of us had communicated with him in months. Elaine was a dingbat. It was easy to get over on her by telling her another lie. "I ran into Daddy's wife's cousin last week. She told me he told her he'd like to get some recent pictures of his kids. I'm going to send him my school pictures."

"Well, when you get in touch with him, you tell him I

said I'd like to get some of that back child support he still owes Mama for us," Elaine snapped. "I'm having a hard time getting by on alimony payments from that hound from hell I divorced."

"Hold still. This won't take long," I told Elaine.

"Hurry up so I can go get ready for my date," she said, looking at her watch. She was impatient, but the fake smile was back on her face. I had her pose in different ways as I snapped away: ten shots in all—hips included in spite of her protests. I knew enough about men to know that they liked a meaty woman. Especially elderly men. When Elaine pranced out of my room ten minutes later, Lola and I headed to the same Walgreens where we had purchased the camera.

We couldn't wait for the photos to get developed, which would take a few hours, not one hour like we had thought. "I'll pick them up tomorrow when I come to get Bertha's prescription filled," Lola volunteered.

We both sent letters to six men each the same night, anyway.

Two weeks went by and only two had responded, both to Lola. It was a real letdown to us both. I was disappointed because nobody had written back to me. And Lola didn't think that the men she'd heard from sounded interesting enough to write to again. Each man complained about all the ailments he had; everything from gout to grippe. Each man said how he would love to have a nice young woman to share his bed with and take care of him. Had I not seen the two different names and two different return addresses, I would have sworn that the same man had sent both letters.

A few days later, I received a letter from a retired farmer in Plano, Texas. He apologized for not responding sooner. He was still recovering from a stroke he'd had last month and had just regained the use of his writing hand. Just like the two men Lola had received letters from, this lonely heart was also looking for a lover and a caretaker. "I don't think it's going to be worth it to write letters to these sick puppies, after all," I told Lola. "The way these dudes sound, they're too weak and sick to even get out of bed to go shopping to buy stuff for us."

"Yeah, you're probably right. I'm sorry I wasted my money and stamps. I could have used it to get my legs waxed."

"Let's not give up too soon. I'll come over to your house after school tomorrow and we can pick out a few more to write to out of a different edition of the magazine. Last night Too Sweet finished reading the one that came this month, so she won't miss it."

A week after we had written letters to several more new pen pals, which included pictures of Elaine, Lola came running up to me in the hallway at school as soon as I got to my locker that Monday morning.

"Girl, didn't you get the message I left for you Saturday? I told that brain-dead Too Sweet to tell you to call me," Lola gushed. I only saw her in such a giddy mood like the one she was in now when there was a cute boy involved. "I couldn't come over because I had a lot of housework to do and I had promised to wash and set Bertha's hair this weekend."

"Too Sweet didn't tell me you called for me last Saturday night. You, of all people, ought to know how forgetful old people can be, and I keep telling you to call me on my cell phone now. If I don't answer, leave a voice mail. That way, your mama won't know how often we talk. So, what's up, anyway? Why is that goofy look on your face?"

Lola looked around first. Then she opened her back-pack and pulled out a stack of envelopes.

"What's all—" I stopped and my jaw dropped. "We got letters from those old dudes?"

"Every single one of those new ones we wrote to responded. Three of the letters came in Friday's mail. The rest came on Saturday. Twelve in all!" Lola said, nodding. "Only one of mine sent me something real nice. The other five said they would if I was sure I wanted to start up something with them."

"Are you kidding me?"

"Nope, I'm not kidding you. Maybe you got something nice too."

"What—what did you get?" I said as she handed me the six envelopes addressed to me.

"I'll show you in a minute! Just open yours."

I was so anxious and curious that I ripped open the first one right away. I was flabbergasted. I couldn't believe my eyes. A cashier's check for five hundred dollars was attached to the letter! I was so busy admiring the check, Lola had to poke me in the side with her elbow to get me to read the letter. I looked around first to make sure none of our classmates and teachers were lurking nearby. I shifted my backpack from my back to my shoulder; then I leaned against my locker and stared at the letter. It was neat, but the writing was so small and written in such a light shade of blue ink, I had to squint my eyes to read it. I read it out loud so Lola could hear:

"My dearest Joan,
"Your letter brightened my day in ways I never dreamed of. I have been in the grip of depression for many years, but now I feel like a new man because of you. You are the angel I have been praying

for since my wife died thirty years ago. Thank you for including your photograph. You look like a film star! You are the most beautiful woman who has ever shown an interest in me! Because of you, I feel alive again! My last lady friend, a woman with health issues of her own, died a few months ago. She was up in age, as were the few who preceded her. I am no longer interested in developing a relationship with another woman in my age group. A young girl like you could keep me alive another ten or fifteen years.

"*As I noted in my profile, I am very prosperous and since I have no family, I enjoy doing nice things for nice people. Each year I donate thousands of dollars to my favorite charities and other worthy causes. I almost wept when you told me in your letter about your financial difficulties and how you and your sweet elderly mother are struggling just to keep food on your table! My dear, that ends today! Enclosed is a cashier's check for five hundred dollars. Even if I don't hear from you again, I will feel good just knowing I gave you a portion of the happiness you deserve. Also enclosed is a more recent photo of myself. The one you saw in the magazine was six months old by the time they featured it and my appearance has changed—for the better I'm proud to say (smile).*

"*With love, Richard Byrd III*

"*P.S. I've dreamt about you every night since I received your letter. And after I kiss your lovely photograph every night, I sleep with it underneath my pillow!*

"*P.P.S. I can't wait to hold you in my arms!!!!!*

"*Until we meet, I send you love.*"

* * *

I struggled not to laugh as I folded the letter and slid it back into its envelope. I looked at Lola and swallowed hard. I didn't know what to say next. But after a few seconds, the words flowed out of my mouth like lava. "Damn, this was as easy as taking candy from a baby. This old dude is already sprung! It's a damn shame he's not better-looking," I said with a shudder.

I had never in my life seen such a homely man; and from the grimace on Lola's face when I showed the picture to her, she probably hadn't either. On top of Mr. Byrd's huge snout of a nose, he had a lazy eye. There was a wool cap on his globelike head, so I couldn't tell what his hair looked like, or even if he still had some left.

"Oh, he's a beast, all right. But wait until you see the *recent* pictures of the ones I got letters from. Their letters are just as corny as Mr. Byrd's. One looks like some swamp creature that ought to be swimming in a black lagoon," Lola said. "The others look even worse. Mr. Royster in Baltimore, the ugliest one of all, sent me a check too. Three hundred dollars."

I was beside myself. Nothing I'd ever done before had been this easy. I opened the five other letters addressed to me and scanned each one for a few seconds while Lola watched. Each man talked about how happy he was that I'd written to him and how sorry he was to hear that my mother was at death's door and in need of a serious operation. The ones who had not sent any money told me to let them know as soon as I could how much I needed and they would send it. I could not believe that in this day and age, suckers of this magnitude still existed! On any given day, the media did stories about scams. I didn't like to hear about people scamming anybody, especially elderly people. Every time I read about some elderly man or woman falling for one of those Internet scams, or a Ponzi scheme, I got mad. A couple of months ago, an eighty-two-year old widow who lived on our street lost most of her life savings to some Nigerian "prince." Somehow he got her telephone number and started calling her on a regular basis. He talked her into transferring money from her bank into his Swiss bank account. By the time the woman's children realized what was happening, it was too late. The bogus prince was a con man of epic proportions, and had been dodging the authorities in eight different countries for two years. As far as I was concerned, people like my elderly neighbor and people like the lonely hearts club members—who were screaming for somebody to take something from them—were from two different planets. Yes, I was getting over on a few old men, but they were taking advantage of me just as much as I was taking advantage of them. And another thing, my time was valuable. With that in mind, time was money. One thing that really jumped into my mind as another justification was the fact that these men had probably been paying for their fun long before they joined Aunt Martha's Friendship Association. One disturbing thought suddenly blew into my mind, and it hit me with such a jolt, I shuddered. That thought was: how would I feel if some greedy con artist was scamming one of my elderly relatives?

"Joan, I—" Lola stopped talking and gasped. "What's the matter? You look like somebody just threw a bucket of cold water on your face."

"Oh, it's just my cramps. My period started this morning," I said. For the first time in my life, I was glad all of my grandparents had already passed. However, I had a few aging aunts and uncles still around and I'd hate for them to get involved with somebody like . . . me and Lola. Despite the money and the "fun" we were going to have writing to senior citizens, I was so conflicted I didn't know if I was coming or going. One minute I was elated; the next minute I was disgusted with myself. But since we had already wet our beaks, it was too late to turn back now. I just wouldn't let Lola know about all these feelings I was having. . . .

"Drink some green tea when you get home. That'll help your cramps. You need to be feeling your best so we can get to the mall and spend some of this money." Lola was so hyped up, beads of sweat dotted her forehead and it was not warm enough in March for anybody to be sweating at all.

Chapter 9

Joan

I TRIED TO REMOVE THE DISTURBING THOUGHT OF SOME-body scamming a member of my family out of my mind, but I couldn't. I was only able to push it to the back behind my other thoughts. "If I didn't know any better, I'd swear a bunch of teenage boys wrote these letters, but I know they didn't. No sane young dude would ever claim to be a senior citizen."

Lola and I locked eyes, giving each other dumb-founded looks. "I'm glad we sent Elaine's picture with the second batch of letters. It sure got the ball rolling!" she whooped. "Just think if we had sent pictures with the first batch. We'd probably have twice as many letters to answer. This turned out to be a piece of cake."

"A 'piece of cake,' my ass, Lola. This is an eight-layer cake with icing. I had no idea getting rich was going to be this easy." Making light of the situation helped keep things in perspective. We were not doing anything bad or wrong; we were just having fun.

"I didn't either. Uh, I'm going to go to the bank after school and cash my check before Bertha 'accidentally' snoops around and finds it. I already have a joint savings account with her at Wells Fargo. I think she's forgotten about it because she hasn't mentioned it in three years."

"You're going to deposit your money into that account?"

"Heck no! With my luck, Bertha would open a statement one month and see the balance. I'm going to cash the check and hide the money in my room."

"I have a Christmas club account in my name only, but I don't know if they'll let me cash a check like this."

"If they don't, maybe I can cash it for you."

"Okay. We'll go to the bank together then. I'll wait for you out front by the bus stop after school."

"Cool!" Lola exclaimed with her eyes sparkling like diamonds.

Had I known it was going to be this easy to get Lola on board this gravy train, I would have shared everything with her sooner. I was about to say something else when I noticed a worried look on her face, and it had not been there a few seconds before.

"What's the matter now?" I asked. "Why do you have that puppy dog face all of a sudden?"

"I don't know. I just had a weird thought. I feel kind of strange about what we're doing. Like a, uh, con artist."

I glared at Lola. I knew that if I confessed to her that I'd had a similar, disturbing thought a few moments ago, she probably would have freaked out. I decided to play it off. In a very casual tone of voice, I said, "So, what else is new? Look, you need to make up your mind. Are you into this or not? Why did you wait until *now* to start feeling strange? And if you don't want that money, you can give it to me."

"No, I'll keep the money, but I'm still a little worried. I've never done anything like this before."

"I haven't either, so we're even," I snapped. It was always hard for me to hide my exasperation with Lola, but I didn't even try to do it this time. I was in too good of a mood. I didn't want my elation to go away too soon, especially for a stupid reason like Lola being a little worried. "Exactly what is it you're a 'little worried' about? All you need to be thinking about is how we're going to spend all this fucking cash!"

"I don't know. Maybe I should have snuck out of church with you during that sermon before that visiting pastor started talking about deceit and the love of money and whatnot. The way people were talking after the service, he'd made a lot of them feel guilty. Thinking about that just now made me think all of a sudden that this might not be such a good idea, after all. It's too good to be true."

"Look, Lola, it's fine with me if you don't want to get more involved now. You don't have to write any more letters, you know. That'd be more men for me to write to."

Lola still had that puppy dog look on her face and it was really getting on my nerves. She took a deep breath and suddenly perked back up. "I can sure use the money. Maybe I'll stick with this for just a little longer. Are you going to respond to all of the letters we received from the new men?"

"I can't think of one good reason not to. Those men sound so pathetic, I feel sorry for them. Just think how happy we can make them just by writing to them and . . . and—"

"Conning them out of their hard-earned money?" Lola tossed in.

"There you go again! That's not what I'd call it, so please don't say that. And how do you know they're not crooks themselves? For all you know, they could have made their money by *conning* people! With all the scams and Ponzi scheme stories we see on TV and read about in the newspaper, I'm surprised that hadn't already occurred to you."

"That's besides the point, Joan. What do you call what we're doing? If this isn't 'conning,' I don't know what is."

"Well, yeah, we are conning them, if you want to split hairs. But this is different from a *real* con. For one thing, our new men friends probably don't see it that way. They were the ones who offered us money."

"But that's only because we told them we had financial problems and because they think we're a gorgeous woman in her twenties who will eventually hook up with them in person. Almost every single one either wants a serious relationship or a wife."

How a superfly girl like me ended up with a wishy-washy BFF like Lola was beyond me. "Look, if they didn't want to give away their money, they wouldn't have bragged about how prosperous and generous they were when they sent their information to be listed in that magazine. These men want some attention. We want some money. You can back out if you want to, but I . . . I'm going to get more prints of Elaine's pictures because I'm going to write to a few more men. I'm going to tell them all about how poor I am and how my mother needs an operation."

"I need to think about this a little more," Lola said, her voice cracking. "I'm glad I got this money, but . . ."

"But what? You feel guilty? If that's the case, like I said, give me the money you received."

"I don't feel *that* guilty," she said, and chuckled. If she was laughing, she couldn't be too concerned about being a "con artist."

Chapter 10

Joan

I LOOKED FORWARD TO EACH NEW DAY BECAUSE I WAS ON a roll. Thanks to my elderly pen pals, cash was coming in faster than I could spend it. Just last week, a real nice man—a retired oil executive in Dallas—sent me a thousand dollars in his second letter! In the last couple of weeks, I purchased all of the latest CDs by my favorite rappers and a few I had just discovered, half-a-dozen new novels, and some very expensive new clothes. Last Monday after school, I got my hair and nails done for the first time at a salon that catered to local celebrities. I didn't know what to spend my money on next! As long as nobody noticed all the new stuff I had acquired, I wasn't worried. I was over the moon. I had just begun to flirt with the idea of buying myself a set of fake D-cup titties, until my busybody cousin Too Sweet said something that brought me back down to earth.

"Joan, you been looking mighty spiffy these days. New clothes, fresh hairdo every week—what's up with all that? Where you getting all this money from? I know you ain't making much by babysitting now and then, and you ain't doing nothing else to be getting paid."

I sat at my desk with my back to the door. Too Sweet had entered the room so quietly that I didn't even know she was present until she started talking. I whirled around, with a lie ready to slide out of my mouth. "I've just been borrowing money from Lola," I said, ignoring the suspicious look on her pig face.

"Lola? Hmmm . . ." I hated when my cousin sucked on her teeth and looked at me out of the corner of her eye. She reminded me of a mighty oak tree standing there with her hands on her hips. "She ain't got no job. Where is *she* getting money from, all of a sudden?"

"Oh, didn't I tell you? Her daddy had a real big life insurance policy with the bus company he drove for, so he left her a pretty penny when he died. Her stepmother just recently allowed her to start spending some of it."

"I see," Too Sweet said with a skeptical look. One thing that had always been in my favor was that she didn't have much authority in our house. Right after she moved in, she tried to throw her weight around and boss me and my siblings. With her old-school notions, she assumed she could give us whuppings the way Mama and Elmo did when we misbehaved. My brother Chet was thirteen at the time. After being a resident for only three days, Too Sweet attempted to whup him with one of her double-wide, extra-long leather belts for sassing her. Not only did he cuss her out so bad it brought tears to my eyes, he hauled off and sucker punched her in the chest and knocked the wind out of her. She never attempted to whup him again, nor any of the rest of us. Not even me.

And she had seen me do a lot of things that normally would have gotten me whuppings from Mama *and* Elmo at the same time.

As far as I was concerned, Too Sweet was even lower on the totem pole than I was. Normally, I wouldn't even worry about anything she had to say in my case. However, I didn't want her to say anything that would arouse Mama's or Elmo's curiosity and make them start paying more attention to me and all the new stuff I had purchased.

"Well, that 'pretty penny' must be a mighty *big* penny too for Lola to be lending you the kind of money you've been spending. . . ."

"I don't know exactly how much her daddy left her, and I know it'd be rude to ask. But she told me that whenever I need a few extra dollars, to just let her know. I know you've noticed how nice she's been looking lately too."

"Now that you mentioned it, yeah. But Lola is a real cute girl, anyway." My miserable cousin gave me a hopeless look. For a moment, I thought she was going to cry. "Life is so unfair. If somebody had died and left me a bunch of money, I would have been able to fix myself up better and have a husband and some kids by now. I never thought I'd still be single in my late forties Too bad you and Elaine got all the looks in this family. I bet if I looked like you or her, or Lola, men would be throwing money at me with both hands and I'd have to beat them off with a stick, huh?"

"Yep! You sure would!" I chirped. "You don't have to be a beauty queen to get a man's attention. There are other things you can do." I spoke with caution. My cousin was the nervous type who could burst into tears and expel silent farts at the drop of a hat when something spooked her. And with a gas problem that could bring down the house, I had to handle her with extreme care.

Too Sweet dipped her head and looked up at me with her eyebrows raised. "Where are you going with this conversation?"

"Cuz, have you ever thought about joining a lonely hearts club?"

Too Sweet gave me an incredulous look. "Like them nutcases listed on the back pages in my *Modern Love* magazines?"

"Uh . . . yeah. I glanced at that list one time and some of those men sounded real nice. And rich . . ."

"What's wrong with you, girl? For one thing, those men don't want a woman my age—and I don't want no man my age. And for another thing, when somebody stoops low enough to *advertise* in a magazine for a wife or a husband, something's got to be wrong with them! I ain't about to waste my time on that kind of nonsense! I done waited this long for my soul mate—I can keep on waiting. I think any woman that gets involved with *strangers* through the mail, or strangers any other way, period, is asking for a heap of trouble. They'll end up with an ax murderer, a she-male posing as a full man, or worse. Uh-uh, baby girl. That New Age dating mess is for people with a straight-up death wish." Too Sweet paused and stared at me with a look on her face that was a combination of disgust and disbelief. "Promise me, you will never bring up some foolishness like a 'lonely hearts club' to me again."

"I promise you, I won't," I muttered.

Chapter II
Lola

*A*s the weeks passed, I began to think long and hard about the person I had become—all in the name of greed. I experienced several different degrees of emotion. Those old men would never even meet me, let alone be with me and love me to the end. That made me feel even sorrier for them, but not enough to leave them alone or tell them the truth.

Now when I received letters, especially ones that contained money, I not only felt a little guilty, I also felt a little lonely. Those feelings never lasted that long. The easy money still gave me a rush. I had never been addicted to anything before, but I had a feeling I was now addicted to money. I couldn't get enough. Not only was the cash rolling in like tidal waves, the old men thought they were investing in a future with a beautiful woman in her twenties. That was the part that really made me feel a little guilty from time to time.

* * *

About three months after we'd mailed the first batch of letters, Libby showed up at the house unannounced on a Saturday morning. She and our mailman arrived at the same time! I watched from the living-room window as she parked her car and got out. She pranced up to the mailman just as he was about to deposit a thick stack of envelopes into the box. In addition to all of the other negative things about my stepsister, she was a big flirt whenever she was in the presence of a good-looking man. I couldn't hear what she was saying to the mailman, who was grinning like a fool as he handed her the mail! My heart skipped a beat and I held my breath as I watched Libby walk toward the porch. I was still holding my breath when she barged in. She dropped the stack of mail on top of the small bookcase near the entrance and I let out a sigh of relief.

"Rudy Jeeters sure is cute. If I wasn't married and he wasn't just a mailman, I'd sock it to him," she said with a dreamy look on her pie-shaped face.

"He is cute for a mailman," I said, shifting my eye toward the mail.

"I see Mama still gets a ton of bills. I hope you're making sure they get paid on time." Libby removed her white nylon windbreaker and draped it over her arm instead of placing it on the coatrack by the door, which meant she wouldn't be staying long.

"I do. I mail the payments myself," I said eagerly. I rushed over to get the mail before she had a chance to go back and look through it more thoroughly. I flipped through it as fast as I could. The utility bill was on top. The rest included more bills, junk, and a postcard from a retired teacher Bertha used to work with, who was on vacation in Italy. "Your mama is in her room," I chirped.

Since no new letters had come for me or for Joan, I dropped the mail back onto the bookcase.

Libby stood with her hands on her hips. "This floor looks like hell," she complained, frowning as she stared at the floor.

"Hmmm. That's odd. I just cleaned it two days ago."

"I never would have guessed that. Not with all these dust balls and other shit." She gave me a dry look and then she started to sniff and rub her nose. "Chitlins for dinner last night *again*?"

"You know how much your mama loves chitlins. She'd eat them every day if they weren't so expensive. And the man at the meat market always cleans them for us for free," I reminded. "Uh, do you want me to go tell her you're here?" Libby's visits rarely lasted longer than a few minutes, but even that was a few minutes too long for me. Her demeanor had become even nastier over the years. I couldn't remember the last time she said something pleasant to me or asked any questions about how I was doing in school and such. I made sure she and Marshall knew that I was a straight-A student by posting some of my best test papers on the front door of the refrigerator. I'd won the annual citywide spelling bee last year, but they had never commented on it. They only mentioned me and school in the same conversation when they discussed how I had managed not to get pregnant so far and drop out of school like so many other girls we knew. I always assured them that I was *not* going to get pregnant, and even if I did, I would still get my diploma and hopefully continue my education. Libby had such a bleak outlook when it came to me, she usually just gave me blank stares when I said something positive about myself. "Bertha is constipated again, so she had a rough time last night and didn't get much sleep."

"Humph! She's going to have a lot more rough nights

if she doesn't stop gobbling up hog guts and all the rest of that mess you let her eat."

"I can't tell Bertha what to eat. She pays for the groceries," I said firmly. "I do buy fresh veggies myself when I go to the store on my own, though."

"From the size of your butt, I'm sure you're eating just as much fattening pork as mama is," Libby cackled. "Oh, you know I'm just playing with you. There's nothing wrong with being your size, Lola."

That remark didn't even deserve a response. For one thing, I was still just a size eight. Libby's butt was just as big as mine and the rest of her was even bigger. Apparently, she saw something different when she looked in the mirror or stepped on a scale. I had to look away to keep from snickering.

Just then, Bertha wobbled down the stairs, moaning and groaning. Her hair was all over her head and I could tell from the dried spit on her chin that she had not even washed her face yet or cleaned the dentures she'd been wearing for five years. "Libby, I thought I heard your voice," she said with an anxious grin. She walked over and gave her a hug and a quick peck on the cheek. Libby stood there like a tree with no emotion on her face. "I've left you three or four messages and I was wondering when I'd hear from you, baby."

"I've been busy. Taking care of a husband and a house is a full-time job."

"Is everything all right?" Bertha asked. Before answering, Libby looked at me and nodded toward the door, a hint for me to leave the room so she could have some privacy with her mother.

I cleared my throat. "I'll go start breakfast," I said, easing toward the kitchen. As soon as I turned the corner, I put my ear to the wall.

"Mama, I need another grand."

I heard Bertha gasp and choke on some air before she responded. "For what?"

"Um, the water heater went out last night."

"That's what you told me when I gave you that thousand dollars last month! Libby, please tell me you're not still spending my money in the casinos. You told me you'd stopped gambling."

"I did stop gambling and I did tell you last month I needed money for the water heater. That incompetent stooge who came out the first time didn't do a good job and we're right back where we started."

"Oh. Well, I don't have that much cash in the house. I'd have to go to the bank Monday morning. If you can't wait that long, I'll write you a check and you can get Mr. Thomas at the market to cash it without charging a fee, like one of those convenience stores."

"Write me a check then. And hurry up. I have a lot of things to do today. I still have to go to the beauty shop to get my hair done and then to Macy's to get a dress to wear to Jeffrey's supervisor's son's bar mitzvah today."

"Is that what you need money for?"

"How many times do I have to tell you not to get all up in my business? I told you, I need a thousand bucks to get the water heater fixed. Now, if you don't want to give me that money, just say so and I'll get up out of here and go borrow it from somebody else. I'm sure I can get money from one of daddy's people. . . ."

Nothing hurt Bertha more than to hear that her children still had a relationship with her ex-husband's family. Especially since every single one of them had never accepted Bertha. Libby and Marshall only mentioned that side of their family when they wanted to manipulate her.

"Honey, you don't need to ask your daddy's people for anything as long as there's a breath still left in my body. Let me go upstairs and get my purse."

"By the way, Mama, how much allowance do you give to that girl?"

It was bad enough that Libby was so mean-spirited, but it hurt when she referred to me as "that girl" when she didn't know I was listening.

"I give her twenty dollars a week like her daddy used to do. Why?"

"Last week when I was at the mall in Milpitas, I saw her and that slutty Joan Proctor shopping in Neiman Marcus. How can that girl afford to shop at a place like *Nieman* on twenty bucks a week?"

"Hmmm. I don't know. I hope she's not shoplifting."

"I doubt that she's stealing, but I wouldn't put it past her. They didn't see me, but I saw her and Joan hand cash to the girl behind the sportswear counter for whatever it was they were buying. Probably more hoochie-coochie frocks. And the fact that they already had a few shopping bags with them told me they weren't stealing. At least not in that store." Libby paused. "Can we get upstairs so you can write me that check? I told you I was in a hurry."

"I was hoping you'd stay and visit for a while. I'm getting old and I'd like to spend more time with you and your brother. . . ."

"Mama, I'm telling you *again* that I'm in a hurry. Now, are you going to go upstairs to write me that check or not?"

"Libby, your spending is out of control. Every time I see you, you have on a new dress or a new pair of shoes." Bertha didn't stand up to Libby or Marshall often, but when she did, it made me feel good to know she was not a complete pushover. It was bad enough that I was straddling that same line myself. "After this, don't you come back over here for more money for a while."

"Then you'd better make that check out for three thousand bucks instead of one so I won't have to come back for a while," Libby said dryly.

As soon as I heard them walk up the creaky stair steps, I ran to the wall phone in the kitchen and called Joan.

"Hello," she said in a cheerful voice.

"Libby called you a 'slut.'"

"That heifer! That—that *slut*!" Joan yelled. "Is that what you called to tell me?"

"That's one of the things." My heart was pounding as I leaned toward the door listening for Libby and Bertha to come back downstairs. "I have to talk fast, so listen up. Remember that day you borrowed your stepfather's car and we drove out to the Great Mall in Milpitas?"

"Yeah. What about it?"

"Libby saw us shopping in Neiman," I told Joan in an angry, breathless whisper.

"So, what if she did? A lot of people shop at Neiman."

"Yeah, but she knows all I get is my twenty-dollar-a-week allowance and a few babysitting dollars every now and then. She was telling Bertha about it a few minutes ago and that's when she called you a 'slut.' What will I say if they ask me how I could afford to be shopping in such an expensive store?"

"If she asks, just tell her you went with me to pick up a few items for Elaine. Everybody knows what a high-maintenance woman she is and they know she gets a fat alimony check every month."

"Okay," I muttered. I was a nervous wreck and I couldn't believe how nonchalant Joan sounded. I was glad for that, though. If she had sounded nervous too, I would have been falling apart even more.

"Don't worry about Libby. She has nothing on us." Joan paused and snorted. "Did any new mail come for me today?" I didn't like her casual tone of voice. She didn't seem the least bit concerned about Libby. I didn't want to get into a conflict with her, so I didn't say anything else about it.

"No. And that's another thing. I'm glad nothing came for us today because we had a close call. Libby got here at the same time this morning as our mailman and he handed her the mail!"

"Shit!" Joan yelled. She sounded concerned about Libby now.

"We should rent a private mailbox, just to be on the safe side," I suggested.

"Didn't I tell you that those things cost more than a couple of hundred dollars a year? And they are not even that secure. My cousin Preston has his mail delivered to one. He complains all the time about those idiots putting his mail in the wrong box. What if we rent a box and one of our letters with cash in it gets put in the wrong box and the person at that address opens it? They could be dishonest enough to keep the money, or mean enough to turn the letter over to the post office authorities. It wouldn't take long for them to figure out what's going on."

"Damn! We don't need anything else to worry about, so forget I mentioned renting a private mailbox. I'll just have to be more careful and make sure Libby or somebody else doesn't go nosing through the mail. Until . . ."

"Until what?"

"Until we decide to stop, or until we get caught. . . ."

Chapter 12

Joan

I COULDN'T STOP THINKING ABOUT WHAT LOLA HAD SAID a few minutes ago about us getting caught. I knew we'd eventually stop writing to those old men, but it never occurred to me that we'd "get caught." I pushed those words, and what she had told me about Libby bringing the mail into the house, to the back of my mind. I was convinced that as long as we were careful, we had nothing to worry about. To keep myself busy so I wouldn't have time to worry about Libby or anything else related to our activity, I decided to go on about my day. In other words, it was business as usual. I treated myself to a spa treatment and a very expensive lunch. I ate caviar for the first time in my life.

The following Monday, Lola received a letter from one of her pals that contained eight hundred dollars, all in hundred-dollar bills. I asked myself over and over if these old dudes' brains had become pickled due to age. It was easy for me to see why so many old people ended up being victims. I was glad that most of the money came in money orders or checks. Later that same week, six more letters arrived—three for Lola and three for me. Each one contained *cash*!

When we received checks and money orders, we cashed them at a different location each time. The reason for that was because the bank tellers and the clerks who worked in convenience stores were just as nosy as everybody else. Sooner or later, some of them would start keeping track of two black teenagers cashing checks several times a month and blab enough for some meddlesome investigator to get involved. That was one chance we could not afford to take.

I kept my money in a cigar box, which I hid under a pile of junk in our garage. There was so much junk in there already, Elmo and Mama had to park their cars in our driveway. The only time anybody went into the garage was to store more junk, or to get rid of something else to make room for more.

By the first week in June, I had so much cash in my cigar box, I had to secure it with thick rubber bands to keep it shut. By the first week in July, I had *two* cigar boxes full of money! Even though Mama never asked about the bank account she had opened for me, I was still too afraid to deposit more than ten or twenty bucks at a time, which was what I earned babysitting and running errands for people.

I didn't like the fact that Lola and I couldn't use our money the way we wanted to. We still had no choice but to continue doing our spending on the down-low. We wore our most expensive outfits when just the two of us were together. We ate meals in expensive restaurants instead of the pizza parlors and rib joints we used to eat in. Every week we spent two to three hundred dollars each on spa treatments, manicures, pedicures, and trips to the beauty shop. On a Monday, the week after the Fourth of July, Lola accompanied me to a surgeon's office in San Jose. I had an early-morning appointment for him to remove a hairy mole from the side of my left boob. It was minor outpatient surgery and didn't take long. I paid the doctor two thousand dollars in cash. He told me I had to wear a special bra for two weeks. I wanted to wear a different one every day, so I needed to buy *fourteen*. The cost was forty dollars for each one. I didn't have much cash left in my wallet after paying the surgeon, so Lola paid the five hundred and sixty dollars, plus tax. She also paid another hundred dollars to cover the prescription for the pain pills the doctor thought I might need. On the way home, she treated me to a lobster and filet mignon lunch with all the trimmings. That was another couple of hundred bucks. We were almost living the lifestyles of the rich and famous.

By the time we returned to school in September, I was very comfortable with our routine. I even wrote some of my love letters in Mr. Dowling's history class. I sat in the last seat in the last row, where nobody could see what I was doing. At home I composed letters in my room on my laptop. And I was always careful, or so I thought. One Saturday morning, ten minutes after Too Sweet had rolled out of her bed and left the room, I scrambled out of mine and padded over to my desk. I plopped down into the new desk chair I had purchased a few days ago and turned on my computer. I started a "thank you" letter to a man who had just sent me another cashier's check. I was so preoccupied that I didn't hear the door open.

"Joan, what in the world are you up to this time?"

I whirled around so fast, I felt a crick in my neck. Too Sweet was standing behind me, looking over my shoulder. "I thought you were downstairs eating breakfast," I wailed, minimizing the screen on my computer at the same time.

"I wish I was. Elmo burnt the grits and had to start a new pot," she told me with a frown as she rubbed her nose. She pursed her lips, turned her head slightly to the side, and looked at me from the corner of her eye. "Joan, I hope you ain't messing around with some married man."

"Who me? Why would you say that?"

"I seen the top of that letter you trying to hide. You started it with a 'Dearest something or other' and that ain't the normal way kids talk." There was a suspicious look on her face that was so extreme it looked like it had been tattooed on. I blinked and my mind raced to come up with something that would make her back off. She was as gullible as my pen pals, so I didn't have to use much brain energy.

"Please promise me you won't tell," I began speaking in a feeble voice and blinking even harder. "I don't want to get Lola in trouble."

Too Sweet did a double take and folded her arms. I knew she thought she was about to get a real juicy piece of news that she could spread. "Oh? Is Lola the one fooling around with a married man? Humph! The way she was raised, I ain't surprised. Whose husband is it? How come you writing a letter for her?"

"Her computer is in the shop for repairs, so she couldn't write a letter to the man herself to tell him she wanted to break up because she found out he's married," I explained.

"Why is she calling him 'dearest' if she's breaking up with him? A low-down, funky dog who's cheating on his wife needs to be called anything but dearest. What's wrong with Lola?"

"She still has feelings for him, see. She told me what to say in the letter."

"Do say!" Too Sweet rolled her neck and placed her ashy hands on her hips. "How come she couldn't tell him to his face? And if her computer is broke, how come she couldn't handwrite him a letter?"

"I don't know. I guess she's too upset."

"Or too lazy. So she makes you do her dirty work." Too Sweet gave me a woeful look. "You poor thing. I had a feeling Lola was taking advantage of you. I hope you don't let none of her bad habits rub off on you. A girl like her, who grew up in a house with her daddy's girlfriend and mama living there at the same time, must come up with all kinds of devilment to lead girls like you into."

"I won't let Lola do that to me," I mumbled. I wondered what my cousin would say if she knew that I was doing most of the "leading."

"Do I know the man?"

"What man?"

"That hound from hell Lola's involved with!" Too Sweet said sharply.

"No, you don't know him. He just moved here last month from San Francisco."

"Oomph, oomph, oomph. So he's from *Frisco*? That figures! No wonder he's such a freak. But that ain't no excuse. He's new in town and he's already acting a fool—with a *teenager*. His wife ought to peel his dick with a dull knife."

"Uh-huh," I agreed as I turned off my computer. I rose and stretched. I was glad to see Too Sweet walking back toward the door. "I'll finish this letter tomorrow. I'm getting real hungry."

"Well, let's just hope Elmo don't burn another batch of them grits."

As soon as Too Sweet was out of the room, I locked the door and scurried back to my computer and finished typing the letter I had started. I sealed it in an envelope I had already addressed. This particular man was so antsy, if I didn't reply to one of his letters within the same week, he mailed a new one each day until he heard from me. He had been bugging me for a telephone number so he could finally hear the voice of the "sweet woman" he hoped to marry someday. I wanted to mail the letter as soon as I could to thank him for the money. I couldn't take a chance on him sending an avalanche of letters again in the same week. Some mailmen were just as nosy as bank employees and the people who cashed checks at convenience stores. I didn't want the man who delivered the mail to Lola's house to get suspicious about a pile of letters from the same man in the same week. My goal was to keep everybody at bay so Lola and I could keep the cash flowing a little while longer.

Chapter 13

Lola

TWO DAYS AFTER THE LAST TIME I'D TALKED TO JOAN, I trotted over to the convenience store a few blocks from school to cash a three-hundred-dollar cashier's check I'd received from one of my pen pals.

I was on my way into the store, and a woman I hadn't seen since I was twelve, and thought I'd never see again, was on her way out: Shirelle Odom. I still cared about Shirelle and I still thought of her as my other mother. Her niece, Mariel Odom, had been one of my closest friends, but after Shirelle severed ties with my family, so did Mariel and everybody else in their family.

"Lola, is that you?" Shirelle hollered, grabbing my arm. "You're so grown-up and pretty!"

"Shirelle?" She no longer resembled the woman I used to know who had always worn a long blond weave and enough makeup for two women. Her hair was black and short now and the only makeup on her face was some lip gloss and a little face powder. She was about twenty pounds heavier and in her middle forties now, but she was still a very attractive woman with her big, shiny black eyes and high cheekbones. "I am so happy to see you!" We moved out of the doorway and she gave me a big hug. "Do you live around here now?"

"Um, no. I was just in town visiting my folks," she said quietly. "I live in San Francisco with my husband."

"Oh, you're married now."

She nodded. "I wasn't going to wait forever on your daddy to marry me, and I knew he wouldn't as long as your mama was alive. I, uh, I heard she died and he married Bertha Mays."

"Yeah, he did. He died about three years ago."

"I heard that too. I would have come to his funeral, but I was in Mexico with my husband at the time."

Seeing Shirelle gave me a warm feeling. She had been more like family to me than Bertha, and I hoped she wanted to resume our relationship as much as I did. "I'd love to meet your husband. Where did you meet him? Do I know him?"

Shirelle blew out some air and gave me a pitiful look. When she shook her head, I no longer felt the warm feeling I'd experienced a few seconds before. "No. Um, you don't know him. His name is Harold Ledford and he's from San Diego. He's an architect and we have two little boys already, thirteen months apart." She paused and gave me a guarded look. "Only a few people know I met him on the Internet."

"You met your husband on the Internet? Did you meet him in a chat room?"

"Heavens no! It was nothing that tacky. I met him three years ago on a Christian dating site. We got married four months later. He's a deacon in the church we belong to. He's one of the sweetest and most decent men I've ever known."

I was impressed. But I was shocked to hear that Shirelle, a woman who had grown up in the hood and fooled around with so many other women's husbands, had actually found one for herself on the Internet. "When can I meet him, your husband?"

Shirelle held up her hand, looked toward the street, then back at me. The way she started blinking and shifting her weight from one foot to the other told me she was nervous and anxious to be on her way. "Lola, I'm sorry, but I don't think that'd be a good idea. My husband doesn't know that I shacked up with your daddy in the same house where you and your mama lived at the same time. I don't want him to know what kind of woman I was back then, so it's best if you and I stay out of one another's lives. I'm very happy and I want to stay happy."

"I understand," I said glumly. I was so disappointed; I thought my heart was going to stop beating. "Well, it was nice to see you again. Can we have lunch or something before you go back to Frisco? We can go someplace where nobody will see us."

Shirelle glanced toward the street again. She gave me a pitiful look and shook her head. "I'm leaving to go back home in a couple of hours. I hate to rush off now, but I'm supposed to meet my cousin at her house in a few minutes so we can have a few margaritas. I only came here to pick up a bottle of tequila." She faked a smile and held up a brown bag with a bottle in it and waved it in my face.

"I'm listed in the telephone book if you ever want to call me sometime," I told her.

"That's good to know. I just might do that. Um, I'm glad we ran into one another. You take care of yourself, sugar. Have a blessed day!" She gave me another hug before she rushed out the door. She sprinted to the parking lot and got into a shiny black Town Car and sped off like a bat out of hell.

Right after I cashed my check and got back outside, I pulled out my cell phone and called Joan. She answered right away.

"I just ran into my other mother," I told her, my voice cracking as I walked toward my house.

"Shirelle? Where?" she squealed.

"She was coming out of the convenience store on Grant Street. Guess what? She's married to an architect. They have two little boys and she says she's very happy."

"No shit? A hoochie like Shirelle caught herself an architect? I'd sure like to know how she managed to pull that off! Let's invite her to go have pizza or something. My treat. I'm dying to hear what-all she's been up to."

"Joan, she met her husband on an Internet dating site. He's in the Church, so she doesn't want him to find out about her past. Because of that, she told me we shouldn't keep in touch with one another."

"Oh, well. It is what it is, I guess. So she found a husband in an online lonely hearts' club, huh?"

"I wouldn't call the site she met her husband on a 'lonely hearts club.' She met him on a Christian dating site."

"Well, at the end of the day, all of the clubs on the Internet and in magazines are for people looking for love." Joan snickered. "And money. Gotta run! Talk to you later."

"Later," I mumbled, clicking my phone off and sliding it back into my purse.

It made me sad to know that Shirelle didn't want to have a relationship with me again, so I decided to put her out of my mind and forget about her. But I knew that if she ever changed her mind, I'd be eager to have her back in my life. In the meantime, I decided to focus on the "club" that I belonged to now.

The following Monday after school, Joan rented a small public-storage unit to hide some of the things we'd purchased. We made eight trips by bus and cab to the unit, carrying two shopping bags each that contained clothes, perfume, CDs, books, and other small items. We did it over a five-day period so nobody would notice. An hour after the last trip on the fifth day, we went shopping again and had to make another trip to the storage unit the same day. At the rate we were buying things, we were going to run out of space real soon.

"We're going to need a much bigger place if we keep shopping so much," I told Joan a week after she'd rented the storage unit. It was a Tuesday evening and hotter than usual for early October. We had both scored A's on a math test that morning and had decided to celebrate with a nice dinner at Angelo's Grotto, a very expensive Italian restaurant not far from downtown San Jose. "Between the two of us, we can easily afford an apartment. And it has to be one located in a neighborhood across town so we won't run into anybody we know."

"Let me think about that," she said. "We don't need to get too carried away."

I tilted my head to the side and sucked on my teeth. "'Carried away'? *Duh?* Don't you think it's a little late for you to be saying that? How much more 'carried away' can we get?"

Joan huffed and gave me an impatient look. "I know that, so don't even go there. We have enough to worry about. We don't know what might happen if we get into this *too* deep." The silence that followed was spooky.

After almost half a minute, I exhaled and locked eyes with Joan. "Is there something you're not telling me?"

"No," she replied with a shrug. "It's all good."

Joan's cousin Larry had recently moved in with her family while his apartment was being painted. He'd let her borrow his ten-year-old minivan to drive to the restaurant.

"Just thought I'd ask." I sniffed and pursed my lips. "I've been thinking. . . . If we had an apartment, one with a garage, you or I could buy a decent vehicle. I'm tired of cruising around in your cousin's hooptie. And you had the nerve to park that jalopy right next to a brand-new Jaguar! I'd love to cruise around in a brand-new Mazda or a Jetta."

Joan took a bite of the garlic bread we had ordered to go along with our steak and lobster dinners. "Be serious, girl. Hiding our new clothes and other stuff is one thing. How would you or I explain a new car while we're still in school and unemployed? Even if we hid it somewhere, sooner or later somebody would see us in it and want to know who it belongs to. Forget about either one of us getting a car." Joan snorted, gave me a dismissive wave, and shifted in her seat. It was time to change the subject. "By the way, are you still sneaking Bobby Hayes into your house after Bertha goes to bed?"

My eyes rolled back in my head. "He came over last night. He was so hot he couldn't even wait for me to take off my panties. He ripped them off," I recounted, swooning. "Bertha came downstairs to get a glass of milk and almost caught us getting busy on the living-room couch. Thank God we'd finished our business in time." I giggled and slid my tongue across my bottom lip.

"I thought you said, once she went to bed, she slept like a corpse."

"She usually does. But every now and then she'll get back up and wander down to the kitchen for a snack or something to drink. I really like Bobby and I'm going to do everything I can to hold on to him. The last boyfriend I had kicked me to the curb after one date because he couldn't deal with Bertha."

A very cute Italian waiter delivered our main courses, but the smell of all that spicy food was very potent. Joan rubbed her nose and excused herself before she made a mad dash to the ladies' room. When she returned about ten minutes later, I folded my arms and looked at her with both eyebrows raised. "I was just about to come check on you. I thought you might have fallen into the toilet."

"Don't worry about me." Joan collapsed back into her chair and drank from her water glass. "I'm fine." She lifted a napkin and wiped her mouth.

"You don't look fine. You've been acting weird and looking sick lately. Right now you look pretty bad—dark circles around your red puffy eyes and all. What's up?" I asked, spearing one of the asparagus spears on my plate with my fork.

Joan took a deep breath first and then she started talking again with a grimace on her face. "There's something I need to tell you. I've been putting it off, but I can't do that any longer. You and everybody else will know soon, anyway. It's the reason I don't think we should rent an apartment or buy a car." She sighed. "I don't know what's going to happen to me in the near future. . . ."

"Oh no!" I said in a hoarse whisper. "Please don't tell me you're dying too! I've lost my parents and I don't think I could go on if I lost you too. Do you have a health issue that—"

Joan interrupted me by holding up her hand. "No, I don't have any health issues. Well, in a way I do."

"Joan, stop beating around the bush and tell me what the hell is going on."

She took another deep breath and wiped her mouth again before she continued. "We have enough on our plate already, so we don't need to complicate things. How long do you think we could keep the news about us renting an apartment hidden from the big mouths?"

"Joan, you're talking in all kinds of circles. Exactly what is this 'something' you're holding back that me and everybody else is going to find out soon, anyway? And how does it involve us getting an apartment or a car?" I narrowed my eyes and looked at her with my lips pressed together. I beckoned with my hand for her to continue.

"You know I don't believe in abortion, right?"

My eyes got big and my face froze. "Did I miss something? How did we get from talking about us getting an apartment and cars to the subject of abortion? Is one of your sisters pregnant again?"

She shook her head. "I wish," she replied, just above a whisper.

"Speak up and get to the point." I glanced at my watch, then back at Joan, with a distasteful look on my face now. "I'd like to finish eating and get up out of this place before midnight."

Joan snorted, coughed to clear her throat, and sat up straighter in her chair. She placed her hands, palms down, on top of the table, as if she was about to participate in a séance. "Remember that going-away party I went to back in July that my hairdresser hosted for a young dentist she went to high school with?"

"Uh-huh. The one who started his practice last year. He was going away to participate in some program to assist some dentists in Haiti for a few weeks, right?"

Joan nodded. "Reed Riley. And it was Martinique, not Haiti."

"I saw his picture in the paper the other day about some charity function he helped sponsor. Hmmm. Not only is he impressing a lot of folks, he's cute. Too bad you didn't get a chance to get to know him, if you know what I mean."

"I did. . . ."

"Oh? I thought he left the country the day after that party."

"He did. We really hit it off and I went home with him after the party. We were drunk, so I don't have to tell you what happened when we got to his place."

I sagged back in my seat and muttered some gibberish under my breath. Then I looked at Joan with my eyes squinted. "No, you don't have to tell me. I'm just ticked off because you hadn't told me before now. So, are you telling me that you slept with that man?"

She nodded again. "Reed's a nice catch, good family, fantastic job. He's going to make some woman a good husband someday. I know he's several years older than me, but he's only twenty-seven. Mama was sixteen and Daddy was twenty-five when they got married." Joan stopped talking and stared off into space for a few seconds. Then she started talking in a slow, controlled tone of voice. "Lola, I know I'm young, but I know what I want—a good-looking, smart, successful husband, a nice home, and a few children." She stopped talking again, and gave me a mysterious smile. "I want to have a lot of fun too."

"I want all the same things," I declared, swallowing a lump in my throat. "That's every woman's dream. Are you trying to tell me you want to marry this man?"

"Maybe."

I looked at Joan like she had just sprouted a goatee. "Are you serious?"

"Yes, I am serious."

"Well, if you want to be with him and he wants to be with you, go for it. The age difference is not really that big. My mama was still in her teens when Daddy married her and she was already pregnant with me. He was almost thirty." I gave Joan a thoughtful look and then I giggled. "Let me know if Reed has any single friends." I quickly paused and gave her a suspicious look this time. "Why are you even thinking about marriage while you're still in high school?" I whispered. "And what was that abortion comment about?"

"I'm pregnant and Reed is the father," she blurted out.

"Pregnant?! You?!"

"Lola, stop talking so loud. Put your eyes back into your head," Joan advised. "It's not the end of the world."

"But you're going to have a baby. And after all the times you reminded me to keep a stash of condoms in my purse."

"Lola, I never said I was perfect. Everybody is entitled to at least one big mistake. Even me." Joan lowered her head and stared into her lap for a few seconds. When she looked back up, I was staring at her with a look of pity that was so extreme, it made her squirm. "Stop looking at me like that!" She stopped talking long enough to grit her teeth. "I already feel pitiful enough. I hope you're not too disappointed in me," she whined.

"I'm not disappointed in you, but I am surprised. You were the one with all the big plans for your future—writing for magazines and traveling all over the world."

"I know, I know. But things happen."

"Apparently." I blew out a loud breath. "Does Reed know?"

"Not yet. I looked up his home number in the telephone book yesterday. I called to see if he had returned from the islands. His voice mail was full and I couldn't leave a message, so I called his office this morning. He's back, but he was with a patient and couldn't take my call. I told his receptionist to let him know that I need to talk to him as soon as possible about an extremely urgent matter. He hasn't called me back yet, and if he hasn't called by tomorrow, I'm going to storm his office."

"Joan, how the hell did you let something like this happen? And with a man who's almost thirty! You're the last girl in our graduating class I expected to get into a mess like this! The busybodies are going to roast you alive."

"Fuck the busybodies. They've been bashing me since kindergarten. And for your information, we did use a condom. But, as everybody knows by now, those damn things are not foolproof."

"Are you sure you're pregnant? Maybe you're just a little late."

"I've been early before, but never late. Besides, I took two different pregnancy tests three days apart and they were both positive. I would have told you sooner, but . . . well . . . I wasn't ready to talk about it until now."

"What are you going to do?"

"That all depends on what Reed wants to do."

Chapter 14

Joan

"YOU HAVE NO IDEA WHAT YOU'RE IN FOR. YOUR LIFE won't ever be the same again," Lola told me, giving me the third or fourth pitiful look in the last five minutes. I didn't appreciate that look because there was nothing pitiful about me, now or before. Motherhood was going to be a new beginning for me and I was going to do whatever I had to do to make sure it was a positive one.

"Don't you get crazy on me. I'm *just* pregnant, girl, not dying."

"Remember when Ann Brody got pregnant? She had to drop out of school and go on welfare. She lives with her baby in a shack on some backstreet—"

I held up my hand and waved it in Lola's face. I had to cut her off before she went too far. "You stop right there!" The last thing I needed was my best friend going off on a tangent. As long as we'd been BFFs, we had never had a serious falling-out. "Ann was a skank. Her family is trifling and in no position to help her, so that's why she had to go on welfare. You know my family will be there for me. I don't know why you think things are going to change that drastically. I'll still be the same person after I have my baby."

"I sure hope you're right, Joan," Lola said in a heavy voice.

It was a very tense ride home. When she told me again that my life was never going to be the same, I flat out told her to shut up or talk about something else. After that, we were as silent as mutes until I pulled up in front of her house. Before she piled out of the van, she gave me a hug and told me, "I don't care what happens next. I've still got your back."

"And I've got yours," I told her.

Things changed drastically for me the very next day. Reed called me that morning just as I was about to leave for school. He didn't mention his trip to the islands and I didn't bring it up. I figured we'd discuss that after we'd discussed the reason I needed to see him. I gave him my address.

"Joan, I don't know what this is about, but I will be there right after I finish up with my last patient this evening," he assured me.

I was surprised that he had agreed to come, even though he didn't know why I needed to talk to him.

Then his voice got real soft and gentle. "I've been thinking about you ever since that night we met and, uh, you know. I couldn't send you a note or a postcard or even call you while I was away because you didn't give me your telephone number or your address. And none of the folks who'd attended my party would give that information to me when I asked. Is everything okay?"

"Uh, yeah," I muttered. I had a feeling Reed knew the reason I needed to talk to him, but I was going to make him wait to hear it from me.

He had not met my family yet. I'd casually mentioned him to them the night I'd hopped in a cab and gone to that party, but nobody had seemed interested. When he showed up at the house in his light green scrubs a few minutes before six P.M. the day we had spoken, you would have thought Dr. Phil had walked into our living room. I was glad that only Mama, my stepfather, Too Sweet, and Elaine were present. Had some of my more unsophisticated relatives been on the premises, Reed might have freaked out, especially when he didn't even know what I needed to talk to him about.

"We ain't never had no dentist come to the house before," Too Sweet said, plopping down on the arm of the couch next to Reed. She looked at him like she wanted to eat him. So did Elaine and it was no wonder. He was tall and he had an athletic body. With his slanted black eyes, curly black hair, pecan-brown complexion, and thin lips, he was way more handsome than most of the men Elaine dated.

Mama was beaming like a high-powered flashlight. She couldn't take her eyes off Reed. Even my lanky, hard-to-please stepfather was impressed. Elmo couldn't stop grinning, showing off his tobacco-stained teeth and the deep lines around his mouth and cloudy gray eyes. He offered Reed some of his best scotch. Mama invited him to stay for dinner. Reed took a rain check on the dinner invitation, but he didn't hesitate to accept the scotch and he probably needed it to calm his nerves. The conversation was neutral. We discussed sports, current world events, and even some TV shows. I could see that Reed was uncomfortable, so I was not going to prolong his visit.

"We'd better leave soon or they'll give up our restaurant reservation," I said, looking at my watch.

Reed had only consumed half of his drink, but he glanced at me and then finished what was left in one swallow.

"Reed, I'm glad you ain't one of them grumpy old men like Dr. Thompson, the only other black dentist I know of in this town. It's nice for us to have such a nice-looking, young black dentist for a change." Too Sweet grinned at him.

"Sure enough," Mama agreed, still beaming like a high-powered flashlight. "Reed, honey, are you sure you don't want to stay and have dinner with us? It's a mean one today—mac and cheese, pig ears, greens, corn bread, and peach cobbler."

After hearing Mama describe one of our typical meals, Reed looked like he wanted to puke and bolt. I didn't know him well, but he was a dentist and he probably socialized with a lot of sophisticated people of various ethnicities. I had a feeling that the black people he associated with no longer ate pig ears and greens and whatnot—if they ever had.

"Uh, no and thanks for asking again," he chortled, blinking hard. "Maybe next time."

Right after he set his shot glass down on the coffee table, he and I rose at the same time. With everybody asking him all kinds of mundane questions about his practice and his recent trip to Martinique, it took another ten minutes before I could get him out the door and into his car. I decided not to waste any more time to tell him the reason I needed to see him. Just as he was about to turn on the motor of his Lexus, I blurted it all out.

"Reed, I'm going to have a baby."

His hands froze on the steering wheel and he let out a loud gasp. He whirled around to look at me. There was such a stunned look on his face that it could have stopped a clock. "What did you just say?" he croaked.

"I'm pregnant. And you're the father." I sniffed. "I know a man like you is probably in a serious relationship with another girl, and I'm not trying to cause you any trouble. But it is what it is."

Reed narrowed his eyes and blinked nervously. A few seconds went by before he spoke again, and it was in a very shaky and hoarse tone of voice. "I was involved with someone a couple of weeks before I met you, but it didn't work out." He paused and shook his head. "Well . . . I . . . are you sure you're pregnant?"

"I'm pretty sure," I said with a nod.

"Does your family know yet?"

"Uh-huh," I replied with another nod. Last year I thought I was pregnant. When I told the boy who was responsible, the first thing out of his mouth was *"By who?"* I was so glad Reed had not said something that insensitive and insulting. "I told them yesterday. They were disappointed and my parents fussed at me for ten minutes nonstop, but they told me they'd be there for me, no matter what."

"Hmmm. I'm glad to hear you have such an understanding and supportive family. I never would have guessed that they knew already, as nice as they were to me. I'm lucky your stepfather didn't kick my ass."

"Two of my sisters were pregnant before they got married, so me getting pregnant is no big deal. I just wanted you to meet some of my folks today, my parents especially. I told them not to mention my condition until I had told you."

I glanced out the window and saw Elaine peeping from one living-room window and Too Sweet peeping from another. Elmo and Mama were so bold, they stood in the doorway; Elmo had his hands on his hips, and Mama was smiling and still beaming as they stared toward Reed's car. They saw that he drove a shiny new Lexus, so I knew they were all on cloud nine, for sure, by now. I was glad when they all disappeared back into the house a few moments later.

I knew that when I got back home, those four and everybody else who'd be home at the time would get all up in my business.

Reed sighed and then he touched my shoulder and looked at me for a long time with his lips parted just enough for me to see his teeth. They were perfect and his breath was minty fresh. But I'd never known a dentist with a mouth full of yellow rotting teeth and foul breath. What Reed said next made my heart sing. I was suddenly so overwhelmed with joy and relief, it was hard for me to hold back my tears.

"Joan, I really do care about you and I certainly care about the child you're carrying. If I'm the father, I intend to do the right thing."

"Meaning what?" That other dude had offered to drive me to and from the abortion clinic and pay for any medicine if I needed it. I'd told him right away that I did not believe in killing unborn babies. When I found out that same night I was not pregnant and called him to let him know, he told me to "stay the hell away" from him. "What is the right thing, Reed? I'm not getting an abortion!" I said quickly.

"I should hope not! God is the only one who has the right to take a baby's life!" he yelled. I was so glad to hear that we were on the same page about abortion. "I promised my mother that if I ever got a girl pregnant, I wouldn't hesitate to marry her," he said with a serious look on his handsome face.

I couldn't believe my ears. Reed's reaction to my news

was way more positive than I had expected. The moment I'd realized I was pregnant, I started fantasizing about being married to him, but I had not expected him to suggest it so soon, if at all. I would have been happy if he had only told me he'd support the baby and have a relationship with him or her.

"You'd marry me even though we don't know one another that well? And even though I'm still in high school?"

Reed shrugged. "Well, if you don't want to get married, I will make sure you and the baby are taken care of. I know you're still very young, and if being a mother gets to be too much for you, I'd be more than happy to take full custody of the child. Mother's been praying for a grandchild to fuss over."

"Are you serious?"

He started the motor. "Yes, I am very serious. I didn't think I'd get married before I turned thirty, but things happen."

"We can get a DNA test done so you'll know I'm not lying about you being the father," I offered.

Reed turned toward me with his mouth hanging open. "DNA?" he said with a loud gulp. "Will that be necessary?"

"No, but I don't want you to have any doubts."

"Were there . . . uh . . . any other men around the same time as me?"

I shook my head. "The night I met you, I hadn't been with anybody for months. And I haven't been with anybody since that night. And I hope you don't think I'm lying."

"Joan, I believe you. Now, if you want to get a DNA test just for the sake of it, we can do it. I liked you the first time I saw you, and . . ." Reed stopped talking and chuckled. "I thought I'd never tell you this, but even before I

got you alone, I told my buddies at the party that I was
going to marry you someday."

"You did?"

"Uh-huh. I knew you were young when I first saw
you, but the lighting was dim and I had been drinking, so
you looked at least eighteen. Now that I've seen you in
better lighting, you look about fourteen or fifteen. Had I
known you were only seventeen and still in high school, I
would not have approached you."

"I told my hairdresser I was eighteen. She wouldn't
have invited me to the party if I'd told her my real age."

"Well, I guess I'm glad you lied about your age."

"I'm glad I lied too." I was so elated it was hard for me
to keep myself from giggling like a giddy teenager—
even though that was exactly what I was. "I'd be happy to
be your wife—if my parents let me get married. I mean, I
hardly know you."

"True. Would you rather wait a couple of years so we
can take our time and really get to know one another?"

"If you're willing to marry me now, that's fine. I don't
want to wait a couple of years to get to know you, but I
can wait a couple of months. That's enough time for us to
get to know one another . . . I think."

"What do you really want to do, Joan?"

"I want to be married before I have my baby. That's
what I really want to do."

"Then we'll get married. All you have to do is let me
know when you want to do it."

"Okay," I mumbled. Tears of joy slid down the side of
my face. I smiled all the way to the seafood restaurant we
went to. We held hands in a candlelit booth while we
made plans for our future.

Chapter 15

Joan

ONE THING I DIDN'T LIKE ABOUT THE WOMEN IN MY family was that they all gained a huge amount of weight when they got pregnant. Losing my shape was one of my biggest fears. But since I was probably going to blow up like a blimp, anyway, I promptly ordered a whole loaf of garlic bread for myself.

Reed and I decided not to tell anyone else, not even his parents, about my condition until we were absolutely sure. He volunteered to make an appointment for me with one of his doctor friends for the following week.

Lola sounded happy when I called her up later that night and told her what Reed and I had discussed. She wished me well, but after a few minutes, her tone changed. Her well wishes now sounded like complaints. "I don't know what I'm going to do now. I'm going to miss hanging out with you," she whined.

"Nothing will change between us when Reed and I get married," I insisted.

"The hell it won't. No married man is going to let his wife keep running around with her single friends. Him being a dentist, you'll be meeting all kinds of upper-class folks. And once you have your baby, you'll be carpooling, and planning PTA events, and having lunch with soccer moms. Next thing I know, you'll be joining the country club and going to tea parties. . . ."

"Lola, please don't spoil things."

"I'm not spoiling things! You're the one who got pregnant!"

"I didn't plan this," I shot back. "I thought you were happy for me."

"I am. And I'm sorry for . . . Oh, Lord! I just thought of something! *What about those old men?*"

"What about them?"

"Are you going to keep writing letters to them?"

"Of course I am. I don't see why I should stop right away. Besides, some of the letters are a hoot. Last week my old dude in Tulsa sent me a picture of his dick! I never laughed so hard in my life!" Joan guffawed. "Thank God he included a couple of hundred dollars with it."

"But with the kind of money Reed must be making, you won't be needing money from your pen pals."

"What if he's stingy and puts me on a strict budget? That's one thing. Another thing is, for all I know, he and I might get married and not even stay together. My sister Elaine and her husband didn't stay married a year."

"Well, I'm happy if you're happy. I just didn't think things would change so drastically, all of a sudden. With a husband and a baby, you're going to be so busy you might not have time to keep writing to your pen pals, or time for me. . . ."

"I will make time for you! Until I know how things are

going to go with Reed, I'm going to keep writing to my pen pals. What about you?"

"I guess I'll keep writing to them too," Lola said dryly. "Why not?"

I could tell that she was more than a little concerned about the future of our relationship. She suddenly wanted to end the call and asked me to call her the next morning so we could have our usual Saturday-morning chat.

Even with Too Sweet snoring, I went to sleep as soon as I laid my head on my pillow and I slept like a baby.

I got up early the next morning. As usual, there was a ruckus going on downstairs, so it was hard to sleep in, anyway. I planned to call Lola after I had polished my nails. Before my polish had even dried, she called me. The moment I heard her frantic voice, I knew something was wrong. I was not prepared for what she told me.

When she told me that she had just gotten rid of the wife of one of my pen pals who had come to her house a few minutes ago *to kick my ass,* I knew it was time for us to get off our gravy train. I was afraid, and from the panic in Lola's voice, I could tell that she was too.

I was just about to bolt and head over to Lola's house so we could send "breakup" letters to all of our pen pals when Mama accosted me in the hallway outside my bedroom. "Don't you leave this house, gal, until you finish that laundry you started last night," she barked, hands on her hips.

"Yes, ma'am," I mumbled as I scrambled downstairs to the laundry room. I plucked clothes out of the dryer and folded everything as fast as I could. Then I did a few more chores that Mama had been badgering me about. It was over an hour and a half before I was able to head over to Lola's house.

When I arrived, stomping up the front porch steps like a clumsy mule, Bertha snatched opened the door. She never attempted to hide her annoyance with me. She parted her chapped, liver-colored lips just enough to give me a blunt greeting. "Hello, Joan. You over here again?"

"Lola told me to come over," I said defensively as I eased over the threshold, almost stepping on Bertha's flat bare feet. She stepped out of my path and waved me toward the staircase.

I rushed up to Lola's room, entered, and locked the door. She stood in front of her dresser with a pen in one hand and a sheet of paper in the other. "It's about time you got here," she said sharply.

"Mama made me do all kinds of shit first and I had to go pick up the stamps so we can mail the letters today," I explained, my voice dropping almost to a whisper. "I got here as fast as I could." I had run up the stairs, so I was huffing and puffing and even had to cough a couple of times to catch my breath.

Lola gave me a concerned look as I approached her. "Joan, are you feeling all right? You look terrible," she said.

"I feel fine," I said with a dismissive wave. "I'm just a little bit woozy and tired."

"Well, you'd better get used to that." Lola glanced at my stomach, then at my face, which was beginning to feel hot. I didn't know if it was because of my condition or the real reason I had come to visit. "I still can't believe you hadn't told me about the mess you got yourself in sooner than you did," she complained. "Pregnant at seventeen!"

"You didn't tell Bertha about it yet, did you?"

"No, I didn't tell her yet."

"She sure was looking at me like she knew something."

"That's nothing new. She always thinks you're up to no good," Lola pointed out. "Do you want some tea or milk or something? Bobby left some weed the last time he was here. I could roll you a blunt."

"You mean a *joint*? Lola, what makes you think I want to smoke some dope, especially in my condition?"

There was a scared look on her face. "I figured you'd be a little nervous after what I told you about that woman coming to beat you up. I thought you might want something to calm your nerves."

"I'm fine," I insisted. "And if I did need something to calm my nerves, it wouldn't be some weed. I didn't even know you smoked that shit."

"I don't and I never will. But like I said, Bobby left some here. He's fooling around with Cathy Harbor now, so I probably won't hear from him again, and I don't know what else to do with a bag of weed."

"I'd like to stay on Elaine's good side, so I'll take it home and give it to her. Now let's get this letter writing shit over with. I can't stay long. Reed's coming back today so we can continue discussing our plans," I said as I plopped down onto the neatly made bed. I opened my backpack and dumped out the stamps and several pens. She had already placed the stationery and envelopes on her nightstand. She produced the list that had the names and addresses of her pen pals, and I removed mine from the front pocket of my backpack. Despite her ugly off-white furniture, the old-fashioned venetian blinds covering the windows, and the baby-shit-colored walls, I enjoyed spending time in Lola's room because it was a lot more private than mine.

I was going to wait until I got home to write the final letter to Lee, that love-struck woman in Miami. I had changed my mind about telling her that lie about me having to take my mother to Mexico to live with my uncle

Alex. Now I thought it would be better to tell her a stronger lie: I had just accepted a job with the Peace Corps and would be moving to Brazil and would write to her again once I got settled. With a story like that, I was convinced that she would not attempt to find the "man" she'd fallen in love with. I still didn't want Lola to know that I had posed as Leroy Puckett and conned a female.

"I have a few things to do myself today, but I'm not doing anything until I get all my letters written," she told me. I noticed her hands were shaking as she grabbed an envelope and began to address it. "I'm never doing anything like this again," she snapped, giving me a menacing look.

"I'm not either," I responded in a meek voice.

After we had composed all of the letters, we trotted to the mailbox at the corner. Since we had so many to mail, we decided that it might not be such a good idea to put them all in the same box at the same time. We dropped off only a couple at the first location. Then we roamed around to ten more boxes, with at least two or three blocks between each one. At one point, I got dizzy, so we stopped and sat on a bench at a bus stop for a few minutes. I couldn't believe that I had already begun to feel like shit so early in my pregnancy. After I felt better, we left the bus stop and resumed our mission. I was so relieved when we dropped the last batch into a mailbox in front of the main library.

We were exhausted by the time we made it back to Lola's house. She was just as surprised as I was to see Bertha standing in the doorway with a frantic look on her face and the telephone in her hand. "Lola, I was just about to call the police and have them come here so I could give them one of your blouses," she wailed.

"Why would you give the cops one of my blouses?"

Lola asked as she brushed past Bertha, with me close behind.

"For the dogs to sniff and help find your body, that's why. I didn't know if a sex maniac had grabbed you and Joan off the street or what. You didn't tell me where you were going when you left, so I didn't know what to think."

"Um, you were in the bathroom and we didn't want to disturb you. We went to get something to eat and w-we, um, lost track of time," Lola stammered.

"There's a kitchen full of food in this house," Bertha pointed out.

"It was my fault. I wanted a Big Mac, so we had to go to McDonald's," I explained. I could tell a storm was brewing and I'd been in too many storms already. "I guess I'd better get on back home before Mama has the police out looking for me." I excused myself and rushed back out the door before Bertha could do or say anything other than suck on her gums and give me an annoyed look.

Lola and I held our breath for the next couple of weeks. Most of the old men, and the Lee woman in Miami, didn't respond to our Dear John letters. But a few, ironically the ones who had sent the least amount of money, continued to send letters, but no more money. They begged us to reconsider our decisions to "move to Canada" with our new boyfriends. It was so pathetic and I felt so bad about the misery I had caused some innocent old people. But we did what we had to do. To make sure no more letters addressed to me came to Lola's address, I filled out a change-of-address form. My "new address" was actually an empty warehouse several miles across town, next to a vacant lot. Lola didn't want to fill out the same form because she thought that if we both did it, and one or more of those old men filed a complaint, it would look mighty suspicious to the postal authorities. So a few more letters addressed to her trickled in.

By the end of October, all of Lola's pen pals had stopped writing to her. And that woman who wanted to beat me up never returned. Now I was totally convinced that she was the wife of Mr. Blake in Reno because he never wrote to me again and I hadn't even sent him a Dear John letter. I promised Lola, and myself, that I'd do my best to walk the straight and narrow for the rest of my life.

I was about to become a wife and mother and it was time for me to grow up and behave more responsibly. I just hoped that would be enough to keep me from losing my way again.

Chapter 16

Joan

I WAS NOT READY TO BE A MOTHER, BUT I WAS READY TO accept the consequences of my actions. Had it not been for the support of my family, Lola, and Reed, I don't know what I would have done.

Reed and I decided not to wait for me to graduate in June, but I was going to put off getting married as long as I could because I wanted to enjoy my freedom just a little longer. After all, I planned to spend the next forty or fifty years with him, so there were lots of things I wouldn't be able to do when I got married. But remaining footloose and fancy-free was not so easy.

From the day I told Reed that I was having his baby, he became a frequent visitor. When he was not sitting in our living room drinking scotch with Elmo or in the kitchen with Mama eating pig ears or whatever was on the table that particular day, he was on the telephone, asking me all kinds of dumb questions. His favorite one was "Are you eating right and taking the pills the doctor gave you?" He also wanted to know if I was still seeing other men and he needed to know my whereabouts at all times. Almost every time I saw or spoke to him on the phone, he wanted to know if I really loved him. He began to show up at my school unannounced to have lunch with me or to give me a ride home. No matter what the reason was for him to be keeping such close tabs on me, the attention made me feel special. I was flattered to know that I had a man who loved me so much he wanted me all to himself.

I decided to go ahead and marry him before my graduation to keep him from spending so much money on my greedy relatives. To them, he had become the goose that laid golden eggs. Every time he called, different ones started whooping and hollering and asking what time he was coming over and what he was bringing. Reed often showed up with expensive liquor for Elmo and flowers and candy for Mama and Too Sweet, and a variety of miscellaneous goodies for everybody else. One evening he treated everybody who happened to be in the house when he arrived—nine of us—to dinner in a very expensive restaurant. Three days after that, while I was having dinner with Lola, Reed came to the house and took seven more of my relatives to another expensive restaurant. I knew that it was just a matter of time before they started hitting him up for "loans," the way Libby and Marshall did with Bertha.

We decided to exchange vows on the second Saturday in February, 2000, at three in the afternoon. The ceremony was scheduled to take place in my mother's living room. The night before, I had spotted what I thought was a roach crawling up the wall and I went ballistic. For one thing, we had never had a problem with roaches or any other creature. "Girl, you imagining things. That was probably just a baby gnat you seen," Too Sweet insisted. I had made such a fuss, my stepfather rushed to the hardware store and returned with enough odorless roach paste to coat every wall in the house. He applied it only to areas where nobody would see it. That made me feel better, but our house still couldn't compete with the upscale twenty-five-floor building I'd be moving into with Reed. It was located in one of the most exclusive, gated neighborhoods in town, within walking distance of the country club. His condo was on the eighth floor. His immediate neighbors included a pilot for a major airline and a stockbroker. Most of my family had been to Reed's place a few times; and every chance one of them got, they told me that I was "moving on up" and that I'd "hit the mother lode." Mama was brazen enough to tell me—in front of Reed—that no matter what he did to me after we got married, I'd be a "straight-up fool" if I didn't stay with him until one of us died. That last comment had given me an ominous feeling and I'd immediately pushed it out of my mind. As far as I was concerned, two healthy young people like Reed and me didn't have to worry about dying anytime soon.

We invited forty-five people to the wedding and informed each one that they could bring one guest. Since we knew so many folks who were *never* on time for anything, we didn't tell them that the ceremony was scheduled to start at three P.M. We told them that it would start at one P.M. I had told Lola the actual time and I was glad when she arrived at exactly three P.M. with Perry Washington, a frat boy she had just started dating a week ago. Almost every other guest showed up an hour late, anyway, descending like locusts in groups of four and five. A few stragglers, Bertha included, didn't show up until after the reception had started. Libby, Marshall, and their spouses were the last to arrive—two hours late. Only two dozen people bothered to bring wedding gifts.

My family spared no expense when it came to food and alcohol. My cousin Clifford was the deejay and his wife, Vivian, and her two sisters had prepared most of the food. The honey stung fried chicken wings and the potato salad were both so delicious, Reverend Bailey insisted on fixing a huge plate to take home. I even saw a couple of bold females slip food into their purses. Such behavior was so typical at our events, acknowledging it was never even considered.

Reed's side of the guest list had almost nothing in common with mine. His crew stood off in bunches of two and three discussing politics, the economy, and world events. My crew stood around discussing Tyler Perry movies, how much they hated their jobs, and who was making love to someone other than their mate. Even as happy as I was, I couldn't wait for the day to end!

"Joan, you look so good in that green silk dress. I'm glad the designers are making maternity outfits look more stylish these days," Libby chirped as she gave me a clumsy one-armed hug. A weary look crossed her face when she looked over my shoulder and saw the numerous bottles of alcohol on the table in the middle of the room. She was pregnant with her first child, too. She was eight months along, I was seven, so neither one of us could drink any alcohol. "Girl, I'd give anything in the world if I could have me a few Cadillac margaritas," she muttered.

"I feel you," I told her with a wink.

Marshall came up to me next with his arms outstretched. Hugging him was like hugging a barrel. "Joan, I can't believe you're getting married! I remember when you was a little girl how you and Lola used to throw rocks at me." I wanted to throw a rock at him now, but

Marshall was a guest and this was a very special day for me, so I remained cordial. I even kissed him on his bloated cheek. "I wasn't sure if we were supposed to bring something, but if you run out of food, I can run out and pick up a sweet potato pie," he said. At the same time, his eyes were roaming from one woman to another, even though his wife was on his arm. He and my cousin Arthur played cards now and then. That was the only "social" connection I had to this fool. If Mama had not run all around the neighborhood bragging about me marrying "a successful young dentist" and telling everybody about the reception, I would have insisted on going to a restaurant with just a few relatives and close friends.

Reed was all over the place. One reason he was trying so hard to get in good with my family was because my uncle Grady had told Reed he was not happy about him getting his baby sister's baby girl pregnant, and that if Reed ever mistreated me, he was going to suffer. Other than Uncle Grady's ominous threat, nobody else in my family had said one mean word to or about Reed.

His parents lived in Monterey. His daddy was recovering from knee surgery and his mother had to stay home to look after him, but Elmo had taped the wedding for them. Reed's favorite cousin, Laura, a mannish-looking woman in her thirties, had driven over from her home in Berkeley with her dull husband. It was obvious that they were not party people. They didn't drink or eat anything and stayed only an hour.

The first chance I got to speak privately to Lola, I steered her into a corner away from as many people as possible. "You look good in pink," I told her. "You should wear it more often."

"I will," she said with a raised eyebrow. Then she gave me a misty-eyed look. "Joan, I am so happy for you. You must be the happiest girl in the world."

Mary Monroe

"I'd be even happier if I could have a few drinks," I pouted.

"Well, you can forget about that until you have that baby." Lola wagged her finger in my face before she took a sip of her rum and Coke.

I scanned the room and saw Bertha in a corner with Perry. Her lips were moving about a mile a minute. The way she had his path blocked and from the tight expression on his face, he looked more like a hostage than a wedding guest. "Perry seems like a nice dude. I hope Bertha Butt doesn't run him off, like all your other boyfriends," I snickered.

Lola gazed at them, but she was not amused. She let out a heavy sigh and a groan at the same time. "I hope she doesn't either," she said with the most hopeless look I'd ever seen on her face. "Bertha told me before I left the house that if a girl like you could land a dentist, there's no telling what kind of man I could get."

"A girl like me? What am I, a one-eyed Cyclops?"

We both laughed.

"She thinks you're a little too fast," Lola told me.

"She thinks I'm a 'little too fast.' Now, that's funny. For the record, she didn't waste any time latching onto your father when your mother died." We laughed again. "And now she realizes you will get married someday?" I added in a serious tone of voice with my head cocked to the side and my hand on my hip.

"There was never any doubt about that. The only thing is, she still thinks that when I get married, she's going to live with me and my husband."

"What do you say to that? I've told you more than once that I'm sure your father didn't mean for you to take your commitment to such an extreme."

"I know what he meant," Lola snapped. "I will look after her, but I will have a life of my own."

Chapter 17

Lola

I HAD NEVER SEEN JOAN LOOK AS BLISSFUL AS SHE looked on the day she got married. She was so beautiful in her bright green silk maternity dress as she stood next to Reed in his black tuxedo in front of Reverend Bailey. I was almost as happy as she was and I didn't have a husband in sight. I was barely holding on to my latest boyfriend.

Nobody would believe that Joan was the same girl who had concocted that lonely hearts club swindle that had almost got us both hurt, maybe even killed—not to mention the mess that her unsuspecting sister, Elaine, could have ended up in because of us.

Now that our scheming days were over, I thought back on everything from day one and admitted to myself that I'd been a fool—and a *crook*! My mother had raised me to be a respectable and honest person, especially if I expected to be blessed and go to heaven when I died. I thought if I became even more devoted to Bertha, God would cut me some slack.

Joan made arrangements to stay current with her schoolwork by doing it from home. I agreed to bring it to her. She would only come to school when she had to take a test or meet with one of her teachers. Thanks to the big mouths in her family, almost all of our classmates knew she was pregnant. Some were brazen enough to point and whisper about her when she showed up on school grounds. Joan was aware of it, but it didn't even faze her. Now that she was married, the level she was on was too high for something as small as gossip to bring her down. I was even more impressed. Except for her pregnancy, I still fantasized about trading places with her; to me, it seemed like she was in complete control of her life.

It pleased me to know that my girl was determined to get her diploma. So far, no member of her immediate family had not completed their high-school education, and two of her brothers and one of her sisters had gone to college. To make sure Joan didn't ruin the family's high-school completion record, her mother had told her in front of me and several other people, "You're going to get your diploma if I have to hold my gun to your head." Joan vowed that she would graduate on time, but her diploma would be mailed to her, or she'd have to pick it up.

The newlyweds went to Aruba for a two-week honeymoon. It was one of the loneliest periods of time in my life. The first week was unbearable. Since the day I had become best friends with her in second grade, we had rarely gone more than a couple of days without communicating. Now that she was married, a new fear was brewing in me. Despite her claim that our relationship was not going to change, I was still afraid that I would have to find myself a new BFF. It had taken me a long time to groom Joan, and I knew she felt the same way about me.

But it was what it was, and all I could do now was go with the flow.

I had no idea that a new friend would enter my life while Joan was on her honeymoon. That person turned out to be Libby's husband, Jeffrey. He was a firefighter, so he enjoyed helping people. Everybody adored him. He had always been nice to me, but he was about to get even nicer and do things to help make my life more enjoyable.

A week after Joan's wedding, Jeffrey came to the house to do some maintenance work that Marshall had been putting off for months. I was in the living room reading the newspaper when he called me into the kitchen, where he was gathering the tools he had used to repair a leak in the sink.

"What's up?" I asked as I stood in the doorway with the newspaper still in my hand.

"One of my old air force buddies is coming to the house tonight," he began, speaking with his back to me. "I'm throwing a little get-together in his honor. We were in the same platoon. He reenlisted after I got discharged. When he got his discharge papers last month, he couldn't get back to civilian life fast enough." Jeffrey turned to look at me with his light brown eyes sparkling. There were beads of sweat on his square-jawed, cocoa-colored face. It was hard to believe that a good-looking, nicely built man like Jeffrey had married a plump plain Jane like Libby. "I thought of something nice that you may be interested in."

"O . . . kay," I said with a shrug. I didn't know why Jeffrey was bothering to tell me about one of his "get-togethers." Especially at the last minute. He knew I didn't like Libby and she didn't like me. The last person I wanted to socialize with on a Saturday evening, or any other evening, was her. "What is this 'something nice'?" Libby was due to give birth to her first child in a few weeks. She'd been sick a lot lately, and I felt sorry for her. I'd even taken her some chicken soup and picked up her prescriptions a couple of times, but she was still as mean as ever to me. I was hoping that the "something nice" that Jeffrey was going to tell me was that Libby was too sick to attend the party.

"Mark's younger brother just moved here from San Diego and he's coming too. I thought it would be nice to have a young woman around his age for him to hang out with. Mark told me last night about him wanting to join us tonight. Otherwise, I would have mentioned it to you before now."

"Uh . . . oh," I said, rolling my eyes. "What's wrong with this 'younger brother'?" I rarely went on blind dates and the few I had experienced had been disastrous. I was tired of people pawning off a homely or oddball relative or friend on me. But since it was Jeffrey, I was willing to consider it again.

"There's nothing wrong with the dude," Jeffrey said with a laugh. "He's smart and not bad-looking. But he's kind of shy, so he hasn't made many friends here yet."

"Oh. Well, thanks for the invite, but I think I'll pass. I have a lot of things to do around the house this evening."

Jeffrey stood up straight and placed his hands on his hips. "Lola, I can't do much about the way Libby treats you, but I can do a lot to help you deal with the way things are. If you and Ted—that's my boy's brother's name—hit it off, there is no telling what it might lead to."

"Jeffrey, I really appreciate you being so nice to me. And I am glad that you know how hard it is for me living with and taking care of Bertha and having to put up with Libby and Marshall's . . . well, you know what I mean."

"Oh, I know exactly what you mean. I don't know how

you have managed to live with Bertha all this time without going crazy." Jeffrey glanced toward the door and lowered his voice. "But I will say this, you need to stop letting her control your life."

"I'm still a teenager, Jeffrey."

"Well, you won't be a teenager much longer. I advise you to be strong and start putting some distance between you and Bertha. If something happens to you, God forbid, she'll have to fend for herself or force her children to take care of her. One thing that has always baffled me is the fact that Bertha's not that old and she's in fairly good health. I'm sure that most of her illnesses are in her head—and a way for her to make you feel sorry for her. I have relatives who are old enough to be her mother who still live on their own, and are doing quite well for themselves. My aunt Velma is eighty-six and she still drives, lives on her own, and has a boyfriend. As a matter of fact, most of the senior citizens I know, especially the ones in my family, they would never have a young girl like you underfoot! When my twenty-year-old cousin Ellen offered to move in with my grandmother, Granny Lou cussed her out and told her, 'Hell no, you ain't moving in with me. I need my space,'" Jeffrey said with a straight face. I couldn't stop myself from laughing. He didn't laugh, so I closed my mouth and gave him an apologetic look. He took a sharp breath and continued. "There are a lot of things that senior citizens can do to make old age more manageable. In Bertha's case, as long as you let her, she will depend on you like a baby depends on its mother."

I quickly processed Jeffrey's last statement and it immediately made my head throb. What he'd said was true and it was time for me to start weaning Bertha. "What time will your party start and tell me your air force friend's brother's name again, please?"

Chapter 18

Lola

I WAS GLAD I HAD ACCEPTED JEFFREY'S INVITATION TO ATtend the party at the big white stucco house that his parents had helped him and Libby finance. Despite the ongoing friction between her and me, I loved being in their home, though my visits were few and far between. I hadn't been a guest in two months.

As usual, every room was spotless. Unlike Bertha's dreary residence, which always had a mild musty scent, Libby and Jeffrey's place always smelled like roses. It was a beautiful place with trendy furniture, a fireplace in the living room, and thick maroon carpets on every floor, except the kitchen and the three bathrooms. I knew they had put a lot of money into their place because Libby shopped in the *highest* end of the high-end stores. She wouldn't be found dead in places like Walmart or Target.

I didn't know what kind of money Jeffrey made as a fireman. His father was a retired judge and his mother was from a well-to-do family in Dallas, so I knew he was not hurting for money. He'd attended private schools when he was a boy and had traveled all over the world with his family. What I couldn't figure out was why a man with his background would settle for a position as a fireman. But he enjoyed his job and he loved doing things for other people. Whenever Bertha asked him to come to the house to do maintenance work or to drive her someplace, he never disappointed her. She was thrilled to have such a humble son-in-law, and she mentioned it to me all the time. With a pretentious, loutish ox like Marshall for a son, it was no wonder she felt the way she did about Jeffrey.

No matter what his salary was and how much his parents contributed, apparently it was not enough for him and Libby. There was no doubt in my mind that some of the cash Libby "borrowed" from Bertha helped finance their champagne lifestyle. She drove a Toyota Camry and Jeffrey drove a Ford Bronco and they replaced their vehicles every two or three years.

Despite Libby's presence, I had a good time at the party. She was in a rare mood, which meant she was cordial to me. "Lola, don't you be shy. You can have a few drinks as long as you don't overdo it. I'd hate for somebody to call the cops and blow the whistle on me for letting a minor drink alcohol," she said, stumbling even though she had on flat-heeled shoes. She wore a light blue silk dress with a matching turban, which looked more like a fancy do-rag. There was too much makeup on her face, and the wrong shade. What she had on was meant for a woman at least three shades lighter than her, like Joan.

Just as I was getting acquainted with Ted Mitchell, the man I'd come to the party to meet, the front door flew open and in walked Bertha in one of the outlandish flow-

ered dresses she wore to church. Nobody seemed surprised to see her, but I was. For one thing, she had complained about feeling tired all day, so when she got into
her nightgown around seven P.M., I had assumed the only
place she was going was to bed. Just before I'd left the
house, I told her that Jeffrey's friend wanted me to meet
his brother. All of a sudden, she claimed she didn't feel so
tired anymore. The thought that she'd come to the party
never crossed my mind.

I liked Ted even though he was not as cute as I hoped.
He had an overbite, hooded black eyes, and long, wiry
reddish brown hair. He was a couple of inches shorter
than me, which made him about five feet three inches tall.
I had on two-inch heels so he had to look up at me when
we talked or danced. I liked him, anyway. I was interested in having a relationship with him, and he initially
made me think he felt the same way.

"I'm glad you came tonight, Lola. Jeffrey's told me so
much about you and I'm glad to see that everything he
told me was true," Ted said, looking me up and down,
nodding his approval during our third dance.

"I'm glad I came, too," I told him. He had a sense of
humor, he was charming, and he had the confidence of a
handsome man. That was more than enough for me.

I danced with several other men, and every time I
scanned the room to locate Bertha, she was talking to Ted
and glancing in my direction. I couldn't imagine what she
was saying to him. The more time she spent talking to
him, the less time he spent talking to me. He even turned
me down when I asked him to dance again. That made me
feel slighted. There was nothing worse than being re-
jected by a plain man! Whatever Bertha had said to make
him lose interest in me must have worked. Because by
the time the party began to wind down, Ted had lost interest in me completely. I realized that when I saw him leav-

ing with Betty Jean Parker, the younger sister of one of Libby's friends.

I had come to the party in a cab and so had Bertha, but Jeffrey insisted on driving us home. It was a short but tense ride. She complained about how many "thugs" had been at the party and how bad her knee was aching.

"I didn't see any thugs," I said quickly, turning to face Bertha. I was in the front seat with Jeffrey; she was in the back, slumped in a corner, with her arms folded and a sour look on her face. "Everybody was well-mannered and well-dressed and I'm sorry I didn't get to spend more time with Ted. I hope I hear from him," I admitted, hoping I didn't sound too eager.

Bertha rolled her eyes and grunted. "He seemed nice enough. I guess it helps to be nice when you look like him. . . ." I cringed and waited for Bertha to complete her bad review of Ted. "What happened to his face?" she asked, her voice catching in her throat. She followed that question with a hacking cough.

"His face? What do you mean?" I asked when she stopped coughing.

Bertha geared up the way she always did when she was in an insulting mode. She sucked on her teeth for a few seconds and then she leaned forward, placing her hands on the back of my seat. "Was he in a car wreck or did he walk into a wall or something? I hope he was not born with that wide, flat face. Hmmm. He probably was. His brother's got the same problem. Can you imagine how the other kids are going to tease and pick on Ted's kids if he ever has any?"

I refused to egg Bertha on by responding to her unflattering comments.

"Looks aren't everything, Bertha. A person's character is a lot more important. And from what I hear, Ted's a righteous dude," Jeffrey said, glancing sharply in my direction. "Lola, I guess you didn't hit it off too well with him, huh? The way he pounced on you when you first arrived, I thought we'd have to pry you two apart. I don't understand why he shifted gears and ignored you the rest of the night."

"Maybe he didn't like Lola after he'd talked to her for a while," Bertha said with a grunt.

"I guess he didn't," I agreed.

I had given Ted my telephone number a few minutes after we'd met. I figured he'd be good for a few dinners and maybe a few bedroom games. He didn't call me the following day like he had said he would. So when Donald Akins, a hottie and one of the best quarterbacks on our football team, invited me to go to the movies with him that Wednesday, I went.

Things went well between Donald and me for a few days. We went out three times. Then he suddenly stopped calling. He even stopped speaking to me in school.

I was glad when Joan returned from her honeymoon exactly two weeks after her wedding. We chatted on the telephone that Saturday and a few times the following week. She had been home two weeks when I visited her for the first time in the swank condo she shared with Reed. It was a Sunday afternoon. After she had told me all about Aruba and showed me a couple dozen pictures, I brought the attention around to myself. "I don't know what got into Donald all of a sudden. Things were going just fine. Bertha was nicer to him than any of my other boyfriends, so I don't think she scared him off. Anyway, after our last date, he suddenly dropped me like a bad habit," I complained as we sat on the side of the huge bed in her lavish bedroom.

Every few seconds, we glanced toward the door. Joan

had already warned me that Reed was a high-level snoop. He liked to lurk around outside in the hallway when she was in the bedroom with one of her relatives or friends. We had to be careful because he could barge in at the drop of a hat. She looked at me and blinked rapidly several times—a habit that annoyed me. It usually meant she had something to tell me that I didn't want to hear.

"I know what got into Donald," she whispered. "Bertha Butt."

"What in the world are you talking about? I told you she was always nice to him when he came to the house. When he ate dinner with us one evening, she insisted on fixing him a plate to take home because, as she put it, 'his Nigerian mama knows nothing about how to cook a good American meal' and blah, blah, blah. I made sure not to leave him alone with her for more than a minute or two, so she couldn't have had enough time to say something too stupid or crazy about me."

"Reed's cousin Minnie was at Kandy's beauty shop one day when Donald's mother was also there."

I groaned and braced myself. "If you're trying to tell me that the beauty shop hens have been talking about me, please do so *now*. You know I don't like to be kept in suspense."

Joan exhaled and hunched her shoulders, which looked like they belonged on a linebacker these days. She had gained a lot of weight since she got pregnant, but it didn't bother her at all. She just bought bigger clothes. Today she wore a bulky red flannel maternity top with a white collar and white cuffs. She was eight months along now and if she had a white beard, she'd look like Santa Claus. She noticed me staring at her outfit, so she gave me a slightly dirty look before she brushed off her sleeves and continued talking. "We both know what a cesspool of gossip that beauty shop is."

"Cut to the chase," I said in a loud voice, snapping my fingers.

"Anyway, Donald's mother blabbed that you screwed anything with a dick and that you had infected several of your boyfriends with STDs. She even called up her witch doctor uncle in Nigeria to get his advice on what to do in case her son caught something from you."

I was so horrified I almost fainted. White-hot anger ripped through me. "What? Who does that woman think she is, spreading lies like that about me? I saw her only once in person and talked to her on the telephone a few times and I always treated her with respect. I thought she liked me."

"Minnie told Reed, and he told me, Donald's mother told everybody in the beauty shop that day that she was going by the word of a reliable source."

My shoulders slumped and I clenched my fists as I sat there, staring at Joan in stunned disbelief. I didn't even realize my crossed legs were shaking until one bumped into Joan's. I uncrossed them and unclenched my fists, but I was so angry it felt like my entire body had been put on hold. "Reliable source, my ass! Who in the world would say something that low-down about me?" I yelled as soon as I was able to move my tongue and lips again.

Joan gave me a distressed look. "I didn't want to tell you this, and I'm surprised nobody else told you before now, but somebody sent Donald's mother an anonymous note."

I gasped so hard I almost had a panic attack. "And she's going by what somebody wrote in an anonymous note? Well, it's a goddamn lie! You know if I had a problem with an STD, you'd be the first to know. Remember that clap incident I went through a few months ago? I told you I had been infected before I even went to the clinic to get it taken care of and that was before I met Donald." I had to pause so I could catch my breath. I was hopping mad. Had we been in my bedroom sitting on my bed, I would have punched my pillows several times by now. "Yeah, I've dated a lot of boys, but I've only had sex with four. They were all clean, but I made them use condoms, anyway—except Arthur Turner, the nasty buzzard who gave me the clap! That's why I refuse to let another boy touch me now unless he's wearing *two* condoms."

"Shhh! Don't talk so loud. Reed could be outside listening. He's too nosy and too clingy for my tastes these days."

I lowered my voice and continued. "Who and why would somebody tell a bald-faced lie as mean as that about me? I'll bet it was that bitch from the Washington Projects Donald used to kick it with." I stopped talking and gave Joan a curious look. "Who else could be mean enough to send Donald's mother an anonymous note about *me*?"

Joan gave me a look that made me feel like the most pitiful person on the planet. "Well, one thing for sure, it was somebody who didn't want you to be with Donald." She paused and calmly added, "Or any other boy."

"What else are you trying to tell me?"

"I think you know."

I knew that Joan was thinking the same thing I was thinking. "You're talking about Bertha, aren't you?"

Joan gave me a steely look and nodded. "Yep. Who else?"

"Oh, come on. Bertha is an oddball, but she wouldn't do something like that. Would she?"

"There's only one way to find out for sure—ask her."

Chapter 19

Joan

LOLA DIDN'T WAIT FOR ME TO SAY ANOTHER WORD. WE knew one another so well that it was not hard to know what was on each other's mind.

"I know you think Bertha sent that note to Donald's mother," she told me.

"Uh-huh. She's the only person who has something to gain by spreading lies about you," I said. I was so angry even my jaw was twitching. "You need to get in her face and tell her to stop fucking up your relationships!"

"What good would that do? I can't prove she sent the note. If I ask, I'm sure she'll deny it and get so upset. Then I'd have to deal with that too." There was a hopeless look on Lola's face *again*.

I continued talking with my jaw still twitching. "That girl from the projects that Donald was fooling around with, she hooked up with some dude from Berkeley. I heard she complained about how lousy Donald was in bed."

"Well, that's one thing I'll never get to find out about the boy."

I gasped. "Do you mean to tell me that you never did it with him?"

"I would have told you by now if I had. Every time he came to the house, Bertha sat in the living room with us until he left. When he took me out, she called where we went so many times we couldn't enjoy ourselves."

"Lola, for you to be such a smart girl, you sure do some dumb shit."

"So you keep telling me. By the way, the same thing is true of you."

"So you keep telling me. You shouldn't answer your cell phone when you're out with a boy if Bertha's number is on the caller ID."

"It doesn't matter if I answer or not. I always tell her where she can reach me, and when I don't answer my cell, she'll call wherever I'm at. One time when I didn't answer or take her call on the restaurant phone, she hopped in a cab and came to the place."

I had to hold my breath to keep from laughing. "Why are you still telling that silly old woman where you and your dates are going to, girl? Haven't you learned anything from me when it comes to giving folks the slip?"

"I tell her because she makes me feel like shit when I leave her in the house alone at night. Then she goes on and on about how important it is for her to be able to get in touch with me in case she has falls or something."

"Please don't mention that deathbed promise you made to your father."

"I wasn't going to bring that up. For the record, Miss Thing, the last few times we discussed that subject it was because *you* brought it up."

"Oh, well . . ." I paused and glanced around the room. I didn't like what I saw, especially the beige curtains, the dresser with its round mirror, and the plain white comforter on the bed. I had plans to visit a furniture store within the next few days to replace the items Reed had decorated his condo with that I didn't like—which was almost everything. I turned back to Lola and let out an exasperated sigh. "I have to find something to help keep me from getting bored. I'm going to spend as much as possible redecorating this place."

"I don't blame you." Lola glared at a huge picture on the wall of a white horse standing on its hind legs. "Joan, I have a feeling there's something you want to tell me—and I hope it's not something else about Bertha."

"What makes you think that?" I asked, my voice rattling like a broken bicycle wheel spoke.

Lola was the only person I knew I could trust with my deepest, darkest, and most intimate secrets. And the secret I had been keeping for weeks was that I was already so miserable being married to Reed Riley I wanted to scream.

I loved the child in my belly who was due to be born in about three weeks, and I thought I loved Reed. But he was not the man I thought he was. For one thing, he was stubborn and already set in his ways. He was a neat freak of epic proportions and that really bugged me. *Everything* in our condo had to be in its place at all times. He checked every day, several times each day, for dust. One time he actually squatted down on his knees and slid his fingers on the floor under the living-room couch. He made sure all of the dishes were neatly stacked in the kitchen cabinets and every condiment had to be in alphabetical order on the shelf. The clothes in the closets, as well as the baby items I had received at the shower Elaine and Lola hosted for me last week, had to be stored in a color-coded manner. According to him, I used too much bleach when I did the laundry and I didn't fold his shirts properly. I didn't iron the towels and bed linen well enough. I drew the line when he suggested I iron his *underwear and socks*! I cussed him out so thoroughly he made arrangements to have his shit cleaned by a professional laundry service until—and these were his exact words—"You learn how to be a real woman. . . ." And my cooking—oh, how that set him off! Everything was always either undercooked or overcooked, and had too much or not enough seasoning. So far, he had not complimented a single one of the dishes I'd prepared. "My mama doesn't cook like that" was his favorite line. No matter how hard I tried, it was literally impossible for me to please him.

"If your face gets any longer, it'll be on this bedroom floor," Lola said as she gently touched my shoulder. "So tell me what's wrong."

With relief I looked in her eyes and began to let it all out. "Reed is not the man I thought he was."

"Uh-oh. I hope he didn't suddenly get stingy with his money."

I shook my head. "I wish it was something that simple. It's much worse."

Lola gave me a wide-eyed look. "Is it another woman already?"

I shook my head again. "No, it's not another woman, as far as I know. But I could deal with that." I exhaled and then I told her in great detail all the things I didn't like about Reed. "I don't know how much longer I can stay with him."

Her response stunned me to say the least. "Is that all?" she asked.

I gasped and had to tap the side of my head because I had a hard time believing the words that had slid out of Lola's mouth. "What the hell do you mean by that? Did you not hear everything I just told you?"

"Yeah, I heard everything you told me. But I don't

think any of that is all that bad. Hell, other than Jesus, no man is perfect. No woman is either, for that matter. I'm sure that Reed has a list of things about you that drive him crazy. What do you think about that?"

"I think you need to stop while you're ahead. Whose side are you on, *Dr. Lola*?"

"I'm on your side, Joan. But give the man a chance. You should be glad he's not a drunk, a wife-beater, a compulsive gambler—or all three. Him being a neat freak is not that bad. With his money, you can afford a house-keeper."

"If he did any one of those three things, I'd have been long gone by now, and my brothers and uncles would have beaten his brains out. And I don't want to be bothered with a housekeeper. What I do want is my old life back!"

Lola looked at me like I was speaking Gaelic. "You've only been married to that stud for a few weeks, girl!"

"And that's a few weeks too long. Reed was a totally different man before we got married. I realize now that he was wearing a mask. That's the main problem. He tricked me! I was duped!" I paused. The amused look on Lola's face did not surprise me. I padded to the door, opened it, and peeped out. I had to make sure Reed was still out of earshot before I brought up the next thing on my list of complaints. I returned to the bed and sat even closer to Lola. "On top of everything else, the stud is a dud," I whispered with a grimace on my face.

Lola's face froze. "Get out of here! With his long, muscular legs and that tight butt, I never would have guessed they were only for show! I thought Reed was a spark plug in the bedroom."

"Humph! That's a laugh. If anything, he's a butt plug in the bedroom! When we do make love, I'm usually the one who loosens him up."

"Joan, didn't you know he was lousy in bed before you married him?"

"I guess I forgot to tell you I made love with him only that one time before we got married. When I told him I was pregnant, we didn't sleep together again until our wedding night. And get that surprised look off your face. It was his idea for us to wait until we got married."

"Hmmm. He must have a real low sex drive if he could wait that long."

"And that's another thing. Not having sex on a regular basis doesn't even bother him. He claims he'd only been with four other women before me. I've got more experience in my little finger than he has in his . . . well . . . you know what I'm trying to say. I don't need to get too explicit. I avoid talking or thinking about sex when I can. You know how horny I get when you and I discuss that subject." I winked at Lola.

"Joan, you didn't *have* to get married. I know your mother and Elmo would have let you stay on in the house with your baby. You would have eventually met a man that you would have been a lot happier with—if you had really taken the time to get to know him." Lola shook her head and gave me a sympathetic look. "I'm telling you now, I am not going to marry any man until I am convinced that I know him inside out. I don't care how long it takes."

"I hope I live long enough to see that day," I snickered. "If you had really developed something with one of those old men in the lonely hearts club, you might have had a chance to enjoy a normal life."

"Yeah, right. And how would I have had a chance with any one of them?"

"Come on now. You're not *that* dense. The way those geezers were coming on, wanting to send us tickets to come marry them and live happily ever after and all, you could have left Bertha's house right after graduation."

"I doubt that. Those men thought it was Elaine they were in love with! If I'd been stupid enough to go meet one, I would have had a lot of explaining to do. And what if the older man I wanted to be with already had a wife? Did you forget about that woman who came to beat you up?"

"No, I haven't. But I don't think about her that often anymore, and you shouldn't either," I said with a dismissive wave. "That's all in the past. We've learned our lesson about playing with people's feelings."

"And taking their money."

"Yeah, that too."

"We're lucky we didn't end up in jail for using the mail to commit fraud. Maybe even elder abuse too," Lola said. She pursed her lips and blew out some air. Then she stood up and shuddered. "Just thinking about that gives me a chill. We dodged one heck of a bullet."

"Maybe we did this time, but life is full of bullets. We're going to do a lot more dodging down the road," I said.

Chapter 20

Lola

*I*T RAINED ALMOST EVERY DAY IN MARCH. WE DESPER-
ately needed it, but I was glad when it finally ended. I had
a habit of losing umbrellas when I went out in public. By
the time I'd misplaced two different ones before the month
ended, I was at the end of my rope. I was glad when April
rolled around. The warm, dry weather did a lot for my
morale.

Nothing significant had happened in my life recently. I
hadn't seen Libby or Marshall in weeks, so I was pretty
relaxed and optimistic. And Bertha was currently in a
really good mood—for her. It had been more than a week
since she'd complained about her health, and she had
been unusually cordial to a couple of males who'd come
to visit me. That was very suspicious, but I didn't spend
too much time trying to figure out what was really on her
mind. My life was much more pleasant when she was in a
good mood. On the last day in March, I got real bold and

decided to mention something to Bertha that I had been putting off.

"Somebody sent Donald's mother a nasty note about me," I said casually during breakfast that morning. I occupied a seat at the kitchen table and had almost finished eating.

Bertha was standing in front of the stove scrambling her second helping of eggs. She was still in her bathrobe and more than a dozen pink sponge rollers dangled from her head. She whirled around so fast to look at me, one of the rollers flew off her head. There was a stunned look on her face. "Huh? What did the note say?"

"A bunch of lies about me having sex with a lot of boys, spreading diseases and stuff."

Bertha gasped. "Who in the world would say something like that about you? Um, do you have any idea *who* sent the note?"

"The person didn't sign it, so I have no idea who. Anyway, it worked. Donald doesn't even speak to me anymore."

"Tsk, tsk, tsk! That's a damn shame!" she hollered. "I'll bet it was some jealous girl that wanted to break you and Donald up so she could have him."

I sighed. "Yeah. I'm sure that's who it was." Bertha looked relieved. There was only a *slim* possibility that one of my rivals had sent the note. For one thing, the girls I knew didn't bother with petty things like sending anonymous notes. Whenever they had an issue with another girl, they got up real close and personal in her face and they did it in a very public way so everybody would know about it. I was practically convinced that Bertha was the culprit. I knew she'd never admit it, so I decided to drop the subject and never mention it to her again.

* * *

The first Saturday in April, Bertha rented a car for me to drive her to Berkeley to visit one of her friends who had recently moved to the East Bay Area. The three of us had a very spicy lunch at a popular Chinese restaurant, got manicures and pedicures, and spent a couple of hours rooting through the bins in a thrift shop. We didn't find a single item we liked enough to buy, but it had been an enjoyable excursion. I didn't miss shopping in the upscale stores, or eating in the expensive restaurants that Joan and I used to go to when we were behaving like greedy idiots. I realized that being broke, or close to it like I was now, was a lot less stressful than having a lot of money. In our case, more money—especially dirty money—had meant more problems. It had been a hassle to keep it hidden from other people, and we were worried about getting in trouble for using the mail to commit fraud to get the money. I wondered how wealthy people stayed sane.

When Bertha and I got home around seven P.M., the first thing I did was check the voice mail messages. Reed was the only one who had called. Joan was due to give birth any day, so when I heard his tired voice telling me to call him as soon as I could, I did. Before I could finish dialing his cell phone number, Bertha joined me in the kitchen, huffing and puffing like she had just run a footrace.

Reed answered my call right away. "Is everything all right?" I asked.

"Who are you talking to?" Bertha wanted to know, standing so close to me I could smell and feel her breath on my face. "What's happened?"

I held up my hand and shook my head.

"Joan had a really rough time," Reed said. "She wouldn't agree to a C-section, like I suggested, but after another hour of that unholy pain, she was screaming for the doctor to cut her open."

"So she had to have a C-section?" I asked, rubbing my stomach. The thought of being cut open terrified me. I glanced at Bertha out of the corner of my eye and saw a look of relief on her face. I figured she had thought something bad had happened to one of her children or Libby's little boy.

"No, thank God. Just as they were about to prepare her for that, our son came," Reed said, his voice cracking.

I unbuttoned my windbreaker and fanned my face with my hand. "Is she all right? When can I see her and the baby?"

"I'm on my way to get something to eat, but when I go back to the hospital, I'll tell her to give you a call. I wasn't going to tell you this, but, uh, after it was over, you were one of the first people she wanted to talk to."

I smiled and tears flooded my eyes. "Well, you tell her I can't wait to talk to her and meet little—"

Reed cut me off and blurted out with a chuckle, "Reed Junior. We had decided on the name six months ago."

I didn't get to talk to Joan until the following Monday morning. She called me a few minutes before I left for school while I was at the kitchen table with Bertha finishing the smoked sausages and grits she had prepared. I got up to answer the phone and she continued to eat, but her eyes were on me. "Joan, I am so happy to hear your voice! How are you feeling? I know being in a hospital is no fun," I hollered. As soon as I mentioned "hospital," Bertha's hand froze in midair above her plate and a concerned look appeared on her face. I held the telephone away from my ear and mouthed, "It's just Joan."

Bertha bobbed her head like a rooster and returned her attention to the food on her plate. My plan was to skip my last two classes and go visit Joan. I was surprised when she told me she'd be home in a few hours.

"You're doing that well?" I asked. "I thought they kept

women in the hospital at least two or three days after giving birth."

"They used to, but they don't do that anymore, unless there are some complications. A woman who came in two hours before me last night gave birth to her baby girl a few hours ago and she's already gone home."

"Then I guess I'll come see you at home this evening?"

"I'll see you then, Lola." Joan sounded so happy and strong, I envied her.

I couldn't wait to be in her position, more than ever now. Despite my feelings of envy, I was happy for her. I was also happy that she had not complained about Reed in a few days. But I was saddened because things were happening that would definitely cause more changes in my relationship with her. I could feel us drifting apart and it scared the hell out of me.

Reed had bought Joan a brand-new Audi three weeks ago and she'd told me that whenever I needed a ride to let her know. But so far, every time I'd called her for a ride, she was busy. Now that she'd had the baby, she'd be busier than ever.

After school that evening, I attempted to call Joan, but she didn't answer. I called the hospital to confirm that she'd been released. When the receptionist told me she had been a few hours ago, I took a cab to her new residence. I was about to burst open; I was so anxious to see her and the baby. I was probably as elated as she was. My elation didn't last long. Reed's mother opened the door for me with a scowl on her moon face. She wasted no time making me feel unwelcome.

"You should have called before you came over here!" she snapped in a voice that was way too husky for a woman. "What was your name again?" I'd been in Mrs. Riley's presence half-a-dozen times since Joan and Reed got married. Each time she'd asked me my name.

"My name is Lola," I answered meekly with both of my eyebrows raised. "I'm Joan's best friend," I added in a firmer voice. Since Mrs. Riley was looking at me with such contempt on her rust-colored face, I was not about to waste a smile on her.

"Well, Lola, Joan is taking a nap. She needs her rest, so I am not going to let you disturb her. You can go in the nursery at the end of the hall and take a peek at the baby, but don't pick him up or touch him. And don't you stay in there but a couple of minutes. Do you hear me?"

"Can I stay here until Joan wakes up? I spoke to her this morning and she's expecting me."

"No, I don't think that's a good idea. I don't have time to entertain you, so it would be better if you leave and come back when she's awake. And please be considerate enough to call first!"

Despite Mrs. Riley's rudeness, I managed to remain civil. "Yes, ma'am."

Not only was Joan's son adorable, he was the image of her. I couldn't take my eyes off him. I got to spend about three minutes in the nursery gazing at the baby in the bright blue bassinet before Mrs. Riley barged in.

"Young lady, didn't I tell you not to stay in here but a couple of minutes? Now scoot!" she barked, waving me out the door.

I let out a heavy sigh combined with a groan and left without another word.

The next day, I got to see Joan a total of eight minutes before her mother-in-law shooed me away again.

Chapter 21

Joan

NOW THAT I WAS A MOTHER, I KNEW THAT MY LIFE WAS going to change in ways I never imagined. I didn't know what to expect next. For one thing, I didn't like the way my body looked now. I had cellulite on my thighs and butt too hideous for words. And even with all the milk in my breasts, they had begun to droop! I was still a teenager, so I was not about to walk around with a rack that looked like it belonged on a woman in her thirties! I had already ordered some kind of exercise contraption that was supposed to restore the perkiness.

Another thing I was concerned about was the shape of the rest of my body. I had gained only thirty-two pounds during my pregnancy, but my stomach still looked bloated. And as if that was not bad enough, I had the most hideous stretch marks. Luckily, they were below my belly button and on the lower part of my butt, so I could still rock a bikini.

One thing I had not expected was Mother Riley, Reed's

bossy mother, coming into my house and trying to take over. That woman got on my nerves and I fantasized about slapping her face! I was glad she didn't live in South Bay City and didn't like to travel the fifty miles from her home in Monterey, so I would not have to see her and Reed's whiny, meek father that often.

"That girl named Lula or Lola or some other countrified name like that keeps calling here for you. I keep telling her you can't talk or spend time with her. I hope the rest of your friends don't pester you like that," Mother Riley told me as she hovered over my bed.

I had stirred around too much since I'd come home from the hospital and now I was paying for it. My ankles were swollen and my lower back felt like somebody had been dancing on it. Last night I actually fell to the floor when I tried to get up from the living-room love seat too fast. It scared Reed so bad, he almost had a baby himself. He leaped up from his La-Z-Boy and shot across the floor like a bullet. His mother and father wobbled up from the couch and ran to me. With three frantic people attempting to assist me, I fell again. This time I hit my head on the edge of the coffee table. A bump rose on my forehead and I immediately developed a headache that wouldn't quit. My doctor ordered me to stay off my feet for a while. I'd been lying in bed off and on for hours at a time.

"Lola's my best friend and I'd like to see her. When she calls or comes by again, let me know," I said firmly. "If I'm asleep, wake me up."

Mother Riley snorted and gave me a guarded look. "Now, look—"

"No, you look," I said as I rose up into a sitting position. "This is my home and my rules. If you don't like them, you don't have to stick around." I knew Reed's parents, and most of his other family members, didn't care for me and the feeling was mutual. When Lola told me how my mother-in-law spoke to her when she called and when she visited, it made me furious. When I told Mama I was going to tell Mother Riley off, she didn't think it was a good idea.

"Baby, you don't want to create tension between you and Reed on account of his mama. Let that uppity heifer have her way when she's here. As long as she don't get too far out of line, ignore her," she advised. "And if she do get too far out of line with you, baby, let me know and I'll straighten her out."

I didn't want a civil war on my hands so I decided to take my mother's advice. I was glad that she and Reed's mother were rarely with me at the same time. Despite all the attention I was getting from family, the one person I wanted to see the most was Lola.

When she called me up that evening and updated me on Bertha's antics, I laughed. I didn't laugh long, though, and I didn't say anything on the subject. I knew that Lola didn't want to hear what I had to say about her step-mother again or how she needed to start working harder on being more in control of her own life. I kept my comments to myself, something I didn't like but had learned to do well over the years because I didn't want to upset my BFF.

I called Lola the next day around five P.M. Even though I had talked to her the evening before, I was so glad to hear her voice again. "Hey, let's go out this coming Friday evening," I suggested. "I'll check today's newspaper to see what movies are playing."

"You?" she exclaimed. "Do you think you should be going out so soon?"

"I'm doing just fine and I'll be doing even better once I get back into the swing of things. I have so many telephone messages to return too. Hey! I heard you got asked to the prom by two different dudes. Humph. I'm jealous."

"Don't be. I turned them both down."

I could hear the pain in Lola's voice, which didn't make sense. One of the many things she and I had talked about since middle school was going to our senior prom. I obviously was not going to make it, but I assumed she would.

"What?"

"It was two of the biggest assholes we know," Lola hissed. "Clint Kirksey and Neil Dobbs."

"Girl, they're two of the hottest dudes in our school. Clint is captain of the football team. What's the matter with you? Do you think I would have turned either one of them down, had I not gotten myself into the mess I'm in?"

"Before I could make up my mind which one to go with, Joy Rogers told me that her boyfriend told her Clint and Neil had been talking trash about me in the locker room about what an 'easy piece of ass' I was. They had a bet going. If the one I went to prom with 'hit it' afterward, he would win twenty bucks from the other one. They said that was the only reason they asked me to go. I haven't slept with half as many boys as most of the girls who go to South Bay High."

"I wish I could say that," I muttered. My scorecard had already run out of space by the time I got to Reed. I couldn't count the number of times I wished I had kept my panties on more often, like Lola had done.

"Anyway, I'm not going. If you're not busy that night, and if Reed doesn't mind, let's go out for pizza."

My jaw dropped. "Are you telling me you'd pass up senior prom to go have a pizza with me?"

"I sure would. You're a much better friend to me than any of the boys I know. Besides, I know I'll have a good time with you."

"O . . . kay. It's a date. If you change your mind, I won't be disappointed."

Chapter 22

Lola

A MONTH AND A HALF AFTER JOAN HAD GIVEN BIRTH, she and I spent prom night in Angelina's Pizzeria, sharing a large pepperoni pizza. I couldn't remember the last time I felt so relaxed. The cute boy behind the counter, who had graduated the year before, was one of Joan's castoffs, but he still liked her. He was cool enough to slip us some beer in Pepsi containers.

To my surprise, Libby and Marshall and their spouses attended my graduation ceremony the following week. Libby's two-month-old son, Kevin, was with a babysitter. I prayed that since she was a mother now, she would be a nicer person. Her attendance and behavior today (so far) were hopeful signs and that made my big day even more special to me.

It was an occasion I would never forget. Not only had Libby told me how nice I looked in my cap and gown, she had actually smiled most of the evening. And she was the first person to give me a hug after I received my diploma.

"I hope you have plans for your future," she told me, patting my shoulder.

"Uh, I'm going to get a job and work for a year or two and then I'll decide what I want to do about my future," I responded. I ignored the worried look on Bertha's face when I turned to accept a hug from her.

We celebrated by having dinner at a French restaurant. No matter how "nice" Libby and Marshall acted to me, which was so rare, I got suspicious when they did. Tonight was no different. I kept expecting one of them to say something inappropriate to or about me. To my surprise, they didn't. The evening actually ended on a good note.

Five days after graduation, I landed a job as a cashier at Cottright's, a mom-and-pop grocery store five blocks from Bertha's house. It was within walking distance and I could purchase groceries and get a 20 percent employee discount. That pleased Bertha.

I liked my job immediately and I was thrilled to death to know that I'd be getting a paycheck every other Friday. However, it saddened me to know that my lifelong dream to have a real career as a teacher or a nurse someday probably wasn't going to come true anytime soon. For one thing, my senior year grades had not been quite good enough for me to get a scholarship. And Bertha didn't know if she'd be able to afford helping me continue my education. Libby and Marshall had been putting the bite on her wallet so frequently, and for so long, I suspected she was probably close to being bankrupt. My only hope was to work for a few years and save some money, and then pray for the best. Either I'd continue my education and pay for it on my own, or I'd get married and let my husband help me do it. But the way things were going with my love life, landing a husband was as much of a dream as going to college. I had not met a man yet who stayed around more than a few weeks once he got to know Bertha.

Eddie Burris, a bank teller I'd recently met, was the most recent one. On the last of his four visits, Bertha had sat like a sphinx on the seat across from us in the living room, staring and blinking at him. After being silent for about fifteen minutes, she abruptly told Eddie that she and I were a "package deal," and where I went, she went. He didn't comment on that, but he looked from her to me with a confused expression on his face. He left ten minutes later, dashing out the door with me stumbling behind him. We stood on the front porch steps and chatted for a few moments. When I went back inside, Bertha was standing in the middle of the living room with her arms folded. She looked like she had just swallowed a canary.

"That boy sure left here in a hurry," she commented.

"He won't be coming back," I said dryly.

"Oh? What did you do to him?"

"I didn't do anything to him," I said, struggling to keep my voice from showing my frustration. "He decided not to pursue a relationship with me because he didn't think I'd be able to spend much time alone with him." I expected Bertha to be apologetic or at least sympathetic. I was wrong.

"'Time'?" she shrieked. She put her hands on her hips and continued in a loud, angry voice. "Ha! That mole-faced so-and-so ought to be glad you even gave him the little 'time' you did! By the way, I heard that he treats his own mama like a dog, so there's no telling how he'd have treated *me*. I'm glad he won't be coming back." Bertha's eyes lit up and a crooked smile appeared on her face. She even had the nerve to clap her hands. "You're too sweet for that Eddie, anyway!" After a long sigh, she added, "I don't know what I'd do without you, Lola. I'm so glad I can still count on you. You do spoil me! I love you as much as I love Libby and Marshall." Then she gave me a bear hug and a kiss on the cheek.

Even though Bertha continued to frustrate me with her clinging-vine behavior and her abusive attitude when it came to my male friends, I tolerated her because I felt so sorry for her. She was one miserable woman. Her relationship with her children was so messed up it broke my heart to be a witness to the way they mistreated her. And despite the fact that she got on my last nerve, she was still a good woman and I still cared about her.

"Lola, I thank the good Lord every day for sending you to take care of me. I'm so glad you decided to take a job close to home. You need to be close in case I fall or something," she told me a month after I'd started working at the grocery store.

I had filled out applications all over the place, including several upscale stores at all of the local malls and a couple in San Jose. A few of the cool kids who had graduated with me had already secured jobs in some of the same stores. I thought it would be fun to ride on the commuter bus to and from work with them. But since I was so anxious to get out of the house during the day and have a paycheck, I had eagerly accepted the grocery store job offer when Mr. Cottright called me up the day after I had applied.

Things could have been a lot worse, so I counted my blessings. I still had a lot more going for me than some of the kids I knew. But my life still had enough glitches in it to keep me on my toes. One thing I was determined to do was stay out of trouble. I went out of my way not to offend people or do anything else that would earn me a spot on their shit list. Now and then, something happened that made me think about the angry woman who had come to my house last year looking for Joan. Every time I saw a gray-haired, middle-aged woman in a pantsuit, it brought back memories of that incident and I panicked. I knew that I was just being paranoid, but I couldn't help myself. I had more important things to think about than the angry wife of one of Joan's former pen pals, or any other angry woman for that matter, coming to my house to have a showdown about her man. Incredibly, another angry woman did come to the house and this time it was for *me*. And it was the last woman in the world I expected: Libby!

It happened on a Saturday afternoon in July, two weeks after I had attended another party at Jeffrey and Libby's house to celebrate his thirtieth birthday.

The only reason I had gone to that party was because Joan had canceled a movie date with me. We had gradually begun to resume our lengthy visits and telephone conversations. However, with a cranky baby in her arms most of the time, our visits were not nearly as much fun as they used to be. I couldn't wait for Reed Junior to get older so he'd be less trouble. Until that happened, I had to find other ways to spend my time.

I had not been too excited about going to another party at Libby's house. And had it not been Jeffrey's birthday, I would not have gone. Ted, the man I'd met at the party back in February, had also been invited. He had come alone, but he paid very little attention to me, not that I cared anymore. The way he had treated me at the previous party after he'd huddled with Bertha, I had written him off, anyway. Most of the other men had come with dates. Eventually a man I had never met before asked me to dance. But he was so drunk he could barely stand up, let alone dance. If Jeffrey had not danced several dances with me, I would have spent most of the night sitting on the couch alone.

"I apologize for not inviting more single dudes," Jeffrey told me during my fifth dance in a row with him. Under normal circumstances, I liked slow dancing, especially if it was with somebody I was attracted to. Slow dancing to one of Luther Vandross's most romantic old-school tunes with Jeffrey was like dancing with a preacher. But being a normal, red-blooded young man, touching a woman's lower body with his had the same effect on him that it had on every other man I'd ever slow danced with. His dick suddenly got as hard as a piece of steel. From the tight look on his face, I knew he was embarrassed, to say the least. I pulled back enough so that I couldn't feel his hardness pressing against me. It didn't bother me that Jeffrey's face was so close to mine; but from the corner of my eye, I noticed a frown on Libby's face.

"I thought that Ted would pay more attention to you this time," he told me with his cheek touching mine. "You're the best-looking woman in the room."

Libby walked up just in time to hear his last remark. No woman in her right mind, especially one who thought she was as hot as Libby thought she was, appreciated hearing her man make such a bold statement to another female.

"This is one of my favorite old songs," she growled, thumping Jeffrey on his shoulder, but looking at me. If looks could kill, I would have dropped dead on the spot. "Lola, do you mind if I dance with my husband?"

"Sure, Libby," I replied with a forced smile. I eased out of Jeffrey's arm and waded through the crowd. I was glad I had left my sweater on the back of the couch, so I didn't look so conspicuous when I grabbed it and started inching my way to the door.

I saw a few people glance in my direction, but the only one I was concerned about was Libby. I didn't like the menacing look on her face, and I didn't want to wait around to find out why it was there.

When I saw her lead Jeffrey by the hand into the kitchen, I ducked out the front door. I jumped into the first cab that came along five minutes later.

Since I had had such a miserable time at the party, Jeffrey had tried to make up for it. He took me to lunch the next day and for pizza and other snacks a few times after that.

"I sure hope Libby doesn't mind you spending so much time with me," I said when he drove me home from our last dinner date.

"Well, what she doesn't know won't hurt her. This will be our little secret," he said in a conspiratorial manner. We both glanced up toward Bertha's bedroom window. I was sure he was as pleased as I was to see that her light was still out. We had not left the house until she'd gone to bed.

"Jeffrey, I appreciate everything you do for me, but you don't have to keep spending time with me. And you certainly don't have to invite me to every party you and Libby have. You have a wife and a little boy and I know they need you more than I do."

A sad look crossed his face. "Yeah, but sometimes that's the reason I need to get out of the house." He let out a dry laugh before we piled out of his Bronco. With his arm around my shoulder, he walked me to the door and gave me a long hug.

I went to bed right away and got up early the next morning so I could take a long shower before I headed off to work. I only worked Monday through Friday, but I had eagerly agreed to work that Saturday because the woman who normally worked on that day had been out for the past three days because of a nasty cold.

But since this was the first weekend in the month when the people on public assistance received their benefits, it meant a busy and hectic day dealing with the EBT cards and other government vouchers. Some of the recipients were rude, hostile, and pushy. They wouldn't hesitate to threaten or cuss out me and whoever was on the second cash register if we refused to let them purchase cigarettes, condoms, lottery tickets, alcohol, or any other unauthorized items with their EBT food card or WIC coupons. It didn't matter how many times we explained to them that it was against the state's rules.

This particular day was even more hectic than usual. It was times like this that I wished I had held out for a better job. Two days after the Cottrights had already hired me, Macy's offered me a job in the shoe department.

"Get the hell up out of that grocery store and get your tail over to Macy's! We can get a lot of mileage out of your employee discount," Joan advised when I told her.

"I'm staying right where I'm at. The Macy's job might not work out and I feel a whole lot more secure working for the Cottrights. Since most of my pen pal money is gone now, I need something to fall back on in case I have to move out of Bertha's house at the spur of the moment. You know how volatile Libby and Marshall are. Now that I am a little more independent, things might get even worse between them and me. Besides, I promised the Cottrights I'd stay at least a year," I explained. "You, of all people, know I never go back on my promises."

"Tell me about it," Joan snapped. I knew she was referring to the deathbed promise I had made to Daddy, even though she didn't say it. I was glad that I was a person people could count on.

Anyway, this day, "welfare day" as the Cottright employees called it, was getting on my nerves. I couldn't wait for it to end. I had even skipped my one-hour lunch break so I could go home at three P.M. instead of four. One reason I wanted to go home early was because Bertha had gone shopping with two other retired teachers, so I would have a few hours to myself in the house.

I had been home for about ten minutes when I went into the kitchen to microwave a potpie to eat for dinner. Before I could set the timer, I heard the front door open and then slam shut.

"Lola! Get your black ass out here, BITCH!" I couldn't remember the last time I'd heard Libby's voice sound so angry. And she had never made a reference to my "black ass" before. What was even more disturbing was the fact that nobody had ever called me a "bitch" in my presence.

I took a deep breath and scrambled out of the kitchen and into the living room, already in a defensive mood. "What's wrong now?" I asked with my arms folded.

"HOW LONG HAVE YOU BEEN FUCKING MY HUSBAND?" she roared.

Chapter 23

Lola

*B*EING ACCUSED OF FOOLING AROUND WITH ANOTHER woman's man was bad enough, whether it was true or not. Had I not been as alert and lucky as I had been the day that woman came to the house looking for Joan, I don't know what might have happened to her—or to me. Every now and then, I think about how that large woman could easily have mowed me down and stormed Bertha's house the same way Libby had just done.

If she had accused me of fucking the fat, lazy cat she rescued from the animal shelter last month, I could not have been more stunned. Other than Marshall and God-zilla, Jeffrey was the last male on the planet I wanted to have sex with. I loved him to death, but I was no more at-tracted to him than I was to a *cat*! "Huh?" was all I could say.

"Don't you stand there and deny it! I know all about it! He told me all about the pizza dates and other dates you and him went on—but only after I asked him! I always knew you were a little on the slutty side, but I never expected something this low and nasty from you! And after all my mama has done for your ass! You ought to be ashamed of yourself, Lola Poole!"

Words could not describe the look on Libby's face. On the anger scale from one to ten, I rated her eleven. And words seemed to be stuck in my mouth. All I could do at first was babble. "I—I—"

She cut me off sharply, shaking her fist at me. "What do you have to say for your nasty self?"

I winced and shook my head so hard it felt like marbles were inside rattling and bouncing off my brain. I was dumbfounded "I don't know what to say. You think me and Jeffrey are—" Before I could finish my sentence this time, she lunged at me.

For the next two or three minutes, she was on me like a wildcat, biting my arm, pulling my hair, and punching me in the face. She bit my fingers when I tried to pry hers from around my arm. She suddenly stood stock-still and started cussing at me at the top of her voice. "You no-good whore! You nasty, skanky, sex-crazed bitch! I hope you didn't give my husband herpes or something worse!"

I glared at her in stunned disbelief as I rubbed the teeth prints she'd left on my arm. I was aching in every spot where she had bitten, punched, scratched, and mauled me. "I don't know what the hell you are talking about!" I hollered.

All these years I had endured Libby's hostile attitude and I had managed to remain cool. Well, I could no longer say that. Just as she was about to bite me again, I took a very deep breath, reared back, and punched her in the stomach so hard she stumbled all the way across the room and hit the wall with a thud.

"You . . . you hit me," she whimpered as she slid to the

floor with a horrified look on her face. "I can't believe you hit me!"

"You're damn right I hit you and I will hit you again if I have to! What did you expect?" I shrieked. "Did you think I was going to stand here and let you whup my ass without trying to defend myself? You've got some fucking nerve coming up in here and accusing me of sleeping with your husband and attacking me!" I was sizzling with rage. I stomped across the floor and stood over her with my fist still balled.

"Stop lying, whore! You *have* been sleeping with my husband!" she screeched as she rubbed her stomach.

"Who told you that? Jeffrey is like a brother to me and he's never shown any romantic interest in me. Even if he had, I would never sleep with him, or any other married man!"

"You're a damn slut and a damn liar! Never mind who told me! I know all about it! How long did you think you could get away with this shit before I found out? I know you were with him last night!"

My head felt like it had been turned upside down. I couldn't imagine who had told Libby that I was sleeping with Jeffrey. Then it dawned on me. Last night when he hugged me at the door, he must have held me in his embrace for a full minute—a long time for a hug. That must have looked pretty intimate to some of my neighbors. I had noticed a few peeping from their windows. Hester Springer, one of Libby's few friends, who was just as much of a bitch as she was, lived directly across the street from Bertha's house. She instigated more conflicts and other confusion among the people on our block than anyone else I knew.

"Did Hester tell you she saw me and Jeffrey together last night?"

"What if she did? Last night is not the first time you were caught with my husband!"

I stared at Libby with my mouth hanging open. "What do you mean 'caught'? Nobody 'caught' me doing anything with your husband. Did you ask him?"

"Yes, I asked him and he denied it too. But I'm no fool! Yes, Hester did tell me she saw you and my Jeffrey together last night, and she wasn't the only one. I got information from other people as well. I ran into Edie Caruso just this morning. She told me how often you and Jeffrey come into the pizzeria that her grandfather owns and snuggled up in a booth like newlyweds."

"Yes, Jeffrey has taken me out to eat several times. He's even taken me to the movies a few times. But we've never 'snuggled up' anywhere. I've never 'snuggled up' with any other man in public either! Your husband was just trying to be nice to me, since you and Marshall treat me like a piece of shit," I explained.

"That's because you are a piece of shit!" Libby slowly rose up off the floor, rubbing her stomach some more. "You think I believe you?"

"You need to leave," I advised. That was probably the last thing I should have said to her.

She looked at me like I had turned into the devil himself. "Me leave? Hah! You've got some fucking nerve telling me *I* need to leave! This is my mama's house, which your displaced, orphaned ass has been living in rent-free for years!"

"Is that what this is *really* about? You have a problem with me living here? If you had said something about that before, I'd have been long gone by now and you wouldn't be feeling the pain of my fist. I can be up out of here in fifteen minutes," I said evenly. "I've been wanting to leave for a long time, anyway, and now is as good a time as any. Tell Bertha I'll let her know where I'll be staying as soon as I get settled—" Before I could say another word, the telephone rang. I scurried over to the stand at the end of the couch and grabbed it. "Hello!" I yelled.

"Lola, thank God you answered!" It was Jeffrey on the other end. His voice was hoarse and he was breathing hard. "Did you get my message?"

"What message?"

"I left you one about half an hour ago."

"I haven't retrieved any yet."

"Is Libby there? She's on the warpath." Jeffrey was talking so fast his words ran together. I could tell from the tone of his voice that he was frantic. "She's got a crazy notion that you and I are having an affair! I left you a message telling you that she had called me up at work and said she was coming over there to have it out with you! She asked if it was true that I'd been taking you out and I told her that it was. I called you as soon as I got off the phone with her."

"Yeah, she's here. She's been here for a few minutes," I muttered. "She's been hearing all kinds of shit about you and me having an affair. I told her it was not true. She didn't believe me, though."

"Did she . . . Did she hurt you?"

"No, not really. I'm not sure I can say the same for her. . . ."

"Oh, shit!"

"I didn't hurt her too much, but if you don't get here in time, she might come at me again and I am not going to be responsible for my actions."

"I'll see you in a few minutes." Jeffrey hung up and I placed the telephone back into its cradle. Libby was leaning against the wall brushing off her clothes, glaring at me like she wanted to attack me again.

"Your husband is on his way," I snapped. In a much

calmer voice, I added, "In the meantime, I suggest you keep your hands to yourself before somebody gets hurt real bad."

The expression on Libby's face was priceless. I had never seen her look more stunned. "Are you threatening me?"

"Yes, I'm threatening you!" I shrieked, wagging my finger in her direction. I also stomped my foot and gave her the most hostile look I could manage.

Now there was a dazed look on her face. She stared at me in silence for a few seconds. What she said next surprised me. "Look . . . um . . . maybe I overreacted. You know I'm a reasonable woman."

I couldn't believe my ears! I didn't know whether to laugh or cry because of what she'd just said. "Yeah, right," I said, my voice dripping with sarcasm. "For the record, Libby, I know plenty of men. I don't have to mess with your husband! I wouldn't do that to you. And I would never do anything that trifling because I know how much it would hurt Bertha if she found out. But like I said, I can be out of this house in fifteen minutes. I don't have much to pack—"

"I . . . I can't lose my husband. My period is two weeks late, so I could be pregnant again already."

My heart felt like it had dropped down to my feet. "Oh?" The fact that I had hit her in her stomach concerned me. I would not have hit her at all if I'd known she could be pregnant.

"You can get that scared look off your face. That little baby tap you just gave me didn't hurt me."

"I'm sorry. But I'm especially sorry for you because I don't know what to do to get along with you. You have never liked me and I can't seem to do anything about that and I'm tired of trying."

Libby held up her hand and actually smiled. "Look, uh . . . Mama really depends on you. I can't take her in and neither can my brother and we can't afford to hire somebody to come look after her. Besides, she's crazy about you. You don't have to move out. You're living here rent-free and I know you are not making much money at that pooh-butt grocery store. The only place you'd be able to afford is a shack on a backstreet or a rat-infested room in a cheap motel."

"I could deal with that if I have to and I'm sure I'd eventually find somebody to share a decent place with," I shot back.

Before I could say another word, and before she could respond, Jeffrey arrived. He immediately ran up to Libby and wrapped his arms around her.

"Baby, are you all right?" he began, jerking his head to look from her to me and back.

"This woman almost killed me," she blubbered, trembling like a true victim. Snot and tears suddenly appeared and began to slide down her face. I was not surprised that she had turned on a dime. She had replaced her smile with a ferocious scowl. "Take me home before this *savage* jumps on me again!" she boomed.

"I will, honey. Baby, I swear to you, Lola and I are not having an affair!" Jeffrey exclaimed, looking at me again with an extremely apologetic look on his face. "I'm sorry about this, Lola. I assure you it won't happen again." He glanced around. "Did Bertha . . ."

I held up my hand. "She's not here."

"I don't think we should mention this misunderstanding to her," he said with his eyes on Libby. She was writhing in his arms and moaning like she was already in labor. There was a helpless look on Jeffrey's face now. But the look on her face was the one that confused me. She had turned on another dime. She actually looked remorseful. In addition to a puppy dog expression, she surprised me again with another smile.

"Lola and I just have to figure out a way to get along, I guess," Libby said in a demure voice I'd never heard her use. "I . . . I told her I'd overreacted. I had my doubts from the get-go because I *know* you're not Jeffrey's type, Lola. I've known him most of my life and he's never been attracted to women like you," she whimpered.

"Uh, Lola, can we overlook what happened here today?" Jeffrey asked, looking like he was about to pass out. "Let's pretend this little incident never occurred. I mean, you know how the neighbors are. It's a good thing it took place inside, where they couldn't see or hear enough to call the cops."

Libby appeared to have renewed her strength. Now instead of a whimper, her voice came out loud and clear. "I'd hate to get the police involved. The ones in this town take domestic abuse very seriously," she pointed out, shooting a smug look in my direction.

I had never been in trouble with the police before in my life. Just the thought of me getting arrested for hitting a pregnant woman—even though it had been self-defense—made my head swim. "I can forget any of this happened," I said. My heart was racing and my blood was boiling. Even with Jeffrey present, I was prepared to defend myself again if I had to.

Libby's face looked like it had turned to stone. "Yeah," she growled. Then she blinked hard and narrowed her eyes until they looked like slits. "This is over, as far as I'm concerned."

"Let's keep this among ourselves. The three of us," Jeffrey suggested.

"Marshall knows. I called him just before I left the house," Libby said quickly. "He said he was going to straighten Lola out too."

"Well, you can tell Marshall that there is nothing to straighten out!" I yelled. My ears were ringing and my chest felt like it was on fire. The longer Libby remained in my presence, the more miserable I felt. I almost wished that Jeffrey had not come in time, so I could have really whupped her ass. Had that happened, I knew there was no way I could have remained in Bertha's house.

"I'll deal with Marshall. He's got enough problems with his own marriage. We don't need to have him sticking his nose in ours." Jeffrey shook his head. "How about a group hug?" he asked with a lopsided smile.

I took my time walking over to them. The "group hug" was about as fake and clumsy as it could be. The rest of Libby's body felt like it had turned to stone too.

After apologizing to me like he was the one who had attacked me, Jeffrey quickly ushered Libby out the front door. I was still in such a state of shock, you could have knocked me over with a feather.

I couldn't wait to talk to Joan.

Chapter 24

Joan

*T*HE DAY WAS DREARY WHEN I GOT UP THAT SATURDAY morning. The rain was coming down hard; the wind was howling; the sky looked like a gray blanket. It was the kind of gloom that depressed and bored some people. It was July, when the sun was supposed to be out. The Fourth of July was coming up in a couple of days, but I was not really looking forward to it. Today I was more depressed and bored than ever before and it wasn't because of the weather. Reed was the source of my misery. I promised myself that I would live through the mess I'd gotten myself into, no matter what I had to do.

It was way too soon for me to be thinking about a divorce, but it was not too soon for me to be thinking about things I could do to spice up my life. Shopping and hanging out with Lola and a few other friends helped, but it was not enough. Being that I was a very sensuous woman (at least I thought I was), I was convinced that the only way I was going to remain sane was to have an affair. And as soon as I ran into the right man, I would. It seemed like almost everybody I knew was doing it. All three of my sisters and two of my brothers had cheated on their mates. So had Daddy. With all that in mind, I felt cheating was in my DNA. Having affairs was a family affair! I told myself that if I couldn't beat 'em, I'd join 'em. The difference between me and my family was, they had been caught and had suffered the consequences. Mama told me once that "anything done in the dark eventually comes to light." Well, I was going to be the exception to that stupid rule.

I shopped most of the afternoon and returned home a few minutes before five P.M. Reed decided to spend most of Saturday slumped on the living room couch watching ballgames he had recorded—which was the reason I'd gone to the mall and stayed so long. My cell, which was in my purse, was ringing when I opened the door to let myself in, so I set my shopping bags down so I could answer it. Reed was sprawled on his back on the living-room couch, flipping the pages in one of the numerous medical magazines he subscribed to. "Junior," who was now three months old, was snoozing on the opposite end of the couch.

"Hi, Lola."

As soon as I mentioned her name, Reed closed his magazine and sat bolt upright and focused his attention on me. With his eyes wide and tufts of his hair on top of his head sticking up on both sides, he looked like an owl.

"Can you talk?" she asked in a tentative tone of voice.

"A . . . little," I replied with hesitation. I was still standing near the door.

"So the good Dr. Riley is nearby, huh?"

"Something like that."

"Well, don't worry. I won't say anything he'll be able

to use against you. I left you a voice mail a little while ago."

"I was out shopping and had turned my phone off. I just got home, so I haven't had time to check my messages."

At this point, Lola's voice got louder. "Girl, you are not going to believe what went on in this house today! When you respond, say something that'll get Reed out of the room. When I tell you what happened, you won't be able to talk with him close by because you might have to do some serious cussing."

"Uh-huh. Um, I'm sorry I missed that Tupperware party you had last night. I forgot all about it. With all those hens you invited, tell me what each one bought and who they roasted this time," I said.

Nothing bored my husband more than me on the telephone talking about things as mundane as hen parties. It was the fastest way I could think of that would make him leave the room. He didn't move fast enough for me this time. He didn't budge at all. Just as I opened my mouth to tell him to take the baby to his room, where he'd be more comfortable in his bassinet, Reed got up and left on his own, carrying Junior over his shoulder.

"He's gone," I whispered into the telephone. "What happened?"

"I'm so fucking mad I'm about to bust wide open!" Lola shrieked.

I listened with my mouth hanging open as she told me about Libby's accusation and the violence that had transpired. I almost cheered when she told me that she had fought back. "It's about time you showed that fucking bitch your stuff. I wish you had broken a few of her goddamn bones!"

"I'm glad I didn't. She might be pregnant again and I punched her in the stomach," Lola said with a groan.

"Oh, shit!"

"Don't worry, she's okay. I didn't hit her that hard."

"Well, it sounds like you were just defending yourself."

"Yeah, but when you hit a pregnant woman, the cops throw you in jail and ask questions later. Thank God we didn't get the cops involved, though."

"Maybe you should have. You could have told your version of the events and had something on record."

"Why would I want to do that? I don't want Bertha to know what happened, and I don't want to have to deal with the cops."

"Libby could change her mind in a day or so and go to the cops, anyway."

"That's a chance I have to take, I guess."

"Suit yourself," I snorted. "I can't for the life of me believe she actually thought you and Jeffrey were having an affair. And I can't believe you're still going to stay on in that house after what happened today!"

"I will stay for a little while longer, I guess. After all, like Libby and Marshall keep reminding me, I am living rent-free. If I can hang on for another couple of years, I'll have saved enough money to move out with."

"And what will you do about Bertha? Put her in a nursing home?"

"That's not up to me. And she's not that old, so she's hardly ready for a nursing home."

Lola vented for another ten minutes before we ended our conversation.

When I went into the kitchen, Reed was sitting at the table, slurping from a bottle of Coors Light. He had a look on his face that told me things were about to get ugly.

"What's the matter with you this time?" I asked as I stopped in front of the doorway and placed my hands on my hips. The foul mood I'd been in for several hours had intensified, so it would not take much for me to go off the deep end. If Reed was looking for a fight with somebody, he was looking at the right person. "I'm getting sick and tired of that suspicious look on your face. One of these days, I'm going to slap it off," I threatened.

I couldn't believe how suspicious and paranoid he had become. And I had just about had it! Only a miracle could get me to spend the rest of my life with Reed! My marriage was already in the toilet, just waiting for me to flush it. The more I thought about my bleak situation, the more I realized I *had* to leave Reed.

"Joan, are you cheating on me?" he asked.

I was surprised that he didn't comment on the threat I'd just made. There were tears in his weary eyes. On top of all his numerous other flaws, the man was a damn crybaby. Seeing that he was about to shed some tears made me want to cry. The last thing I wanted to deal with was him boo-hooing in my presence.

Reed's question caught me completely by surprise. It was hard for me to keep a straight face. "What? You've got some nerve asking me that!"

"I'm not dumb, Joan. You're almost never home when I call during the day. And you've been spending a lot more time on the telephone lately. Who was that you were just talking to?"

"You know damn well I was on the telephone with Lola!"

"So you say! If you're fooling around, stop before it's too late!"

"Too late for what, Reed?"

"Too late for everything!"

"*What* makes you think I'm fooling around?"

"You!"

I was so mad . . . I was shaking. If I had been close enough to him, I would have slapped his face. Instead, I backed up a few steps so I wouldn't be tempted to shoot across the floor and pounce on him. "What have I done?"

"Joan, you slept with me the same night I met you. Who does that?" he asked, standing up, waving his arms.

I moved another step back, not because I was afraid of what he might do to me, but because of what I might do to him. *"You did!"*

"I'm a man—"

"Don't you pull that double-standard bullshit on me, motherfucker!"

"Well, yeah, I had sex with you on the first night we met, but you didn't have to let me do it! If you were that easy with me, how easy are you with other men? I am not going to tolerate you sleeping around! I won't stand for it!"

"So I guess you want a divorce, huh?"

His eyes got big and his lips began to quiver. With a loud gasp, he sagged back into his seat. "Divorce? Oh, Lord! I will *never* give you a divorce!"

"Well, if you don't stop fucking with me, I will file for a divorce myself."

Reed slammed his beer bottle down onto the table. Then he closed and rubbed his eyes; he shuddered so hard I thought he was having a spasm.

"Are you okay?" I asked, rushing over to him. I helped him up and led him to the living room, where he dropped down onto the couch like a rock.

"Joan, I love you and I can't live without you," he declared, wheezing like a man twice his age.

I let out an exasperated breath and rolled my eyes. "I'll get you a stronger drink," I said, already heading toward the liquor cabinet next to the huge stereo system across the room.

"Stop!" he hollered, holding up his hand. "I don't need another drink."

"You look sick. I'll get you an aspirin then."

"Honey, come sit next to me," Reed rasped. I sighed impatiently, but I joined him on the couch, anyway, groaning under my breath. "Joan, I meant it. I can't live without you."

I had never seen him, or any other grown man, look so distressed since Mama gouged out Daddy's eye. I listened to him sob for about a minute. I got sick of looking at his tears and the snot oozing out of his nose, so I jumped up and ran back to the kitchen to get some paper towels to dry him off.

He muttered some gibberish under his breath and we didn't resume our previous conversation. I stood in front of him as he mopped his face with the paper towels. Then he stretched out on the couch and began to stare up at the ceiling.

With a disgusted snort, I spun around and returned to the kitchen and dialed Lola's number.

"You think you've got problems," I began in a low voice as soon as she answered.

"Joan, what's the matter?"

"Reed just told me that he can't live without me."

"So? Love-struck men say stupid shit like that all the time. One time a dude told me that on our second date. He only stuck around for a month."

"That was different. Reed and I are married and he just told me that he would never give me a divorce."

"'Divorce'? Are you guys having problems serious enough for 'divorce' to come into the conversation?"

"I have a feeling that'll be our final destination."

"I hope it doesn't come to that, Joan. You have so much going for you. I'd hate to see you throw it all away too soon and have to start all over again."

"Lola, what's wrong with starting over again? People do it all the time."

"Yeah, but you're different."

"'Different'? In what way?"

"For one thing, you're a free spirit. You were the boldest girl in our school. You did things I would never do and you never got caught."

"Thanks, I guess. I don't think there's anything unique about the way I do things."

"Yeah, but you do your things so well. You live your life the way you want to and I think that's only because you always make the best of a bad situation. I wish I could be more like you."

I wondered what Lola would say if she knew I was planning to find a man to have an affair with. "Be careful what you wish for," I warned.

Chapter 25
Lola

*I*OFFERED TO MEET JOAN FOR COFFEE AT WOODY'S, A trendy café a few blocks from her condo, but she declined. She explained that Reed had accused her of seeing other men and that it was in her best interest to lay low for a few days.

"Reed can't be serious about you having an affair." I laughed. The idea of Joan cheating on her husband was ridiculous. She was a "hot mama" with a huge appetite when it came to sex, but she had assured me that she'd taken her wedding vows very seriously.

"What's so funny?"

"*You* having an affair," I said, laughing some more.

"You think that's so funny? I'll have you know, married people have affairs all the time. After that thing with your daddy and Shirelle, you should know that better than anybody."

"Joan, you're right and I'm sorry. I know my mother

never complained about Daddy moving his girlfriend into our house, but it had to be painful for her. There's nothing funny about cheating. But since it's you we're talking about, I don't know what to say."

"You can say whatever you want to say. I'd rather you say it and not just think it. You and I have never bitten our tongues, so don't start now."

"Okay. Would you cheat on Reed?" I held my breath as I awaited her response.

"Let's talk about this again at a later date," she told me with a dry tone of voice. "I'm going to hang up and go fix myself a strong drink." Joan sounded so tired and weak. If she hadn't ended the call when she did, I would have.

I missed not talking to Joan for the rest of the week. I had things on my mind that I wanted to discuss, and she was still the only friend I could confide in.

In the meantime, I had enough going on in my life to keep me occupied.

Since my altercation with Libby, she had not been back to the house when I was present. But according to the neighbors, she and Marshall often dropped by while I was at work.

Last Wednesday, as I was leaving for work a few minutes later than usual, I saw Marshall cruising toward Bertha's house in the brand-new Mercedes he had purchased a month ago. The man couldn't even pay his bills on time without his mother's help and here he was driving a *Mercedes*! Bertha must have known he was coming, because she had gotten up that morning before me.

A couple of days later as I walked toward home after work, I saw Libby prancing out the front door with Bertha close behind her. I stopped and ducked behind a bread truck parked in front of Husat's Bakery. I waited a few moments before I peeped around that truck. I shook my head and cussed under my breath when I saw Bertha and Libby hugging each other on the front porch steps. I didn't come from my hiding place until I saw Libby dash off the porch and get into her car.

I thought it was amusing that Libby and Marshall felt so intimidated by me that they'd go out of their way to avoid me. But then again, I wasn't sure if I intimidated them or if they just despised me that much.

Jeffrey had also stopped coming around when I was home and he no longer called to chat with me. I missed him, so about a month after my fight with Libby, I called him on his cell phone. I was surprised that he had not changed his number.

"Hello, Jeffrey. It's Lola," I said when he answered.

"Hello there, Lola!" He sounded like he was glad to hear from me. "I've been meaning to call you, but . . ."

"But you don't want any more trouble with your wife. I understand. You were on my mind and I just wanted to hear your voice. I hope things are going well for you now."

He let out a loud breath and responded in a very somber tone of voice. "Libby lost the baby a couple of days ago."

"Oh! I'm sorry. I hope she's all right. Bertha didn't tell me!"

"She didn't even know Libby was pregnant again. We didn't want to tell too many people because she's . . . Well, she's had two previous miscarriages. Bertha didn't know about those either, nor did anyone else. We want at least two more children." Jeffrey's voice cracked and he paused for a few seconds. He cleared his throat and continued, talking in a slow, controlled manner. "Libby wants a daughter so she can relive her childhood. She thinks a daughter would be an extension of herself."

I held my breath because the thought of two versions of Libby sent a chill up my spine.

"I hope you'll keep what I just told you about the miscarriage to yourself."

"I will. And I really am truly sorry about the miscarriage. I know I'm not one of Libby's favorite people, but I do wish her nothing but the best. I'll let you get back to whatever you were doing."

"Take care, Lola. Maybe when things cool off, I can take you out again."

"Yeah . . . sure."

Two more weeks went by and Libby and Jeffrey, as well as Marshall and his wife, still only came to the house during the day when they knew I'd be at work. I was surprised that it took Bertha so long to notice this new development.

"I wonder why the kids don't come by in the evening and on weekends the way they used to," she said over breakfast one Sunday morning just before she left for church.

"I don't know," I muttered.

"I guess they're so busy with their own lives, they have to come by when they can. Oh, by the way, that soldier boy you went out with a few times called last night while you were at the mall with Joan."

I was surprised that Bertha was talking about Maurice Hamilton in such a pleasant tone of voice. During his first visit, she had casually told him that he had a "generous" nose, but he was "still cute." Stunned, he had laughed and quickly changed the subject and she never mentioned his nose again.

Until now.

"Too bad such a cute young man has such a meatball nose," she crowed.

"Yeah, but he's still cute," I countered. "Thanks for letting me know he called. I . . . I r-really like h-him," I stammered as my mind wandered back to the first time I'd encountered Maurice.

He was a sexy, twenty-year-old marine I had met a few weeks ago at a Dollar Tree store. In addition to his uniform, his tall, muscular body and his cute baby face had immediately caught my attention. I had been gathering a few miscellaneous household items when I bumped into him in the cleaning-products aisle. He looked so confused, holding three different brands of spot remover. I offered to help him decide which one to purchase. We clicked and exchanged phone numbers.

When he came to visit me two nights later, Bertha was her usual self. She promptly told him about some of her ailments and what a blessing it was to have a daughter like me to take care of her.

A few minutes after she had insulted his nose, she jokingly told Maurice that she and I were "joined at the hip," something she eventually told almost every man who came to see me. He didn't respond directly to Bertha. Instead, he turned to me and said right in front of her, "Lola, I can live with that if you can. I'd still like to get to know you." From the sour look on Bertha's face, it was obvious he had said something she didn't like.

"Your food is getting cold," she now said, interrupting my thoughts. Maurice was so heavy on my mind . . . I had almost forgotten I was at the kitchen table.

"Huh? Oh, yes. I'll give him a call later on today," I mumbled.

It had been quite a while since I'd been with a man that I liked as much as Maurice. I called him after I finished breakfast and I went out with him the following three nights in a row. He had only six more days left on his leave and I wanted to spend as much time as possible with him—without Bertha in the vicinity blowing her nose and saying one stupid thing after another.

"Lola, I know we haven't known each other that long, but I'd like to take our relationship to the next level," Maurice told me as soon as we were alone on his next visit. I was glad Bertha had left the room a few minutes ago.

"What are you trying to tell me?" I asked, glancing toward the doorway. I was relieved when I heard the toilet flush. That meant she was still in the bathroom upstairs. It would take another couple of minutes for her to wash her hands, take her various pills, and make it back to the living room. I turned quickly back to Maurice, blinking at him as I anxiously awaited his response.

"I know we don't know one another that well, but I know you well enough. I've told my folks about you and they want to meet you before I leave."

"Oh. I . . . uh, I'd like to meet them too," I said with hesitation, hoping I wouldn't be stupid enough to make the same mistake Joan had made by marrying Reed too soon. If Maurice asked me to marry him, I planned to take the time to get to know him better. Besides that, I needed to ease him into the notion that Bertha might live with us.

Chapter 26

Lola

*T*HE DAY AFTER MY LAST DATE WITH MAURICE, JOAN and I decided to give up the storage unit, where we had stashed most of the expensive items we'd purchased with the money from our pen pals. She had access, where she and Reed lived, to a unit of the same size in the garage. He never used it, so we decided it made no sense for us to keep paying rent on one when we could use his for free.

Just as we were about to leave Joan's place to go remove our belongings and load them onto the truck she had borrowed from one of her cousins, we got one hell of a surprise. The storage facility manager called and told her that thieves had broken in the night before and looted several of the units. The only things the crooks had not taken from ours were two dozen unread hardback mystery, romance, and street lit novels, and a large, framed velvet picture of Dr. Martin Luther King Jr. hugging a baby. Nobody had ever stolen anything from me before, so this really bothered me, especially since the items had been purchased with "stolen" money, so to speak.

There were other things related to the lonely hearts club money that also bothered me. A cell phone I had purchased with money I'd received from a ninety-year-old man in D.C., and a stereo Joan had purchased with money from her sugar daddy in New York, had conked out beyond repair *on the same day* two months ago. A week after that, I dropped and broke a bottle of some very expensive Versace perfume. Other peculiar things had happened with some of the other items we had purchased with that money, which I now thought of as tainted. What really spooked me was last week I lost my wallet, which contained five hundred dollars of the last grand I had left.

Joan agreed with me when I told her that maybe karma was kicking us in the ass for being so deceitful and greedy. Now that she had Reed's income and I had a job, we could pay for some of the things we wanted. By this time, she had spent all of her pen pal money, anyway. Since I couldn't return any of the money that I had left to my elderly "boyfriends"—and most of them had probably died of old age by now, anyway—on the same day of the theft, I donated my last five hundred dollars to an organization doing research for Alzheimer's disease. A few hours later, we carted the items that the thieves had left behind to the nearest Salvation Army facility. I no longer wanted to associate with *anything* that I'd obtained in such a deceitful manner. I felt good about my decision. There had been numerous times during our pen pal scam when it had seemed like I was leading a double life. I'd even felt like half a person on some days. Now, because all of that was behind me and I'd repented, I felt *whole* again.

The next day, I made arrangements with the director of the Happy Meadows nursing home to spend a few hours, a couple of times a month, doing things for the residents, like reading to them or running errands. Joan agreed to come with me when she was available and do whatever she could to try and make up for what we'd done to those old men. We were going to do whatever the nursing home supervisors asked us to do for *free*. We felt better because we knew we were doing the right thing. We also felt redeemed. If the karma theory was fair, there were better things in store for both of us.

Right now one of the better things in my life was Maurice.

A week after the storage unit theft, I told Bertha that he wanted me to meet his family. She and I were having breakfast that Friday. I immediately regretted mentioning him while she had food in her mouth.

She coughed so hard, a piece of Canadian bacon shot out of her mouth and landed back on her plate. "Meet his family?" she gulped, swallowing the rest of her food. There was a distraught look on her face. "Why?"

"Well, in case things get more serious between us," I answered. I shrugged as if what I'd just said was no big deal. And it wasn't to me. But I knew it was to Bertha. The sooner I told her something she didn't want to hear, the easier it was to deal with it and move on.

"Serious? You mean serious like *married*?" The way she started blinking and biting her bottom lip, you would have thought that I'd just told her I had a terminal disease.

"That's a possibility. I know I haven't known him that long, but I really care about him and he cares about me."

"Hmmm. Well, if you're going to marry anybody, he's probably your best bet. He's got a good head on his shoulders, a secure future with the military, and he's rather cute—even with that meatball nose propped up on his face. There is no telling what his kids are going to look like. I feel sorry for them already. . . ."

"Well, if I marry Maurice and our kids have his big nose, I'd still love them," I stated. "And I'd like to start my family right after I get married to whoever, and whenever that is."

"Oh, I'm sure you would, Lola. That's a good thing." Bertha bit a huge plug out of her wheat toast and chewed and swallowed it within seconds. "I'm sure Libby and Marshall won't mind. . . ."

"'Won't mind' what?" I asked dumbly. I knew what she was talking about.

"There's plenty of room here, so Maurice—or whoever you marry—can just move in with us and you can start working on the first baby lickety-split. It'll be nice to have some kids in the house again. Marshall's old room would make a nice nursery. As a matter of fact, I still have the crib he slept in when he was a baby. Libby took hers when she found out she was pregnant with Kevin."

"Uh, there's one more thing about Maurice that you need to know."

Bertha reared back in her seat and gave me a bug-eyed look. "What?" she asked, her voice cracking. Steam was rising from her coffee cup. And I could have sworn that steam was coming out of her nostrils too. She looked like she was angry enough to cuss out the whole world.

I had to clear my throat before I could answer. I wanted to make sure I got the right words out so Bertha would have no doubt about what I'd said. "He's going to be stationed in Germany. If things get serious enough for us to marry, I'll eventually have to go where he goes." It was too soon to be thinking about Maurice and me getting married, but I wanted to put the idea in Bertha's head, anyway. If I was going to have to wean her, now was a good time to start.

"Germany?" She spat out the word like she was spitting out vomit. The way her lips quivered, it must have tasted like vomit to her too. "After the way that racist-ass Hitler destroyed so many millions of Jews, not to mention the way he reacted when black athletes were over there for the Olympics, I don't understand why any black person would agree to move to such a hellish country."

"Hitler was a long time ago, and for your information, there are a lot of black folks and Jews in Germany these days and they are doing just fine."

"But you don't speak German!"

"I'm not worried about the language. I won't be interacting with the Germans that much, anyway," I said quickly. I stopped talking long enough to reorganize my jumbled thoughts. "If Maurice does get shipped off to Germany and I go with him, or join him later, you won't be able to come with us. We'll be living on a military base. But I am sure you can visit us from time to time, though. Or we can come visit you." I couldn't believe we were having this conversation. Especially since Maurice had not even asked me to marry him yet!

I massaged my chest and took a long, deep breath. Bertha looked like she was about to take her last breath. "Uh, I don't feel too well. I think I'll go up to my room and lie down," she mumbled. Sometimes when she got upset, she seemed to age temporarily before my eyes. Right now she looked as old as Methuselah.

"Are you all right? Do you want me to get you an aspirin?" I got up and walked around the table and attempted to wrap my arms around her shoulders. She pushed me away with both hands.

"I'll be okay, I guess," she said with a loud sniff. "I don't want you to lose your job, so don't even think about taking the day off to stay home with me. . . ." As if on cue, Bertha let out a loud, hacking cough and, with a moan, even rubbed her chest, which was meant for my benefit. I knew what she was up to.

"I'm going to call in sick and stay home with you," I said, moving toward the telephone. I dialed my work number to let my coworkers know that I needed to take the day off so I could take care of a personal matter. It was the first time I'd taken a day off, so my bosses didn't have a fit the way they did when one of the other cashiers couldn't come to work. When I told Bertha I'd be spending the day with her, she perked up for a few seconds. Then she hoisted herself up out of her chair and shuffled up the staircase to her room.

After I made sure she was comfortable in her bed, I did some housework, answered a lengthy e-mail from a girl I'd graduated with, who had moved to Atlanta, fixed Bertha some lunch at noon, and then I watched a few game shows on the living-room TV. When the last show ended a few minutes before five, I decided to check on her again. I usually knocked before I entered her room. This time I just pushed open the door and walked in.

"Bertha, I just wanted to see how you were feeling now," I began.

"I don't feel too well, but don't you worry about it," she muttered.

"Maurice called a little while ago and invited me to go see a movie and have dinner with him this evening. I wanted to make sure you didn't need anything before I left," I said, moving slowly toward the bed. Bertha lay on her side propped up on four pillows. She was on top of the covers in her black-and-white nightgown. She looked like a penguin.

"I . . . I don't need anything, I guess," she said in a

weak voice, slowly focusing her eyes on me. "I'm just feeling a little blah."

I was surprised she didn't cough again or do anything else to make herself seem "sicker." Her "feeling a little blah" was not reason enough for me to cancel my date. Besides, I'd been cooped up in the house all day and I needed to get out and get some fresh air if nothing else.

"After we leave the theater, we'll be at Jeanette's Steakhouse in case you need me." I gave Bertha a strong hug and promptly left the room.

Lately I had been putting my cell phone on vibrate when I left the house. Ten minutes into my dinner with Maurice, I excused myself to go to the restroom to check my messages. I was surprised to see that I had *eight.* I'd only been gone a little over three hours. I was even more surprised to see that Bertha had not been the person who had called me eight times. She'd left only four messages—each one a whiny complaint about being in the house alone—all within an hour after I'd left the house.

My heart skipped a beat when I saw that Marshall had left all of the other messages. All he'd said was "call me back ASAP," so I had no idea *why* he had called. "Shit!" I hissed. He was the last person in the world I wanted to talk to. My stomach turned and bile rose in my throat. That sucker had never called me on my cell phone before; so whatever he had called about, it had to be serious. I immediately dialed his cell phone number, cussing until he answered on the fifth ring.

"Where the hell are you? I've been calling and calling!" he bellowed.

"I'm out," I snapped. "Why did you call me?"

"I'm at City Hospital with my mama, that's why I called you!" he boomed, choking on a sob.

My head felt like it had been kicked by somebody wearing steel-toed boots. "The hospital? Oh, my God! What happened? Is Bertha all right?"

Marshall sniffled and choked on a few more sobs for several moments before he was able to speak clearly again. "I haven't talked to the doctor yet, but we think she had a heart attack."

"Oh no! She told me she wasn't feeling too well before I left the house."

Marshall gasped so hard, it sounded like somebody was choking him. "Well, if you knew that, why did you leave my mama alone? Why didn't you call me or Libby so we could have come over there and looked after her, so you could go gallivanting all over town? What's the matter with you, Lola? Don't you ever think about anybody other than yourself?"

That last sentence stunned and angered me. I could not believe my ears. I didn't know of anyone who thought more about themselves than Marshall and his sister. Normally, I would have lit into him with a few choice words of my own. One reason I didn't was because I knew I'd get that opportunity again real soon.

"Exactly where the fuck are you, girl?" he yelled.

"I'm out with Maurice," I said firmly.

"Who the hell is Maurice?"

I couldn't respond fast enough. "The man I'm currently dating—"

"No wonder you didn't take any of my calls earlier," he interrupted. "I should have known! You've got some nerve taking your *hot* ass out with one of your studs and leaving my mama in such a bad way, all by herself!" Marshall was yelling at such a high volume, I could have tossed my phone across the room and still been able to hear him.

I ignored his crude comments. For Bertha's sake, I didn't want to waste any more time on a verbal confrontation with him. "Is she really that bad?"

"Hell yeah, she's 'really that bad.'"

My mouth dropped open. The thought that Bertha might have already died made my head swim. "She's not . . . she's not—"

"She's not dead, if that's what you're trying to say. But from the way she's moaning and groaning and the way she looks, she's probably close to it. She keeps asking for you."

"I'm on my way," I said.

Chapter 27

Lola

I WAS GLAD MAURICE WAS WITH ME AS I STOOD BY THE side of Bertha's hospital bed. I was also glad that Libby and Marshall had come and gone.

The sight of my pitiful stepmother lying on her back, looking like she belonged in a mummy's tomb, was excruciatingly painful. It reminded me of the last image I had of Daddy.

"I . . . I'm so glad you're here," she rasped, struggling to sit up. When she realized Maurice was with me, she froze. A profound frown appeared on her face and she coughed a couple of times. "Who is this strange man, Lola?"

Maurice gave me a puzzled look and we shrugged at the same time. I forced myself to smile as I returned my attention to Bertha. "This is Maurice. Don't you remember him? You and I talked about him before I went out tonight."

She rubbed matter from the corners of her eyes and

blinked. "Humph!" Then she looked at Maurice with so much contempt, it made me flinch. The next few words shot out of her mouth like missiles. *"How could I forget that nose?"*

Maurice sighed and dropped his head. No matter how many times Bertha said something unkind to or about him, he always maintained his composure. He and I had discussed her desperate attempts to keep me in her life on her terms a few times, and I had assured him that I'd do whatever I felt was best for *me*. I was glad that I had not yet told him about the promise I'd made to Daddy. Maurice was totally devoted to his family, so I knew he was the type who would honor a deathbed promise.

"Bertha, I'm sure you'll be up and about real soon, as long as you do everything the doctor tells you to do," he said. The smile on his face was just as fake as mine. "My grandmother tells my grandfather all the time, 'God ain't through with you yet.' He's had three heart attacks and a stroke and he's still with us."

Bertha did not comment on what Maurice said. She just glared at him, with one eye twitching and her lips quivering.

"How are you feeling?" I asked.

She turned to me with a blank stare. "I might make it and I might not!" she snapped coldly.

Despite the chill in Bertha's voice, Maurice's tone was gentle and warm. "I'll be praying for you day and night," he told her.

"Don't waste your breath! *You* don't have to do that or anything else for me, Mister Man! I'm in God's hands. I don't need any help from *you*." I was shocked at how strong she suddenly sounded and the coldness in her eyes as she continued to glare at him.

Maurice shifted his weight from one foot to the other. There was so much tension in the room now that even a sword couldn't cut through it. "I think I'll split so you two can have some privacy," he said, clearing his throat. I had a feeling he knew that *he* was the reason Bertha was in the hospital. "I'll call you," he said as he squeezed my hand. He didn't kiss me or offer me the hug I needed.

"All right," I mumbled. He bolted so fast I didn't have time to say anything else to him, or give him a hug like I always did when he departed. Something told me that this might be the last time he and I would be in the same place at the same time.

The doctor entered the room a couple of minutes later. He greeted me and introduced himself with a nod and a wall-to-wall smile on his moon face. Then he strolled over to the side of the bed and felt Bertha's forehead with his hand. "How are we feeling today, Mrs. Poole?" Dr. Brown asked. He smiled some more. I didn't care how much Bertha moaned and groaned and twisted her lips as if the Grim Reaper had already entered the room; I knew that the doctor would not be so cheerful if her condition was as serious as she wanted me to believe it was.

"I guess . . . I'm doing all right," she blubbered, looking more pitiful than ever. Tears were threatening to spill out of her eyes and her lips were trembling so hard I could hear her false teeth click-clacking. I knew that this was all as much for the doctor's benefit as it was for mine.

"How serious was the heart attack?" I asked in a quiet voice.

Dr. Brown whirled around so fast to face me, the stethoscope around his neck slipped to the side. "'Heart attack'? What *heart attack*?" he mouthed with one eyebrow raised as he adjusted his stethoscope.

"My stepbrother led me to believe that she'd had a heart attack," I explained with a gulp.

"Well, I'm pleased to tell you that your stepbrother

was wrong." Dr. Brown chuckled and shook his head. Then he got serious. "This was nothing more than a severe anxiety attack." He paused and turned to Bertha with an amused look on his face. "Mrs. Poole's heart is in better shape than mine."

"So she's going to be all right?" I asked with my heart thumping hard as I silently prayed for a positive response. I grabbed Bertha's hand and squeezed. It felt like a piece of cold wood.

"My dear, she's going to be 'all right' for a very long time." The doctor gave me a hopeful look and patted my shoulder. "You can expect your mother to be around for at least another twenty to twenty-five years."

"Oh" was all I could say at first. It took a few seconds for me to process Dr. Brown's prognosis. *Bertha could live another twenty to twenty-five years?* It sounded like a prison sentence for me; and in a way, it was. Or was it? What if I married Maurice and things didn't work out? I cared about him, but marriage was a huge step and could be another form of prison—especially with a man I had known for such a short period of time. With him, I could end up with a "sentence" twice as long as the one with Bertha! For all I knew, he could have bad habits and other faults too hellish to imagine. Then I'd be in the same boat Joan was in with Reed! One thing I could say about Bertha was that I had learned how to read her like a book. There were no more surprises with her, not even her fake heart attack. What if I married Maurice and moved to some faraway location and things didn't work out and we parted ways? With my skills and work history, no matter where we were, landing a job that could cover rent and other living expenses would not be easy. Then I'd really have something to worry about, such as me wanting to move back in with Bertha and her not letting me.

No matter what I did, if it impacted Bertha, Libby and

Marshall would get involved. It would be just like them not to let me move back into her house. My life had become such a mess. There were times when I wished I could go to sleep and wake up and find out that the last ten years had been a bad dream. I would have given anything in the world to have Daddy, Mama, and even Shirelle back in my life. But I was not dreaming. I was determined to find a way to be happy again whether I gave up marriage and stayed on with Bertha (another twenty or twenty-five more years!) or not.

I could still hear Dr. Brown talking to Bertha, but I had no idea what he was saying. It was only when she addressed me that I put the thoughts running through my head on hold.

"Lola, you can go on home. I'll be fine," she insisted, sounding much stronger.

Dr. Brown gave me a guarded look. "I'd like to keep her overnight. She can go home tomorrow morning between ten A.M. and noon."

I dialed Maurice's number as soon as I got home. "Baby, we need to take a break for a while. My stepmother needs more time to get used to you," I told him when he answered. I braced myself and held my breath. The inside of my mouth tasted like I had been sucking on a cotton ball. I had to swallow hard to keep from gagging.

Maurice took his time responding. He grunted and began to speak in a hard, detached voice. And that didn't surprise me. But I was surprised that he was still speaking to me at all after the way Bertha had talked to him in the hospital. "I've been expecting you to say something like that."

"She's getting old and she really depends on me to

take care of her. She's afraid that the more time I spend with you, the less time I'll have for her."

"Lola, that woman has two grown-ass children. They both live just a couple of miles from her. Shouldn't the bulk of the responsibility of taking care of her be on their shoulders? This woman is only your stepmother."

Maurice's last comment was a sad song that I'd been singing to myself since the day Bertha latched onto me. It didn't matter to me that she was only my stepmother and that her children lived nearby. The emotional tug-of-war, which I couldn't seem to get rid of, had won another round. "I have to hang up now. Can we talk more about this some other time?"

"I guess we'll have to." He paused for a few seconds. Then he began to speak in a voice that sounded even harder and more detached than a few moments ago. "You've made your decision. Good-bye, Lola."

"Good-bye, Maurice." I had a feeling this was our last "good-bye."

I was right. I never heard from him again.

Three weeks after Maurice had dumped me, Joan took it upon herself to "cheer" me up by playing matchmaker. "Reed's friend Paul Sibley just broke up with his wife. If I invite him over for dinner, will you come?" she asked during a brief telephone conversation.

"I don't think so. I never have much luck with blind dates," I told her with a dry laugh. "And Bertha would probably scare him off too."

"Not Paul. Nothing scares him. He's the only one of Reed's friends I know who can really stand his ground. His ex mother-in-law was a real bitch, but it never bothered him."

"Hmmm. What does he look like?" I wanted to know.

"Now, you know I wouldn't set you up with an owl!" Joan laughed. "He's tall, dark, and handsome—picture a young Denzel Washington."

I gasped. "A man like that doesn't have a new woman yet?"

"Relax. He's only been back on the market for a couple of weeks. So if you're interested, you'd better move fast. The other bitches are in heat."

I laughed. "Well, why not? I need something to take my mind off Maurice." I sniffed and swallowed hard. "I'd love to meet a man that Bertha couldn't scare. How soon can I meet him?"

"He works on weekends, so is this coming Monday soon enough?"

"Sounds good to me. What kind of work does he do?" I was more than a little excited by now. Most of Reed's friends were in the medical profession. His closest friend was also a dentist and another one was an eye doctor. "Is he a doctor too?"

"Something like that." When Joan paused, I got suspicious.

"Uh-oh. What does that mean?"

"He's the assistant coroner. . . ."

"Oh." My heart skipped a beat. "So his 'patients' are dead people. . . ."

"I guess you could say that."

I let out a dry laugh. "I think I'll pass." I recalled the image of Mama laid to rest in a yellow dress. A guest at the funeral had told me that it looked like me lying in that coffin. Then there was that eerie picture that Joan had taken of me lying on her bed with my eyes closed while wearing a yellow blouse. I looked like a dead girl. The last thing I wanted in my life now was a lover who was so closely associated with *death*.

I didn't sleep much that night. And when I did, I had a dream that was so chilling it woke me up. In the dream, I lay dead in a coffin dressed in a yellow shroud.

I stayed busy so I wouldn't think about Maurice too much or the "premonition" of me being dead—which I kept telling myself was ridiculous! I waxed the floors twice as often as I used to and I ran more errands for neighbors.

Last Saturday, a month after my last conversation with Maurice, Joan and I spent almost three hours doing volunteer work for the senior citizens at the Happy Meadows nursing home. This was the second time in the same week. I washed and braided two old ladies' hair; Joan trimmed one old man's toenails; we played Chinese checkers with two other residents; we read the newspaper to two more. Afterward, we both felt real good about ourselves and couldn't wait to return and do something else. The director stopped us on our way out and told us not to come back because a few staff members had complained about us taking work away from them and were threatening to go to the union. Getting "fired" was bad enough, but to add insult to injury, they had a security guard escort us out of the building! We were just as stunned as we were disappointed.

"They *fired* us! Do you believe that?" Joan hollered as we trotted to the lot across the street where she had parked.

"And to think we were giving up our time to work for free. So much for that," I said as we climbed into her car.

When she stopped for a red light at the corner, we looked at each other and burst out laughing. "I guess we'll have to figure out other ways to make up for taking money from those old men," she said, laughing some more.

But at least we had made some amends for our crime

by helping out at the nursing home. Now that that was over, I was going to look for other ways to redeem myself

Each new day, I felt a little better about myself and how much I had grown up since Daddy had died. I was determined to be the kind of woman he and Mama would have wanted me to be.

I often thought about my past and how happy I'd been during my childhood, even when Daddy was having affairs. Because of my age back then, I could not have said or done anything about what he was doing. I still wondered what made him do what he did, and what made Mama put up with it. One thing I knew for sure was that I was not going to be like her. If my future husband cheated on me and flaunted his affairs in my face, I'd leave him in a heartbeat.

Chapter 28

Joan

2012

IT WAS HARD FOR ME TO BELIEVE THAT I WAS NOW THIRTY years old. It was even harder for me to believe that I was still with Reed.

Even though I was still a young woman, I felt old. Life was passing me by and I didn't like it. I was not going to wait too much longer before I did something about it. Years ago I had considered having an affair. But I'd put if off because I hadn't been able to find the right man in the bars, parties, and other social gatherings I'd attended back then. I'd even flirted with a bank teller at Citibank until he invited me to have lunch with him. When I told him over Whoppers and fries in the Burger King across the street from the bank that I was married to a dentist, all he suddenly wanted to talk about was his financial problems. He was so brazen, he had the nerve to tell me he hoped I'd be able to help him out from time to time. "Just a few dollars now and then, baby." I had no desire to be some broke-ass man's sugar mama back then, or now. I started going to a different branch of Citibank to do our banking, but I kept looking for the right man.

A few days later, a handsome dude in a suit approached me on a busy street downtown. I told him I was married, but he still insisted on giving me his telephone number and told me he wanted to get to know me. When I called his number that night to see when he wanted to get together, a woman answered. Thinking she was his mother or some other female relative, I told her the reason for my call. She cut me off in the middle of a sentence, cussing and threatening to kill me if she ever caught me with her husband. I couldn't get another word in edgewise, so I abruptly hung up.

After that fiasco with the lonely hearts club, I had no desire to get involved with another woman's husband. I kept looking and it took a couple more months before I came across another man I liked enough to cheat on Reed with. He was the son of one of my stepfather's friends. Before we could get together alone, I found out he was addicted to crack cocaine and had just come out of rehab for the second time in the same year. I wasted no time scratching him off my list.

I gave up on finding a lover and my life went on, more miserable than ever.

Despite everything I had, I was too unhappy for words. I was so bored and dissatisfied with Reed I wanted to scream. Our marriage had gradually become so stale, I could barely stand it. We hardly ever went out anymore, and some days we went for hours without speaking to one another. We had so little in common with each other's relatives and friends, we didn't have many visitors and we rarely visited anybody together. That was how we managed to hide how bad things were between us. But it was hard to hide too many things from Junior.

"Mama, how come you and Daddy don't talk no more?" he asked. The three of us occupied the same living-room couch, watching *Toy Story* on DVD. Other than when I yelled at the characters on the TV screen, Junior was the only one I had spoken to in the last two hours.

Reed sat on one end of the couch; I sat on the other. Junior, who was a little pudgy for a twelve-year-old, sat squeezed between us. He was only half-watching the program and fiddling with some baseball cards at the same time.

Reed and I glanced at each other at the same time. I blinked. He scratched the back of his head. Even though my son had directed his question to me, it was Reed who responded. "Your mommy and I do enough talking when you're not around," he said with a weak chuckle.

His answer wasn't enough for Junior. Not only was my son big for his age, but he was inquisitive for his age too. He turned to me, tugging on the sleeve of my blouse. "You don't hug and stuff no more, either, like you used to when I was a little boy."

"Honey, your daddy and I are still very much in love. But as adults get older, they show their feelings in different ways."

"What ways?" Junior asked, looking so confused I felt sorry for him.

Just before I was about to offer another feeble response, the telephone rang and somebody knocked on the front door at the same time. Reed leaped up to go answer the door and I leaned over to pick up the telephone on the stand at the end of the couch.

Brandon Martin, the airline pilot who lived next door, had come to advise Reed to put his brand-new Lexus in the garage. It was street-cleaning night, which meant no parking on the street between the hours of seven and nine. That got Reed out of the house and I was sure he was relieved. Brandon was rather long-winded, so I knew he'd detain him for at least ten minutes. The telephone call that had saved me from making a fool of myself in front of my son was from Too Sweet. She wanted to remind me to bring the extra bottle of bath salts I had promised to bring to the house on my next visit. To keep her talking, I asked about everybody *individually* in the house at the time, which was quite a mob. By the time I got to the sixth person, my sister Marguerite's best friend, Nancy Dixon, Too Sweet could stand no more. "Look, Joan. I don't have time to sit here all night. *Everybody* is doing all right. So let me get off this phone."

A few seconds later, Reed came back inside, but he didn't return to the living room. He went to our bedroom, where he stayed for the rest of the night.

I was apprehensive about tucking my son in for the night because I was afraid he'd say something else about me and Reed. But he didn't and I breathed a sigh of relief. I rushed out of his room as quickly as I could and returned to the living room, where I leafed through a stack of recent family photos of just myself, Reed, and Junior. We all looked so happy. But I didn't know how much longer I could keep up my part of the act. Had it not been for my precious son, I probably would have lost my mind by now. He was the glue that held the family together. But a young boy could only do so much in such a fragile situation.

An hour after I had made sure Junior was in bed and not playing around on his new computer, I peeked in on Reed. He was snoring like a bull. I got a blanket and some pillows out of the hallway linen closet and made up a bed for myself on the living-room couch.

I wanted to have several more children, but there was no way in the world I was going to have another baby with Reed. Our marriage had been on life support for a long time and I thought about pulling the plug, more and more, with each new day.

So far, Lola was the only person I had confided in.

"I don't know why you stay in a relationship that makes you so miserable," she told me during happy hour at Tiny's Bar, a hole-in-the-wall of a building in the same block where she worked. It was a Thursday evening, a week after the awkward conversation with my son. I had not called her first to let her know I was coming. But when I showed up at her work a few minutes before she clocked out, she was happy to see me, anyway, and eager to go join me for a few drinks and some of the delicious complimentary fried chicken wings "Tiny" served if you bought at least one drink. In less than an hour, we were already on our third drinks.

I had nibbled on only two of the wings in the basket on our table while Lola gobbled them up, left and right, and signaled for the waiter to bring another basket. We still weighed about the same, but a few things on my body had shifted. She was still as firm as ever and rarely worked out. I had not done much to stay in shape during my pregnancy. Now I had to work hard and eat right to look good in my clothes.

Lola kept chewing like a rabbit, but her eyes got big when I responded to her comment. "You're a fine one to talk! At least I'm in a miserable relationship with a man. You're in a miserable relationship with your stepmother. You could have married Maurice and be living God knows where in the world by now."

"I'm dating regularly, so I'll eventually meet someone

I can work on a future with. And you're also a 'fine one to talk.' You told me that you and Reed go for weeks without having sex. Knowing what a 'hot mama' you are, that must drive you crazy." Lola laughed but I didn't find her comment funny.

"Sometimes we do 'go for weeks without having sex.'"

"That's what I just said."

"That doesn't mean *I* go for weeks without having sex, Lola."

"I'm not sure your masturbation sessions count," she said, rolling her eyes.

"That's not what I'm talking about. . . ."

A digital camera couldn't have captured the look of disbelief on Lola's face. You had to see it in person to believe. "Lord have mercy," she mouthed. "Are you going to confess to me that you're having an affair?" I could tell from the amused look on her face that she didn't think I was serious. It took only a few seconds for her to realize how serious I was.

I sniffed and smoothed down the sides of the fresh hairdo I had treated myself to at the beauty shop a few hours ago. I took my time responding. "Something like that . . ." I stopped talking and looked in Lola's eyes and winked.

That made her mouth drop open so wide I could see bits and pieces of chicken on her tongue. "Woman, don't you dare go silent on me now. If you are getting it on with another man, you'd better tell me. I know you too well, so I'll know if you're lying or not telling me everything." Lola had no idea that she was about to find out she didn't know me as well as she thought.

"Yep! This woman is 'getting it on' and on, and on some more," I quipped. It took a few moments for her to react to my words.

Her hand froze in midair with another chicken wing inches in front of her mouth. "Did you just say what I think you said? You're having an affair?"

I nodded.

"You little devil." Lola dropped her piece of chicken back into the basket and took a long drink from her wineglass. After a mild belch, she continued. "I should have known something was going on with you. The way you've been smiling and glowing these past few weeks. Reed was right! You're involved with another man. Is it somebody I know?"

"Well, it's not just *a* man. . . ."

"There's more than one?"

I had planned to tell Lola sooner or later the dirty little secret I had been keeping from her, and now seemed like a good time. "I've been visiting some dating sites." I heard Lola suck in some air, but I didn't give her time to respond. "I should have done it years ago, but I kept putting it off, hoping things would improve between Reed and me. I eventually got so frustrated I changed my mind and jumped on the bandwagon, so to speak. I spent hours on my computer the first night. I didn't bother with any of the mushy sites like eHarmony and Christian-Mingle. They cater to people who are interested in serious relationships or marriage. The sites I'm focusing on are for people who are interested *only* in casual, no-strings-attached sexual relationships with like-minded people."

"*You?* You're looking for a man on the Internet?"

"Why not? And don't sound so surprised. I'm talking about a little bedroom activity now and then, not a walk on the moon."

"When did you start doing this?"

"I started Googling the sites last month. I've already . . . uh, met some really hot men online," I confessed with a shy smile. "Really nice, good-looking, professional dudes with good reputations who have some of the same frustrations I have." I was not prepared for the loud groan that came out of Lola's mouth and the bug-eyed look that appeared on her face. I folded my arms. "Don't sit there looking at me like I just turned into a pillar of salt. Say what you want to say, so I can say what I want to say," I challenged.

The waiter set another basket of wings on our table. I casually plucked one out and bit into it while Lola stared at me with her mouth hanging open again. She closed her mouth and shook a finger in my face. "Are you the same woman who told me she was going to be more serious in her marriage than her mama and her sisters and half of her other female relatives?"

"I'm the same woman," I replied with a shrug.

"What's the matter with you? Don't you read the newspapers and watch the news? People are getting into all kinds of trouble with people they meet in chat rooms and whatnot. You're the one who told me about that 'Craigslist Killer,' the one they made a Lifetime Channel movie about!"

"Calm down," I advised, holding up my hand. "Don't get all crazy on me."

"I know Internet dating works for a lot of people, but I don't think I'm brave enough to do it . . . yet. "

"You can think what you want. That Craigslist Killer went after prostitutes. Most of the women I've read about who got in trouble with men they met online were also involved in prostitution and all kinds of other shady shit, drugs, robbery, and scams, to name a few."

"Speaking of 'scams,' what about the mess we got ourselves into with those old men in that lonely hearts club?"

"We were stupid teenagers, remember? And there is a huge difference between what we did back then and what

I'm doing now. I'm not taking money from the men I hook up with. Like I said, I'm dealing with professional, respectable men with good reputations. Most of them are married. I feel safer with them than I would a man I met in a bar or anyplace else these days. My new friends have a lot to lose if they do something stupid."

"Joan, don't be naïve. Just because a man's a professional this or that and is married, it doesn't mean he can't also be a psycho. What about that big case in Oakland a few years ago? That computer big shot who killed his wife and buried her in a shallow grave? What about that doctor in Santa Barbara who chopped up his wife and dumped her body parts in three different cities? And must I remind you that Ted Bundy was a law student? Don't you talk to me about professional men being safer. You can't be that gullible."

"I am not naïve or gullible. I meet these men in very public and crowded places. Before we get too comfortable, and certainly before we check in to a room, I ask to see his business card and ID. I show them my ID, too, because I could be a criminal myself, for all they know."

"So what? What if one goes off the deep end and comes to your house?"

"Pffft! They don't know where I live. I always cover the address with my finger when I show them my ID. Where they work is listed on their business cards, but other than the city and state, I don't know where any of them live either. These men are my friends and I consider my relationships with them as a 'friends with benefits' arrangement. You should use your computer for something other than games and Googling for coupons and other mundane shit!"

"You're a grown woman and I can't tell you how to live your life." Lola's voice and demeanor had softened. But I knew she didn't approve of my new activity. "I just don't want to see you get in a mess of trouble with a man."

"Lola, I'm already 'in a mess of trouble with a man,' and his name is Reed Riley. I am going to leave him soon because I can't go on like this. I have to do what's good for me. I had never been as sexually frustrated in my life as I was before I went looking for love on the Internet. It didn't take long for me to find out that there are a lot of men out there who are just as frustrated with their mates as I am with mine. Well, those men want to be with me, and I want to be with them. I don't intend to keep doing it on the down-low. You know what a free spirit I am. I like to express myself, no matter what it is I'm doing. Shit."

Lola let out a sigh, squeezed my hand, and gave me a sympathetic look. "You do what you have to do," she said gently. "I may not like what you do, but I'll continue to watch your back and be there for you. Don't just think about what's good for you. Reed has feelings, so think about what's good for him too. The sooner you let him go so he can move on with his life, the better for both of you. I just hope he doesn't take it too hard. That man loves the ground you walk on. I know he is a major pain in your ass, but I still like him. For his sake and mine, let him down gently."

"I will," I vowed. "Reed is a rational man. If I handle the breakup right, he'll politely go his way and I'll go mine. And for our son's sake, he and I can remain friends."

Chapter 29

Lola

THINGS HAD CHANGED A LITTLE BETWEEN BERTHA AND me over the years, but not much for the better. She had become even more dependent on me. Most of her close friends had either passed or moved away. Maxine Sweeny, one of her bingo-playing buddies, had a massive stroke two months ago that left her totally disabled. Her forty-five-year-old divorced son, Douglas, who made Libby and Marshall look like Mother Teresa and Gandhi, promptly dumped her into a nursing home and practically forgot about her. He never visited or called to see how she was doing. She died three weeks later. Bertha was so devastated she didn't eat or sleep for two days. Four days before her stroke, Maxine had warned Bertha that women like them were doomed and would end up getting "tossed out like the garbage" sooner or later. Now more than ever, Bertha was afraid she'd end up like Maxine.

"I just know my kids are going to put me in a home

someday," she'd wail several times in the same conversation on a regular basis.

I promised her that I would do everything within my power to make sure that didn't happen. I assured her that if her kids put her in a nursing home, I would visit her two or three times a week. That always pleased her for a few days. Then she would resume her usual behavior: meddling in my relationships and acting like she couldn't go on without my assistance.

The more Bertha leaned on me, the more creative I got as far as my love life was concerned. Each time I met a man I liked enough to consider having a serious relationship with, I put off letting Bertha know about him for as long as I could.

Libby had had her own phone with a separate number when she'd occupied the bedroom that I had now. To reduce the chances of Bertha answering a call from one of my men friends and spewing a bunch of nonsense, I had that line reactivated. I did it when she was at the beauty shop because I didn't want her to know about it. I turned the ringer off when I had to go out; and I turned it down so low when I was in my room, I was the only one who could hear it. Instead of a traditional answering machine, I had voice mail service through the phone company and a pin number was required to retrieve messages.

I didn't stop there. I came up with an even more brilliant ruse. I opened an independent account with the phone company where people could dial a number at a call center and leave recorded voice mail for me. Joan disguised her voice and left an outgoing message using the name "Liza Mae Ford," a bogus handicapped friend I frequently "visited" at night when I wanted to be with a new man that I didn't want Bertha to know about. Each time I left the house and used the ruse, she called the number several times and left one convoluted message after another. It was usually something as ridiculous as a "suspicious man" walking back and forth in front of the house, or a "vicious stray dog" lurking around in the backyard.

I didn't like deceiving Bertha in such an elaborate manner, but I couldn't think of any other way that I could live a fairly normal life while I was still living under her roof. She bought the story about the invalid friend hook, line, and sinker. "That poor Liza Mae, confined to a wheelchair for the rest of her life. Tsk, tsk, tsk. She's so blessed to have a friend like you who's willing to spend so much time with her. How long has she been paralyzed from the waist down?" Bertha asked as I stood in front of the full-length mirror behind my bedroom door, dressing to go out one night. She plopped down onto my bed, fanning her face with a rolled-up copy of *Ebony* magazine.

"Uh, since she got hit by that speeding car last year," I replied, stepping into a pair of low-heeled black pumps.

"Hmmm. I'll bet the driver had been drinking."

"Uh-huh. And it wasn't his first accident. He'll be in jail for a while."

"And he should be! It's a damn shame poor Liza Mae has no family. It's a good thing she's got a couple of other friends and that home care nurse coming to see her when you can't be there. If I wasn't so close to disablement myself, I'd offer to go over there with you sometime to help that poor girl out. The Lord blessed me with sweet children, but I wish they were more like you. . . ."

Things had not changed much among me and Bertha's "sweet" children. I was pleased that Libby and Marshall still didn't come to the house that often when they knew I was home. If I answered the telephone when they called to talk to Bertha, they rarely said more than a few words to me.

Bertha had had a few serious health issues over the

years, but nothing life-threatening or serious enough for her to consider a drastic change in her lifestyle. Several of the small group of women she still had relationships with had moved into a gated senior citizen apartment complex, like sixty-three-year-old Becky Roberts, who used to live across the street, had done. Another acquaintance, who had some heart problems, had moved into an assisted-living facility. No matter how hard I tried to encourage Bertha to consider doing the same, she balked and reminded me about what had happened to Maxine Sweeny.

"What's wrong with you, Lola? I thought you told me you'd do everything within your power to make sure I don't end up in a home. Did you already forget how poor Maxine died less than a month after her scoundrel of a son put her into one of those places? Your daddy, may he rest in peace until I join him, told you to your face that no matter what happened, don't you dump me into a nursing home. Did you forget about that too?"

We were in the living room that Wednesday evening watching *Wheel of Fortune*. My eyelids fluttered and my face got hot. "No, I didn't forget," I whimpered. As soon as I said that, Bertha's eyes danced with delight.

"You can do whatever else you want to do—get married and have six kids and a dog—but you can't break the promise you made to your dying daddy, girl!"

"I won't," I replied with a dramatic sigh. I gulped in some air and continued. "Daddy really put me in a spot, you know." I had not wanted to add that last sentence, but by now I was sizzling with rage.

Bertha's jaw dropped. "You think your daddy put *you* in a spot? What about the spot he put me in? Do you think I would have married him if I'd known he was going to die so soon and leave me with a young child to raise after I'd already raised two other kids on my own? I'm in a bigger spot than you ever were! At least you're young and still in good health."

There were days, like this particular one, when I got so agitated I wanted to pack up in the middle of the night and disappear. No matter how much I cared about Bertha and my commitment to her, the reality was that I was not only being played by her, but I was also being played by her children. She knew that as long as she had me under her thumb, she didn't have to worry about being on her own. Libby and Marshall knew that they didn't have to worry about her welfare, as long as I lived under her roof. Lately it had really begun to bother me in a way that was disturbing. Some days it bothered me more than others. When I was in a relationship with a man, it bothered me the most. When I was between lovers, and couldn't catch up with Joan or anybody else, I was almost glad I had Bertha to keep me from feeling lonesome. I'd never admit that to Joan. She would be appalled to hear such a declaration coming from me after all the complaining I'd done to her about Bertha. Just thinking about some of the things that Joan would say made my chest tighten.

After I had composed myself, I continued. "I am not talking about a nursing home. Becky Roberts lives in a two-bedroom unit in a senior citizen building that is very much like the same place she lived in for ten years with her son until he got married."

"Uh-huh. And I bet she wishes she was still in that same apartment she lived in for ten years—with her son until he married that snooty woman who made him get rid of his own mama. Last week Becky slipped on a bar of soap in her shower in that old folks' home and couldn't get up. She laid there for eight hours before somebody found her."

"I didn't know that."

"You know it now. Just about anything can happen to a

woman like me in the best of one of those homes!" The fear in Bertha's eyes made me shudder. "The patients are just bodies to the people who work in those homes. And when they're not neglecting and abusing them, they're raping the women—"

I held up my hand and cut her off. "Let's change the subject," I said with another dramatic sigh. That look of fear was still in Bertha's eyes; so with a whole lot of hesitation on my part, I decided to say something I knew she wanted to hear. "You don't have to worry about something like that happening to you as long as I'm alive." That statement, even though it was just a smoke screen, was one way to keep the peace for the time being.

Despite what I was feeling toward Bertha whenever we had these tense conversations, my plan was that when I did marry, I was going to leave her point-blank. I didn't think about the promise I had made to Daddy as frequently as I used to, unless she brought it up. The main thing that was keeping me with her now was the fact that I still couldn't afford a place on my own. I had purchased a four-year-old Jetta six months ago, which I still had two and a half years left to pay on. And I had almost maxed out four of my five credit cards. Before I moved anywhere, I needed to get out of debt.

Otherwise, I had a fairly happy life. I still worked at the grocery store and I had a social life that I was comfortable with. My love life was still somewhat sporadic, but I was fairly certain that I would eventually meet my soul mate.

A couple of weeks after Joan had told me about her online romances, I opened a Facebook account. I wanted to reconnect with some of the people I'd been friends with in the past. I had no interest in hooking up with an online lover—at least not yet.

During the next few days, I chatted back and forth with former classmates and a few ex-lovers. It didn't take long for me to get bored. Most of them were living lives duller than mine. I finally decided to try and locate Mariel Odom, my other mother's niece and one of my former best friends. If anybody was doing something interesting, it would be her.

It was not as easy as I thought it would be to locate Mariel. I had no way of knowing if she had a Facebook account. There were several other women in various cities with the same or a similar name. Finally one evening, around five o'clock, a week after I'd opened my account, I clicked on a "Mariel Odom-Porter," who lived in Seattle. Her profile included the high school she had attended and the names of a few of her relatives, so I knew I had the right Mariel. I immediately sent her a friend request and twenty minutes later she accepted. When I responded, I included my e-mail address and she sent me a message right away, which included her home phone number. I logged off my computer and called her up immediately. She must have been sitting real close to the phone because she answered halfway through the first ring.

"Mariel, I am so happy to hear your voice after all these years!" I squealed. "I wondered what had happened to you. What have you been up to?"

"Well, a lot has happened to me since the last time I saw you. I have a perfect life—an awesome husband, two beautiful children, and a lovely home. I have a great career too. I teach fourth grade in one of the most prestigious schools in Seattle. What about you?"

Just hearing that Mariel was doing so well made my

eyes water, not because I was jealous, but because I was happy for her. Especially the part about her teaching, a dream I still had. "Remember that grocery store a couple of blocks from where you used to live?" I replied.

"Yikes! You mean Cottright's, that dingy little place with the gummy floors, the jacked-up prices, and the moldy-looking meat?"

"Uh, yeah. . . ."

"Yuck! What about it? I hope the city has finally closed down that dump."

"No, it's not closed down. I started working there as a cashier right after I graduated. It's not nearly as gloomy as it used to be."

"Oh. Well, a girl like you can give a place like that some class."

"Thanks," I said dryly. "Anyway, when I get my vacation, maybe I can come visit you. I've always wanted to see Seattle."

"I'd like that very much, Lola. We have so much more catching up to do. Since my grandmother passed, I don't visit South Bay City that often anymore. Hey! What's Joan been up to?"

"She's married to a very successful dentist. They have a son and they live in a gorgeous condo facing a lake."

"A dentist? Humph! I wonder how a ghetto-fied sex addict like Joan landed a dentist. I'm sure he looks like that Shrek character in the movies. What else is wrong with him?"

"Nothing. He's real handsome and he adores Joan."

"Oh, well. They say 'truth is stranger than fiction' and love *really* must be blind. So she's a happy housewife now, huh?"

"Something like that." I didn't want to say that Joan was more of a "desperate housewife" than a "happy housewife." I was glad when Mariel steered the conversation in another direction.

"How is life treating you, Lola? Are you married yet?"

"Uh, no. I want to enjoy the single life a little while longer," I chirped.

"Well, did you get your degree? I know you wanted to teach too."

"Uh, no," I said again.

"Hmmm. I guess you must be happy with your life if you're not ready to get married and you settled for a job in a *grocery store*. Oomph, oomph, oomph."

"I don't plan on being a cashier too much longer. And I don't plan on staying single too much longer either." I didn't want Mariel to ask about my love life so I jumped into another subject. "Before I forget to ask, how is my other mother?"

"Your 'other mother'? I used to laugh to myself every time you called Aunt Shirelle that!" Mariel chuckled. "She's doing even better than I am. She has two sons and a daughter now and her husband treats her like a queen. They just moved into a fantastic house in San Diego and she couldn't be happier."

More tears flooded my eyes. I was happy for Shirelle, but I felt like she had deserted me when I'd needed her the most. Had she stayed with Daddy, Bertha would not have snatched him up and I wouldn't be in the mess I was in now.

Chapter 30

Lola

I WAS ELATED TO HEAR THAT THINGS HAD GOTTEN EVEN better for Shirelle since I'd run into her at that convenience store thirteen years ago. At the same time, I felt sad for myself. It seemed like everybody else had moved on with their lives while I stayed stuck in the same place.

"You know, Mariel, some women always get what they want. Some of us don't." I hoped that what I'd just said didn't make me sound jealous. That was not the case. I truly was happy for Shirelle. "I'm happy to hear that my other mother is doing so well," I admitted. "I guess her joining that dating site was the best thing she ever did. Apparently, finding a husband online worked out for her."

Mariel mumbled something unintelligible under her breath.

"What? I didn't understand what you just said," I let her know.

"Oh, it was nothing. It's just that I am surprised Aunt Shirelle told you how she met her husband."

"Uh, yeah. Maybe I shouldn't have opened my big mouth. . . ."

I wanted to bite off my tongue. Then I reminded myself that Shirelle had eagerly shared her online experience with me. She had not said anything to me about keeping that information to myself.

"Oh, honey, don't worry about it. It's no secret anymore. Aunt Shirelle was the one who convinced me to join a dating site. And thank God I did."

I didn't think there was anything else Mariel could say that would surprise me. But what she'd just said almost knocked the wind out of me. "You too?" I exclaimed. "How did it work out for you?"

"Great! That's how I met my drop-dead gorgeous husband, Christopher," Mariel answered, sounding like she was swooning. "He's an architect, like Aunt Shirelle's husband, and owns his own company. I had to kiss a lot of frogs before I met my prince, but I had a lot of fun along the way." She paused and remained silent for a few seconds. Then in a patronizing manner, she said, "Other than that grocery store job, what else are you doing for yourself? I thought you'd at least be married by now."

"Oh . . . well, I'm sure I'll find my, uh, Mr. Right soon."

Mariel wasted no time jumping on my clumsy statement. "Well, you'd better look harder! We are the same age, so I advise you not to take too much longer. Thirty is not old, but a lot of my husband's unmarried friends are looking for girls no older than twenty. The strange thing is, when I was that age, hardly any man worth looking at wanted me. And they didn't get interested until I got online and skipped all that bullshit a woman goes through in bars and every other meeting place. The Internet is where people cut to the chase."

"So I keep hearing," I muttered. I knew that when I told Joan about Mariel's Internet experience, she'd use it as leverage the next time she tried to convince me to join a dating site.

We chatted a few minutes more, discussing everything from my parents' passing to my situation with Bertha. Mariel didn't have much to say about her, but what she did say didn't surprise me. "Lola, you always did go out of your way to please people, whether they deserved it or not. Sometimes you're too good for your own good. That's positive, but it could turn on a dime into something negative. It could cause some serious emotional problems for you if you don't keep it under control. Sooner or later, you're going to snap and do something totally out of character for you. Maybe even something violent. Remember that meek man who went berserk at that dairy farm when we were in middle school?"

"The one people described as a 'very nice man'?"

"That 'very nice man' snapped one day when he got passed over for a promotion. He went home, got his gun, and went back to work and shot and killed everybody in sight."

I recalled that grisly incident with a shudder. I was disappointed that our conversation had taken such a grim turn. "You don't have to worry about me. I wouldn't hurt a fly." I forced myself to laugh. "Life is too precious to me."

"Speaking of life, did they ever find that young black woman who disappeared on her way home from work?" Mariel asked in a stiff tone of voice.

"What young black woman? When? With all the crime in California, it's hard to keep up with it all."

"Oh, that happened several months ago, maybe even

last year. She was a nurse and she lived in South Bay City, just four blocks away from that house you lived in with your parents before they died."

"Oh, yes. I vaguely remember reading about her. The newspaper said she worked at City Hospital. Did you know her?"

"No, I didn't know the poor woman. Her mysterious disappearance was a big story up here because she was from Seattle and her family still lives here."

"I don't read the paper every day or catch the TV news, but far as I know, they haven't found her yet."

"Brrrr! Just thinking about it gives me chills. Whoever that maniac is that kidnapped her, I hope they catch him soon."

"'Kidnapped'? How do you know that's what happened to her?" I asked. "Just because somebody disappears doesn't mean some maniac snatched them. A few months ago, another local young black woman disappeared. She worked as a secretary for some big law firm. There were so many rumors that her ex had done something to her, the police got all over him like a cheap suit. There was no evidence that he'd done anything to her and he had a solid alibi, but that poor man lost his job because of those rumors. A week later, they found the woman's car with her body in it at the bottom of the Berkeley Marina. She had had a few too many drinks at an office party and lost control of her car on her way home."

"Well, as far as I'm concerned, drowning is as bad as some maniac chopping you up into a dozen pieces. Dead is dead." The conversation had taken a turn that was downright ghoulish to me, but Mariel kept running with it. "If I ever get in a life-and-death situation, I hope it's over quickly. I hope I'm already dead if my killer decides to dismember my body. And I hope somebody finds what's left of me before I turn to dust. At least my family could give me a proper burial, and they'd have some closure. Can you imagine the pain that the missing nurse's family must be in, not knowing where she is or if she's even still alive?"

"I can't imagine their pain," I said with a mournful sigh. This conversation had begun to depress me. I *had* to lighten it up a few shades. "Uh, I still plan to get a degree someday, either teaching or nursing."

"I certainly hope so! I can't imagine you working in a grocery store for the rest of your life! Jeez! And I am hella surprised to hear that you still live at home with your stepmother. For goodness' sake!"

I saw no reason to tell Mariel the complete details of my situation with Bertha. Like her aunt Shirelle, she was so opinionated I knew she'd say something that would upset me if I told her *why* I was still living with my stepmother and how I allowed her to manipulate me.

As much as I enjoyed chatting with Mariel, I was glad when she had to end our conversation to go break up a fight between her sons. We agreed to talk again soon, but I wasn't sure I wanted to hear too much more about her "perfect life." It would have done more for my morale if she had told me she had a few problems in her marriage, like Joan and other couples.

After I hung up, I decided to give Joan a call. I thought that if I shared the news that Mariel was so happy, it might give her some hope. A male voice I didn't recognize answered her phone.

"Joan ain't here," the deep voice informed me. "Who's calling?"

I cleared my throat and said firmly, "I'm Lola, a close friend of hers. And you are?"

"You probably don't remember me on account of I

don't come around that much. I'm Derrick Foster, Reed's cousin. I was the one you were dancing with at Joan and Reed's wedding reception when her cousin Too Sweet had one too many drinks and fell into the preacher's lap."

"Oh, yes, I do remember you, Derrick. Uh, do you know when Joan will be home?"

Derrick took his time answering my question. "To tell you the truth, that's hard to say. She's still at City Hospital. I'm hanging out at the condo to keep an eye on things until things get back to normal. . . ."

My first thought was that Reed had hurt Joan. She had confided in me that the last time she mentioned divorce, he had threatened to beat some sense into her.

I gasped. "She's in the hospital? Oh, my God! What happened to her? Is she all right?"

"Naw, she ain't all right. She's in pretty bad shape. She's a train wreck, if you ask me."

I could feel my heart pounding inside my chest as I braced myself for more bad news. "What did Reed do to her?" I asked angrily, balling my hand into a fist at the same time.

"He didn't do a damn thing to her. That dude would never hit a woman. Joan ain't the one the ambulance hauled away. It was Reed."

"*She* hurt *him*?" Joan had been rough and tough as far back as I could remember. She had had a lot of fights in school and with various members of her rambunctious family. But she had become less volatile over the years. Or had she? "What happened?"

"Well, she got up in his face and started talking that trash about leaving him again. I guess he finally got tired of hearing it so that damn fool swallowed a bunch of sleeping pills! Suicide ain't never the way to fix a problem!"

The next word shot out of my mouth like a torpedo. " 'Suicide'?"

"Uh-huh! I read somewhere that one of the highest suicide rates in the country is among the dentists. For some reason, they like to end it all by jumping out windows, blowing their brains out or swallowing a bunch of sleeping pills. I—somebody's at the door, Lola, so I have to get off this phone."

Derrick hung up before I could say another word. I was stunned! I couldn't sit or stand still. I began to pace the floor like a panther. If I didn't find out soon exactly what had happened, I'd go out of my mind. I immediately dialed Joan's cell phone number, but she didn't answer. In the next hour, I left her three messages, so now all I could do was wait until she called me back.

Chapter 31

Joan

I COULD NOT BELIEVE HOW MUCH MY LIFE HAD UNRAVeled since the day I married Reed, especially in the last couple of years. It seemed like just yesterday that I was a superfly, intelligent, fun-loving, ambitious young girl with my whole life ahead of me. Now I was a desperate, sexually frustrated housewife with a future as bleak as a rainy day. But I was an awesome mom—there was no doubt about that. I would not hesitate to die for my son. He was crazy about his father so no matter how much Reed got on my nerves, I didn't want anything bad to happen to him. Oh, he'd made me mad enough to want to slap the shit out of him and send him to the emergency room on numerous occasions, but I had always managed to control myself.

Now, of all things, that jackass was lying in a hospital bed half dead, anyway! If somebody had told me that Reed was capable of taking his own life, I would have called them a big fat liar. Yes, he had told me several times in the past that he would not want to live if I left him. But he had never even hinted that he would commit suicide!

It happened on a Monday evening while I was out on one of my random dates. I had called Reed at his office earlier that rainy afternoon and told him that I was going to go visit my family. Elmo was recovering from hip replacement surgery and was down in the dumps, so I wanted to go over and cheer him up. The weather had played a part in the way I was feeling that day. I had always hated rain, black clouds, and any other form of gloom associated with bad weather.

When I was six, while visiting one of my aunties in Alabama, there was a tornado that had destroyed almost everything in its path, including my auntie's house—with us in it. Somehow we had managed to survive with only a few minor injuries. I couldn't get my butt back to California fast enough. I had nightmares for months about being swept up in a tornado and dumped off in some faraway place where nobody could find me. My fear was so severe, in fact, I could no longer stand to watch *The Wizard of Oz,* and it had been one of my favorite old movies.

Anyway, this particular day had me so antsy I had to get out of the house, even if it meant I had to be outside during the rainstorm. I wanted to be somewhere that would make me feel safe and relaxed. Nothing relaxed me more than some *good* old-fashioned sex.

Having a husband didn't mean automatic sex. Even if Reed had been in the house with me that day, I would not have wanted to have sex with him, anyway. Making love with him had become unpleasant and felt more like a punishment. He was too quick, too unromantic, and sometimes funky as hell. There was nothing more disgusting to me than having sex with Reed when he needed a shower. The last time he climbed on top of me, after working out at the gym for two hours and not taking a shower, I almost gagged. I couldn't believe he was the same man who nagged me about keeping the condo clean.

I had not had sex with him in over a month, so I was "hotter than a six-shooter," a phrase I'd heard my sisters use when they were horny. My family still had no idea that Reed and I were having problems in our marriage. They still thought he was the best thing that had ever happened to me or to our family, for that matter. Having a successful dentist in the clan was a huge feather in my mother's cap. I got sick of her spending hours at a time on the telephone with some of her friends, or leaning over the bannister of her front porch, bragging to neighbors about how well I had turned out. "We thought the girl would marry some dreadlocked creature with a mouth full of gold teeth," she said one day.

While I was holed up in a Sheraton hotel with an Italian stallion from the Bronx, who was in town for a management-training program, Reed was snooping around trying to find me. He left four messages on my cell phone. We had been so out of tune with each other for so long, I ignored the fact that it was my birthday. He had left his office early so he could come home and do something special with me. I told my mother and the rest of the folks in the house that if he called, they were to tell him I was out shopping with Elaine. She used me as a cover when she fooled around on her current lover, so she owed me. The problem was, I had not been able to reach her before I left to go on my date, so I couldn't brief her. And nobody told her in time what I'd told them to say in case Reed checked up on me. When he went to Mama's house looking for me a couple of hours after I'd left for my afternoon tryst, Elaine blew it. She told him that she hadn't even seen me in a week and that I was the last person she'd go shopping with.

If that was not bad enough, my clueless stepfather told him he'd overheard me on the phone talking to somebody about how I couldn't wait to see him, blah, blah, blah. Well, Reed put two and two together and assumed I was with another man. He had assumed right. I had had a fantastic time with my date. So fantastic that I drank one glass of wine too many, dozed off, and stayed way longer than I'd meant to. Had I stayed a few minutes longer, it probably would have been too late.

I got home just in time to find Reed unconscious. I was horrified when I saw him stretched out on the floor in the bathroom connected to our bedroom. Luckily, the sleeping pills he had swallowed were not as strong as he thought they were. A brief, unsigned note and the empty sleeping-pill bottle were on the floor next to him. He had typed the note on the same computer that I used to find lovers online. All it said, in bold, upper-case letters, was: I TOLD YOU I COULDN'T LIVE WITHOUT YOU. PLEASE TAKE CARE OF MY SON.

I was fit to be tied! I couldn't believe that he was inconsiderate enough to pull a stunt that could have hurt so many people! I decided right away not to mention this to anyone except my family. Now I thought it was important for them to know just how far Reed would go to keep me. One thing I gave my family credit for was that if they were told not to blab our business to anybody outside of the family, they didn't. Lola was the exception. I had told her almost every little one of my relatives' secrets.

Right after I had called for an ambulance for Reed, I ripped up the note and flushed the pieces down the toilet. My story to paramedics was that my husband had "accidentally" taken too many sleeping pills. We didn't need to have the cops or newspaper busybodies nosing around.

A suicide attempt could have cost Reed his practice. I was convinced that at the very least, most of his patients would desert him if they knew what he'd done.

The doctor who treated him was his father's cousin, so I knew he wouldn't blab to the wrong people. "Just make sure he doesn't have access to any more prescription sleeping pills," Dr. Franklin told me with a dry look. "We don't have that many black dentists in this town, so we can't afford to lose Reed."

Chapter 32

Joan

I T WAS AN HOUR BEFORE REED REGAINED CONSCIOUS-
ness. During that time, I remained by the side of his bed,
biting my nails, cussing to myself and at him, and wondering how in the world I was going to tolerate him now!

Right after the doctor checked his vitals and left the
room, Reed sat bolt upright. His lips were chapped and
his eyes were bloodshot.

"You didn't tell my folks, I hope," he wheezed. "This
would kill my poor mother. Nobody in my family has
ever done anything like this before!"

I shook my head. "And I am not going to tell them or
anybody else. But . . . my family knows. You know the
Proctor family likes to share everything."

We stared into each other's eyes for a few uncomfortable seconds.

"Joan, were you with another man?" Reed didn't give
me time to answer. "If you're cheating on me, I don't

want to know," he choked out, his voice sounding much stronger. "If I am going to lose you . . . I don't want to know that either."

I sucked in some air and shook my head. "Don't you think it'd be hard for me to leave you for another man and not let you know?"

"I . . . I don't want to go on," he whimpered with a tortured look on his face.

I glanced around the room just long enough to regroup my scattered thoughts. When I returned my attention back to Reed, he looked even more pathetic. "You have a lot to live for. You've got a successful practice, lots of friends, and a family who loves you."

"None of that means much to me if I don't have you!" he boomed. His tongue snapped brutally over each word as he continued. "I am not going to let you mistreat me and get away with it, Joan!"

"So you'd rather kill yourself, huh?"

"Well, you've got me acting like a fool!"

"If you're acting like a fool, it's because you are a fool!"

"Humph! Don't put the blame for my, uh, accident all on me! You couldn't be more responsible if you had shoved those pills down my throat yourself!" Reed lifted his chin and looked at me with so much raw contempt, I felt like stretching out in a hospital bed myself.

He frowned when I folded my arms, so I quickly unfolded them and put my hands on my hips instead. I didn't want him to know just how upset I was, so I forced myself to keep my voice calm. "I know I lied about where I was going, but I was not with another man. I don't know why you think I was. . . ."

"Where were you then? Several times in the past few months, I couldn't locate you when you were supposed to be at home. And what's the point of you having a cell phone when you rarely answer it when you're not at home?"

"This time I was at the mall," I said flatly. "I'm always forgetting to take my cell phone with me when I leave the house."

"Mall, my ass! If I weren't such a nonviolent gentleman, I'd jump up out of this bed and *maul* your head with my fist!" The frown on Reed's face was even more severe now. I moved back a few steps, in case he overlooked the fact that he was "such a nonviolent gentleman" and jumped out of his bed and attacked me. "Joan, I've found matches from various hotels in your coat pocket—more than one time. I've even *smelled* another man on your body—more than one time! If you're going to screw around, the least you could do is be clean about it. Wash the stink off your ass before you come home! There is nothing more irritating to a man than a woman's funky-smelling body!" I couldn't believe how harsh he sounded now, and I couldn't believe that this stinky mother-fucker—who often smelled so bad now, I had to rub my nostrils to keep them from stinging—had the nerve to be implying that I was unclean! He was not done with me yet; and the more he berated me, the more he pissed me off. "And rinse out your mouth. I don't like to taste another man's slimy dick on my wife's lips when I kiss her like I have MORE THAN ONE TIME!"

I wasn't going to waste my time telling Reed about all the times I'd endured his sweat and funk during moments of intimacy. It would only prolong his rant. I decided to play "nice" and remain civil.

"How come you never said anything before now?" I asked calmly with my eyelids fluttering. I was so busted, but I was not about to admit it.

"Because I thought that if I ignored the problem, it

would go away. Having you tell me to my face that you've been with another man would kill me."

"Reed, you're imagining things." He flinched when I patted his shoulder.

"Bull doo-doo! Don't tell me you haven't cheated on me!" he screeched.

"Can you prove it? So what if I had matches from hotels in my coat pocket? I go to buffets in a lot of different hotel restaurants with Lola, and every time I go, I pick up some matches! So there!" I shot back. I paused just long enough to catch my breath. "And another thing, how do you know the dick you tasted on my lips wasn't yours? I know we don't get busy like we used to, but the only dick I suck is yours. To tell you the truth, your last performance was such a letdown I didn't bother to clean myself up afterward the way I usually do. I didn't shower or rinse out my mouth until the next day."

"Humph! So now you're telling me you're not as clean as I thought you were? How did I let a skank like you trap me into marriage?" he wailed. The more he ranted, the more desperate he looked. "I—I knew I should have married that Fisher girl like my mother and everybody else in my family wanted me to!"

"Pffft!" I spat, waving my arms. I was not just "hot" as in anger. I was hot as in *hot*. I could feel sweat forming on my face. "You're coming up with all kinds of ridiculous shit! And you don't have to stay in a marriage to a 'skank' like me if you don't want to. I'm sure that if you still want Velline Fisher, she'd be glad to have you as soon as she gets out of prison. . . ."

The way Reed's eyes popped out, you would have thought that I had just pulled out an Uzi. "I didn't know Velline was in jail. What did she do?"

"Something about an armed robbery," I reported. "She

and that drug dealer she and her three kids—by three different men—were living with."

"Oh." Reed look embarrassed as he cleared his throat. "It's a good thing I didn't marry her, I guess. I'm glad I married you, and I married you for life. I don't care what you do. I will have to just deal with it. I strongly suggest you forget about ever getting a divorce."

"Then I 'strongly suggest' you stop talking about me cheating on you."

"I'm tired," he said, lying back down. That tortured look was back on his face. "Joan, I'm willing to forget everything I just said. I know you're not perfect, but you're perfect for me. I don't want to lose you."

I cussed under my breath and rubbed my neck, which felt like all the muscles in it had been stretched to the limit. "You get some rest," I said, patting his shoulder again. I reluctantly gave him a quick peck on his sweat-covered forehead. "I hope you never try this again," I whispered.

"That's up to you. I was serious about not wanting to live without you. . . ."

"So you're telling me, you'll try to kill yourself again if I do leave you?"

The look in his eyes answered my question, but he confirmed it with a statement that made my skin crawl: "Like I said, *I will not live without you.*"

At his request, Reed was going to spend two or three nights in the hospital. I didn't leave until he had gone to sleep about fifteen minutes later. As soon as I heard him snoring, I bolted. I needed to talk to Lola.

There were not many people in the hallway or in the waiting area, but I still decided to go outside to use my cell phone. My call went straight to her voice mail. I glanced at my watch and realized it was almost ten P.M. I went home, but I didn't sleep much. I called her again, around seven the next morning, hoping I'd catch her before she left for work.

Lola answered right away. "I am so glad to hear from you!" she hollered. "I called you yesterday and Derrick told me what happened. I left you some voice mail messages."

"I know. Sorry I'm just now calling you back. I've been busy."

"Derrick told me what he did! I am so sorry. Poor Reed. He was so full of life. Are you at the morgue?"

I gasped so hard that I almost choked on some air. "'Morgue'? Lola, Reed is not dead. I found him in time. He's in the hospital."

"Thank God! Derrick had to hang up before I could find out everything. Is Reed going to be all right?"

"He'll be fine. Don't worry about him. He wasn't really trying to kill himself. He was just trying to get my attention."

"Well, overdosing on sleeping pills is a hell of a way to try and get somebody's attention!" I hollered. "What was he thinking?"

"I don't know what the hell that jackass was thinking. All I know is, he's willing to do anything to get his way, and I don't like it one damn bit!"

"I don't like it either, Joan. But the important thing is, he's still alive, and as long as he is, there is hope for you and him."

"Pffft!"

"You don't think there's hope for your marriage?"

"Uh, yeah, whatever." Joan snorted. "Listen, I'd appreciate it if you didn't mention this incident to Reed when you see him again. I want to put this behind us as soon as possible."

"Oh, I won't say a word to him about it. It's none of my business, anyway. Is there anything I can do for you?"

"He won't be coming home for a day or so. Can you call in sick and come spend the day with me?"

"I'd love to, but the Cottrights are going to be in Napa today to check out some new wineries they want to start buying their wine from. It'll just be me and their nephew working the store. How about lunch?"

"Uh, I'm going back to the hospital to visit Reed this morning and I don't know how long I'll be there."

"Can you call me whenever you get home from the hospital?"

"I'd rather talk to you in person. How about lunch to-morrow?"

"Well, if that works for you, it works for me. Is noon okay?"

"That's fine. Don't come to the house. You'd use up too much of your lunch hour. I'll meet you at that deli across the street from your work."

"That'll do."

"Lola, he thought I was with another man."

"Were you?"

"I was. And because of how bad things are between us, I doubt if I can stop seeing other men—especially ones I don't have to even leave home to find. Some days I feel so lonely and bored, I could scream. I walk around the house, wondering what to do with myself. With Junior being in school most of the day, I don't have much to keep me occupied. And I am not about to settle for a life of watching talk shows and doing housework. You know I'm a woman who always likes to be involved in some-thing . . . something fun. I've always been this way."

"Tell me about it. Why don't you go out and buy a cat? Having to clean up behind a pet will keep you so busy you won't have to worry about being bored and lonely. And you should never mention the word 'bored' to me. That's the reason we got caught up in that lonely hearts club thing back in high school."

"There are times when I wish I still had those old pen pals to write to," Joan admitted with a mournful sigh. "At least it was fun."

"Look, if you do start writing corny love letters to a bunch of old men again, I don't want to know about it!"

"Oh, you know I'll never do anything as foolish as that again. But getting a pet is out of the question. Cleaning up behind Reed and Junior is enough. I'm not about to be cleaning out a litter box too. And the online clubs I am into now are nothing like that lonely hearts club. This is a whole different ballgame."

"Then if you don't want a pet, and if you don't want to let that online shit go, why not join a book club? As much as you like to read, I'm surprised you haven't joined one already. There are dozens of other hobbies that you can take up. If you find one that suits your needs, it might keep you from getting bored."

"I did . . . and it's men. Lola, dudes are all over that Internet looking for women like me. Most of them request married women so they can keep the hookups casual."

"Listen, 'Mrs. Desperate Housewife,' you don't have to tell me that. I watch TV. I read the newspapers and most of the magazines where they talk about this stuff. I don't want anything bad to happen to you, Joan. If you are going to keep having affairs, please be careful. Reed killing himself might not be the only thing you have to worry about."

"Please don't give me that warning about Internet serial killers and maniacs again. I've met some nice, good-looking men online and not a single one had a violent bone in his body. They were all very sweet men."

"Most serial killers were 'very sweet men,' too, until they started killing innocent people."

"Stop already! You've gone out with some pretty shady characters that you met the normal way. Remember that dude you went home with from the Blue Goose bar last year who tried to bite off your nipples?"

"Please do not remind me about that! I've learned my lesson about one-night stands. Yes, I make a lot of stupid choices too."

"Then relax. You don't need to beat me over the head. I get the point you're trying to make," I said.

"I'll see you around noon tomorrow. And do me a favor when I see you, tell me something good."

Chapter 33

Joan

REED WAS ASLEEP WHEN I GOT TO THE HOSPITAL A FEW minutes after ten that morning. I waited around two hours for him to wake up. "Joan, please leave me alone for today," he told me as soon as he saw my face. "I'd like to pull myself back together before we talk some more."

"I can wait," I said, giving him a weak smile. I was happy to see that he didn't look so tortured today. "Embarrassed" was the best way I could describe the look on his face now.

"No! I want to be by myself," he insisted. "Go on home!"

Not only was I exhausted, I was not in the mood to argue. I needed to pull myself back together, as much as he did, so I left.

* * *

As much as I ignored it, I finally admitted to myself that I no longer loved my husband. I wasn't even sure I ever really had! He had impressed me in the beginning of our relationship, and I thought that with all he had to offer, he could make me happy. I should have insisted on waiting until I got to know him much better before we got married! I was angry with him for putting me in the position he had put me in by attempting to kill himself. I realized now that he was a weak, miserable man and had probably been that way his whole life. It explained why he had targeted a girl my age. I couldn't see a woman his age tolerating his behavior. Well, he could play his games as much as he wanted to. I was not about to let him use suicide to hold me hostage! I would play along with him, just enough to keep him "happy," and do everything I could to please myself too. But there was no way that I could stay with Reed and please myself *without* seeing other men. . . .

I was sorry I didn't have a date lined up for the evening. With Reed in the hospital, I would not have had to make up a story about where I was going. And spending a couple of hours with a man I was not committed to would certainly take my mind off the man that I was committed to.

Too Sweet had promised to pick up Junior from school and take him to Mama's house until I picked him up, so I had a few hours to myself. I refreshed my makeup and drove around for about twenty minutes before I decided to get on the freeway. I had not planned to do anything in particular, but when I approached the exit to a mall, I decided to spend a couple of hours shopping before the stores closed.

I picked out a few items for myself and for Junior; and just to make it look good, I purchased a new robe for

Reed. I had a feeling he would not want to wear the one he'd been found in after his suicide attempt.

On the way home, I stopped at a Starbucks to have a cup of coffee. Someone had left a newspaper on the only available table; it featured a story on the front page about the three local young black women who had all turned up missing in less than a year. It was a disturbing article, but it was the pictures of the women that gave me a chill. *They all resemble Lola,* I thought. I folded the newspaper and stuffed it into my purse, wondering if she had seen it.

I was anxious to pick up my son from Mama's house, so I finished my coffee and got back on the freeway

"Joan, how is poor Reed?" Mama asked as soon as I made it into the house. She was still in her ugly gray prison uniform.

I heaved a heavy sigh. "He's fine. He'll be home in a couple of days, but I don't think he'll want too much company for a while, so don't come see him."

"Well, none of us will come to see him until he feels up to it, but I'll keep him in my prayers." Mama reared back and looked me up and down, giving me a pitiful look. "You look terrible, baby. Come sit with me for a little while." She led me by the hand to the living-room couch. "You're just in time. Elmo made a pitcher of margaritas. And I hope you can stay for dinner. Elaine made gumbo."

"I can't stay for dinner. Before I left home, I put a steak in the sink to thaw out. Where's Junior?"

"He's next door visiting the Carter boy." When we reached the couch, Mama stopped abruptly and gave me a wild-eyed look. "I hope you don't tell Junior his daddy tried to commit suicide!"

"Of course I won't tell my child that. If it's up to me, he'll never know."

"I'm glad to hear that." Mama looked relieved. "Well, he sure won't hear it from nobody in our family."

Mama dropped down onto the couch with a groan and a complaint about a pain in her back. I sat down next to her, glad that Elmo had already placed a tray that contained a margarita-filled pitcher and several salt-rimmed glasses onto the coffee table. One thing I could say about my stepfather was that he was a "handyman" in every sense of the word. He went to his job and worked just as long and hard as Mama did every day. But he did a lot of the cooking and other things around the house too.

"You know how heavy-handed Elmo is with the tequila. His drinks are pretty potent, so be careful." Mama filled two glasses and handed one to me. I immediately took a sip and so did she. "I don't care how many times I get on that man's case. His head is still as hard as a brick! Just like his daddy and all three of his brothers. They're all lucky they married the right women. Even though I keep my husband on the straight and narrow, he still wants to do things his way, but he ought to know better by now." Despite Mama's complaints, she smiled and rolled her eyes in mock exasperation. She worshipped my stepfather and everybody knew it.

"I wish I had married a man more like Elmo," I said in a flat, weary voice. I didn't have the heart to tell Mama that her husband reminded me of an obedient dog. She probably knew that, anyway.

"What's wrong with you, girl?" Mama gasped so hard, she almost choked on her drink. "You caught you a *dentist*! If I could have got me a man like Reed, I wouldn't have given Elmo the time of night!" Mama snickered, but something told me she was serious.

I gave her a puzzled look. "Then how come you

haven't bounced a brick off Elmo's head to make him mind you better, or gotten rid of him the way you did my daddy and that conniving Jamaican you married before you met Elmo?" I took another sip of my drink, glad that the buzz had dulled my senses. Otherwise, I would never have fixed my lips to ask a woman like my mother such a bold question.

"Humph! My mama didn't raise no fool! Since it's this late in the game, I'd rather keep Elmo than train a new man." She paused and gave me a critical look. "Now you look here, girl. I don't care what's going on between you and Reed, you better go with the flow or fix it! As long as he don't beat your ass or let you catch him with another woman, you ain't got a damn thing to complain about. I wish when they got married, your sisters had hit as big a jackpot as you did. You marrying a dentist took this family to a whole new level. *Shit.*"

"There you go again! What's so great about me being married to a dentist?" I huffed. "Reed is still just a man and he can get on a woman's nerves just as quick as any other man."

Mama placed her hand on my shoulder. "Baby, people look up to men in professions like Reed's. Dentists, or any other kind of doctor, get almost more respect and admiration than a preacher. Prestige like that goes a long way in the black community. You ought to know that by now."

"Well, I'm here to tell you that being married to Reed is not a walk in the park. And now that I know he's capable of trying to hurt himself, I wonder about his mental state. How would you feel about having a psycho in the family?"

"Oh, pshaw! Please stop being so dramatic, girl!" She laughed, dismissing me with a wave of her hand. "Reed wasn't trying to kill himself. If he had really wanted to

die, with all he must know about medicines and shit, he
would have given himself some kind of lethal shot or
whatnot that would have done the trick in no time. Or, he
could have driven to Frisco and jumped off that Golden
Gate Bridge like a *practical* suicidal person would have
done. That man knew what he was doing. He was just trying to scare you. Why he felt he had to scare you, I
wouldn't know, unless you want to tell me. . . ."

"I'd rather not talk about that right now." I could tell
from the disappointed look on Mama's face that she
wanted to get more information from me so she could
blab to the rest of the family. But this was one time I was
not going to go there. There was already enough chaos
going on that didn't involve me. With stories such as the
elderly Asian man across the street who'd been arrested
last week for beating his wife, as well as the snooty West
Indian family who had moved into a house a few doors
down, my family had enough subject matters to keep the
gossip pot boiling for weeks. They didn't need to stir Reed
and me into the mix. I knew that they eventually would,
anyway, and I wanted to delay it for as long as I could.
"How was work today?" I asked. Mama claimed she hated
her job, but she was always eager to talk about it.

Her eyes lit up and she wiped her wet, salt-covered
lips with the back of her hand. I knew I had chosen the
right subject to steer her in another direction. I was sorry
I hadn't done so sooner.

"Baby, I'm so glad you asked me that." Mama rubbed
the back of her neck and grimaced. "I can't wait to retire
from that snake pit. I'm getting too old for the kind of shit
I have to put up with. I had to break up three fights
today." There was an exasperated look on her face as she
complained. "The black women can't get along with the
other black women. The Hispanic women can't get along
with the Asian women, and the white women can't get

along with anybody, not even us guards! I don't know what this world is coming to. I tell those bitches all the time, if they hate being locked up so bad, they should have thought about that before they broke the law!" Mama paused and caressed my cheek. "Joan, you don't look good to me." There was a concerned look on her face now. "Honey, Reed's going to be just fine. When he gets out of that hospital, I'm going to make him some chicken soup."

"Thanks. I'm sure he'll like that."

"Now sit here until that margarita wears off before you get back in your car. You know how I feel about drinking and driving. When you get home, I want you to read the Bible. You got a lot to be thankful for. Pray for Reed. Pray that you won't have no more turmoil in your marriage." Mama snorted and looked at me with a wan expression on her face. "By the way, how is Lola these days?"

"She's fine. I'm having lunch with her tomorrow."

"That's nice. I know she's your girl, but if she tries to talk you into leaving Reed, don't listen to her. He is the best you can do, and I know you know that! I'm glad I don't have to worry about you ending up in the arms of another man while you're still married, the way your sisters did."

Mama's last comment almost made me laugh. For a woman who'd married three different men, she was clueless when it came to love and marriage. I couldn't wait to end up in the arms of another man again!

Chapter 34

Lola

"YOU REMEMBER MARIEL? SHIRELLE'S NIECE?"

Joan and I had been talking for ten minutes, and so far, we had not mentioned Reed's suicide attempt. I had decided that I wouldn't be the one to bring it up. She'd already told me that he was doing okay, so that was all that really mattered. If she wanted to discuss it, I'd listen and hopefully not say anything that would make her feel any worse.

"Yeah, I remember her. She was nice for such a cute girl. You know I can't stand good-looking females who think their shit don't stink."

"You're not like that, Joan," I teased.

She gave me a menacing look and shot back, "You're not either. What about Mariel?" She bit a huge plug out of the ham-and-cheese sandwich she had ordered for lunch at the deli, where I ate lunch at least once a week. Cottright's had a sandwich-and-soup counter, which was where I usually got my meals while on the job. Even though my work agreement included free snacks up to fifteen dollars a day, I liked to get away from the grocery store from time to time. I had been looking forward to my lunch date with Joan.

"Can I have your pickle?" she asked.

One thing I could say about Joan was: No matter how big of a problem she had, it rarely interfered with her appetite. If my husband had just tried to kill himself, I'd probably be in a catatonic state. She was not a callous person, so I knew she was dealing with the situation in her own way. She appeared to be as upbeat and casual as usual. And I wanted to seem as normal myself, so Mariel was a neutral enough subject for us to discuss.

"She's married and so happy with her architect husband in Seattle," I replied as I plucked the dill pickle spear off my plate and dropped it onto Joan's.

"Well, do say," she sneered. "I thought I told you yesterday to tell me something good today."

"I thought I just did."

"With my marriage being such a wreck, I don't want to hear about some other married woman being 'so happy.'"

"Are you ready to talk about Reed some more?" I asked in the gentlest voice I could manage.

Joan dropped her head. When she looked up at me again, her big brown eyes were shiny with tears. "I don't know what to do about him. All I know is, I can't stay married to him and be happy."

"Then don't stay with him. When he gets out of the hospital, give him time to get his bearings back and then tell him you want out of the marriage."

"It's not that simple, Lola. I don't think I'll find him in time, the next time. I couldn't live with another suicide in my family." Ten years ago, Joan's favorite aunt had shot herself to death when she found out she had terminal cancer. Joan rarely mentioned it, but I knew it was always on her mind.

"Do you honestly think he'd attempt suicide again if you do leave?"

"I don't think he'll '*attempt* suicide' again. He'll succeed the next time."

I looked around the deli to make sure nobody we knew was close enough to hear our conversation. "Joan, no matter what happens, I'll support you."

"I know you will." She took a long drink from her Diet Pepsi. Then, to my surprise, she smiled. "How did a dull woman like Mariel land an architect?"

I was tempted to tell Joan that Mariel had asked how she had landed a dentist. "I guess she was in the right place at the right time." I continued without hesitation. "She met her husband online. Just like Shirelle!"

Joan's eyes got wide and her smile got even bigger. "They both married architects that they met on the Internet? Get out of here!"

I nodded. "Mariel and I are Facebook friends. I checked out some of the pictures she posted of herself, her sons, and her husband. The kids are real cute and the husband's not a bad-looking man. And he looks to be about our age."

Joan gave me a thoughtful look. Then she waved her hand and exhaled. I couldn't tell from her gestures what she was thinking or what she was going to say next. With a profound sigh, she asked, "Is Shirelle still married to the man she met online?" The way a grimace suddenly covered her face, it seemed as if she wanted, or expected, me to answer her question with a negative answer. I was glad I had more good news to report.

"Yes, she is. And according to Mariel, she couldn't be happier. She has a daughter now too.

"That's wonderful! I'm happy that Shirelle finally has

a husband of her own. She was 'the other woman' in her mens' lives too long."

"I guess the Internet works out for some women," I admitted. "I'm glad you're having so much fun fooling around with your cyber boos."

"My 'cyber boos,' now that's real cute." She snorted. "The way your love life is going, I'm surprised you haven't taken the plunge and landed you a few 'cyber boos.' There are tons of them up for grabs. Face it, honey. Internet romance is the future. It's going to replace almost every other thing we've been doing to meet new partners."

"I can't stop thinking about the ones it didn't work out for. I'm through with the bar scene. I'd like to meet my soul mate at church." I swallowed hard and gave Joan a tentative look.

She stared at me like I'd just said something ludicrous and after I'd thought about it for a few seconds, I realized I had.

"So you think that just because a man is in the Church, he's safe?"

"Maybe—"

"Remember the woman who used to play the piano at Second Baptist Church?"

"Of course I remember Norma Yates. What about her?"

"You forgot how she married the choir director and he stabbed her to death a year later when he caught her in bed with another man"

"Yeah, but—"

"What about the church secretary and the usher? He shot and killed her when she told him she wanted to marry another man."

"There are exceptions to every rule."

"Exactly. Men in the Church are no safer than men in a

crack house. You can sit here gnawing on that turkey sandwich like you know it all, but you don't."

"Yeah, but I think you should really work on your marriage and stop fooling around with your Internet Romeos."

"Now that's even cuter than 'cyber boo,'" Joan snickered.

I gave her a look so critical, it made her shudder. I knew she was going to do more than that when she heard what I said next. "Your wandering eye is going to get you in the biggest mess! I've known you most of my life and I'm just now finding out how shallow and superficial you really are—"

Joan twisted her mouth and frowned. "Lola, kiss my ass and go to hell," she snarled, attempting to rise. I grabbed her wrist; gripping it so hard, I could feel her pulse. "When you are ready to talk to me like a mature woman, call me. You're the *last* person who needs to be judging me!" In spite of what she'd just said, and with my fingers still around her wrist, she plopped back down into her seat and took another sip of her Pepsi.

"I didn't mean that the way it sounded!" I hollered. I removed my fingers from her wrist and patted the top of her hand. "I'm so sorry. You're no more shallow and superficial than I am, I guess." I could feel my face burning with shame. Had Joan called me "shallow" and "superficial" first, I would have been just as upset as she was.

"I'm glad to hear the pot apologize to the kettle," she said with a smirk.

I shrugged and tapped my fingers on top of the table for a few seconds as I looked around, still trying to make up for the stupid comment that had slipped out of my mouth. "From now on, I'll keep my opinions to myself," I said. "Especially when it comes to your sex life." It was then that I noticed the daily newspaper sticking out of Joan's purse. "Are there any sales or coupons today?" I asked, nodding toward the newspaper. She pulled it out of her purse and placed it faceup on the table between our plates.

"Why don't you take a look yourself," she suggested, pursing her lips.

"This is yesterday's paper," I said, glancing at the date.

"Look at what's on the front page first," Joan ordered with a reserved look on her face.

I silently read the lead story's headline: POLICE ARE BAFFLED BY MYSTERIOUS DISAPPEARANCE OF THREE LOCAL WOMEN.

"Well, say something," Joan prodded.

"This is so sad," I replied, feeling a pang of sadness as I read a few lines in the first paragraph. I stared at the faces of the three women who had disappeared within a twelve-month period of time. "This reporter seems to think these disappearances are related and the cops are still investigating. Whoever is responsible for these women missing must be one smart cookie—or three smart cookies, I should say. They've all probably done something crazy to women before, and if the cops don't stop them soon, they'll do it again." When I looked up, Joan was staring at me with the strangest look on her face. "What's wrong with you? Why are you gazing at me like that?"

"Lola, look at those women and tell me what you see. I noticed it when I read the paper yesterday."

"What's the matter with them?" I asked.

"Take a real good look at those three women and tell me what you see," she insisted.

I gazed at the pictures again. "They're all black, attractive, and in their thirties. So what?" I said with a shrug. I held the newspaper closer to my face and squinted. "One was a newly wedded secretary, one was a nurse—she must be the one from Seattle that Mariel mentioned to me—and the other one was a stripper." I let out a loud

breath and looked at Joan. "I'll bet the nurse and the secretary had mean men and those men are involved. Hmmm,"
I said as I scanned the lengthy article some more. "The
nurse's boyfriend even admits that he'd argued with her
the night before she disappeared, and the woman who
lives in the apartment across from hers says she had to
call the cops to break up one of their fights the day before. And the stripper? There's just no telling what happened to her, with all the creeps she must meet in her line
of work. Well, if you lay down with dogs, you're bound
to get fleas." I shivered and shook my head.

"Lola, those women look enough alike to be sisters."

I looked at the pictures *again*. It took me a few seconds to see all of the similarities. And it was true. The
women looked enough alike to be related. "You're right.
They do resemble one another. The article doesn't say
anything about them being related, though." I hunched
my shoulders and gave Joan a puzzled look. "Am I missing something here?"

"They are not related. They were random victims. Isn't
there something else about them? Look at those faces real
hard."

"They're all very pretty," I said.

"And . . . they all look like *you,* girl!"

"Me?" I blinked and looked at the pictures again. I
didn't know why I had not noticed it before. But all three
of the missing women did resemble me. I swallowed hard
and looked in Joan's eyes with my heart beating like a
drum. "So you think a maniac is going around killing
women who look like me?"

"What do you think?"

"I think it's just a coincidence."

"One missing woman who looks like you is a coincidence. To me, three sounds like some clever criminal's
MO. That's what I think."

I gave Joan a dismissive wave and said with a chuckle, "I think you need to stop watching so many crime TV shows."

"Well, maybe you're right. It's just a coincidence. But it just seems mighty peculiar to me."

"Girl, any and everything can be called 'peculiar' if you think about it," I insisted.

"Oh, well. I'm glad three women who look like me aren't missing."

We laughed. Joan folded the newspaper and slid it back into her purse and we finished our lunch.

Chapter 35

Lola

I WAS GLAD JOAN AND HER FAMILY HAD DECIDED TO KEEP Reed's suicide attempt a secret. Other than myself, Bertha was the only other person who knew about it. She found out when she overheard me talking on the kitchen telephone with Joan yesterday and she promised me she wouldn't tell anybody else.

Gossip was a powerful weapon and it could cause a lot of damage to a person's life. That was why I didn't run around town yip-yapping about Reed's suicide attempt.

Despite the fact that he was driving Joan up the wall, I didn't want anything bad to happen to him. I certainly didn't want him to take his own life or ruin his career. I had no idea how things worked in the medical profession when it came to a doctor doing something as stupid as trying to commit suicide. But I knew enough about human nature to believe that if Reed's patients found out about his suicide attempt, they wouldn't want such an unstable person to be drilling on their teeth or doing anything else that involved their health and well-being. I was glad that I had decided to stay with the dentist I'd been with all my life. I was not about to have Reed snap while he had a drill or a needle in my mouth. Joan felt the same way. She told me that the only thing she'd let him stick in her mouth now was his dick. She had made an appointment with a new dentist for her next routine teeth cleaning.

"I noticed Joan don't come around as often as she used to," Bertha commented during dinner a week after I'd had lunch with Joan. "I'll bet that husband of hers is jealous and controlling, huh? And since she is spoiled and likes to have her way, she won't take too much of his mess. She's from a family of thugs, so if he treats her bad enough, he won't have to commit suicide. Either she or one of her kinfolks will put him out of his misery."

"Reed just got out of the hospital. I hope he doesn't do anything that'll make somebody hurt him and send him back. But you're right, he is controlling and jealous."

"I'm not surprised. I heard from a reliable source that his daddy is like that. Reed makes her carry a beeper in her purse so he can keep up with her every time she leaves the house. Bad habits generally run in families." Bertha stopped talking long enough to bite into a fried chicken leg. After she had swallowed, she said all in one breath, "I just hope Reed does not do a repeat performance—and succeed. I don't have one decent black frock in my closet to wear to his funeral."

Ten minutes after I had put away the leftovers and washed the dishes, Bertha started yawning. It was only a few minutes past seven. Almost every night around eight, she would be in bed, snoring like a dragon. Sometimes she stayed up to watch a TV show with me or call up somebody to exchange gossip. An hour after I entered the living room and made myself comfortable on the couch, she waddled in and dropped down onto the love seat. She didn't want to watch *Jeopardy!* so she reached for the telephone on the end table and called Libby.

As usual, Libby was too busy to talk more than a couple of minutes to her mother. Bertha hung up and dialed another number. "Oh, Marshall can't come to the telephone right now? Well, tell him his mama called and to call me back when he can." It was impossible not to notice the hurt look on her face. With all of the emotional pain and stress Libby and Marshall had put her through, I was surprised she had not keeled over from a stroke by now. She had aged so much in the last few years. Her hair was completely white and she didn't attempt to hide it with wigs and hair dye, the way she used to. There were dark circles around her eyes and bags underneath them. Deep wrinkles stretched from one side of her face to the other. I was also surprised that she was still trying to win her children's love after all these years. That made me sad.

"I guess I'll go on to bed," Bertha said in a weary voice as she set the telephone back into its charger. "I had wanted to talk to the kids about us all doing something special for their upcoming birthday next month. . . ."

"We can do a real nice steak and lobster dinner with all the trimmings, including a bottle of champagne and invite them and their spouses over to celebrate," I suggested. "I'll get everything from work so it won't cost us much and I'll do most of the cooking myself." There was probably nothing I wanted to do less than host a birthday dinner for Libby and Marshall, but I was willing to do it because I knew how much it would lift Bertha's spirits. I hoped that I would never experience the kind of pain she had to live with every day.

Shaking her head, Bertha wobbled up from her seat.

"That's real nice of you, Lola. But since we tried to do the same thing for them last year and they only stayed long enough to fix a plate to take home, maybe that's not such a good idea this time." She gave me a tight smile. "You are such a sweet young woman. Thank you for asking. Lord knows what I would do without you. . . ."

"Thank you. I appreciate you saying that. Why don't I fix you some of that green tea you like so much?"

"Yes, please do so. That and a nice hot shower will do me a world of good. Wait about fifteen minutes before you bring the tea up, because I need to do my constitutional first. I've been blocked for two days, so I know I'll have to sit on the commode for a while. And if you don't mind, would you come up and read a few lines of Scripture to me before I go to sleep? My eyes don't focus as well as they used to at night. After you finish reading to me, we'll pray together for Reed."

"Okay," I mumbled. I cleared my throat to keep from groaning.

After I made the tea for Bertha and read a few pages of Scripture to her, I went to my room and turned on my computer. I deleted a penis enlargement ad and several other pieces of useless junk before I decided to turn off my computer and check my cell phone messages. Joan had left a frantic voice mail message an hour ago. She told me to return her call as soon as I heard her message, no matter how late it was.

When I didn't feel comfortable talking to Joan on her home phone, I dialed her cell phone number or sent her a text message. Last month during one of our landline conversations, Reed picked up the extension in the kitchen and eavesdropped for ten minutes. We knew he was on the line because we could hear him breathing. All he'd heard was our discussing a sale at Ross. Now when I called her, I usually tried her cell phone first. I couldn't dial that number fast enough this time.

"What's up?" I began as soon as she answered.

"I need you to cover for me tomorrow evening," she said quickly.

"Don't tell me you've arranged another hookup already!"

"If I don't get laid soon, my poor pussy is going to explode!"

"What about Reed? I thought things had improved between you two since his . . . uh . . . accident."

"Puh-leeze! His dick was so limp last night, I couldn't have turned him on with battery cables."

"Hmmm. Maybe all those pills he took messed up his sex drive."

"It was not much better before he took those pills."

"Joan, I know he's still kind of young, but have you considered Viagra?"

"Viagra?"

"Maybe you should get some and slip it into his coffee or something."

"No way. That's more trouble than I'm willing to go to."

I resumed my end of the conversation with caution. "Okay, now, Joan, don't you think you should slow down with that Internet dating thing?"

"Honey, I'm just getting warmed up. One afternoon last week, I spent two hours Googling. I came across a site that even you won't be able to ignore. It's way more classy and better organized than the others I've been dealing with. And it has a lot more variety of hookups to choose from. They even have a sex therapist available that you can call up and chat with on the radio so other members can listen to the conversation. I won't bother with that. I don't think I need to talk to a sex therapist—yet. And I don't want to share my business with an audience." Joan had not sounded this excited since her wedding day.

Even though I was still apprehensive about Internet romance, I was curious as to what this new site was. Especially if she thought it was something that even I couldn't ignore.

"What's the name of this site?" I asked.

"It's called Friends with Benefits: Discreet Encounters. They make it real easy to find a club member you like. You enter the gender, age, and ethnic preferences in the search box on the home page. You can narrow your search by plugging in other preferences like what the person is into. I was shocked when I saw how many people were into bondage, group sex, and other kinky shit."

"What about you? Those people sound kind of scary to me."

"I'm not interested in anything but some good old-fashioned sex and I made that clear when I did my profile. I was so intrigued, I took notes. Listen to this." Joan paused and I heard her shuffle some paper. "Okay . . . as of today, they have four thousand four hundred and one members. Five hundred and fifty-two members updated their profiles and pictures. And since last week, fifteen people have joined in the last three days, ten canceled their membership, and, most important of all, *twenty-five* members have viewed my profile since I became an official member two days ago! They have a weekly newsletter and a schedule of events for the members who want to take their hookups to the next level. Uh, like getting together in groups. But I'm not into orgies."

"I don't know what to say," I said with a gulp.

"I know what to say, I think I've hit the mother lode!" Joan was swooning, not even trying to hide the excitement in her voice. The more she talked, the more excited she sounded.

Her behavior was making me feel excited, but I was not about to tell her. "What's so great about this particular site? Aren't they all basically the same?"

"This one is *only* for people who want to have a casual encounter, nothing more. I did a lot of research and I found out that most of the members are either married or in committed relationships. And they are almost all professionals."

"So? What's so great about upscale booty calls? Sex is sex."

"Well, all men are not created equal when it comes to sex, if you know what I mean. The club members on this site get to the point real fast. The men I've communicated with so far are willing to pay to have a good time with an amazing woman like me." Joan laughed. Even though I was in my room, where she couldn't see me, I shook my head and rolled my eyes.

I could not believe what I was hearing! Joan and I had done a lot of stupid things over the years, but she had gone too far this time. "Woman, have you lost your mind? Do you know what you're getting into?"

"What?" she asked dumbly.

"When a man pays a woman to have sex, it's called prostitution!"

Chapter 36

Lola

"'Prostitution,' my ass! Quit putting words into my mouth!" Joan scolded. "There is no money involved!"

"You just told me the men *pay* to have a good time with you. A good time that involves sex."

"Let me lay it all out for you, because I don't think you're getting the picture. The men reserve a hotel room, they pay for a nice dinner, and sometimes you might get a nice little gift or something. It's no different than when I—or even you, for that matter—go out with a man. When that dude took you up to Reno for your birthday last year and spent a ton of money on you, and you screwed his brains out, were you prostituting yourself then?"

Just thinking about the two days I'd spent in Reno with a shoe salesman named Ricky Oliver sent a chill up my spine. He was only thirty-five, but for the hell of it, he'd started taking Viagra and had almost worn me out that weekend. We'd spent more time wallowing around in bed than in the casinos. When I'd complained about all the time we spent having sex, he reminded me how much money he was spending on me.

A few hours before we checked out of the lavish hotel suite in the Peppermill Resort, a hotel clerk delivered a receipt for our expenses while Ricky was in the shower. I was stunned when I saw that the two nights, all of our meals, our train tickets to and from Reno, and six hundred dollars in free slot play had all been comped! Ricky had not spent a *dime* of his money on me. I was furious. He had a temper, so I didn't want to confront him during the train ride home. But I had decided that I would never see him again.

When we got back to the Amtrak station in San Jose, where he had parked his car, he told me I had to pay for the parking and buy him enough gas to get back to his apartment in Oakland. When I refused and told him I'd seen the hotel receipt, he cussed me out and literally shoved me out of his car. I had to take a cab home. I never told Joan everything about that fiasco because she would have teased me for weeks.

"No, I—I wasn't prostituting myself when I spent that weekend in Reno with Ricky!" I sputtered, with my face burning. "All right. You've made your point. So, what you're telling me is that this new thing you're involved in is just sex with people you don't have feelings for?"

"And please pay more attention to what I'm saying and stop getting the wrong idea. I'm not looking for a soul mate!" Joan yelled. "And for the record, the *initiator* is responsible for the hotel."

"I'm sorry, but you've lost me," I said.

"Say you're a female club member traveling to an out-of-town location for business or other reasons. You see the profile of a man, *or of another woman,* in your destination that you want to hook up with. You contact that member. If he or she is interested, it's your responsibility to book a hotel. If dinner is included, and a show or some other activity, the dude would probably pay for that—and maybe even the hotel! You know how upscale men like to show off."

"If a woman pays for sex, it's still prostitution. What's your point?"

I could tell from the sharp sigh Joan huffed out that I was annoying the hell out of her. "Are you still not listening to me? This is all about sex—that's my point. Look, 'Miss Queen of the Friends with Benefits Club,' do you want me to remind you about all the times you got busy with a man you didn't have feelings for, just for a little fun? And unlike a few of my other dates on those other sites, who were really looking for love—which is the reason I searched until I found this one—*none* of the folks on this new one are looking for love."

"You can dress it up all you want, but I thought that meeting somebody to develop a relationship with was the whole point of these dating sites. Every time I turn on the TV, that eHarmony commercial comes on and the members are talking about how they just got married, blah, blah, blah. Even that ChristianMingle site, and that other one that's just for senior citizens. And I don't care what you say, the bottom line is *everybody* is looking for their soul mate—"

"Lola, I'm going to e-mail you the link to this amazing Web site. Unless you become a member, you'll only be able to see the home page and a few sample members' profiles, and some of the reviews that members post about their encounters with other members. You can't log in and connect with a member until you create an account. Just check it out. I know you must be horny as hell by now, so we don't have any time to lose. You haven't been with a man in over a month. I feel sorry for you."

"You don't have to feel sorry for me," I shot back. "I know lots of men. I could call up any one of them if I just wanted to have some quick sex."

"Sure you do. Busboys, chauffeurs, cooks, thugs. Most of the men on this site are doctors, lawyers, and businessmen. The dude I'm meeting tomorrow at the Hilton is a Harvard-educated medical technician at a New York clinic. He's here for a conference. He's happily married and not looking for anything more than a couple of hours—"

"How do you know he's telling the truth about what he says he is? He could be a cross-eyed cabdriver with a clubfoot, for all you know."

Joan let out a long groan and muttered a few cusswords under her breath. Her exasperation didn't faze me. She was the one who had brought up this subject. She started talking again, speaking in a slow, controlled manner as if I had suddenly turned into an idiot. And maybe I had. . . . "Unlike the sites I used to fool around with that would let the boogeyman and his brother be a member, this one does a thorough background check before they let you join. That's another reason you don't have time to lose. The background check, at least in my case, took four days to be completed. It keeps the crazies out."

"I see. What kind of background check would this glorified booty call club do on a person like you? You're just a housewife."

"Even a housewife can have a closet full of skeletons. But since you asked, they check to make sure a potential member doesn't have a criminal history and is not in the fugitive database. They even check to see if you have any outstanding warrants. This outfit is more thorough than the government."

"That's pretty thorough. But tell me this, why would some hotshot medical technician from the East Coast be interested in a housewife?"

"Because I'm what a lot of men are looking for! Wait until you see my profile. I've already received almost a *dozen* requests for dates. I'm not going to let this get out of hand like we did with those lonely hearts club old men. The main thing is, I will never ask one of these men for money or tell them a bunch of lies about how poor I am so they'd send money the way those old men did. I can't say it enough, all I want is some good company and some good sex. This club has so many members, with tons of new ones joining all the time, I can milk this cow for years! And if I'm going to be stuck with Reed, for God knows how long, I need a long-term backup plan."

"You've got a point there, I guess."

"I advise you to take a long, hard look at yourself, Lola. If you don't get the spirit, you're going to get left behind."

"I've been left behind before!" I cracked. "And I turned out all right. Another thing I want to know is, what would your family say if they knew what you were up to?"

"I'm glad you brought that up. I have the most broad-minded relatives in the world, but I think they'd draw the line about me being in a sex club. Some of them are probably doing shit way worse, and I don't want to know if they are. What I don't know about them can't hurt me, and what they don't know about me can't hurt them. The bottom line is, everybody is into something."

"Not me."

"Well, you should be. Maybe you wouldn't be so up-tight. Let's get back on the subject. The deal is, Jeremy, that's the guy I'm meeting tomorrow, he said that as soon as he saw the picture I posted of myself, he got an instant hard-on. I had on that red bikini I bought for the vacation in Mexico that Reed canceled on me at the last minute last year. And, like I said before, and I'll say it *again,* this is all about sex. Nothing more. Besides, this dude is white. He said he's always fantasized about sleeping with a black woman."

"Hmmm. Well, what if you hook up with some dude that can't screw worth a damn? Then what? What if this Jeremy's got . . . a . . . teeny . . . weenie."

"Honey, I think that's one problem I won't have to worry about. This white boy has had eight hookups so far this year. Each one gave him a five-out-of-five-stars review and comments that would make a porn star horny."

"Is he good-looking?"

"Try to imagine a cross between George Clooney and Brad Pitt. He's also on Facebook, so I'll send you his full name and you can check out his picture there. Maybe you can party with him on his next trip to California. One thing about the men in this club is they have the kind of money that if they want to send you a ticket to meet them somewhere, they can do it. I read one woman's review about a guy—a CEO for a software company—and she said that's what he did for their hookup. She lives in Baltimore. He lives in L.A. and had to go to Tokyo, Japan, for a bunch of meetings. He paid for her to meet him there."

"Can't those horny people find other horny people closer to home?"

"Didn't we have a similar discussion about those old men we used to write to?"

"Yeah, we did."

"When you have money, you can do whatever you

want and it doesn't have to be logical, or make sense. I'm sure that the average billionaire is not concerned about finding a woman in his own backyard when he gets horny. A woman who would travel a few thousand miles to be with him would be so grateful to get a free trip, she'd go out of her way to show him a good time."

"The more you tell me, the more this deal *still* sounds like prostitution. This new site you've joined is *selling* sex, point-blank."

"Lola, the new site I joined is *networking* sex, so I wish you would stay off the subject of prostitution. I know there's a thin line between somebody handing me a few bucks just for sex and somebody inviting me for a rendezvous just for sex. Both may sound like prostitution to you because somebody is paying for a room, and dinner, and whatnot. But they are not handing me money for having sex. They are spending money so we can have a nice place to fuck." Joan moaned for a few seconds. "This conversation is giving me a headache!"

"You're the one who brought it up," I reminded.

"All right," she said with a heavy sigh. "The thing is, if you want to get technical, every woman who goes on a date with a man—even her husband—and accepts dinner, gifts, or anything else, is a prostitute."

"Joan, I know what you're saying. I'm just . . . Well, I just don't want you to get into something you can't get out of."

"Honey, don't worry about me. Worry about yourself and all the money you spend on batteries for that vibrator you hide under your mattress. . . ."

I ignored Joan's last comment. I didn't want to know when she had snooped around in my bedroom and found my sex toy. That would have been more uncomfortable to discuss than the sex site. I cleared my throat and said in a mocking tone of voice, "For your information, I just might call up Vincent Lopshire this weekend. You remember the bartender I met last summer?"

"Please!" Joan croaked. "How could I forget *him*? While you're in his flabby arms, I'll be humping—"

"Woman, shut up!" I laughed. "If you're trying to make me jealous, you've done that. Call me at work tomorrow and tell me what I'm supposed to say in case Reed calls me while you going at it with your George Clooney/Brad Pitt honey."

Chapter 37

Joan

"*EEEEEEEEOWWW!*" MY HUSBAND SQUEALED, LIKE A stuck pig, as he climaxed. He remained on top of me another ten seconds before he abruptly rolled off and back to his side of the bed, breathing through his mouth. "Was it good for you, baby?" he asked in a raspy voice.

"Uh-huh. You're still the best," I lied. I reached for my see-through black negligee, which I had flung to the floor.

"Hey!" Reed stiffened. "Don't put that damn thing back on yet. I'm going to be up for seconds as soon as I recharge my, uh, *D* battery," he added with a chuckle as he slapped his limp dick on the side of my thigh. That was the last thing I wanted to hear out of my husband's mouth. "I may need a drink first, though!"

I needed a drink myself to get through another round with him. I stood up and got into my gown, anyway. "You know how chilly it is in the kitchen this time of night. What do you want to drink?"

"Fix me a rum and Coke." Reed gave me a hard look and shook his finger at me. "And, Joan, make sure you put it in a clean glass."

As soon as I made it to the kitchen, I sat down hard at the kitchen table and moaned. Intimacy with my husband had become so boring and unfulfilling, his touch made my skin crawl. *Two* minutes after Reed squeezed my right tittie, blew his foul breath on my face, scrambled on top of me, and slid his limp penis between my thighs, he was climaxing all over the place.

Ten minutes later, when I returned to our bedroom with two large glasses of rum and Coke, he was snoring. "So much for a second round," I said with a sigh and a silent "thank God."

I went into the living room with the drinks, clicked on a lamp, and eased down on the couch. I sat for several minutes, thinking and drinking. After I had emptied both glasses, I glanced around the room, admiring the blue velvet couch and matching love seat I had purchased last month. Then I glanced at the wall clock above the love seat. Even though it was after midnight and I had a buzz, I reached for my cell phone on the coffee table and punched in Lola's number.

"I hope I didn't wake you," I said when she answered on the fourth ring.

Lola and I had engaged in a lot of late-night telephone conversations lately. She didn't sound the least bit surprised or annoyed to hear my voice at such an ungodly hour. "I'm still awake. I was just lying here watching TV. What's up?"

"I . . . I just wanted to talk to somebody."

"Well, somebody's listening."

I heaved out a loud, sour breath before I spoke again. "Reed just gave me his midnight express special."

"Huh?"

"The last time I rode on his train, it took three minutes. Tonight it took two." Lola was the only person I'd share something so disgustingly pitiful and intimate with.

"Two minutes tonight? I guess that was an express. I rode on an express train once. His name was Earl."

Lola's attempt at humor didn't amuse me. She laughed; I didn't.

"So, are you still going to meet your online friend later today?"

"I sure am. Especially after the ordeal Reed just put me through. Did you check out that site? Did you see my profile? Did you take a look at the dude's picture on his page?"

"Yes, I checked out the site. I couldn't believe your profile and that sexy picture you posted! Girl, I am scared of you! If I didn't know you, and I were a dude, I'd be checking you out too."

This time I did laugh with Lola.

"And you're right. That guy you're going on your first date with is really handsome."

The silence that followed Lola's statement was frightening.

"Lola, are you still with me?"

"Yeah, I'm still with you. I was just thinking about all the sex crimes we read about in the newspaper almost every day. Are you worried about that?"

"To me, a 'sex crime' is not getting any. Let me tell you again. This site is for 'discreet encounters,' which means straight-up sex."

"But is it really safe? Do you believe it's just a networking site for horny, consenting adults and not a playground for sex offenders and other predators?"

I let out an impatient sigh and mumbled a few cuss-words under my breath. "If I didn't think it was safe, I wouldn't be involved with it. Did you read the reviews?"

"I did. I couldn't believe how giddy some of those folks sounded."

"Tell me about it."

"It was funny to see Wall Street men, who had all probably attended Harvard or Yale, using words like 'poontang' and 'nookie' in their reviews. The women were just as bad. One female *lawyer* described a man's penis as a 'tallywacker.' Now, how corny is that? I have never heard anybody use such hokey-sounding words, *period*. Not even those geezers we used to write to. Well, I have to admit, it sure sounds like the members of that club are having a ball."

"Tell me about that too." I chuckled.

"What if I wanted to join? What would I have to do, and how much does the membership cost?"

"The membership is free. I thought I told you that. This site, like a lot of other sites, makes its money from advertisers. All you have to do is create a profile and post a picture of yourself. You don't even have to use your real name or give out personal information, like your telephone number or address, on your introductory profile, which I'd advise you not to do, anyway. You only have to give that information to the site people so they can do the background check. Once you agree to a date with a man, then you tell him your real name and any other information you feel comfortable sharing."

Lola was so quiet during the next few moments; I knew she had all kinds of outlandish thoughts swirling around in her head.

"I could use a fake name, give a fake address, and tell those site people all kinds of lies. How would they know?

Background check or not, I could still be a maniac," she said in a mocking tone of voice.

I was sorry now that I had shared my secret with her so soon. "Look, if you're not going to take this seriously, let's forget about it. And in the first place, what I'm into is probably out of your league. Maybe you're not the type of woman who should get involved in something this sophisticated. . . ."

"Why not? I'm just as attractive and 'sophisticated' as you are, and I love sex as much as you do," she complained—just like I knew she would.

"You're also a scared little chicken. You probably wouldn't make it through the first date without having a meltdown." I didn't care how much Lola protested; I read her like a book, so I knew she'd eventually come around.

She proved me right when she replied in a tone of voice that had perked up within a matter of seconds. "You said that people always meet up in nice hotels, right? Not any of those off-the-freeway motels with a vibrating bed and a broken toilet? That was the kind of place the last man I dated took me to. If that wasn't bad enough, his credit card got declined, so I had to pay for the room!"

"Men with class and money don't go near places like that, and I can assure you that their credit cards don't get declined. I'm meeting Jeremy at the Hilton. I logged in again a couple of hours ago and saw I had more messages. A professional football player from Denver wants to get together with me in the Ritz-Carlton next week. I'll e-mail him back in a couple of days, so I won't look so anxious." Joan practically squealed.

"You're not wasting any time, are you?"

"Nope. I want to get while the getting is still good. Life is too short."

"You're just in your thirties, Joan. You've got plenty of time left."

"Yeah, right. I could get run over by a bus tomorrow. The bottom line is, I'm not getting any younger. Twenty years from now, it'll be a lot harder for me to attract men like the ones I attract now." I snorted. "Well, I'd better get some sleep. I'm going to need all of my strength for tomorrow." I chuckled again.

Lola took her time responding, and when she did, she said something that shocked me. "Joan, get some for me."

"Oh, I will do that and more. Since you are too scared to get some for yourself."

"I'm not scared. I'm just cautious."

I covered my mouth with my hand to keep from laughing again. From the way the harshness had gradually eased out of Lola's voice in the last few seconds, I could tell she was getting weak. "Uh-huh. You're beginning to get weak, aren't you? Well, when you get weak enough, you'll change your tune. In the meantime, you can sit around and wait for one of your exes to give you a booty call. I don't mind having enough fun for both of us. I'm used to it."

Chapter 38

Lola

I WENT TO BED RIGHT AFTER I ENDED MY CONVERSAtion with Joan, but I couldn't go to sleep. I couldn't stop thinking about everything we had discussed. For one thing, I *had* begun to weaken. Even with all of the negative media attention online dating had received in the last few years, now I was real curious about the new site Joan had discovered. I didn't want to find a husband online, the way Shirelle and Mariel had, but it was not something I wouldn't consider—*if* I ever decided to take the plunge and create a profile on a dating site.

Joan called me at work on my lunch hour the next day. She told me she had rented a car to drive the two and a half hours to San Francisco to meet her date. The minivan that Reed had purchased for her three years ago was being serviced, and he never let her or anybody else drive the second new Lexus he had purchased in four years.

Joan's instructions were that if Reed called me, I was

to tell him that she and I had had lunch, and as a favor to me, she'd driven to San Mateo to pick up some beauty products for a mutual friend. The "mutual friend" was Liza Mae Ford, the same wheelchair-bound woman I had created to fool Bertha. We were getting a lot of mileage out of this fictitious woman. I still used her as a cover to dodge Bertha, who was impressed with me for being so devoted to Liza Mae. One night Bertha told me that I should let her know if I ever needed *her* to help out with the "poor little thing."

Being devoted to other people was one thing I had gotten used to. I had had a lot of practice with Bertha, and Joan, too, for that matter. Because I was still trying to make up for scamming my elderly pen pals, I felt obligated to be nice to my elderly employers, Maisie and Samuel Cottright. I was determined not to ever let them down. But they were so good to me that I would have been just as devoted to them, anyway. Not only did they encourage me to take home complimentary bags of groceries almost every day, they told me regularly how much they depended on me. Their only son, Marvin, was in San Quentin doing life without parole for killing his ex-wife on the day she was to marry another man. Their grandson and nephews and nieces, who often took turns working one of the other cash registers, rarely showed up on time; and when they did, they spent most of their shift goofing off or hiding out in the storeroom to use their cell phones. Cynthia, their niece who had graduated with me, rang up customers' groceries and texted at the same time. After so many customers complained to the Cottrights about how she had overcharged them for something, or didn't give them the attention they expected because she was too busy texting, they suspended her for two weeks. I didn't care for Cynthia; she was as flaky as they came. But the rest of the Cottright family members were not much better. Whenever I was alone in the store with one of them, they took advantage of the situation excessively with extended lunches, personal telephone calls, and so on, since they all knew they could depend on me. Because I spent so much time manning the store by myself, a few customers thought I was the new owner.

I rarely complained to the Cottrights because I had a good thing going. I had a dream job that I could walk to and from and take off when I needed to (as long as I had somebody to cover for me). It didn't pay that much, but I was still making out like a bandit. In addition to the complimentary groceries, free lunches, and other perks, I had been voted employee of the month twice in the last six months and each time it had included a two-hundred-dollar bonus.

"I hope you don't let that job go to your head," Bertha told me the last time I was employee of the month. "And don't let the Cottright family take advantage of you too often. You spend enough time and energy helping out that Liza Mae. And you have *other* obligations to attend to. . . ."

Bertha was probably never going to let me forget about my "obligation" to her. In a twisted way, I was glad Daddy was no longer around. Had he not died, he would have been the one under her thumb.

I still resented the fact that because of her, I had not seriously pursued another relationship with a man that might have led to marriage. After the mess with Maurice, I promised myself that when the next potential husband came along, nothing was going to stop me from accepting his proposal—if I felt he was the right one. I regretted the way I had given up so easily on him, until I heard that he had been dishonorably discharged from the service for using drugs. I'd also heard that he'd recently married a woman from the Silicon Valley, whom he controlled and beat. If that wasn't bad enough, he was also a serial cheater.

According to the rumors, he had a mistress, who was pregnant with his baby! Ironically, Bertha's interference may have saved me from being in Maurice's wife's shoes.

Half an hour after my conversation with Joan at noon, Reed called me on my cell phone from his office. I happened to be in the employee restroom, sitting on the commode, but I answered his call right away.

"I thought you were having lunch with Joan," he started, speaking in that annoying whiny voice I had come to hate. "She's not answering her cell phone."

"We did have lunch, but she couldn't stay the whole hour," I said evenly.

"So she should be on her way back home, huh?"

"That was her original plan. But one of our friends called while we were eating lunch. You remember Liza Mae Ford, don't you?"

"The woman who is confined to a wheelchair? Joan keeps putting off introducing her to me, when she knows I like to be familiar with all of her close friends."

"Uh, well, yeah. Anyway, Liza Mae asked Joan to pick up some beauty products for her from this beauty consultant in San Mateo and bring them to her."

Reed remained quiet for a few moments. "I'm surprised that a woman who can't even walk still cares about beauty products."

"Well, this one does. Two months before that drunk driver hit her and paralyzed her for life, she won a beauty contest. She still likes to wear makeup and stuff. . . ."

"I see. Well, if you hear from Joan before I do, tell her to call me as soon as possible. I'd like to take her to dinner tonight. She's been kind of down in the dumps lately and I'd like to try and cheer her up." Reed paused and I heard him suck in some air. "I'm sure she's told you, but things are really working out well for us. As a matter of fact, I'm planning to ask her over dinner tonight if she's ready to have another child. I wish we had started working on it years ago so they'd be closer to Junior's age. I want at least two more, and I'm going to make it clear to Joan that I want them to be only two or three years apart."

I had to hold my breath to keep from gasping. "Hmmm. That's nice to hear, Reed. Joan always said she wanted at least two or three children." I couldn't wait to talk to Joan again.

About three and a half hours after my conversation with Reed, I glanced at my watch. I had only a few minutes to go before I clocked out for the day.

"Lola, can you stay a little longer?" Mrs. Cottright asked with a pleading expression on her chipmunk-looking face as she finished ringing up a customer. She had been working the other cash register all day. "Tyrone just called and said he's stuck in traffic. I knew I was going to have a problem with that oafish grandson of mine getting here from Oakland on time every day." I hated working on the days when twenty-year-old Tyrone was supposed to come in. He was almost always twenty to thirty minutes late.

From the sweat on Mrs. Cottright's face and the way her gnarled hands were shaking, I could see that she was pretty well-frazzled. I didn't want to add to her distress, so I answered eagerly and without hesitation. "Yes, ma'am. I'd be glad to stay."

"God bless you, Lola," she said. Her cloudy black eyes lit up and a crooked smile appeared on her thin lips. She patted the side of her frizzy gray wig and smiled even harder. "I told that man of mine that we can always count on you. Before you leave, grab a few packages of them smoked turkey necks to take home and tell Bertha I said 'hello.'"

I didn't care how much longer I had to work on this particular day, I had no place to go except home, anyway. And I had something important on my mind: I was worried about Joan. She had promised to call me as soon as she ended her date, which should have been a couple of hours ago. She wasn't answering her cell phone or her home phone.

Tyrone finally showed up around six P.M. I gathered my purse and Windbreaker and ran over to the meat counter. I plucked out two packages of turkey necks, then scurried to the time card area and punched out.

As soon as I got outside and started walking toward home, I dialed Joan's home phone number from my cell phone again. I was surprised and happy when she picked up on the first ring.

"Where the hell have you been?" I hollered. "I was worried sick!"

"I was in heaven," she cooed.

"This is not funny! What time did you leave that hotel?"

"Oh, I left when I said I would. We didn't even need the whole two hours." She began to talk in a low, sultry voice that I only heard her use when she was flirting with a hot dude. "Jeremy was wonderful."

"Forget about Jeremy. Have you talked to your husband? He called and I told him that story about you going to pick up some beauty products for Liza Mae."

"Pffft! Don't worry about him. On my way home, I stopped off at his office. I waited until he finished performing a root canal on his last patient for the day. Then I lured him into the copy room, locked the door, leaned him up against the Xerox machine, and unzipped his pants. By the time I got through whipping some hot pussy on him, he was purring like a kitten." Joan snickered. "Men are such fools when it comes to a piece of tail." She snickered again. "I hate to rush, but I have to get ready for the dinner he's taking me to tonight. You remember that pasta place downtown with the hot Italian waiter named Carlo?"

I purposely ignored Joan's last question. The last thing I wanted to talk about was that "hot Italian waiter named Carlo."

"Shut up and listen to me, with your slutty self. Reed told me he's ready to have another baby."

She guffawed. "Humph! It won't be with me!"

"I know it's none of my business, and I know you're going to do whatever you want, but he sounds like he's really trying to make the marriage work. Do you really think this dating site is something you ought to be involved with right now?"

"I'm seeing Jeremy again when he comes back out here next year. And next week I have a date with that football player I told you about. Does that answer your question?"

Chapter 39

Joan

*I*T HAD ALREADY BEEN A YEAR AND A HALF SINCE MY FIRST date with a fellow Discreet Encounters club member. Since then, I'd been with more than two dozen others, and I had had some unforgettable dates.

One Thursday afternoon last month, I hooked up with a forty-five-year-old oil executive from Dallas named Edgar Strickland. Just like his screen name—"Big-Nasty"—he was big and nasty. But he had a problem getting and keeping an erection. After fumbling around for over an hour, he asked me to give him a hand job. I eagerly agreed to that, but it only made the situation worse. I rubbed his penis so long that by the time he got hard, he was also sore. I was stunned when he started *crying*. It was a sight to see this big strapping multimillionaire—who ran a big company and supervised dozens of people—naked and crying like a baby. I wondered if he cried in front of his employees and business associates when he had work-related problems.

"I am so sorry," I said as I rushed to get dressed.

"Not as sorry as I am," he sobbed. "I've never had a problem like this. I . . . I think I drank too much!"

I left him sitting on the bed, crying and pleading with me to stay. I felt sorry for the man, but the date was over for me.

I was glad Reed was still at work when I dashed into the condo, took a quick shower, and fixed myself a strong drink. An hour later, BigNasty sent me a text: **Can you come back ASAP? I've solved my problem.**

I texted back right away: **Not today. Let me know when you'll be back in town.**

My next unforgettable date was two weeks ago with Rabin Mahanta, a charming man in his late thirties from Bombay, India, who owned a chain of high-end restaurants there. His screen name was "Rockin'Rabin." He had come to the States with his wife to spend two weeks celebrating their tenth wedding anniversary in San Francisco, where he had booked a suite for them at the Four Seasons.

On the third day of their visit, after sightseeing and riding the cable cars for several hours, he tucked his wife away in their hotel suite and told her to stay put so he could go out and do some networking with some local restaurant owners. After his last meeting, he hired a car service to transport him to the Hyatt in San Jose, where he had reserved a suite so he could do some "networking" with me too.

Within minutes after I showed up, he started bragging about his beautiful wife and their amazing three sons, and his mistress and their amazing two sons.

Rabin was very religious. He could not stop talking about how "blessed" he felt to know that a beautiful woman like me wanted to have sex with him. He was an intelligent, witty, very likeable man; and he was good-looking, with his jet-black hair, hazel eyes, and bronze-toned skin. But he was a *midget*. The top of his head barely touched the bottom of my waist.

Rabin had not listed his height in his profile and his picture was a head shot. After we had chatted for about half an hour, he glanced at his watch and jumped up off the bed, where we'd been sitting, sipping wine, and looking at snapshots he carried in his wallet of his family.

"We must hurry! My driver has to get me back to San Francisco in time to take my wife to dinner!" he hollered as he removed his hideous touristy flowered shirt and khakis.

I gasped when I saw his nude body. It didn't bother me that he was plump, ashy, and hairy, but his penis looked like a big toe. Except on my son when he was an infant, I'd never seen such a tiny penis on a human being. I was devastated because I knew I was not going to have much fun on this date. But what he said next relieved me. "You will only masturbate me, and I will only give you oral sex. And I shall do you first. Lie on bed and spread your legs."

I agreed to that; but once his head ducked between my thighs, I regretted it. He was very good with his tongue—so good that I got carried away and clamped my legs around his little body to hold him in place. I didn't realize he was in trouble until he started moaning, writhing, and slapping my thighs. I had almost smothered the man!

As soon as I released him, he rolled off the bed, gasping for air. I was mortified and immediately started apologizing as I helped him up off the floor. But he took the whole incident in stride.

"Don't worry. God is good. I still had a blessed time. You must go now," he told me with a dismissive wave.

Since he was so anxious for me to leave, I didn't hang around to take a shower. Five minutes after I'd put my clothes back on, he hugged me, puckered his thick lips, and kissed me.

When I got back to my car in the hotel parking lot, I sat there for a few minutes, thinking about what had just happened. I almost fainted when I realized I could have been responsible for Rabin being hauled out of the hotel in a body bag. From that day on, I asked my dates their height.

The date with Rabin had been such a disaster, I was anxious to hook up with somebody else as soon as possible. There were several messages in my club in-box, so I didn't have any trouble lining up another quick date.

I spent several hours with a young computer executive from Hong Kong named Mr. Ting. He had come to the States to meet with a bunch of those Silicon Valley geeks to discuss new software. And he'd eagerly admitted to me, "To get some African-American pussy for the first time."

It was a first for us both, because I had never been with a Chinese man. I had the time of my life. Not only was I getting laid properly and frequently these days, I was being exposed to different cultures and lifestyles. I replayed part of my conversation with Mr. Ting in my head for the rest of the week.

"Joan, you are the most exciting woman I have ever known," he'd told me in his heavy Chinese accent as I lay in his arms. We'd spent the afternoon in his swank hotel room at the San Jose Marriott on Market Street. He had just told me some charming stories about his childhood.

He had grown up in a mansion with nineteen siblings and his wealthy father, who had three wives. "You make a velly good mistress." Before I could respond, Mr. Ting leaned over and kissed me on the lips. "If only you lived croser to me, I'd be a velly happy man. I never *clum* so good and hard in my life before today. I make you clum too?"

"Uh-huh, you sure did make me . . . clum," I replied, hoping he didn't think I was making fun of his accent by pronouncing "cum" the same way he had.

I still had a couple more hours of free time. (I had told Reed and everybody else I was going to drive to Sonoma with an old school friend to visit our favorite winery.) So Mr. Ting and I decided to watch an adult movie on the huge TV facing the king-size bed. Ten minutes into the movie, he got excited again and climbed back on top of me. Had he not been so sweet and nice, and a great lover, I would have declined the second session. After our tryst, he invited me to have dinner with him, but I declined that.

One thing I didn't want to do was spend too much time with the same man. Some of the men I'd been with had gotten attached to me very quickly. That flattered and frightened me. But each time that happened, I recalled a few lines and scenes from the movie *Fatal Attraction* and Lola's paranoid ramblings about online sex fiends and serial killers. That was enough for me to decline offers to stay a little longer on a particular date, or to "keep in touch," the way some of the men suggested.

I had not set any solid ground rules yet, so there was a possibility that if things continued to go well, I'd see more of the same men more than once—I'd already done so with a couple. Until then, I planned to play it safe and rub all the fun I was having in Lola's face.

* * *

"I wish you would stop bragging about the fantastic time you had the other day with Hop Sing, or whatever his name was," Lola complained, rolling her eyes and moving her head like a bobble head figurine.

I had been talking about Mr. Ting for ten minutes straight over drinks at the Green Rose, one of our favorite bars. "Be nice now. His name was Wei Li Ting and he was one of the best lovers I've ever had." I gulped half of my second glass of wine. "Pssst," I said, leaning forward. "Ask me how long his tongue was?"

Lola gave me a mock look of disgust. "How long?"

"Long enough to make any woman very happy. The way he licked and slurped—"

"Enough already," she hollered, holding up her hand in front of my face. "I get the picture."

I spent the next five minutes talking about a couple of other dates. But by the time I got around to Nigel Bascomb, a gorgeous Nigerian banker who lived in London, who had come to San Jose to attend his godson's wedding, Lola was drooling like a hungry baby.

"He had me screaming louder than I screamed when I was in labor!"

"Shhh!" Lola said, with a finger up to her lips. "You don't have to get that explicit."

"Then I guess you don't want to hear about his tongue skills either, huh?"

She blinked and bit her bottom lip. "Well, since we're in that territory already, anyhow, how was he in that department?"

"Honey, some men can't even lick a lollipop or a stamp properly. But that man could lick like an anteater."

Lola laughed. Then she gave me a peculiar look. She glanced around, then back at me. "Guess what? I joined Discreet Encounters."

My breath caught in my throat and my jaw dropped. "*You?* When?"

"Last week."

"'*Last week'?* Bitch, how come you're just now telling me?"

"I didn't want to say anything until they'd done the background check on me, in case they didn't let me join."

"Yeah, right. There's nothing in your background that would keep a sex club from not letting you become a member."

"With all those doctors and lawyers, and other high-end men in the club, I was afraid they'd think nobody would be interested in going to bed with a grocery store cashier."

"If those same men are interested in an ordinary *housewife* like me, they'll be interested in a cashier. Especially a hottie like you. I keep telling you this is all about sex. As long as you're not doing something illegal, this club doesn't care what you do for a living. A lot of the members are waiters, valets, fry-cooks, cabdrivers and what-not. Day before yesterday, I heard from a high school janitor—an unemployed one at that. Men like that can't afford to show women a good time in a fancy hotel and treat them to a gourmet meal and fine wine. Unless you want to fool around with one in a Motel 6 who'll buy you a Big Mac and a soda, I advise you to ignore them like I do. I received a request last night from a gorgeous part-time school bus driver in Ohio. He's coming out here for his vacation in a few weeks."

"Well, are you going to see this georgeous school bus driver? If he can afford to come to California from Ohio for his vacation, he can't be too broke."

"Puh-leeze! I stopped reading his message and deleted it as soon as I got to the part about him being a part-time school bus driver. He probably had to borrow or save his money for years just for his vacation. Stick to the men with money, honey."

"Anyway, as soon as I got the green light, I created my password and a club user's screen name, 'BrownSugar.' Then I posted my profile with a picture of me in that white string bikini I wore when we went to Stinson Beach last summer. Within an hour, eight men had logged in and contacted me."

"BrownSugar? Couldn't you come up with something more original?"

"You can't talk! Do you think yours, 'HotChocolate,' is more original?"

Joan laughed. "I'm just kidding. It's cute and it's an appropriate screen name for you. Last night I chatted with a man whose screen name is 'TrickyDick.' And the night before, I received an e-mail from 'LongJohn.' I'm going to check the reviews on those two. If their screen names mean what I think, I'm going to have to line up a date with each one."

"What's Mr. Ting's screen name?"

"You won't believe it!" I threw my head back and snickered long and loud. I had tears in my eyes when I looked back to Lola. "Remember that old song 'Wild Thing' that they still play on the old-school radio stations?" I asked, wiping my eyes with my cocktail napkin.

"The only 'Wild Thing' song I remember was the one by Tone Loc. Daddy had it on a cassette tape and used to play it so much I'd hear it in my sleep."

"Mr. Ting dropped the *h* and calls himself 'Wild-Ting.'" I laughed again and couldn't understand why Lola wasn't laughing too.

"You think that's funny?" she asked, giving me a pensive look.

"Well, it may not be funny, but it sure is appropriate."

She took another sip of her wine and looked directly

into my eyes. "Joan, I hope this works out for me. I'm sick of you having all the fun."

"It'll work out for you. Just be patient and let things fall into place. Have you lined up a date yet?"

"Not yet. If I'm really going to get into this thing, I'm going to do it right. I am not going to rush, because I don't want any of those men to think I'm desperate."

I took another sip from my wineglass. After a mild belch, I continued. "You know, you never cease to amaze me. Do you think any of these men care if you're desperate or not? They all want the same thing we want. Chances are, you won't see any of the same ones more than once or twice, anyway. Did you at least respond to any of them yet?"

"Just a few." Lola suddenly looked so serious, it scared me.

"What's wrong?"

"Girl, one of the dudes I responded to is *so* good-looking. He's been on my mind ever since he sent me a message three days ago."

"What race is he, and where does he live?"

"He's a brother, and he lives in San Jose."

"Hmmm. Just a word of warning, you might want to avoid the ones who live too close. San Jose is almost within walking distance. All of mine are from other states and other countries. I think it's safer if there's some distance between the dudes and us."

"'Safe'? I thought you told me these men get checked out by the site people before they let them join. If that's true, why are you worried about them being safe? And distance doesn't mean a damn thing! What about that woman who came looking for you to beat you up for fooling around with her husband when we were in that old folks' lonely hearts club?"

There were times when having a conversation with

Lola made me want to scream. She could be so exasperating! "Are you ever going to let me forget about that episode? For God's sake, we were *seventeen*!"

"Well, in some cultures, seventeen is practically middle age." We both laughed. Lola continued talking. "The point is, distance didn't keep that man's wife from coming after you. So . . . what if I do get involved with a man who lives so close to me?"

"You can get involved with the man from next door, as far as I'm concerned. I personally will not date men who live within a thousand miles of me." I shook my head and gave Lola a guarded look. "But whatever you do is your business. Oh, well," I said with a smirk and a shrug. "So, what does this San Jose dude do for a living?"

"He's a long-haul truck driver. He drives one of those huge eighteen-wheelers we hate to be in front of on the freeway. He hauls lumber, merchandise, and all kinds of stuff from Washington and Oregon to various cities in California, mostly around San Diego and beyond. He spends a lot of time on the road. He's one of the most interesting men I've ever communicated with."

"Dude must have really impressed you. You haven't been this giddy in years." I stared at Lola for a few seconds. "You've already spoken to him?"

"No, we've only communicated by e-mail a few times, and once on Facebook. Not only is he fine as wine, he's a war hero. He was stationed in Afghanistan and saved a couple of men's lives."

"Hmmm. That is interesting. But a *truck driver*?"

"Why should I care about what the man does for a living, as long as it's not something illegal? For your information, I Googled around and found out that truck drivers make a hell of a lot of money. And he likes to eat out, watch old black-and-white movies, and do a lot of other things I like. He even likes kids."

"A regular TV sitcom kind of guy, huh?"

"What's that supposed to mean? You're the one who is all hung up on the men on this site being professional and whatnot."

"Let me remind you, this is not eHarmony or any of those other sites for women who are looking for a serious relationship with Mr. Right. This is a straight-up fuck site, and *fucked* is all you're going to get."

"I know what kind of site it is. But I'd still be more interested in spending time with a man I have a few things in common with. I mean, I'd like to converse with the dude, before and after the . . . uh . . . session."

"When are you going to see him?"

Lola hunched her shoulders. "I have no idea. It'll be a while before he's even available. He told me that he has some back-to-back hauls and wouldn't be back in the area for more than a couple of days at a time for another couple of months. He just wanted to introduce himself for now."

"Well, at least you've made it this far. I promise you, you're going to have some experiences you will never forget."

Lola reared back in her seat and looked at me as if I'd just revealed the secrets of the world. "That's exactly what Calvin told me!"

"Calvin?"

"That's his name. Calvin Ramsey and his screen name is 'RamRod.' He's thirty-three, divorced, and has no kids. Check out his profile and his picture. Nice firm body, a fantastic smile with snow-white teeth, and piercing black eyes."

"Calvin Ramsey, aka RamRod—ooh, that sounds sexy. I'll bet he can 'ram' into a woman like nobody's business." I got so turned on I had to cross my legs to make my crotch stop twitching. "You'd better know I'm going to check out his profile. I wonder why a man like him is not married now. So far, all of the men on this site I've heard from are married."

"I didn't ask him why he's no longer married, but he included that information in one of his e-mails, anyway. He said his ex-wife got involved with another man while he was in the Middle East. She wasted no time divorcing him after he got discharged and returned to the States."

A sad feeling came over me. I felt sorry for a man I'd never met, and probably never would. I couldn't think of too many things more disgusting than a woman cheating on her husband while he was risking his life in that damn war in Afghanistan. Even I wouldn't have stooped that low!

"I'm surprised he's still interested in women after all that."

"Calvin said it took him a while to get over it. He's only been dating casually since. He says he'd love to get married again eventually. In the meantime, he's more interested in just having some fun."

"You can tell him for me that he's come to the right place." I winked at Lola and beckoned for the waiter to bring another round of drinks. "And if you don't mind, I just might check him out myself after you're done with him."

Chapter 40

Calvin

*A*S A TRUCK DRIVER, I DIDN'T MIND GETTING MY HANDS soiled. When I went out on the road, I always carried my own soap because that crap in truck stop restrooms didn't do the job the way I liked it. I didn't mind washing my hands several times a day and scraping the greasy dirt and other grime from underneath my fingernails, but I did mind when it included blood. Blood on my hands, or any other part of my body, annoyed me—especially when it was somebody else's blood.

The last hitchhiker who had been stupid enough to accept a ride from me had left so much blood, it had taken me a whole hour and two bottles of bleach to restore the cab of my big rig to the pristine condition I kept it in. She had been too much trouble, period. That husky, corn-fed heifer from Montana had put up a hell of a fight before I got her under control. I couldn't remember the last time I'd had to use my fists, the pocketknife I'd won during a

Boy Scout event more than twenty years ago, and a rope to get someone under control. Hitchhikers and women in bars had become too risky. I realized that if I wanted to continue my mission, I had to change my method of hunting. Being a smart dude, I picked one where horny women were screaming for trouble: the Internet.

I never thought I'd resort to the Internet to find potential victims and some casual sex. There was a lot of both up for grabs. One night last month, I spent three hours browsing various dating sites. I had no interest in the namby-pamby Christian-related sites, even though I was in the Church myself. But a woman with a Christian background was usually too conservative and had too many meddlesome associates. I didn't want to spend weeks, if not months, wooing a bitch just to figure out a way for her to become one of my projects. By the time I would get a piece of ass—if I did—I'd probably be so frustrated by then, I'd get careless and get caught. I'd maybe even end up on death row!

Just as I was about to give up for the night and browse some more in a day or so, I stumbled upon a site that sounded like a predator's playground, compared to some of the others. The club's corny name drew me in like a Venus flytrap, Friends With Benefits: Discreet Encounters. Below the name, in smaller bold italic letters, was *No Attachments, No Commitments*. I was impressed because this site did not beat around the bush. They got right to the point on the home page.

I checked out the site's history, read some of the sample reviews posted by club members, and the bios and vision of the husband-and-wife team located in Memphis, Tennessee, who had created this fuckfest. I was thrilled to learn that there were people outside of the porn industry who were not shy about expressing their sexuality. I wanted to know more, but I'd read everything that a nonmember had access to. I'd already made up my mind. I immediately completed the online application for membership and gave them permission to do a background check on me. My record was flawless, so I wasn't worried about them denying me membership.

While I awaited a response, I checked out craigslist and a few other sites. The first woman I contacted was pregnant. She was looking for a man to pose as her fiancé just long enough to fool her rich parents so she could collect part of the fortune her grandfather left behind when he died a couple of months ago. She offered me five hundred bucks to do so. I declined her offer.

Another woman had the nerve to tell me she'd only sleep with me if her husband could watch. "We might even make a tape of it," she'd told me. I was not interested in participating in a peep show and having it put on a tape.

I eagerly hooked up with the third woman, who was interested in me. During one of my runs from Sacramento to Long Beach, we met up at a Best Western hotel she managed in Modesto. She had ordinary features and was a little on the heavy side, but she was a spark plug in bed. We had some great sex that night. I enjoyed her company and body so much, I even let her ride down to Long Beach when I resumed my run. I stopped counting the number of times we stopped along the way, to and from, to get busy in the cab of my rig.

After her, I spent a night with a thirty-year-old lesbian, who had never had sex with a man. She had finally decided to see what it felt like. She had been disappointed and so had I. "From now on, I'm sticking to females!" she had angrily told me. "So am I!" I'd shot back.

I was glad when I received a "Welcome Aboard" e-mail the following week from the Discreet Encounter site masters and the club's short list of rules and regulations. What a joke that list was! Explicit photos were not acceptable, nor were reviews that included obscene language, and a member was not allowed to reveal another member's real name or any other personal information. I chose a screen name that I thought was as clever as some of the others: RamRod. When I saw that another dude used "HotRod" as his screen name, I almost changed mine, but decided not to. RamRod fit Calvin Ramsey to a tee.

I checked out about a dozen of the other male club members. It was always good to know what the competition looked like. I was surprised to see so many handsome dudes. The only fly in the ointment was the picture of a good-looking brother whose screen name was "FingerLickin'Good." He was in raggedy jeans and a dingy-looking T-shirt. That was tacky enough. But what got my goat was the *do-rag* wrapped around his head and the smirk on his face! I thought I was looking at a mug shot! Dude was in his late thirties and old enough to know better. What sophisticated woman—which was the way the site described all of the female members—would want to hook up with a man who looked like a damn thug? So what if he claimed to be a restaurant manager. It was probably a rib joint in the hood that also served fried chicken wings and catfish sandwiches. I was pleased to see that the rest of the other black men were well-groomed and dapper. My picture would fit in nicely among that batch. The only concern I had was my profession. The other males I'd checked out were professional athletes, doctors, lawyers, accountants, bankers, a few actors I'd never heard of, and so on. Oh, well, if the women ignored me because I was a truck driver, I'd move on to another site.

I got giddy when I checked out some of the females.

Two claimed to be models, one was the lead singer in a band I'd never heard of, two were stockbrokers, and one said she was an actress who had once appeared on one of the daytime TV soaps. I was very impressed. I decided that until I found my next victim, I planned to enjoy myself as much as I could.

Chapter 41

Calvin

AS STUPID AS THE COPS WERE, I KNEW I DIDN'T HAVE TO worry about them. Black women disappeared all the time. But when three from the same area, who also happened to resemble one another, disappeared within the same year, a busybody reporter started making a lot of noise about it.

The day the article appeared in the *South Bay City Tribune* newspaper, I happened to be entertaining Sylvia Bruce, a woman I had chosen to use as a cover. She was a pharmacist in a downtown drugstore and five years older than me, but she didn't look it. I'd met her one Saturday afternoon three months after I'd murdered my wife. I'd gone to get a prescription filled for a minor eye infection I'd contracted.

Sylvia had been alone behind the counter that day and she'd been very friendly, so we'd chatted about a few mundane things. She'd been the one to suggest continuing our conversation over dinner. We'd been a couple ever since. She was perfect for a man in my position. She was gullible, docile, and always willing to please me. Although she was a little too thin for my tastes, she had a cute Cabbage Patch doll face and thick, medium-length brown hair, which she always wore in a conservative do. She worshipped the ground I walked on, and I played my role as the perfect boyfriend to the hilt. I gave her flowers and candy on a regular basis. I took her to boring plays and concerts—both of which I could take or leave. She knew I was not a big reader, except for the newspaper and a few crime publications, but she frequently recommended reading material to me. To show her that I was receptive, I even read some of the books she liked: crap such as romance novels, mysteries, and celebrity bios written by people who had the nerve to call themselves "authors," when they were nothing more than "creative typists," with savvy publishers.

Sylvia had so many good qualities. In addition to being an adequate piece of tail, she was always well-groomed. I couldn't count the number of times somebody said something to me like, "Man, you and Sylvia make such a good-looking couple—and both of you in the Church makes your relationship a double blessing." Whenever I heard comments like that, I always grinned sheepishly and agreed.

Leading a double life was hard, even for a clever dude like myself. I had to keep people believing that I was as normal as the boy next door. And what a laugh! Every serial killer in the world had been "the boy next door" to someone at some point in his life.

Anyway, Sylvia had come to my house a few hours earlier so she could do my laundry and cook our dinner. As if she didn't have enough going for her, she was also a good cook. I often teased her by saying to her, "It took your face powder to get my attention and your baking powder to keep my attention." In addition to all my other great qualities, I had a sense of humor. Several times a week, she spoiled me with some of the best home cooking I'd eaten since my grandmother died. Sylvia had just turned thirty-eight a month ago and had an amazing metabolism. I had to work hard to stay in shape. She could eat just about anything and not gain an ounce—at least not yet. I shuddered when I thought about what she'd probably look like after she had a few babies when Father Time caught up to her.

"This reporter is convinced that these three missing-women cases are linked," she said with the newspaper in her hand. We had just finished the pot roast she had prepared and had moved to my living room with our wineglasses. Sylvia crossed her legs and cringed, her eyes still on the newspaper article.

"What three missing women?" I asked with a yawn, sounding as casual as I could. The last thing I wanted anybody to think was that I had a special interest in missing women.

"That nurse from South Bay City who disappeared one evening after work last year. She had told some coworkers that she was going to stop off at a bar on her way home and have a drink. The police think she might have met up with somebody she didn't know at the bar and . . . well, we both know what can happen to a woman who is stupid enough to trust a stranger she met in a bar. The police found her car parked on the street across from a bar two days after her fiancé reported her missing. One of the women was a stripper, so *anything* could have happened to her. Don't you remember me telling you about this a couple of months ago? The other woman was a secretary."

"I do remember us talking about that a while back," I

said with a shrug. "Maybe they all disappeared on pur-
pose. There was a TV news report a few weeks ago and
they said the stripper had been having some stalking
problems with an obsessed customer. This dude had done
some hard time in the joint for assaulting a few other
women. The managers had to ban him from coming back
to the club when he threatened the stripper. I could see
why a woman in her predicament would pack up and take
off."

"True. I saw that same news program. The nurse didn't
take any of her clothes, her car, or anything else. Her
credit cards have not been used and none of the money
she had in a savings account has been withdrawn since
her disappearance. She had a little boy that she doted on.
Her mother said that no matter where the woman was, or
what she was doing, she always called or came to visit
her child on his birthday, which was two days after she
disappeared."

"Here, let me pour you some more wine." I refilled
Sylvia's wineglass and then my own, hoping she'd change
the subject. She didn't.

"And the nurse had just moved into a new house with
her fiancé. I don't think she'd up and run off. None of her
credit cards have been used either. She didn't even cash
the paycheck she'd received the same day she disappeared." Sylvia took a sip from her wineglass and dropped
the newspaper onto the coffee table. "Why would these
women run off and not use a credit card or cash a paycheck? I'm sure they didn't all take off on a lark. Especially the secretary, who'd just gotten married and
promoted at work."

"Sweetheart, marriage can be overwhelming. That and
a promotion is a heavy load for a young woman in her
twenties to handle. Maybe she realized that and wanted
out of the marriage, and the husband didn't go along with

it. I think the cops should be taking a long, hard look at him. . . ."

"Uh-uh," Sylvia said, vigorously shaking her head. "He passed a lie detector test and they have no evidence that he had anything to do with his wife's disappearance. He didn't have life insurance on her, or any other reason to want to get rid of her. Three women have vanished and nobody knows why."

I took a deep breath and remained as nonchalant as possible. "The thing about going underground is, you have to do it in a way so that nobody can track you down. Check the Internet and you'll see. Women and men drop out of sight on their own every day in this country for various reasons. With all the bills I have, walking away from my current life crosses my mind from time to time." A hearty laugh followed my last comment.

"I certainly feel you on that one." Sylvia laughed, too, and rolled her eyes.

"I would not leave a paper trail by using credit cards or making a bank transaction. I'd also get new credit cards using a fake Social Security number and an alias. I'd even get a fake passport in case I wanted to leave the country."

"I'm sure people who want to walk away from a difficult life do just what you said. Something tells me that that's not the case with these three women."

"Well, this busybody reporter thinks the same person killed these three women. What do you think?"

With a loud gasp, Sylvia looked directly into my eyes. There was a frightened expression on her face. " 'Killed'? How do you know they're dead? So far, all we know is that they are just missing."

I didn't like that look on her face, and I didn't like that I'd slipped up and said something stupid! Again I shrugged and maintained my position of indifference.

"Did I say 'killed'? Hmmm. I just thought that after all the time they've been missing, somebody must have kidnapped and killed them. Like that young Mexican girl they found in a shallow grave in Berkeley last week. I hate to say it, but when women and young kids disappear, they usually turn up dead. Unless, of course, they're lucky like that Jaycee Dugard, the girl who went to the same school you attended when your family lived in Tahoe. She was held captive for eighteen years and had two babies by her kidnapper. And don't forget that poor little girl in Utah who was snatched right out of her own home in the middle of the night while her parents were in another room."

"Elizabeth Smart. Thank God she and Jaycee made it back to their families. There are a few others who came home after being missing for a long time, *years* in some cases, so maybe there's hope for at least one of the three missing black women." Sylvia took another sip of wine and blinked. I was glad she had finally gotten a buzz. She'd be even easier to control once she got good and drunk. "Calvin, we black folks have more than our share of problems, but this kind of shit is done mostly by white folks. I would hate to think that a black man is responsible for the disappearance of these three black women."

I didn't bother to shrug this time, but I wanted to. Instead, I took another sip from my wineglass. "Maybe some white dude who prefers dark meat snatched those three black chicks. . . ."

"Yeah, that's a possibility. But whether this freaky maniac is black or white, I hope I never run into him."

I was tempted to tell Sylvia, "You already have, honey," but this was nothing I wanted to joke about. And like I said, I didn't want anybody to think I was too interested in this subject. "Why don't you join *this* 'freaky maniac' in the bedroom?" I said in a low voice, already tugging on her blouse. For a small woman, she had big juicy breasts and a nice meaty rump that I liked to slap and squeeze sometimes to the point of causing her great pain. She was so tiny and fragile-looking, she made me feel like the Big Bad Wolf.

"That's not a bad idea," she purred, rising. "I'm still a little sore from that session we had just before dinner, so can you be more of a lamb this time?"

"Baaaaaa," I said, tickling her chin. Despite my humor, I knew that once I got her into my bed, I was not going to be responsible for my actions. Women brought out the Big Bad Wolf in me. . . .

After I made love to Sylvia, she rolled over and promptly went to sleep. I didn't like it when she stayed over. But it was past midnight and I didn't feel like driving her home.

I lay on my back with my arms folded across my chest for the next hour or so. Thoughts rolled around in my head like tumbleweeds in a desert storm. My head began to throb like hell. I was surprised I didn't have these excruciating headaches more frequently. I had a secret that had almost consumed me, and would remain a secret until the day I died.

I often wondered what people would say or think if somebody accused me of kidnapping and killing women. I had to hold my breath to keep from laughing out loud because such a notion was not even a possibility.

I finally fell asleep. Unfortunately, sleep was not a refuge for me. What I had become was *always* on my mind. The dreams I had of women dying by my hands (some I had not even met yet), their eyes rolling back in their heads as I strangled the life out of them, haunted me almost every single night since my troubles began eight years ago. . . .

Chapter 42

Calvin

I DON'T KNOW WHO CAME UP WITH THE SAYING "MONEY is the root of all evil," but that's a goddamn lie. The root of all evil is women! I grew up in the Church and I believed in the Bible all my life, despite its inconsistencies and fairy-tale–like stories. If creation began the way the Bible claims, then Adam was doing all right until Eve came along. That hardheaded bitch started it all!

Despite the havoc women wreaked, I had once loved all of the women I knew and treated them with nothing but respect. That all ended when the woman I had loved— more than life itself—caused me to slide headfirst into a bottomless pit that I would never climb out of.

Her name was Glinda Price. I found out too late that she was a bitch from hell.

We'd met a little over eight years ago at the birthday party of a mutual friend, two and a half months before I joined the marines. At the time, she was working as a waitress. The first time I laid eyes on her, I knew I had to have her.

Glinda had come to the party with another dude, but that didn't stop me from making my move, and it didn't stop her. The fact that she had disrespected her date should have been my first warning that she was a she-wolf in sheep's clothing. But I still didn't care. She left the party with me without hesitation and we walked the three blocks to my house, holding hands and smooching all the way. We made love for hours; and when it came to sex, she was as good as she looked.

Glinda was too beautiful for words. She was twenty-four at the time, a year younger than me. She had cinnamon-brown skin, large slanted brown eyes, a smile that could brighten the darkest room, and long, thick black hair. She was petite, the way I liked my women. I loved tall, full-figured women too. But since I was only five feet nine and barely 150 pounds, having a woman larger than me would be too intimidating and difficult to maneuver be-tween the sheets. I had almost married a woman my height, who outweighed me by thirty pounds. But one night when she caught me flirting with one of her friends and got the better of me during the fight that ensued that night, I decided to avoid larger women.

What I didn't know the night I met Glinda was that she was one of the biggest sluts in town. Not only did she get around like a centipede, she had previously worked as an escort for one of the most notorious services in the state. And when I did find out a week later, it was too late.

"That woman is so hot to trot, I'm surprised she ain't caught on fire by now," one of my buddies warned me.

"I can say that about every woman I've been with," I mused. "You can too." This same busybody friend had once dated three women at the same time.

"No, this one gets *a-round*. Glinda spends more time

on her back than a corpse. Poke that pussy as often as you want, but you'd better wear a heavy-duty condom—maybe even two—every single time."

I did use protection when I slept with Glinda. But one night when we were both too drunk and frisky to care, I didn't. A month and a half later she told me she was pregnant with my baby. I didn't hesitate to ask her to marry me, but she was hesitant to accept my proposal.

"I know your whole family hates my guts, as well as most of your so-called friends," Glinda told me with a grimace on her face. "After all, marriage is a big step."

"Having a child is just as big a step as marriage, if not more. It'll probably be less trouble for us both if we're legally married by the time I leave for Camp Pendleton. Uncle Sam is tricky enough. I'd hate to get tangled up in a bunch of red tape when it comes to arranging benefits for you and my child."

I married Glinda in Vegas two months after I'd met her. And because of that, Mama stopped speaking to me. I was hurt because I loved my mama to death; she'd always been the most important female in my life. But I'd been taught—in the same church she used to drag me to when I was a kid—that when a man got married, his first allegiance was to his wife, not to his mother. I didn't just lose my mama, siblings, and a lot of my other family members, I lost most of my male friends. The women of the ones who were married, or in committed relationships, felt threatened by Glinda. My only sister, Vickie, told me in no uncertain terms not to bring her around. She was married to a man who would screw a female snake, so having a woman like Glinda within his reach would have been too much of a temptation.

She was not pregnant, after all. As much as I wanted a child, I was glad it had been a false alarm. "Let's not start our family until I complete my commitment to Uncle

Sam. I know I'll be getting deployed to Afghanistan and I'd hate to be over there worrying about you and a baby," I told her.

"That's fine with me," she replied, looking and sounding very relieved.

As much as I adored Glinda, I began to see things in her that I found disturbing. At the time, I owned a large tabby cat I called Georgie. He'd been with me since the day he was born. One morning, the week before I left to go serve my country, I saw something that made me flinch. Out of the corner of my eye, I saw Glinda kick Georgie when he brushed against the side of her leg. I let it go that time.

The very next day, she kicked him in front of me, sending him scrambling from the room, howling like a banshee. This time I had to say something. "I wish you wouldn't do that anymore," I said, trying not to sound too harsh. "I know you're still upset about not being pregnant and me leaving next week, but I wish you would stop taking out your frustrations on my pet."

"You know I'd never really hurt Georgie," she told me in a serious tone of voice. And I believed her.

To this day, I regret that I didn't make arrangements for my beloved pet to stay with someone else until I returned home. In the first correspondence that she sent to me, she told me toward the end of her one-page letter: *I accidentally ran over your cat the other day and he died.* I was inconsolable.

Georgie had been like a family member to me. And the fact that I was somewhat estranged from most of my family made losing him even more painful. I grieved for days. And I got careless.

On more than one occasion, I had almost lost my life

by not being alert and following instructions. In one week, I saw three of my comrades get blown to pieces by suicide bombers. I came close to ending up in the same situation myself, more than once. I eventually pulled myself up out of my depression when I realized the kind of hell the war in the Middle East was.

One gloomy day one of my comrades tacked a large photo of Jesus on a wall in our barracks. A few hours later, someone scribbled on it with black ink: *I know I'm going to heaven because I'm already in hell.* I was in hell in more ways than one.

I sent Glinda at least two or three letters a week. I was lucky if I received one a month from her. However, some of the few friends I still had wrote to me often, and they all eagerly told me about some of the things she was up to. She was spending time with other men, and she was doing it in the house I owned! Not only did I fear losing my life in a senseless war several thousand miles away from home, I feared losing my woman.

Despite all of the reports I kept receiving from my friends about Glinda, I prayed that she would still want me when I returned. I told myself that if I could survive the war, I could survive my wife's bad behavior.

I never mentioned the reports to Glinda in my letters, and I didn't plan to mention them when I saw her again. I had planned to spend my first leave since my deployment making love to her nonstop, or close to it. I had changed my mind about waiting to start a family. I wanted to get her pregnant as soon as possible. I thought that motherhood would make her change her ways and become a better mate.

My first leave did not go the way I hoped it would. Glinda did not greet me at the airport with open arms, but with a scowl on her face and a cold embrace.

"Honey, I'm so glad to see you," I told her, nuzzling my nose in her hair, which was longer and more beautiful than ever. "You look tired," I said before I could stop myself.

The last thing I wanted to do was upset her. I wanted her to be in a very good mood when we got home. I had told my friends not to call or come to the house for at least two days because Glinda and I were going to be busy creating our first child. She had other ideas.

"I'm fine," she mumbled. She walked with her head down, talking in a low voice. "The stove is on the blink," she grunted as we headed toward the nearest exit.

Dozens of people stared and smiled at me in my dress blues—the sexiest, most recognizable, and prestigious uniform in the whole military worn proudly by marines, and envied by all. Several civilian dudes saluted me as I strolled by. It saddened me to know that complete strangers were more excited than my wife about seeing a man who had put his life on the line for America. I was thinking about all the ways I was going to make love to Glinda and she was telling me that the stove was on the blink!

"We can get a new stove or get the old one fixed," I said. "In the meantime, I'd rather talk about the bed . . ."

Her body stiffened when I put my arm around her shoulder. When I mentioned "bed," I had never seen a more disgusted look on a woman's face than the one on Glinda's face now. She looked like she wanted to puke.

"That'll have to wait. My period just started this morning," she informed me. That was the last thing I wanted to hear, because nothing turned me off like a bloody pussy. I told myself that if I could survive several months without sex and still be sane, I could wait a few more days.

"Oh. Well, it's a good thing I'll be home for a couple of weeks," I said, forcing myself to laugh. She responded with a sharp grunt. We remained silent until we got into our four-year-old Prius and headed toward the freeway.

"Glinda, is something wrong?" I finally asked.

"Nothing's wrong," she snapped. She kept both hands on the steering wheel and both eyes on the road.

"Something *is* wrong," I insisted. "I know you quite well and I've never seen you act this way."

"What way, Calvin?" She glanced in my direction. The look of contempt on her face was so profound, it made my chest tighten.

"You're making me feel like an unwanted, ugly step-child, but I still love you. You don't seem happy to see me, and you don't have much to say to me. I've been away for a long time and the least you can do is make me feel welcome to be back home."

Glinda looked even more disgusted by now. With a heavy sigh, she said, "I'm just tired and I can't wait to get home so I can get some rest."

We were like two strangers when we went to bed that night . . . after I had repaired the stove. With our backs to one another, she slept on one edge of the king-size bed and I slept on the other.

She felt like a piece of wood when I made love to her four days later, when her alleged period ended. But I had not been with a woman since the last time I saw her, so I didn't care what she felt like. I took my time and I didn't release her until I was thoroughly satisfied. When I finally slid off her body, she scrambled out of bed, moaning and groaning, and scurried into the bathroom. I didn't wait for her to return. I was exhausted from our marathon lovefest, so I went to sleep immediately.

The next morning was only slightly better. Around nine o'clock, I shuffled into the kitchen in my pajamas. Glinda had on a frumpy brown dress, a pair of shabby house shoes, and she had pulled her hair into a severe ponytail. Despite her dowdy appearance, she had on as much makeup as she would wear to a nightclub. I was pleased to see that she had prepared a lavish breakfast. I had not eaten grits and bacon since the last time I visited my mother's house. And probably wouldn't again, at least not at Mama's table. She was still angry with me for marrying Glinda and had not even written to me.

My older brother, Ronald, one of the few relatives I had who still communicated with me on a fairly regular basis, had written to let me know that Mama had been experiencing some serious health problems. I'd written to her immediately and even called her house a couple of times. She had ignored my letters and refused to take my calls.

The fact that I had given up so much for Glinda made me even more determined to keep her. I was not about to let my marriage end without a fight.

Chapter 43

Calvin

SIX MONTHS AFTER MY LAST VISIT HOME, I RECEIVED MY honorable discharge papers.

By the grace of God, I made it through the war unscathed. In spite of everything I had to look forward to (or *not* look forward to) once I resumed my civilian status, I couldn't wait to get off the plane and step back onto American soil again. The most important reason I was so anxious to return home permanently was so I could work on my marriage.

I had written two letters a week to Glinda in the last six months, she had written me a total of three times in the last year. I had called the house several times, but not one time had I caught her at home. I didn't bother to call any of my friends or any of Glinda's friends and associates. It wasn't necessary for them to tell me what I already knew: she was running around with other men.

Not only did she not pick me up when I landed at the

San Jose airport, like we had agreed she should, she was not answering my calls. I waited for an hour, hoping she'd eventually show up. She didn't. I didn't attempt to call a friend or a neighbor to come fetch me, because I would have been too embarrassed to let them know that my own wife had let me down. I finally crawled into a cab.

When I got to my street and saw our Prius in the driveway, my first thought was that something had happened to Glinda. All kinds of grim thoughts ran through my mind. I pictured her in the house, stretched out on the floor, unable to speak or move. Her falling and hitting her head on something would have been bad enough, but I cringed when I imagined rampaging thugs beating and raping her during a home invasion. My chest tightened; my head felt like somebody had batted it with a brick. I was afraid of what I might have to deal with.

Robert Franklin, a chubby divorced man who lived next door, was in his driveway when I got out of the cab. Before I could go inside, he trotted over, gave me a "welcome home" hug, and clapped me on the back.

"I'm glad to be home," I told him. "Why don't you come over in a little while and join me and my wife for a drink?"

I knew something was wrong when Robert gave me another hug. After he released me, he reared back and gave me a pitiful look. "Oh, so she's back?"

"Who's back?" I asked, puzzled.

"Uh, I saw your wife leaving with a dude in a blue van around this time yesterday. She had two suitcases with her. . . ."

"Oh," I said in a very small and weak voice.

"My brother told me that when he was at a bachelor party in a strip club last week, Glinda was one of the strippers."

"Oh," I said again, this time much stronger. "Do you know which club?"

"I'll have to ask my brother." Robert looked at the ground, then back at me. He looked almost as sad as I felt. "I'm sorry, man. I'll still come over when you get settled so we can have a few drinks."

"Maybe not tonight. I'll call you," I said. I let out a sigh and dragged my feet toward my front door. I felt so weak I could barely carry the duffel bag that contained some of my military gear. I was glad I had my house keys on me. When I got inside, I went straight to the telephone. I called up everybody I knew and nobody was able to tell me where my wife was.

I let two weeks go by before I attempted to file a missing-person report. The cops laughed in my face when I told them my wife was a stripper and that she'd been seen leaving home with suitcases and a man. They practically chased me out of the police station.

Three days after I'd made a fool of myself with the cops, Glinda moseyed into the house a few minutes after eight P.M. without the suitcases Robert told me she'd left with. There was a smirk on her face and a huge chip on her shoulder. She wore a tight purple skirt and what looked like a bikini top under a white windbreaker. Her hair was askew and she had on enough makeup to paint the side of a barn, and she reeked of alcohol. She didn't say hello or ask how I'd been doing. All she said was "I just came by to get some more of my stuff."

"Did you come alone?" I asked, glancing toward the front window.

"I'm alone. I came in a cab and I'll be going back in a cab," she snapped.

"Wh-where the hell have you been? And where is it

you're going to go back to?" I demanded, following her across the floor into our master bedroom. My hands were balled into fists and a knot was in my stomach. "What's this I hear about you *stripping*?" I could barely get the word out of my mouth. "Wasn't being an escort bad enough? I thought you left that wild lifestyle behind when we got married." I was frantic. I was also glad to see my wife. I wanted to grab her and never let her go. She looked at me like I had scabs all over my face.

"I thought you'd be gone by now," she said casually, rolling her eyes. I couldn't believe my ears! She stopped in front of the mirror behind the closet door and began to fuss with her hair. She didn't comment on the new brass bed and the gold-and-red brocade drapes at the windows I'd purchased the day before.

I was so stunned I had to grope for words. "Gone where, Glinda?" I asked through clenched teeth. "This is my home and I'm here for good," I added as I made a sweeping gesture with my hand. I couldn't believe that this was the same woman I had married. "Glinda—" I didn't even get to finish my next sentence. She whirled around and glared at me with her eyes narrowed into slits.

"Look, fool, I've got better things to do with my time than sit around here waiting on your lame ass to come home."

Again I couldn't believe my ears. "Glinda, talk to me. You need to tell me what's going on. If something is wrong, we can fix it."

"Get outta my face, fool!"

I folded my arms so I wouldn't be tempted to grab her and shake some sense into her hard head. "Are you involved with another man?"

She moved to the bed and sat down hard, kicking off a pair of four-inch black stilettoes. "What if I am?" she asked as she began to massage her feet. "What was I supposed to do? And don't tell me you haven't been dipping your spoon into some . . . something." She threw her head back and laughed. "I know those women over there in the Middle East are probably not as easy to get to as the ones in other foreign countries, but don't think for one minute that I believe you've only been jacking off."

I moved closer to the bed and stood a few feet in front of her. "I have never touched another woman since I met you," I told her. And it was true. I had not even looked at another woman since the night I met Glinda. "Please talk to me," I begged.

She rolled her eyes again, then jumped up and strutted over to the dresser, where she began to root through her underwear in the top drawer. She had a pair of red thong panties in her hand when she let out a loud breath and turned to me.

"What are you going to do now? Go back to that dead-end–ass job at the utility company?" she sneered.

I shook my head. "I didn't want to go back. I received a fantastic job offer a couple of days ago. And it's a position that suits me better."

"Humph. I can't imagine a job that 'suits' you . . . other than a clown in that circus that comes through here every year."

"I'll be driving an eighteen-wheeler, hauling lumber from Oregon and Washington to various cities in Southern Cal. I may be gone for days, even weeks, at a time. I hope that's all right with you. I would have discussed it with you when they offered it, but . . . I didn't know how to get in touch with you."

Glinda dismissed me with a wave of her hand. "I don't care what you do."

"You should care, Glinda. I'm your husband!"

She looked me up and down, shaking her head and muttering under her breath. I could not understand why there was an amused look on her face. "Yeah, you're my husband, but not for long!" she snarled.

My breath caught in my throat and I couldn't get a word out. I stood there like a mute, wondering what Glinda was going to say next. She could not have stunned me more if she had dropped a stove on my head.

"I want a divorce," she said as calmly as if she'd just requested a glass of wine.

"A *'divorce,'*" I mouthed. The word tasted like bile on my tongue. My head was spinning and I couldn't even feel my legs. You could have knocked me over with a toothpick. "You can't be serious!"

"Well, I am! And you can't stop me! You make me sick!" she taunted.

"Is there someone else?" I asked dumbly. My heart was pounding so hard and loud, I could hear it. I was amazed that I had not fainted or burst into tears.

"Yes, there is someone else." Those words hit me like a speeding train. I wanted to holler, hit the wall with my fist—anything that would redirect my anger and keep me from wrapping my hands around her throat. Except for the war, I had never hurt another human being in my life. I had always avoided physical confrontations. I had never even had a single physical fight with any of my siblings, friends, or the school and neighborhood bullies. I knew that if somebody ever provoked me enough to get violent, I would make up for all the times I had managed to run away in time or had talked my way out of a fight.

As if what Glinda had said so far hadn't been painful enough, she hit me with another blow, which almost knocked the wind out of me. In a high-pitched voice, she told me, "And he wants to marry me." There was a crooked smile on her face, so I thought she was just joking.

"Glinda, please tell me you're joking," I pleaded, wringing my hands.

"Am I laughing?" she boomed, waving her hand and snapping her fingers.

I still couldn't bring myself to believe she was serious. How I was able to remain so composed was a mystery to me. At the same time, everything inside my body was falling apart. "But you can't just—"

"I'm pregnant," she announced, even more calmly than she'd said she wanted a divorce. "He wants to marry me and I can't do that until I get rid of your lame black ass." She shook her head. "I don't know what I was thinking when I married you."

"You . . . you said you loved me," I fumbled, struggling to swallow the huge lump in my throat.

"Well, I must have been drunk."

"Glinda, we can get past this. If you give up this other man, I will raise the child as my own. Nobody but us ever needs to know the truth. I won't even tell my family."

"Fuck your family! To hell with them and you! I know they hate me, and I hate them!"

"You can talk about me like a dog all you want to, but I don't appreciate you bashing my family!" I hollered. Some of the same relatives who had shunned me because of Glinda had recently started coming back around. Their support meant a lot to me. But it was too late for me to restore my relationship with Mama and tell her how sorry I was that I had disappointed her so severely. She had passed while I was still deployed. Nobody bothered to tell me until after the funeral, because that was what she had told them to do. I couldn't believe that I had caused her to be that angry with me. The woman responsible for the falling-out between my mother and me was not fit to live! A voice I had never heard before told me, *"Kill her. . . ."*

"They don't give a shit about you, and neither do I! You're a bigger fool than I thought you were. And for the record, that other time when I thought I was pregnant, it was by this same man, not you."

I felt so light-headed by now, I thought I was going to float up off the floor and hit the ceiling. "Then why did you marry me?" I couldn't believe how weak I sounded. My legs felt like jelly and everything else on my body felt even worse. Somehow I managed to remain on my feet.

"I don't think you really want to hear the real reason," she warned.

"Yes, I really do want to hear it."

"Because the other man was married at the time. And everybody told me what a gullible fool you were! I figured I could quit my damn job at that fried chicken restaurant and sit back and enjoy your military benefits. I knew that you would take good care of me and I could still do whatever I wanted. But . . . but my skin crawled whenever you touched me. The last time you fucked me, I douched with vinegar after you fell asleep. Kissing you is like kissing a week-old litter box! You're lousy in bed anyway. Do you want to hear more?"

I grabbed Glinda's arm and she almost jumped out of her skin.

"That's what I'm talking about! Your touch feels like ants crawling all over me!" She looked at me like I had just doused her with acid. "I don't ever want you to touch me again. Now, if you don't mind, I will pack up the rest of my shit and get the hell up out of here!"

I moved closer to her and folded my arms again. Then for some reason, I guess it was because I wanted to put some temporary distance between us so I could regroup my thoughts, I spun around and trotted to the kitchen. I snatched open the refrigerator and grabbed the first beverage I saw, which was a can of beer. Well, I wanted a clear head, so I put the beer back and reached for a bottle of water. I managed to gulp down half of it, but it didn't put out the raging blaze in my belly. I set the bottle on the counter and returned to the bedroom. As Glinda folded clothes and placed them into the opened suitcase on the bed, she was humming "What's Love Got to Do with It."

I walked casually over to her and gently placed my hand on her shoulder. "Baby, I can't let you leave me." I didn't even recognize my own voice. The words I'd just spoken sounded as if they'd come from another man. The voice I had heard a few moments ago spoke to me again, *"Kill her. . . ."*

War changed people. Several of the men I had served with had come home missing a limb or two. Others had come home with post-traumatic stress disorders, and their lives would never be the same again. I was probably one of the luckiest ones. I was basically the same man I'd been before my deployment. It seemed so ironic that a small woman had had more negative effect on me than the battlegrounds in the Middle East. I had lived my whole life as a decent, law-abiding citizen, but because of that small woman, that was about to change. . . .

Glinda stopped humming and turned to face me. The look in her eyes was so empty and cold; I shivered. "You just watch me, motherfucker!" she shrieked. She pummeled my aching chest with both hands, and then she slapped my face and laughed. I was in the worst pain I'd ever experienced in my life, and she was *laughing* at me!

After tonight she'd never laugh again.

Chapter 44

Lola

SO FAR, SINCE I'D JOINED DISCREET ENCOUNTERS TWO weeks ago, I had responded to, but also had ignored, e-mails from a dozen men. I didn't acknowledge one man because he sounded too aggressive, and that frightened me. I'd ignored a frat boy, attending Nevada State, who told me I reminded him of his mother. There was no way I was going to hop into bed with a man who wanted to sleep with me because I reminded him of his mother! I decided not to even consider any men younger than thirty. Some of the other men I hadn't responded to didn't sound interesting enough or they revealed too much information about themselves that was disturbing to me. Like the man who'd told me, in great detail, how refreshing it was to have a thorough bowel movement immediately after sex and then have the woman, with whom he'd just made love, watch him!

I was finally ready to have my first "discreet encounter." His name was Les Gould. Not only was he gorgeous, we shared a lot of the same interests. I was going to meet him in three days, this coming Friday.

Les was a thirty-eight-year-old surgeon from Boston, who attended medical conferences in California on an annual basis. Even though the site management people had done a background check on him, I called the hospital he claimed he worked for, just to make sure he was telling the truth. That checked out, but I Googled him too. Numerous magazine articles that he had written popped up, so I knew he was on the up-and-up. (I didn't tell Joan I'd done a little background checking on this man myself because I knew she'd make a fuss.)

I had never met a black surgeon before, nor had I seen any man who was as handsome and exotic as Les. I drooled when I saw the picture he had posted of himself in his scrubs. He had the body of a prizefighter, enough thick black hair for two men, smooth light brown skin, and green eyes.

By the time Friday rolled around, I was so horny that I could barely walk. After Bertha had gone to bed around eight-thirty P.M., I slipped out of the house and jumped into my Jetta and took off like a bat out of hell. That was how anxious I was to meet Les. I was also nervous.

I was glad I had decided to wear the cream-colored silk dress I'd purchased on my last shopping spree. I had recently lost a few pounds and never looked or felt better in my life. I was a woman having the best time of my life—finally. And I was going to continue enjoying my life as long as I could.

I had arranged to meet Les in a restaurant located in the Hilton hotel in downtown San Jose, where he had booked a suite the day before. When I approached his table in a corner near the front entrance, he stood up and handed me a single rose. I couldn't believe how dapper he looked in his dark blue pin-striped suit. His complexion looked even more exotic in person. He was not as light-skinned as he looked in his profile picture or in the pictures of him in the magazines he had written for. His skin was more of a medium shade of bronze. Purple skin would have looked good on this man.

"Thank you," I said in a squeaky voice. I cleared my throat and offered my biggest smile. Then I purred, "I hope you're Les Gould."

"If I'm not, I'm wearing the wrong underwear," he said with a chuckle. He pulled out the chair next to him for me to sit. "Yes, I am Les." He had a sexy, husky voice that sounded a lot like James Earl Jones when he voiced Darth Vader in *Star Wars*. I was a fool when it came to men with sexy, husky voices *and* New England accents, so I'd even listen to Les read a dictionary to me. I couldn't wait to hear him talk dirty. . . .

"Uh, I'm Lola." I was glad I had paid a visit to the beauty shop a few hours earlier. My hair was looking its best—a French twist with bangs. There was no telling what it would look like after my romp with the big strapping man in front of me, looking at me like I was something good to eat. The thought almost made me giggle. "I've never done this before." I plopped down so hard into the chair, my tailbone ached and my knee bumped his real hard. I couldn't decide which one of us shuddered the hardest, and for different reasons, of course. He was probably excited; I was nervous.

He nodded. "You told me that in your first e-mail," he reminded. "But don't worry, after you've cut your teeth, you'll get used to it."

"Uh . . . huh," I muttered. I wished that I had arrived first so I could have already had a drink or two to calm my nerves. "What do you want to do? I mean . . . you know."

"I thought we'd have a couple of drinks and then a nice dinner. Do you have a favorite restaurant in the area, or would you like to eat here?" He made a sweeping gesture with his hand.

"I don't know about the restaurants in this immediate area, but if you like sushi and tempura, there's a fantastic Japanese place not too far from here." I glanced at my watch.

"Lola, are you nervous, my dear?"

"Who me? Uh, not really," I replied as I nervously tapped my fingers on the table. Before I could stop myself, Les gently took my hand in his and kissed it.

"We could save time by leaving now and ordering room service," he told me, winking.

"Okay. Let's do that." I didn't wait for him to rise and pull out my chair. I wobbled up and quickly scanned the room. There were only a few other patrons and I was glad none of them were paying any attention to us. But I didn't like the way the bartender kept glancing in our direction. He had been eyeballing me since I walked in the door. He winked at me and nodded at Les when we passed by the bar. My first thought was that he assumed I was a hooker!

"I'm more nervous than I thought," I told Les when we entered the elevator.

"You don't have to be nervous at all. We are two consenting adults who want to enjoy the pleasure of each other's company and, uh, each other's body. But if you don't want to go through with this, I'll understand."

I looked at this gorgeous man standing next to me and blinked. It had been way too long since I'd been in a man's arms, especially one this handsome and sophisticated. Les was certainly a huge step up from the rusty, dusty, musty men I'd been with on "regular" dates. Suddenly I was no longer nervous. As a matter of fact, I kicked off my shoes as soon as we entered his suite. Within minutes after several passionate kisses, we removed our clothes and were wallowing all over that king-size bed in the middle of the room.

Les suddenly sat up and looked at his watch. "I, um, have some notes I have to revise later tonight for my presentation tomorrow," he began, running his finger along the side of my face. "We'd better order room service. The steaks here are incredible."

My whole body stiffened as I lay on my back looking up at him. I knew there had to be a downside! This man wanted to hit and run, as if he had hired an escort to come service him. The only difference was, escorts got paid for their services. And that was prostitution! A split second later, I scolded myself for even allowing that thought to enter my mind again. I had known the score from the get-go. I was giving up my body for free because this was not about getting paid; it was about getting laid.

I took a deep breath and sat up. "I had a huge lunch, so I'm not really that hungry," I lied. I had been so nervous about this date that I had not eaten anything since breakfast. Now I was so hungry . . . I could eat a horse. But since it was obvious, or it seemed that way to me, that Les was anxious to fuck me and get it over with, I decided to go along with that plan. While he was still looking at me, I glanced at my watch again. "I didn't realize it was so late," I said. "I have some work I have to finish when I get home tonight too, so I don't mind if we skip the room service."

I was pleased to see a slightly disappointed look on his face. And I couldn't understand why. He had given me the impression that a "rush job" was what he wanted, and I wanted to accommodate him.

"I see," he muttered. Without another word, he lunged at me. As soon as he got me into the position he wanted, he pried my legs apart with his knee and piled on top of me, slapping his dick on my thigh before he rammed it into me. Once he was completely inside, he began to buck like a wild horse, and so did I.

It was one of the most enjoyable experiences of my life. Les was the kind of lover every woman dreamed about. He was not that well-endowed, but he knew how to work with what he had. Not only was he a fantastic lover, but he was also a "devoted" husband.

Immediately after we had both climaxed at the same time, he rolled over, snatched the phone off the stand, and frantically dialed a number. He breathed through his mouth until the person on the other end answered. "It's me, dear. Uh-huh, I miss you too. Baby, I can't wait to get back home. Kiss the kids for me." There was a lengthy pause and then he said, "This trip is just as boring as the last one."

That was not what I expected to hear from a man who was still huffing and puffing from his tryst with me less than a minute ago. I tried to imagine his wife on the other end of the line, what she looked like, and if she was naïve enough to believe she had a faithful husband. After he'd spoken a couple more sentences, reminding his wife to water his orchids and inquiring about his dog, he told her how much he loved her. Then he abruptly hung up.

The way he was ignoring me now, you would have thought I'd already left the room. He bolted out of bed and sprinted to the bathroom without saying another word to me. His peculiar behavior brought me back down to earth. I could not understand why I suddenly felt like a piece of meat. That thought didn't stay with me long, though. I *was* a piece of meat, and so was Les, for that matter. All we'd wanted was to have a good time. Since we'd accomplished that, I saw no reason for me to hang around. As soon as I heard the water running in the shower, I got dressed and left.

Les Gould's behavior after our encounter had bothered me for a few minutes, but I wasn't going to waste my time thinking about it. What was done, was done—and I didn't regret it. I had had sex with more men than I cared to count, and none of them had satisfied me the way Les had.

Chapter 45

Lola

F IVE MINUTES AFTER I GOT HOME FROM MY DATE WITH Les, I took a shower and got into my pajamas. Then I made myself comfortable in my bed, grabbed my cell phone, and dialed Joan's number. Words poured out of my mouth when she answered. "Is Reed around? I really need to talk."

"His grandmother is visiting from Baltimore. He's spending the night at his parents' house." There was a short pause and then she asked in one breath, "Did you go on your date?"

"Yeah, I went. Les Gould was a nice, gorgeous man. And, boy, does he know how to work a woman's body."

Joan snickered. "Seeeeee. I told you, you'd enjoy it."

"He didn't talk much and he gave me the impression that he didn't want me to stick around after . . . after we finished. I took off while he was in the shower. Should I have hung around?"

"Not unless you and he had discussed a second round. The best way to keep this light and simple is to do what you're there to do, wipe your coochie, get back into your clothes, and then haul ass. There is no need to hang around and cuddle, unless that's something you both want to do. I've been with a couple of guys who wasted no time sending me on my way after they'd gotten what they wanted. Which was always fine with me. I'm not inter-ested in lying around with a man I'll probably never see again, discussing a bunch of mundane bullshit! Some of them have big egos and love to talk about themselves."

"I know exactly what you mean. But I have to admit, I really enjoyed myself with Les. I could get used to this until I meet Mr. Right."

"Ha! I wouldn't count on that anytime soon. And even if you do meet Mr. Right, he might turn into Mr. Wrong sooner or later. Look what happened to me with that pig in a poke I married!" Joan snarled. "And to think, for Reed, I gave up my dream to be a journalist. I was going to travel all over the world."

"You can still be a journalist and travel all over the world, Joan."

"Not with that insecure fool breathing down my neck! Do you think he'd even let me set foot out of this state without a fuss?"

"Only if he goes with you and puts you on a very short leash."

"Have you checked your e-mail today?" Joan asked. I was glad she changed the subject.

"Yeah, I checked just before I went to meet Les. Two new club members sent messages, a surgeon and a sales-man. The salesman says he wants to e-mail chat with me a few times before he commits to a date. The surgeon is going to be in town next month to be a guest on a local

TV medical program. He offered to have a limo pick me up and bring me to his hotel."

"A *limo* and another surgeon already? I am scared of you! Aren't you glad you posted such a sexy picture of yourself? It's going to be hard for you to pick and choose when more members find out about you. They are going to bombard you with requests for dates. Unless you want to do this full-time, you're going to have to turn down some real cuties. I know I have."

"Joan, what if I were to browse around the site and see a man I'd really like to be with? Do I ask him for a date, or do I sit back and hope that he will eventually see my profile and contact me?"

"Didn't I already tell you that female club members can request dates? And, like I also told you, the person requesting the date has to set it up, maybe even travel to the other's person's city and pay the hotel expenses. If the dude is a penny-pincher, the woman will be responsible for every other expense associated with the encounter."

"Oh yeah, I forgot. You already told me. Well, hopefully, I'll be too busy with other dates, so it won't ever come to that."

"You will be too busy, honey. I can't keep up with all the requests I get. There's this auto executive in Billings, Montana, who's coming to California to visit his brother next month. He's sent me a *dozen* e-mails in less than two weeks requesting a date and I keep turning him down. A man *that* anxious to get into my pants scares me. With all the women available on the site, why would a dude pester the same woman over and over again?"

"Your profile and picture must have really impressed him."

"I guess so, but that's no reason for him to be so anxious to be with me. If all he wants is a good fuck, he can get that from any one of the other club members, or one closer to his hometown. That is, if they like his looks well enough. One rule I have is that I don't want to be with a man who is too aggressive before we even meet."

"So now you're telling me you're worried about getting into something you'll regret? Like a *Fatal Attraction* stalking situation?"

"No, nothing like that. I just don't want another clinging-vine man in my life, even if it's only for one date. Another thing I'm concerned about is *me* getting too attached to one of my hookups. Having a serious relationship with another man is out of the question as long as I'm stuck with Reed. But you can."

"I can what?"

"If you meet a hot dude and you two really hit it off, there's no telling what it could lead to."

"Remember the man in San Jose I told you about?"

"No, I don't."

"He was one of the first ones to respond when I posted my profile."

"Oh, you mean that truck driver using the RamRod screen name?"

"Uh-huh. I keep thinking about him. He's so handsome, and the first war hero who's ever approached me. Even if I never meet him, I'm glad he made it back safe and sound from Afghanistan. I'll bet he's got some interesting war stories to share."

"Don't let your patriotic panties get wet too soon!" Joan laughed. "I'll bet he's got a lot more than that to share."

"I'm sure he has."

"Well, are you interested in finding out?"

"I am. But like I told you, I don't want to rush into anything with him. I'd rather spend time with a few other men first. After I've had enough fun, I might want to meet Calvin, and not just for a 'hit it and run' date. From what I know about him so far, I'm really impressed."

"You can't be that impressed if you can put off meeting him."

"Give me a break. I'm not as . . . you know."

"I know what?"

"You know I'm not as loosey-goosey as you are. Ever since you got into online dating, you've been running amok. It takes me a little longer to get into the swing of things. I still can't believe you went on a date while your husband was still recovering from his suicide attempt."

"If you had to deal with a sad sack like Reed, you'd get 'into the swing of things' a lot faster than you do now. One of the reasons I went on a date while he was still recovering was so I could recover from it myself. I'm not ashamed to admit that I love to fuck. I wasn't getting what I needed at home, so I had to do what I did, when I did it." Joan paused to catch her breath. "And another thing, when you get your mojo going up to full speed, you'll feel the same way. There's just one thing."

"What now?"

"I still think that this truck driver lives too close for comfort. If, and I say *if,* he gets too serious after you hook up with him, and you don't feel the same, you might have a problem with him."

"I think we're getting way ahead of ourselves. He's not being pushy or anything like that, so he's okay with me taking my time. I haven't heard from him in a while, and as far as I know, he could have forgotten all about me and moved on to another woman, anyway."

"If you do decide to e-mail him again, or if he contacts you and you decide to go meet him, just be careful. Don't give out too much personal information about yourself."

"I won't," I said.

The day after my conversation with Joan, a man, who sounded even more interesting than Les Gould, left a message in my club in-box and sent a message to my regular e-mail address. Before I responded, I checked out his profile and his picture. Enrique Cortez looked like one of my favorite movie stars, Antonio Banderas. He was a forty-year-old hotel manager from Madrid, Spain. His screen name was "SpanishFly" and he was going to be in L.A. on business in a few days. He eagerly offered to cover my travel expenses if I'd meet him in his hotel room at the Beverly Hilton. If that didn't work for me, he'd fly up to the Bay Area.

I turned off my computer and went downstairs to see what Bertha was cooking for our dinner. She was in the kitchen, humped over the stove, humming her favorite hymn, "I Been in the Storm Too Long," and stirring something in a tall pot. I didn't even have to ask what it was. The smell was all too familiar.

"We're having chitlins *again*?" I asked dryly as I poured myself a glass of water.

Bertha whirled around with an amused look on her face. "Girl, you know you won't waste any time gobbling up a few bowls of these chitlins as soon as they get done." Bertha shook her head and chuckled.

As far as I knew, I was very healthy. But I didn't know how long that would last with all the things I ate. It was hard to believe that I usually ate lobster, caviar, and filet mignon, when I had dinner at Joan's house.

"I'm never going to lose weight if you keep cooking up things like chitlins," I complained.

Bertha laughed again and waved her hand in the air. "Girl, you know black men love women with meat on their bones," she said, slapping her hefty thigh. "You need to stop trying to be skinny, because you're too thin already. Only white men like skinny females." With a thoughtful look, she added, "Maybe that's why you can't find a husband. . . ."

Chapter 46

Lola

*A*FTER ALL THE YEARS THAT BERTHA HAD SABOTAGED my relationships with men, my love life was one subject I avoided discussing with her as much as I could. About six months ago, I'd started doing a little sporadic socializing with a couple of my former male classmates: Barry Jones and Carlton Upshur. Both were only marginally handsome and had endured horrific marriages. Barry's wife was serving time in prison for trying to poison him to death by putting cyanide in his meals. Carlton's wife had left him for a woman. They had told almost everybody they knew that they would never remarry or get too serious about a woman again, and I'd shared that information with Bertha. Since she knew they were not a threat to her position in my life, she didn't have anything negative to say about them.

I rotated Carl and Barry. I accompanied them to tame events such as cookouts, church gatherings, and such. I only had sex with them when I felt like it, which was not very often. I'd only slept with Barry twice and Carlton three times. The sex, mediocre at best, ended when I joined Discreet Encounters, but I'd gone out with Barry and Carlton a few more times. I eventually got so busy with my "secret" dates, I stopped going out with them altogether.

When Bertha asked why they'd stopped coming around, I told her both of them had become too serious; and because of their bitterness toward their ex-wives, I didn't think either one was good husband material for me. It was one of the few things she and I agreed on.

"Maybe I should start looking for a white man to marry."

Bertha's jaw dropped and she narrowed her eyes. "A 'white man'? Since when did you start thinking about white men? Aren't black men good enough for you?"

"I must not be good enough for them. Maurice Hamilton was the only black man who ever asked me to marry him," I said in a dry tone of voice.

"For one thing, you aren't the type of black woman a white man worth anything would want to marry," Bertha pointed out.

"What type is that?"

"Most handsome, well-bred white men will only marry a black woman if she's rich, famous, or both. And I know you wouldn't marry one of those uneducated, low-life rednecks from the trailer park, like the ones Jeffrey and Marshall hang out with."

"Can we change the subject?" I said with a moan under my breath. "You know I'm just messing with you."

"Well, don't mess with me too much. My nerves are bad enough." Bertha padded over to the counter, where she'd left her nerve pills, and swallowed a couple of tablets. "Dinner won't be ready for at least another half hour."

"That's okay. I'm going to go back upstairs and do a little reading."

I rushed back up to my room and turned my computer back on. I immediately responded to Enrique Cortez's request. We made a date for Saturday afternoon. He was going to fly up to the Bay Area that morning.

I was glad Bertha had made plans for Saturday to visit one of the nearby Indian casinos with a couple of our elderly neighbors. They were going on a chartered casino bus and would be gone most of the day. She left Saturday morning around seven, before I got up. I was glad she was going to be gone, so I wouldn't have to tell her another lie about where I was going to spend a few hours.

I drove to the Hilton in San Jose, where Enrique had checked in a couple of hours earlier.

I was slightly disappointed when he opened the door to his suite. He wasn't as handsome in person as he was in his picture, and he was at least twenty pounds heavier.

"I am so happy you want to make love with me!" he boomed as he grabbed my arm and pulled me inside. As soon as he closed the door, he wrapped his arms around me and kissed me on both cheeks. "Shall we get started?" He released me and made a sweeping gesture with his hand toward the bed. I hadn't even been in the room two minutes.

"Uh, can we relax a few minutes first?" I said, dropping my purse onto a chair by the door. I looked around the room and felt a sense of déjà vu. Then it hit me: it was the same room I'd been in with my first date, Les Gould! "Do you mind if we order room service? I would love to have a glass of wine."

"Of course. Excuse me if I seem rude and anxious." He grinned, slapping the side of his head, which had half the hair it had in the picture he'd posted. Either he'd been wearing a toupee or he'd posted a very old picture. That was another thing. He looked more like fifty than forty, the age he claimed to be. I liked him, anyway, and he had a nice body. I'd read the reviews about him on the club's review board and every single woman had raved about his lovemaking.

"I'll order some sangria." Enrique had already picked up the telephone. "And how about some lunch? I haven't eaten since I left L.A. this morning."

"That would be nice." I felt more at ease, so I kicked off my shoes and sat down on the bed. "Anything you order is fine with me."

He ordered a bottle of wine and two steak dinners. Then he stood in the middle of the floor and smiled as he stared at me. I crossed my legs, and his eyes got big. "My, my, my, you are a gorgeous woman!" He sprinted across the floor and stopped in front of me with his crotch level with my eyes. He unzipped his pants and whipped out a long, thick, curved penis and shook it at me. "I will do anything you want me to do, so don't be shy."

"I'm not shy, but don't you think we should wait until room service delivers our orders?"

"Aiyee!" he shrieked, slapping the side of his head again. "But of course, we shall wait until after our dinner."

We cuddled on the bed, fully clothed, and chatted about a few mundane things and watched part of a movie I'd never heard of, until our orders arrived.

After we'd eaten and had two glasses of wine each, we undressed and got loose. For the next hour, we made love in every possible position all over the room: in the bed, in the chair by the door, and even standing up.

When we finally decided to get some rest, we got back into the bed. Enrique lay on his back, with me in his arms. What happened next was the last thing I expected.

He started shuddering, and moaning, and clutching his left arm.

"Are you all right?" I asked as I leaped off the bed and stood up.

"Help me! Help me!" he yelped.

"OH, SHIT!" I hollered. "Are you having a stroke?" I started hopping from one foot to the other and looking toward the telephone. "I'm going to call 911!"

"No. No. You don't need to call anybody. This happens all the time. Just . . . just go to my briefcase on the dresser and remove the bottle of pills."

I scurried over to the briefcase and found the pill bottle right on top of a stack of documents. I ran back to the bed and handed the bottle to Enrique. His hands were shaking so hard, I snatched the bottle back and opened it myself.

Not a minute after he'd taken one, he was back to normal. At least he looked like he was.

"Enrique, what happened?"

"It's my heart. I've been on this medication for it since I was a boy. It's miraculous. It immediately does the trick."

My heart was beating so hard, I was tempted to ask Enrique for one of his miraculous pills for myself. "Are you sure you don't want me to call somebody . . . before I leave?" I had already started putting my clothes back on. I wanted to bolt, but I was concerned about Enrique. If a prominent businessman from a foreign country died in a hotel room while he was with a local woman, it would be in the newspaper. And there was no telling what kind of mess I'd be in. I'd have some explaining to do. Not just to the people I knew, but to the cops. What if they tried to say I'd caused his death?

"I'll be fine." Enrique's voice sounded as strong and healthy as before now. "But you don't have to leave."

"Oh, but I think I should," I protested. All I had to do was put on my shoes and open the door.

And that was exactly what I did.

After I retrieved my car, I sped onto the freeway like the cops were chasing me. I got so paranoid, I pulled off at the first rest stop I saw and called Enrique's room. When he didn't pick up by the fifth ring, I thought about making an anonymous call to the hotel and advising them to have someone make sure he was okay. Just as I was about to hang up and do that, he picked up.

"Cortez speaking."

"Enrique, it's Lola," I said in a meek tone of voice. "I was worried about you. . . ."

"Don't be!" he said with a chuckle. "I'm as good as new and I wish you'd come back so I can show you."

"Um, maybe some other time?"

"Then you'd like to see me again someday?"

I hesitated before I answered. "Sure." I had no desire to see this man again.

After he'd praised my body for the fifth or sixth time since we'd made love, he smacked his lips and made a kissing noise before he hung up.

I checked my club in-box before I went to bed and was stunned to see *twelve* new messages. I was flattered that so many hot men wanted to sleep with me. But after the heart attack situation with Enrique, I was not interested in chatting with anyone else tonight. I ignored the messages; and when I got up a few hours later, ten more had come in.

They all sounded interesting, but the only one I was interested in was a photographer from New York named
Roland McMann. He'd included his cell phone number,
so I called him right away. He was going to be in the Bay
Area to photograph some local models for a European
magazine. He wasted no time telling why he had chosen
"ButtMan" as his screen name and why he'd chosen me.

"I like big butts, big brown bubble butts, the bigger
and browner the better," he chanted several times, making me laugh so hard I got the hiccups.

"Well, my behind is not that big," I mumbled.

"Honey, I'm staring at the picture you posted. Compared to all the flat-ass blond bimbo *snacks* I have to deal
with on a daily basis, what you have is a five-course
meal." He had such an amazing sense of humor—I couldn't
wait to meet him.

I had an appointment for my annual checkup, so I
arranged to take off the whole day the following Wednesday. I told Bertha that after my ten o'clock appointment, I
was going to meet Joan and we were going to go to lunch
and do some shopping.

"I'm jealous," Joan told me when I called her and told
her my date's screen name. "I turned down a date with
him last week so I could take my mother-in-law to lunch."

"I hope I won't regret going to meet a man who practically told me I was fat," I said with a chuckle.

"Stop complaining. You're not fat, and I'm sure that's
not what he meant when he made that comment about
your ass. This dude is kind of cute and he's a great photographer. I've seen some of his magazine work."

"I'll call you when I'm on my way back home."

"Later," Joan said with a snicker.

It was the most peculiar date I'd ever been on. Butt-
Man did not want to have sex with me. The only thing he
wanted to do was stare at my butt! He got naked and sat

on the bed. I got naked and I stood in front of him with my hands on my hips.

With one hand, he masturbated. With his other hand, he turned me backward and forward, and side to side, as he moaned and slapped and massaged my butt. There was a look of pure ecstasy on his face the whole time. With all the turning around, I got dizzy real quick and suggested we do something else. The only something else he wanted to do was take pictures of my butt! He got upset because I wouldn't let him do that. Then he started drinking. Within an hour, he had passed out.

As far as I was concerned, the date was over, so I got dressed and left.

I called Joan as soon as I got to my car. "You're not going to believe what happened!" I yelled as soon as she answered.

"Uh-oh! What's wrong?"

"My date tripped out on me. He's dead drunk. He's so out of it, he wouldn't know if the hotel was on fire."

"Is that all? I was afraid you were going to tell me you'd screwed him to death." Joan laughed.

"He got mad because I wouldn't let him take pictures of my ass, so he started drinking."

"Was he good in bed?"

"We didn't even do anything!" I wailed. "All he wanted to do was look at my butt."

Joan laughed harder.

"I'm about to head for the freeway. I'm so fucking horny! If I had enough nerve, I'd go to craigslist and pick out a male escort and have him meet me somewhere."

"Now, don't you even think about going there! That's way too dangerous. I'll bet there are some new messages sitting in your club in-box right now."

"Yeah, you're probably right."

Joan laughed again and I laughed along with her. I

suddenly got quiet. "I hope that if I ever get a date with
that truck driver in San Jose, he'll make me forget about
the disasters I've run into lately."

"You mean Calvin Ramsey."

"Uh-huh."

"I hope he does too, Lola. I hope he's everything
you're looking for."

Chapter 47

Joan

I WAS STILL MILDLY CONCERNED ABOUT LOLA PLANNING to meet up with that truck driver. Neither one of us had had any trouble with any of the men we had met *so far,* but this truck driver living only about a half hour's drive from us was too close for comfort. But I didn't want to spook her by mentioning it too often.

As a matter of fact, I didn't like to harp on any one man more than was necessary. It helped me keep things in the proper perspective. I had had some fantastic times with some incredible men, but I had to remind myself that I could not get too attached to any of my partners. I still had no desire to establish a permanent or a long-term relationship with any of them. And that was an unlikely possibility, anyway. Not as long as I had a suicidal albatross for a husband.

About once a week, Reed reminded me that he "couldn't live without me." The more he got on my nerves, the more I ran "amok," as Lola put it. While he was in his office, I was having the time of my life. But when he came home, I behaved like the wife he wanted. I cooked his favorite meals, gave him massages, and listened to his boring conversations. Our sex life had become so wretched, we didn't even bother to get completely undressed anymore. I was frustrated beyond belief! By the time he went to sleep every night, I was practically foaming at the mouth. I didn't know what I would do if I had to give up my online activity.

Lola was having just as much fun as I was. Last night she kept me on the phone for over an hour raving about the date she'd had earlier in the evening with a software executive from St. Louis in town for a convention.

"His screen name is 'ImaFreak.'"

"Was he?"

"He liked to tickle my toes and masturbate at the same time. After that, he played with my titties for a few minutes, and he masturbated again. That was all we did."

"Yeah, he's a freak. But tickling toes is pretty harmless and I'm sure you didn't get any satisfaction out of that date."

"No, I didn't, but he was a sweet man and I really enjoyed his company. You know something, sometimes it's not all about sex. I enjoy having a nice conversation with a man. Most of the men I've been with in the club were pretty good in bed and in conversation, so I can't complain."

Even though Lola had loosened up a lot, she was not nearly as thick-skinned as I was, so I wouldn't say anything that would ruffle her feathers and set her off. That was why I waited another week before I mentioned the truck driver again.

"So, what did you decide to do about RamRod?" I asked that Friday night. We were having dinner at Bobo's Bistro, a popular restaurant a couple of miles from Lola's house. We had originally planned to drive to San Jose, but a four-car accident had caused all but one lane on Interstate 880 to be closed. Neither of us wanted to stay out too long, so we decided not to wait for the road crew to clear the freeway. We drove around until we found a place that wasn't too crowded.

"I had almost forgotten about that truck driver. I haven't received an e-mail from him in a couple of months," Lola told me, munching on a breadstick.

"Have you thought about e-mailing him? Just to say hello or something?"

"Not really. Why are you asking? I thought you thought it was a bad idea for me to get involved with a man who lived too close."

"I still feel the same way about that. I was just curious. I didn't know if you were even still interested in him."

"I am, I guess. If he's interested in meeting me, he'll eventually get in touch with me again." A wicked smile crossed Lola's face. "I'm having a lot of fun with my other friends, anyway. Especially that date I had a couple of weeks ago with the fitness center owner from Portland, Oregon."

"Please don't tell me about that muscle-bound Samoan again," I warned. "I got jealous as hell when I checked out his profile and saw the picture of Mr. Jon Gunn in his skintight Speedo swim trunks."

"Shut up and listen. He's going to drive down to Newport Beach to look into a fitness center he's thinking about buying. He wants to stop by here on his way and spend a couple of hours with me. I told him I usually don't see the same guy twice, but he keeps pestering me."

"That's a long drive. Will he be driving alone?"

"I didn't ask. If he's traveling with a buddy or his wife, I'm sure he'll figure out a way to meet up with me without them knowing about it."

"You're right. I mean, this whole business is about discreet encounters."

I didn't mention the Samoan again until a week later.

"When is your date with Jon?" I asked Lola. Even though I had my share of superhot dates, I still got jealous of some of the ones she connected with. It seemed like the more sex I got, the more I needed.

Two nights ago, Reed made love to me for the first time in two weeks. To my surprise, he was quite good for a change. I had almost enjoyed our intimacy that night and it lasted more than the usual minute or two. However, last night when he climbed on top of me, he climaxed *before* he even entered me. As soon as he dozed off, which was about a minute later, I slid out of bed and tiptoed to the guest bathroom across the hall, plucked one of my vibrators from the hiding place beneath the bathroom towels in the cabinet beneath the sink, and finished what he had started. Just thinking about it now made me hot all over. I shook the thought out of my head and returned my attention to Lola.

"I haven't heard from Jon since that last e-mail," she told me, looking confused. "I visited his profile page last night. Well, I attempted to, but it had been removed. I have no idea what happened to him, and it's been bothering me all day."

"That would bother me too," I admitted. "But I can top that."

Lola's face froze and she gazed at me with her eyes stretched wide open. "Is it something bad?"

"In a way." I sniffed and sat up straighter in my seat.

"Three weeks ago, a gorgeous salesman named Phillip Newton told me in his first e-mail that he couldn't wait to give me a tongue bath. He lives in Salt Lake City with a wife and their *eight* kids. The wife's usually too tired to make love, so he has to do what he has to do. We e-mailed each other back and forth for two weeks, but we couldn't set up a date because his schedule kept changing. Last night he told me that he would not be connecting with me or anybody else. According to him, one of his previous connections suddenly found Jesus and she confessed everything to her husband. She even gave the husband Phillip's e-mail address, his real name, and the name of the company he works for! After receiving numerous threatening e-mails from the reformed woman's irate husband in a matter of days, he sent me one last e-mail and told me he had decided to end his membership."

"Damn. Why are you just now telling me this?"

I hunched my shoulders and gave Lola a wan look. "I didn't tell you because I didn't want to listen to more of your paranoid mumbo jumbo."

"I wish you wouldn't keep things like that from me. A woman's deranged husband sending threatening e-mails to a club member is serious, and that's something I need to know about. Will you promise me that if something else weird happens, you'll let me know right away?"

"I will," I muttered. "Any more questions?"

"Just one. How long are you going to date? Having sex with a bunch of men can put a lot of stress on a woman's body. . . ."

"Look, if you were in a steady relationship, you'd be having sex at least five times a week. Multiply that by four. That's twenty times a month. If you have a hot guy, it'll be more. What's the difference between that and you having sex with twenty different men a month?"

"I'd *never* date that many men in one month!"

"But do you see what I'm trying to say?"

"I guess." Lola paused and gave me a thoughtful look. "Joan, you always have an answer for everything, but you didn't answer my question about how long you're going to date."

"I know. But to tell you the truth, I don't know how long I'll do this dating thing. I'm sure I'll get bored with it someday and look for other ways to keep myself occupied. In the meantime, let's enjoy it while we can. Okay?"

"O . . . kay." Lola blew out a loud breath before she said anything else. "I got a message from a guy in Atlanta last night. A software guru. He'll be out here next week for his company retreat."

"You don't sound too interested."

"He wants me to wear a mask to bed."

"Stop!" I started laughing, but Lola remained silent. "I hope you didn't agree to see him. The man has a serious problem. A mask? What kind of mask?"

"I didn't ask. He said he'd wear one too."

"Girl, if I ever find out you went to bed with a man wearing any kind of mask, I'm going to talk about you like a dog for the rest of your life. I hope you didn't agree to meet that fool. Paddling somebody's butt or handcuffing them is one thing. That's standard freak shit and a lot of people do it, even me. But if wearing a mask is not a red flag, I don't know what is."

"I told him, straight-up, I wasn't interested."

"Block him so you won't have to hear from him anymore. I'd rather have you hook up with that truck driver. At least he sounds *normal*."

Chapter 48

Calvin

I RARELY THOUGHT ABOUT THE MEN I'D KILLED DURING my stint in the war, and I had no idea how many. It had been so impersonal. I'd even enjoyed blowing away some of those crazy motherfuckers.

It was hard for me to imagine myself killing a civilian, especially one that I had feelings for. But when it happened, it was a totally different experience. It was almost like killing myself. And that was something I'd never do, even though the pain Glinda had caused me was unbearable. Other people would probably have committed suicide to end the pain. Getting rid of the source was what did the job for me. But only temporarily. Each time I thought I had "healed," the pain resumed with a vengeance.

It didn't take long for me to cross a line I never thought I'd even get close to: I chose to become a murderer, and in the first degree. Glinda had not only "killed" me, but she had caused the deaths of other women whose only crime had been that they had crossed my path.

Glinda had fought hard. She had punched my face and attempted to pry my hands from around her throat, but it had done her no good.

I held my breath so long during the struggle, I thought I was going to pass out before she did. Several minutes later, she stopped breathing and moving. An unholy stench that reminded me of rotting eggs suddenly filled the air. I released her and she crumpled to the floor like a rag doll. I stared at her for a few moments. All of a sudden, one of her legs shuddered and she let out a hissing noise.

I squatted down and felt for a pulse, pleased that I could not feel one. I stood back up and watched as a huge wet stain formed around her ass. She had involuntarily emptied her bowels and bladder, which explained the foul, rotting-egg odor. The mess she had made on my carpeting, and her shit and piss stinking up my bedroom, made me even angrier.

"Look at you now, bitch!" I barked.

I rushed to my laundry room. From my dryer, I grabbed a blanket, which I had washed a few hours earlier, and rolled her up in it, swaddling her from her head to her feet. While she lay on the floor looking like a huge burrito, I went into the kitchen and removed a bottle of carpet cleaner from the broom closet.

After I had cleaned my carpet and sprayed the room with air freshener, I hoisted Glinda's body off the floor and placed her on the floor in my walk-in closet, right next to a pile of other useless items I planned to dispose of. I was sorry I didn't have a live hand grenade to toss in behind her!

Just as I was about to go take a shower, my telephone rang. It was Robert, the neighbor who had told me he'd seen Glinda leaving with that asshole.

"Hey, brother! I'm glad I caught you!" he hollered.

"What's up, dude?" It was amazing how cheerful I was able to sound so soon after committing murder.

"One of my former frat brothers is coming to the house in about an hour for a little celebration with a few friends. He just got back from the war in the Middle East too. I know you're over there by yourself these days, so I hope you can join us. There will be a few single ladies present, so they'll help take your mind off Glinda."

I was delighted to know that people still cared about me. I didn't hesitate to respond. "That sounds like a good plan, my man. Thanks for thinking of me."

It was good to get away from the scene of my crime and have a few drinks with someone other than just myself. I enjoyed meeting some of Robert's friends and dancing and chatting with a couple of the female guests. My euphoria was short.

A mysterious migraine suddenly erupted in my head, which jump-started my imagination. When I noticed a group of guests in a corner whispering and glancing in my direction, I thought they were whispering about me. My head felt like it was going to explode. Maybe somebody had been peeping in my window and saw what I had done to Glinda. Or . . . maybe I was going crazy? At one point, I even thought I saw her spirit floating toward me. When you have the body of a woman you murdered in your bedroom closet, your mind can play all kinds of tricks on you. I stumbled and bumped into a woman who had been giving me the eye since I walked in the door.

"You want some company later on, soldier boy? I heard all about what you're going through with your wife and that's a damn shame. You look like you need some tender loving care," she said. The woman paused and looked down at my crotch. Then she hauled off and squeezed the inside of my thigh, dangerously close to my manhood. "Feels like it too. . . ."

"Uh, maybe so. Where do you live?" I asked. There were times when a man was so conflicted, even an ugly woman looked good. The one coming on to me now looked like a mule.

"On Preston Parkway." She paused and gave me a double wink. "But my husband might sneak up on me, so it'd be safer to go to your place."

"So you're married?" I asked with one eyebrow raised. I couldn't believe that a married woman could be brazen enough to throw herself at another man in front of a room full of witnesses! Had things changed that much while I was overseas? Was infidelity contagious, or had every married woman gone stark raving mad?

"Slightly."

"Well, I don't think I'd like to spend time with a 'slightly' married woman tonight," I said with a snort. "Excuse me, please." I walked away before that horny heifer could say another word.

I had to be alone so I could decide what to do with Glinda's body. I thanked my host and departed. I literally ran all the way back to my house.

I knew I couldn't hide her in my closet too long. She was eventually going to decompose. From what I'd seen on television shows like *CSI* and *Forensic Files*, one rotting body could stink up a whole block. I had to do something, and I had to do it fast.

I didn't even go to bed that night. I sat on my living-room couch with a fifth of Jack Daniel's on the coffee table in front of me. By morning the Jack Daniel's was empty, but I didn't feel drunk at all. I didn't even bother to shower or fix myself a cup of coffee. An hour later, I strolled into Home Depot five minutes after they opened. I purchased an enormous horizontal deep freezer—which ironically looked like a makeshift coffin—that I could easily store in a corner in my two-car garage. I paid extra to have it delivered the same day.

"This is a mighty big freezer for a house as small as yours, brother," one of the two husky black deliverymen commented after the freezer had been put in place. "I've only helped deliver ones this size to restaurants and big hotels, and one to a huge mansion in the hills. It's a good thing you're going to keep this bad boy in your garage, 'cause it'd take up way too much space in a regular-size room." I didn't like the way the man was looking at me. It was almost like he knew I'd purchased the freezer for something other than storing food.

"Uh, I will be moving into a much bigger house soon," I said dryly. "In the meantime, I'm planning to host my family's annual reunion in a couple of weeks. You know how we black folks like to eat." I nudged the man's shoulder and winked. He looked from the freezer to me and nodded. "I'm going over to Costco later today so I can stock up on meat before their sale ends," I threw in.

"Oomph, oomph, oomph. Brother, you must have one huge family." The chatty deliveryman plucked a large white handkerchief out of his shirt pocket and wiped sweat off his face. What he said next made my heart drop. "I bet you could hide a dead body in a freezer this big!"

I laughed. I gave both dudes a generous tip and sent them on their way.

I immediately placed Glinda in her final resting place, still wrapped in that blanket. Then I piled tools, oil-stained rags, and other odds and ends on top of the freezer.

Chapter 49

Calvin

A WEEK AFTER I KILLED MY WIFE, I STARTED MY NEW job driving an eighteen-wheeler for Kessler and Sons, a family-owned trucking business based in Vancouver, Washington. It was a much better position than my former job as an office manager at the utility company, with a micromanaging supervisor I'd despised from the bottom of my heart. There was nothing like cruising the interstate highways transporting fresh lumber. The pay and the benefits were spectacular, and I was going to enjoy the mobility and the independence.

I couldn't believe how easy it was for me to go on with my life. Everybody who knew me and Glinda knew she had left me for another man, so they were reluctant to mention her in my presence. They were all happy when I began to date again. I was not anxious to bring any of my new lady friends to my house at first, but I eventually did. Nobody had any reason to go snooping around in my garage, or any other part of my residence. But I watched every visitor like a hawk, anyway. I kept the garage light off and the door leading to it from the kitchen locked. For more insurance, I picked up half-a-dozen white mice from a pet shop and turned them loose in the garage. *If* a woman did wander in, once she saw those frisky, squeaking rodents, she'd bolt.

About two weeks after I'd returned from my first haul down to the San Diego area, I received a call from my older brother, Ronald. He was one of the few relatives who had not severed ties with me. I was glad to hear his voice.

"In case you haven't heard, Glinda's missing. Nobody has seen or heard from her since last month," he told me, speaking in a low, tentative manner.

"I hope she's okay. Anybody have any idea where she might be?"

"No. Everybody thinks it's a damn shame the way she deserted you. Too bad you didn't get a chance to beat the hell out of her first."

"I've never hit a woman. The way things were going between us, I knew it was a matter of time before she took off, so I was prepared."

"It wouldn't have been so bad if she had not left you so soon after you got out of the military. That was some cold-blooded shit she pulled on you, and it'll come back to haunt her someday. You're a good man, bro. As long as you keep the faith and honor the Lord's Word, you'll be blessed with a woman who will appreciate you."

"I know I will. God is good," I said with a sniff. "When, and if, Glinda turns up, I won't contest the divorce. I won't be happy about giving her anything out of the house, since I paid for it all. And I'm glad I never put her name on the papers to the house. But I can live with having to pay her alimony. The way I know her, she won't be single for long, anyway. The last time I talked to her, she mentioned something about her new squeeze wanting to marry her. . . ."

"You might not have to worry about a divorce, paying alimony, or anything else. I saw on the news this evening that the cops suspect that that ex-con she was involved with is responsible for her disappearance."

"Oh? Why do they think that?" I asked with my fingers crossed.

"He had a violent streak a mile wide. The last two times I saw Glinda, she had a black eye and a busted lip. Her family finally went to the cops last week and they started an investigation. When they asked the ex-con about her, he denied knowing anything and then he disappeared the next day! I have a feeling she's dead and he dumped her body someplace where she'll never be found. Him taking off the way he did is as good as him admitting his guilt."

"I hope the cops find this joker before too long."

"They will. Folks ought to know by now that nobody can get away with murder. There is too much technology now and cops are getting smarter every day. Not that I would know from experience, but it's hard to be a successful criminal these days."

"You're right," I said with my fingers, now trembling, still crossed.

A month after the conversation with my brother, the cops found Glinda's lover's decapitated body on the side of a country road in Juarez, Mexico. Dude was a bigger fish than everybody thought. He had been dealing drugs for a couple of years and had double-crossed some members of a ruthless Mexican cartel, who had made hundreds of people disappear *permanently.* They had also tortured some of his family members, including his eighty-year-old grandmother. And he and Glinda had made several overnight trips to Mexico a few days before her disappearance. It was no wonder people were trying to guess where the cartel thugs had dumped her body. One "reliable source" even told the cops she'd been sold to a brothel in Mexico City. I kept my opinions to myself. I was the only person who knew where Glinda really was, and I wanted to keep it that way.

Hollywood couldn't have come up with shit this good! With all that was going on, who would even tune up their brain to think that I had anything to do with Glinda Price's disappearance?

People eventually stopped talking about Glinda, but I thought about her day and night, seven days a week. On the third-month anniversary of her death, I wandered into Jerry's, a dive bar across town. I had just returned from a haul down to Bakersfield in a very heavy rainstorm. With a lot of maneuvering and luck, I had avoided hitting a deer that had leaped out of nowhere. Less than half an hour after that, I'd encountered an hour-long roadblock due to a mudslide. I was pretty frazzled by the time I got back to San Jose and parked my rig in the company's local lot. I retrieved my personal vehicle, but I didn't want to go home to an empty house, so I decided to stop for a drink to calm my nerves.

Jerry's was located in a pretty rough area and shared the block with the Mahoney Street Projects. The bar was crowded, but I noticed one woman in particular because she was hugging and kissing on a dude at the bar, and making eyes at several others, including me. Another reason I noticed her was because she looked a little like Glinda. Just watching her make a spectacle of herself made my head spin and my blood boil. What I should have done was leave, because what I was witnessing was bringing back some very painful memories.

About fifteen minutes after I'd arrived, a large Wesley Snipes–looking brother strolled in. From the menacing look on his face, I could tell that he had an attitude that wouldn't quit. He looked around for a few seconds; then he strode directly over to the frisky woman and attempted to pull her into his arms. She slapped him, kicked his leg, and bit his hand. Was it no wonder so many women got their asses kicked by their men? Had she been my woman . . . Well, I had a foolproof way of dealing with a slutty woman, so I knew what I'd do *again* if I had to. I didn't even know this woman, and I was tempted to walk up and beat the dog shit out of her myself.

Dude threw up his hands. He left the bar before a huge bouncer, slumped in a seat near the rear and yakking on his cell telephone, even looked up. Ten minutes later, the woman left alone. From the way she was staggering, it was obvious she was quite drunk.

I eased out of the bar and stayed a few yards behind as I followed her to a shabby Ford parked a block away on the opposite side of the street.

She leaned against the door on the driver's side, fumbling with her purse. I kept my distance and waited until she had rooted around in her purse and removed her keys. As soon as she started to unlock her car, I trotted up to her.

"Excuse me," I began. She whirled around. The streetlights were very bright. I was pleased to see such an inviting smile on her pretty face. I tried to look helpless by blinking rapidly and wringing my hands. "Sister, I hate to bother you, but one of my tires is flat. I was wondering if you had a jack I could borrow? I'll pay you."

She looked me up and down and pursed her lips. "Weren't you just in Jerry's Bar?"

"Yes, I was," I replied, giving her the biggest smile I could manage.

"I was going to ask you to buy me a drink, until, well, you saw what happened when my old man walked in," she slurred, totally ignoring my request to borrow her jack. "You want some company tonight? I can make you feel real good," she bragged as she tapped my crotch. I wondered if Glinda had behaved the same way during her prowling escapades. "You have a hard-on already. I don't want to let it go to waste, do you?" she teased.

I was glad she removed her hand, because I was about to snap. "Um, no," I mouthed, looking around. It was after midnight and still somewhat chilly because of the storm, so I didn't expect to see any people out and about on foot in this area. I knew they wouldn't come out to investigate if they heard a ruckus, especially a woman screaming in distress.

I had never lived in a low-rent neighborhood like this one, but I knew the way things worked in these concrete jungles. The residents heard violent commotions and even gunfire on a regular basis and all they did was duck for cover. Most of the time, they didn't even call the cops because they didn't trust them, and they usually had some dirt on their own hands too.

"If you'll get that jack for me, I'll fix my tire and we can be on our way. I don't live too far. You can leave your car here and ride with me, or you can follow me."

"I'll ride with you. I can't spend the whole night, though. I have to get up early in the morning for work," she told me, sounding disappointed. She was already stumbling toward the trunk of her Ford.

"I have to work tomorrow too," I said. This tramp didn't even know my name and she had already agreed to go home with me and let me fuck her!

She opened her trunk and removed a jack and pranced back over to me. "Here," she said, thrusting the tool into my hand. "I think it's going to start raining again and I just got over a cold. I'll wait for you in my car."

I gently placed my hand around her tiny wrist. "Could you hold the flashlight while I change my tire?" I asked very nicely, still holding on to her. "I promise I'll be done before the rain starts."

"Oh, all right," she said with a roll of her eyeballs. "Baby, you have a mighty firm grip," she purred as she caressed my hand, which was still wrapped around her wrist. "I hope the rest of you is mighty firm too. . . ."

This horny heifer was so anxious to get busy with me, I thought she was going to drag me behind a bush or pull me into the backseat of her car.

"That's for you to find out," I growled, poking her between her breasts. "As soon as I change my tire, we'll be on our way. Let me get the flashlight out of my glove compartment."

She held on to my arm as we walked to the Jeep Cherokee I had purchased a couple of weeks ago.

"Hey! You just bought this ride!" she gasped, pointing to my temporary license plate. She stopped walking and placed her hands on her hips. "Didn't a jack come with it?"

"Yes. My neighbor borrowed it yesterday and hasn't returned it yet."

"That's why I don't lend things anymore. I'm sure you didn't think you'd need your jack tonight, but things like this happen when you least expect it."

"That is so true! It'll be a long time before I lend out anything else!"

"Which tire is it?" she asked. That was the last thing she said. She didn't know what hit her when I brought that jack down on her head.

While she lay passed out on the front seat of my Jeep, I searched through her purse until I found her wallet. She had just renewed her driver's license. Her name was

Brenda Betts. She was twenty-six, an organ donor, and she wore contacts. I fished a work badge out of her purse. She was a physical therapist. I couldn't believe that a woman who took care of sick people would hang out in a sleazy bar like Jerry's and try to pick up men. Especially a woman who already had a man!

When Brenda regained consciousness on the floor in my garage, she couldn't scream, or do much of anything else. I had covered her mouth, tied her hands behind her back, and secured her feet with duct tape, which I had purchased at Home Depot the same day I'd bought the freezer.

"Do you love your man?" I asked as I stood over her with my hands on my hips, shining a flashlight in her face.

With tears rolling out of her eyes, she nodded.

"Have you ever cheated on him?"

She hesitated and then slowly shook her head.

"When you were growing up, didn't your mama tell you not to trust strangers?"

She slowly nodded again.

"You love your man, but you were going to fuck a complete stranger tonight? You don't even know my name!"

It took her a few moments to respond; and when she did, she shook her head even harder.

"You like dudes, don't you?" I asked.

She nodded vigorously this time and made moaning noises.

"Well, I'm glad you do, because the next dude you're going to see is Jesus. Oops! I meant to say Satan." I couldn't believe how fast she died after my hands went around her throat.

Chapter 50

Calvin

DURING THE NEXT FEW WEEKS, I SAW SEVERAL MORE women who reminded me of Glinda. I wanted to grab each one by the throat and squeeze it until the light in her eyes went out so that I could relive the experience of killing Glinda.

There was a time when the first thing I looked at on a woman was her face. Then I checked out her butt and breasts. I still looked at those things, but now I paid more attention to her neck than all the rest of her body parts put together. But not on a frumpy woman with a neck as thick and rough-looking as a linebacker. I preferred slim, swan-like, dainty necks; those excited me because they were so fragile and the easiest way to do what I had to do. . . .

I was getting bored and restless. I couldn't wait to initiate my next project.

My obsession had begun to control my life and there was nothing I could do to stop it. There were some days and nights when my hands shook so uncontrollably, my head ached, my chest tightened, and my stomach flip-flopped so hard it was difficult for me to function. When I experienced one of those episodes while I was on the road, I pulled over and waited until the feeling passed.

One night I was close enough to a truck stop, so I pulled in and parked. Within ten minutes, three different prostitutes tapped on my window and offered their services. In less than an hour, five more approached me. One happy hooker even told me that she would suck my dick for five dollars because she liked my looks. I turned them all down. The only thing that saved one of those eight lot lizards from dying that night was the fact that I had already wasted too much valuable time and had to get back on the road as soon as possible.

A week later, while I was having dinner in a restaurant about a mile from my house, I noticed a woman sitting alone across the room. I wanted to take her home and *keep* her. My plan was to follow her when she left and do whatever I had to do to get her into my Jeep. Fortunately for her, two other women and three dudes joined her.

A few days after that, I was cruising around and spotted another potential project as she entered a building on Hudson Street. I made a U-turn and parked in a lot at the corner. Thirty minutes later, the same woman strolled back out with a baby in her arms. That was the only reason she didn't die that night. I would never do anything that would endanger a child.

The next day, I encountered a woman at a street fair who was so drunk she could barely walk straight. She was loud and dressed like a slut, just like Glinda. Just as I was about to move on her, two big husky older females approached.

The larger one gave me a surprised look and said loud enough for everybody within a mile to hear, "I know you!

You're Calvin—uh, I don't remember your last name. You drive one of them big-ass trucks. I met you at Marianne Cundiff's housewarming party in Oakland a couple of months ago!"

I grinned sheepishly, made a few necessary comments, and promptly slunk back out of sight. I visited three different bars that night and had no luck. I was getting desperate. I had a hungry monster roosting inside me that had to be fed real soon.

I regretted not keeping Glinda alive long enough to torture her and make her truly sorry for the way she had hurt me. Whenever I recalled the look of fear in her eyes when she realized what was happening to her, I smiled.

The first hitchhiker I picked up at a truck stop in Eugene, Oregon, was a girl in her late teens.

Kimberly wore jeans, with ripped knees, and a white T-shirt, with a huge picture on the front of Bob Marley smoking a thick joint. She was white and didn't remotely resemble Glinda, but she looked like another female who was just as disgusting to me: Paris Hilton. She had big dingy teeth and long blond hair with black roots. Every time she giggled and belched, which was almost every time she opened her mouth, I wanted to slap her.

After chatting with her for just a few minutes, I realized what a no-good whore she was too. She bragged about all the men she had "got over on" and how she had just left her husband after cleaning out the two thousand bucks he had saved in his bank account. And she had slept with his best friend. I was surprised that nobody had disposed of this beast already. I was appalled, but I managed to control my actions. I even laughed along with her as we cruised down Interstate 5. I stopped laughing when she offered to "pay" me for the ride with sex.

"You really look like a girl who can show a man a real sweet time," I said with a chuckle, knowing a corny statement like that would make her feel even more comfortable.

"Oh, I can show a man the best time he ever had. The guy I was with last night, he wanted me to look him up when he gets back from Sacramento. When I make love to men, they never forget me." She let out a loud giggle and it sounded even more annoying this time.

"I'm sure you'll make me feel the same way," I told her, massaging her knee with my trembling hand.

"By the way, I'll probably never see you again, but I would like to know your name. I'm Kimberly. What do I call you?"

"I'm . . . Thomas," I said.

"Thomas, let's go somewhere and get busy."

Without saying another word, I eased my big rig down a long, dark road, which I had visited many times before when I needed to take a bathroom break. Kimberly removed her clothes and was clawing at mine before I even parked.

We moved to the sleeping section of my cab and I clicked on my interior light and gave her a closer look. I almost threw up. Her pale flesh looked like the underbelly of a fish and she almost had more black hair on her legs than I had on my head.

"Hurry up. I ain't got all night." She glanced at my dick, which was as hard as a brick, and rolled her eyes.

That eye roll confused me because I thought she was anxious to have sex with me.

"I like it rough," she cooed.

Oh, I was rough all right. I rammed my rod into Kimberly in such a frenzied way, you would have thought that she was paying me to do so. I finished as quickly as I could, and she quickly let me know what a disappointment I had been.

"What a fucking *joke* this was!" she griped, shaking her head and looking at my dick at the same time.

Kimberly was already doomed, but then she said something that hastened her demise; something no man ever wanted to hear—especially a black man: "For a brother, you sure ain't *hung* the way I expected. I could have had a better time poking myself with a Tootsie Roll." She glared at me like she wanted to bite my head off.

Chapter 51

Calvin

KIMBERLY SNEERED AT ME AS I SAT FACING HER WITH every fluid in my body boiling with rage. "Ex . . . cuse me?" I said as the monster in my belly growled.

"I always heard that *you people* had real big dicks. Now I know that's nothing but a myth that black dudes probably started! I've seen more meat in a hot dog bun than what you've got between your legs!" she said nastily. Then she laughed.

Her complaining about my performance was bad enough. But she had to go and complain about the size of my penis too! That bitch! That heifer! I couldn't wait to put out her lights. If she didn't have it coming, I didn't know who did. My head felt like it had been trampled on by a huge, angry bull; that was how painful my sudden headache felt. I snapped like a twig. And so did her neck.

When I was sure she was dead, I rifled through her backpack. Her shabby, cheap wallet contained almost two grand, probably what was left of the money she had stolen from her husband. According to her driver's license, her full name was Kimberly Diane Hollenbeck. I stuffed the money into my wallet and put her wallet, with the rest of its contents intact, into the duffel bag I carried on each trip.

I suddenly panicked. I had no idea what to do with the body! I couldn't take her to my house, especially since it would be another day before I returned to San Jose.

There was only one thing I could do. I removed Kimberly's naked body from my truck and dumped her onto the ground and dropped her clothes on top of her. Then I covered her with branches and dead leaves.

I had used a condom, so I was not worried about them finding my DNA in her pothole of a pussy or me contracting HIV. I double wrapped the condom with a large leaf and put it in my jacket pocket. I would flush it down the next toilet I stopped to use.

Two months after the episode with Kimberly, I encountered several more women who suffered the same fate. I *almost* let one go. She was an obese Native American woman named Morning Star. She was in her late twenties and had a mug that could curdle milk: tight beady black eyes, a faint mustache, a hawk nose, and a jawline like Jay Leno's. Her long, oily black hair, slicked back and held in place with numerous bobby pins, reminded me of a beaver's tail. I was surprised to hear that she had just gotten married three months ago.

When I warned her about how dangerous it was to hitchhike, she laughed and said, "Nobody would have to rape me, no how. I love to fuck. And truckers are so lonely, they don't care what I look like."

I was horrified. *Aren't there any women who got married and stayed faithful to their husbands?* I wondered. I asked this booger bear point-blank if she had fooled around on her husband yet. Not only did she admit to doing so, she had done it with her sister's black husband because she hated her sister and she had always wanted to "make it" with a black dude.

Morning Star made it with another black dude that night and her double-wide ass ended up in a ditch in some woods a few miles from Fresno.

There was the girl near Sacramento and the one in Bakersfield, and others. I had collected a lot of trophies: a gold bracelet from a Jewish runaway, a buckskin jacket from another Paris Hilton clone, and a pair of red high heels from a woman I'd picked up at a truck stop in Barstow. I stored my trophies in a cardboard box, which I kept in my bedroom closet for a while. One night when I thought I heard noises coming from the box, I got spooked. I made a trip to a hardware store and I purchased a large metal footlocker. I put the box of trophies into my "treasure chest" and padlocked it before I hauled it up to my attic.

I hadn't opened the freezer since I'd stored the third woman, a stripper with a bad attitude. I'd coldcocked her during a private lap dance in my Jeep a couple of months ago. But I went up to my attic at least once a week to admire my treasures.

I couldn't even remember what all of the females had looked like that I'd picked up on the road, or exactly where I'd left each one. I followed the news religiously. Every now and then, there was a report about a hunter or a hiker stumbling across the skeletal remains of a female in a wooded area along the interstate highway. Since some of the women had probably given me fake names, I had no idea if any of them were the ones that I had chastised or not.

If somebody could "connect" the three missing black women from the Bay Area, the way that busybody reporter had done, it was just a matter of time before some-body realized several female hitchhikers had disappeared in the last six years along the same interstate routes that I drove on the same dates.

I was still mad as hell about what Glinda had done to me, but I had calmed down a little, so I decided to slow down—temporarily. Even as clever and lucky as I was, I didn't want to take too many chances. Some of the smart-est criminals made the dumbest mistakes and I didn't want my name to be added to that list. I even hoped that I would eventually find another way to channel my anger, but I knew it would be a while before I got to that point. The belly of the beast inside me was only half full.

Chapter 52

Calvin

*L*ESS THAN A MONTH AFTER I'D BEGUN SEARCHING THE Web for new projects, I stumbled upon the profile of a woman who brought that beast inside me out of hibernation. She was, of all things, a *grocery store clerk*—a long step down from the lawyers and other high-level female club members I had already acquainted myself with.

Her name was Lola Poole, but it should have been Glinda Price. Lola was a dead ringer for Glinda. Had I not known better, I'd have sworn that they were twins. I felt a level of euphoria that I'd never felt before. The urge to complete another project had returned with a vengeance. I *had* to resume what I had been destined to do. Good God! I felt like I had been reborn! Through Lola, Glinda had returned from the dead so I could kill her all over again. And this time it was going to be even more therapeutic.

Lola immediately responded to the first e-mail I sent to her club in-box. She was interested, but she claimed to have a very "full schedule for a while" and didn't know when we could hook up. Bitch! She didn't fool me. I knew she was itching to lie down with me. But like so many other women, she wanted to play mind games. And I was going to give her a hell of a run for her money. I was going to beat the bitch at her own game because I had a real plan, she didn't. I didn't want to rush things, so I claimed I had a very full schedule too. I planned to develop the relationship slowly. I wanted to savor every moment. And when the time came, that cow would suffer more than Glinda and all the others had put together!

I was glad Lola was in no hurry to meet me. I admired her for being honest enough to let me know that she wanted to dillydally with a few other men first. I had my own theory: This man-eater knew I was a good man, but she wanted to nibble on a few others before she decided to settle down with a dude like me. I figured she was already stringing a few other dudes along, and after she'd sampled each one, including me, she'd pick and choose the one she wanted to string along even longer. Oh, I had her number, all right. She obviously had no solid career aspirations; otherwise, she would not have been working as a grocery store clerk for almost *fifteen* years. Her ultimate goal was to land a husband.

The last messages she left in my in-box made me sick: *Hey, Calvin! I looked at your profile and picture again and I hope we can get together someday soon. Keep in touch!*☺☺ *BrownSugar*

BrownSugar was BrownShit!

I didn't bother responding to that corny dribble right away. I'd get back to her in a few days. I planned to communicate with her just enough to keep her interested. The first time I saw her picture, I knew *immediately* that I was going to kill her.

When we did finally meet, I'd wine and dine her and remain somewhat aloof so I wouldn't make her nervous and scare her off. I wouldn't even object if she wanted to continue seeing other men—as if I could stop a bitch from screwing around on me, anyway! I'd even encourage her to do so. I suspected that before she joined the dating site, she had already hurt some righteous men with her nasty self. With her being involved with several men around the time of her disappearance, the cops would have a very long list of suspects to focus on.

It had been six months since I'd sent Lola the first e-mail. In the last one I'd sent, which was a month ago, I asked for a telephone number so I could hear her voice. But she'd declined. She also told me that she didn't feel comfortable revealing too much of her personal information too soon. I laughed out loud, long and hard, when I read that part of her e-mail. The stupid bitch didn't have to reveal her "personal information" too soon. Everything I needed to know about her was posted on Facebook: her full name and the city she resided in! Her name and home address were listed in the telephone book! In her club profile, she had even included the name of that Mickey Mouse grocery store she worked for and it was listed in bold print in the phone book too.

Like so many other ignorant women on the Internet, Lola had made herself a sitting duck and didn't even realize it. No wonder the body count in America was so high. And it was going to get even higher. . . .

Had I met Lola a couple of years ago, she would be a

Popsicle by now, just like Glinda and the two "room-mates" she shared the freezer with.

Christmas was coming early for me this year. Lola was going to be a gift in every sense of the word. She had re-ceived five-star reviews from club members she'd been with. That was enough for me. So in addition to her being my most important future project, I had a good fuck to look forward to as well.

Lola Poole. It was so ironic that her last name rhymed with "fool." So that she'd keep me on her radar, I sent her another e-mail a few hours ago. I practically begged her for a phone number so I could call and text her. She was so glad to hear from me; she wasted no time giving me her cell phone and her landline number. I called her right away.

"Lola? Is it really you?" I asked when she answered on the second ring.

"Yup! It's really me!" she said, sounding like a fucking cheerleader.

"You sound so young."

"People tell me that all the time. Sometimes I have to remind myself that I'll be thirty-three this year."

"So, have you been keeping busy?"

"Yup."

"I'm sure you have." I chuckled, but what I really wanted to do was scream at this bitch and call her every trashy name I could think of. But I was way too cool to lose my cool. I had come too far to derail the plans I had for this nasty heifer.

Women were like books and I knew how to read them. Every page on Lola's book was in big bold print. She was probably already planning a big church wedding for us! Well, if I had not planned to keep her body after I killed her, she'd still be participating in a big church event, all right: her funeral.

"I know a beautiful woman like you wouldn't sit around the house twiddling her thumbs. I'm sure you're one of the most popular women in the Discreet Encounters club, so I know you get a lot of requests for, uh, discreet encounters."

"Well, yeah, I do get a lot of requests," she said slowly, clearing her throat. "I'm glad I joined the club. I have a date lined up for this Friday night. *I wish it was with you.*"

"So do I," I said, almost choking on the words.

"I . . . I realized there was something special about you the first time I saw your picture. I didn't want just to sleep with you and move on to the next man, I . . ." She paused. "I'm sorry. I'm making a fool of myself, but I just want you to know that you really are special to me."

"I feel the same way about you, Lola," I admitted. She was the most annoying, disgusting, stupid, love-struck female I had ever encountered! Bitch, slut, whore! She had probably picked out the names of the children she thought we were going to have.

"I know we've only communicated a few times, but I can already tell that you are a very interesting man." She chuckled.

Despite my rage, I was actually in a jovial mood, so I chuckled too. "And I can already tell that you're a very interesting woman."

"I've met a lot of other nice men in the club, and I've had a whole lot of fun, but I'm not going to be a member too much longer."

"Oh? And why is that?"

"Well, I'd like to settle down with one man."

"Oh? Is there someone special in your life now?"

"No, but I'm sure I'll meet somebody special soon."

I held my breath and counted to five. Sometimes that helped me control my tongue and my anger. This bitch was lucky I couldn't come through the phone. "My schedule is a little more flexible now. If you're not too busy in the next couple of weeks, maybe you can squeeze me between other dates on your calendar."

"Yeah. I'm sure I'll be able to do that. To tell you the truth, I was beginning to think we'd never even get this far," she said, trying to sound coy. She was about as coy as a madam.

"I guess it has been a long time since I sent you that first message, huh?"

"Almost six months. I printed out your message and it's got the date on it."

Why would a woman do juvenile shit like that and then tell the man? She probably kept a diary, too, and called the Psychic Hotline on a regular basis to listen to their lies about her love life. "If I hadn't had to do so many runs and issues going on at work, we could have gotten together long before now."

"Calvin, you don't have to explain anything to me. I've been just as busy as you."

"I'll give you a call in the next week or so and we can make plans to get together. Are you okay with that?"

"Oh yes! I'm really looking forward to it!" This cow sounded like it was Jesus she was going to meet. Well, she would meet him real soon. . . .

"I have a few personal issues I need to attend to first."

"Oh. I hope it's nothing too serious."

"Don't worry, it's not. A lot of things happened while I was in the military that need to be straightened out. The most serious one is that my ex didn't pay the property taxes for two years in a row, like she was supposed to, so that's a big mess. I have court dates up the ass. But I promise I won't take too long."

Everything that had just slid out of my mouth was untrue. There was only one reason I was putting Lola off, and that wouldn't change: I was taking my time because I wanted to savor every day, hour, minute, and second of the whole experience of killing her from start to finish.

"Okay, Calvin. I can't wait to meet you in person."

Chapter 53

Calvin

I HAD KILLED SEVERAL WOMEN AND I HAD NO REGRETS. What I didn't know yet was if I'd continue to kill after I killed Lola. It all depended on that imaginary beast in my belly. If killing Lola put him to rest permanently, I would be done. If it didn't, I would probably continue to kill until I was too old and physically unable to do so.

In the meantime, I wanted to have some fun.

Discreet Encounters had opened up a whole new world for me. So far, I'd had encounters with some fine-looking, sex-hungry women. It was one of the reasons I was holding off on my first real date with Lola Poole. I had her thinking that it was really because of my work schedule and other commitments, and that was partly true. But if I had really wanted to be with her sooner, I would have made time for her. She was too stupid to see that, though. And I knew women well enough to know when they thought they were getting over on a dude. Lola had been trying to play the same cat-and-mouse game with me that I'd been playing with her. She was so obviously anxious to sex me. No matter what she said in her brief messages to me, I could read between the lines. She claimed to be so busy she didn't know when she'd be able to meet me. With all the competition I had, I wasn't even sure she ever would.

But I was going to get close to her in other ways. . . .

The morning after I'd received her last dumb e-mail, I put on a pair of dark glasses, a hooded sweatshirt, and a baseball cap. My own mother would not have recognized me. I was on vacation for a few days, so I drove to South Bay City so I could check Lola out from a distance. I parked three blocks away from the tacky grocery store where she worked and walked the rest of the way. She was busy flirting with some dumpy security guard, who should have been watching the door, so she didn't even notice me when I swaggered in.

I stopped in front of a counter a few feet away from her station, which contained a pile of bruised fruit. I stood like a pole glued to the spot and gazed at her. I couldn't wait to wrap my hands around that goose neck of hers! When the security guard finally returned to his post, she noticed me. She blinked and a curious expression crossed her face.

"Sir, can I help you?" she yelled, flashing a fake smile.

"No, I'm just looking," I replied in a falsetto voice, and swished away like a drag queen.

I immediately started walking up one aisle after another. She was the only clerk on duty, so I couldn't go up and make a purchase. And, I was afraid that if I got too close to her too soon, I'd snap and all hell would break loose. I would have stayed a little longer if that old-ass hag boss of hers hadn't started following me and giving me the fish-eye. There was not a damn thing in that dump that I wanted to buy, let alone steal!

I had already looked Lola up in the telephone book, so I knew where she lived. That night, a few minutes before midnight, I cruised past her house.

This morning I returned around eight and parked a block from her house. I sat there until I saw her come out, prancing down the street like she didn't have a care in the world.

"Lola, you have no idea what I have in store for you," I said, speaking through clenched teeth. I slapped my steering wheel so hard, the dashboard rattled.

When my mini vacation ended the following day, I had a run down to San Diego. And it was a good thing I did, because I knew that if I continued to stalk Lola, sooner or later someone would notice me.

I had a date lined up with a club member who lived in San Diego: a blond female attorney named Rosemary something. Her screen name was "LustyLady." She had sent me an e-mail three days ago. When I told her I was going to be in her area in a few days, she invited me to spend some time with her in the mansion she shared with her blind husband and their three dogs. I agreed to meet up with her for an encounter, but not in her mansion. I didn't care if her husband was blind, I was not going to disrespect the dude by fucking his wife under the same roof.

This woman was very hot for me, so she was not about to give up. She offered to book a hotel room and I was cool with that. Less than a minute later, she decided she wanted to be in a more intimate setting, so she invited me to come to the beach house she owned in Malibu. I was cool with that too. I parked my rig in one of the designated truck stops on my route, hitched a ride to the nearest car rental business, and I drove to her place.

I had never been to Malibu, but I knew it was a playground for wealthy people. One beach house was just as lavish as the next. There were nothing but luxury cars cruising up and down the palm-tree-lined streets and parked in the driveways. I saw a few prosperous-looking people of color, out and about, but I felt out of place because I was the only one driving a Honda. I envied the people who lived in this paradise, but I preferred the simple life. I believed in that old saying: "Mo' money, mo' problems."

"You're quite a stud, you know. Sex hasn't been this good for me in years," Rosemary told me as we lay naked on a thick shag carpet in the living room of her beach house. I'd arrived an hour earlier and we'd already finished off a bottle of cognac and made love twice. She was attractive for a woman in her middle forties and she had a great body. Nothing sagged and there was not an inch of cellulite on her. She admitted that she'd had every cosmetic surgery procedure, from a face-lift to lifting her butt.

"I've been with other black men, but you're one of the best."

I chuckled.

"What's so funny?" She sat up and gazed down at me.

"Another white woman told me I was a lousy fuck."

"She's a goddamn liar! Do you still see her?"

"Oh no. She's someone from my past."

"Harrumph! You don't look like a violent man, and I don't normally condone violence, but you should have slapped her silly." Rosemary laughed. "What ever happened to her?"

I sat up. "What do you mean?"

"Well, I know you probably never wanted to see her

after she made that comment, but did you remain on good terms with her?"

Kimberly, that obnoxious hitchhiker, was probably still rotting under those branches and leaves where I'd dumped her. "No. I heard she left town and I never heard from her or saw her again."

"Good riddance!" Rosemary stood up and started walking toward the corner where the liquor was kept in a small cabinet. "You know I'm married and I love my husband very much. What about you? Is there anyone special in your life?"

"Oh yes! Her name is Lola and she's very special." I smiled so hard, even my cheeks ached.

Chapter 54

Lola

CALVIN CALLED ME AROUND NINE O'CLOCK TONIGHT and we finally made a date for our first rendezvous. We decided to make love in two days, on Super Bowl Sunday (after that damn game ended).

I was beside myself! I had learned so many new bedroom tricks since I'd joined the club, and I couldn't wait to use them on him.

I was so horny for him by now; I started itching between my thighs, and my stomach started cramping ten minutes after his telephone call. I wanted to scream when I went to the bathroom and saw that my damn period had started a week early!

Joan thought it was hilarious when I called her up and told her. "Blood is usually a bad omen," she told me when she stopped laughing. "Maybe it means you should put off meeting Calvin a little longer."

"Maybe it means I should not meet him at all," I coun-

tered. "I might like him so much, I won't want to date any
other men—and I'm having so much fun, I don't want to
do that right now." I was on the telephone in my bedroom. I could hear Bertha stirring around downstairs, but
I kept my voice low so she couldn't hear me talking. She
still didn't know I had a separate landline in my room, because I unplugged it and kept it hidden when I wasn't
using it. It came in handy because I was bad about keeping my cell phone charged. There had been too many
times when I needed to use it to call Joan and couldn't,
because my battery was too low. Like it was tonight.

"He asked me to meet him in that sports bar on
Franklin Street on Sunday, before the game," I said with a
heavy sigh. "We're going to watch the game together."

"Humph! You hate sports as much as I do. Do you
mean to tell me you're going to sit through that damn
football game and then check in to a hotel to get busy?
Girl, you know how men are. Do you think his mind is
going to be on sex after he's just watched the Super
Bowl?"

"I hope so." I sighed. "It was his idea."

"Honey, you need a new plan. If the team he's rooting
for loses, he'll be pissed off. If his team wins, he'll be too
excited to do you any good." Joan laughed again. "Either
way, you can't compete with the Super Bowl."

"He picked the date, so maybe the game doesn't mean
that much to him."

"If that's the case, he wouldn't have asked you to meet
him in a *sports* bar to watch the granddaddy of ball
games."

"Hmmm. Maybe you're right. This Sunday might not
be a good day for me to meet him, even if my period hadn't
started. If I postpone our date, I hope he doesn't lose interest and not want to meet me, after all."

"And what if he does? There are plenty more where he came from!"

"That's for sure, but . . ."

"But what?"

"I'd really like to meet Calvin in person this Sunday. Even if it's just for one date."

"Look, 'Bloody Mary,' unless the man is a vampire or such a freak he doesn't mind dipping his stick in a woman when she's on her period, the sooner you postpone *this* date, the better. Try to get him to meet you in a couple of weeks when you'll be nice and dry—say, around Valentine's Day. That way, maybe he'll bring you a big box of candy and some flowers." Joan stopped talking abruptly. "Listen, Reed's in a foul mood again, so let me go do some damage control on my end too. Call me back when you can."

I had to call Calvin and let him know I couldn't meet him on Sunday, after all. He answered halfway through the first ring.

"Calvin, it's Lola Poole," I said shyly. "My cell phone is charging, that's why I'm calling you from my landline."

"Hello again, Lola."

His voice was so deep and sexy, and he sounded older than he looked in his picture. *Is he the man he claimed to be?* I wondered. I thought about the people who lied about their ages and backgrounds and posted pictures of better-looking people, claiming it was them—the way Joan and I had done years ago. Maybe Calvin was a frog-faced geezer old enough to be my grandfather who had been running a game on me all these months! Before I could stop myself, I laughed.

"Tell me what's funny, so I can laugh too," he said with a chuckle.

"Oh! Nothing. I just thought of a joke my friend told me earlier today." I cleared my throat. "Um, I know we had planned to get together on Sunday, but something's come up." I eased the words in, pronouncing each syllable like I was reading cue cards. I hoped he wouldn't detect the disappointment in my voice.

"Oh? I'm so sorry to hear that. I was really looking forward to spending some time with you this weekend."

"How about next week?" I said quickly.

"I have several hauls the next couple of weeks, so I won't be available again for a while."

"Oh," I said meekly. Silence followed for several seconds.

"May I ask why you can't see me on Sunday?" he asked, sounding almost harsh.

"If you don't mind, I'd rather not say. It's kind of personal." One thing that I would never tell a potential sex partner was that I had to cancel our date because I was bleeding like a stuck pig between my legs. Just thinking about it disgusted me. There was no telling how it would make this man feel if I told him.

"I see." It was obvious he was disappointed. Hopefully, not enough to put me on a back burner or forget about me completely. "Well, when you are ready, you can let me know. When I finish my hauls next week, I'm going to spend a few days down in San Luis Obispo visiting a couple of former marines I served with. I won't be back up here until the middle of February, and I have hauls lined up from then until March."

Now that I had decided to meet my mysterious truck driver, I didn't want to wait almost another whole *month* to see him in person. "I know we had planned to spend some serious time together in a hotel room this Sunday, and I hope we will eventually, but I could meet you for coffee tomorrow." I held my breath, hoping he'd still want to see me.

"Are you sure?"

"Well, yeah. I was planning to do some shopping in a mall close to San Jose, so I'll be in your neck of the woods, anyway. There's a coffee shop across the street from a Bank of America. It has a huge coffee cup painted on the front window. It's not as trendy as the Starbucks a few blocks away, but the coffee is just as good and it's a lot more intimate."

"I know the place, the Koffee Kupp. I go there quite often when I'm in town." Calvin's voice had really perked up.

"But that's *all* we can do . . . ," I said firmly.

"Just chatting with you over a cup of coffee will be enough for now, Lola. If you change your mind about sleeping with me in the future, I'll understand. I mean, we are two mature adults in a sex club." Calvin laughed. "If we're sophisticated enough to be into something like that, we're sophisticated enough to respect one another's decisions. But since we've communicated by telephone and social media and whatnot, it would be nice to meet up at least once—even if it's just for coffee." He had such an engaging laugh; I couldn't wait to see if he sounded and looked the same way in person.

"Is ten A.M. too early for you?"

"Ten is fine. I look forward to meeting you, Lola. Have a nice night."

I went to bed, but I didn't get much sleep. All I could think about was Calvin. I finally dozed off, but I woke up again before dawn; so I got up, took a quick shower, and got dressed.

*   *   *

After I dropped Bertha off at church a few hours later, I sped onto the freeway and headed toward San Jose, humming Chris Brown tunes all the way. I arrived at the coffee shop before Calvin, but since it was such a small place and there were only four other patrons, I knew he would have no trouble spotting me. When he strolled in less than five minutes later, I gasped. He was even better-looking in person. I stood up from the tiny table near the entrance and waved to him.

As soon as he saw me, he stopped in his tracks and the strangest look appeared on his face. His eyes got big and his lips quivered. You would have thought he was looking at a ghost. When I realized he had on a yellow sweater, I felt like I was looking at a ghost too. I immediately thought about the two pictures that "depicted" me lying in a coffin dressed in yellow. I was not about to let such silly paranormal riffraff ruin my day. I held my breath as he approached me.

"That's a nice shirt you're wearing," I said, swallowing hard. "Yellow looks good on you."

"Thank you. And you're as lovely as your pictures on the club's Web site and the one on Facebook." What he said next made my heart jump: *"I'm sure you'd look good in yellow too."*

"Thank . . . you," I stammered. I would never wear or buy anything yellow again. Not even a banana. I knew that my peculiar fear made no sense, and that was why I'd never tell anyone about it.

Calvin gave me a big hug and then he reared back and looked me up and down. With a glazed look on his face, he stared at my *neck* so long—it made me uncomfortable. He didn't bat an eye until I coughed to clear my throat.

"Earth to Calvin," I teased, waving my hand in front of his face.

He blinked hard and shook his head. "I'm so sorry. I

was admiring your necklace," he told me. "My late mother had one just like it."

"Well," I said, caressing the inexpensive silver chain I rarely wore, "if I gain another pound, I won't be able to fit it around my neck anymore! I almost didn't wear it today. When I put it on and finally got it snapped, it felt like I was being strangled. Maybe it's time to buy a new one."

"Well, you have such a dainty neck. I'm sure you'll find another one you like just as much, if not better."

We sat down at the same time. I couldn't take my eyes off Calvin's handsome face, especially his piercing eyes. And he was staring at my "dainty neck" again. This time, he gazed at it even longer. . . .

"Calvin, I hope that when you get back from your run, we can get together," I said. "Even if it's only for one time."

A strange smile crossed his face. "I'll make sure that happens," he said.

We ordered our coffees and spent a very pleasant hour and a half together. We chatted mostly about mundane things and a little about our backgrounds, but we didn't broach the real reason we were together. Since that reason was to have sex, there was no need to bring it up again—until when, and if, we made a date to "consummate" our "relationship."

He gazed at my neck more than my face the whole time, but that didn't bother me. He was the first man who ever told me that I had a dainty neck.

TO BE CONTINUED

In this page-turning prequel to her thrilling
Lonely Heart, Deadly Heart series, *New York Times*
bestselling author Mary Monroe introduces
Lola Poole and Joan Proctor, fast friends getting
a crash course in love, family, betrayal—and
other little disassters . . .

CAN YOU KEEP A SECRET

Available from Dafina Books and
included here as a bonus for you!

Chapter I
Lola

October 1991

M*Y PARENTS SEEMED SO HAPPY TOGETHER, I STARTED thinking about marriage when I was in the fourth grade. My future husband had to be handsome, intelligent, and a well-respected member of our community. He had to want at least three children, make a good living, and treat me like a queen. I didn't meet a man with all my requirements until I was thirty-two-years old. His name was Calvin Ramsey.*

Calvin was everything I had hoped for and more. He had a great personality and he was good in bed. He was also a war hero and a Christian. Before our relationship even had enough time to develop into something serious, I started planning our wedding and picking out names for our children.

At the same time, the man I had fallen hopelessly in love

with was methodically planning to murder me. And for a
reason too incredible to comprehend . . .

I had a good life with two of the most wonderful and
loving parents a girl could hope for. They were not perfect so they made a few stupid mistakes, but I refused to
blame them for all the stupid mistakes I made.

I had no siblings and other than my parents, the only
other relative I had in California was Daddy's older
brother, Gerald. He lived in Anaheim and had three children and an ex-wife. Uncle Gerald had married a woman
from the Philippines named Narissa Pullon. When they
broke up, she took their children and returned to her native country and never looked back. I had never met
Narissa and my cousins, and I had only seen Uncle Gerald in person once during one of our few visits to Disneyland. At the time, I didn't really care that he didn't seem
interested in having a close relationship with us because
my parents were my world anyway. I thought they were
all I needed. Mama and Daddy were good people in every
sense of the word. They were in the church, had good
jobs, and everybody I knew admired and respected them.

Daddy drove a bus for the city and Mama taught third
grade in the same elementary school I attended. We lived
in a nice big brown house on Fullerton Street in the San
Jose, California suburb of South Bay City; with a popula-
tion of approximately thirty thousand residents.

People told me I was cute and smart so I had a lot of
friends. But Joan Proctor was my main girl because she
was so strong and full of life and not afraid to try anything. I didn't approve of a lot of the things Joan did, but
I usually ended up getting involved in the same things
myself mainly because I wanted to impress her. I loved
going to her house, which was located two blocks from

ours. She had a huge family and they all liked to get loose and loud, something my laid-back parents rarely did. Any day of the week it was party central at Joan's house. There were some days when you would have thought that the dullest people in the world occupied my house. Most of the time, I holed up in my room and read comic books and assembled jigsaw puzzles. At the same time, Daddy would be in the living room sitting on the couch as quiet as a mute watching reruns of old TV shows. Mama occupied another room, grading papers or chatting on the telephone with one of her friends or one of the other teachers. During dinner, my parents compared notes about how bad the world had become and how fast I was growing up. They both advised me on a regular basis to always stay on the straight and narrow; which was their way of warning me not to get pregnant before I finished school and got married.

Despite my parents' peculiar behavior, I envied the relationship they had. Daddy was very affectionate, so whenever Mama got close enough, he squeezed her hand or kissed her. When they went out together in public they held hands and occasionally smooched like a couple of love-struck teenagers. That was the kind of relationship I wanted to have with a man someday. I didn't think there was anything better than a man showing his wife how much he loved her the way my daddy did. But a lot of his friends called him a player and he loved it.

My ninth birthday was October 11, 1991; the same day the TV evangelist Jimmy Swaggart was caught with a hooker that he had picked up to have sex with. When we saw the story on the six o'clock news the next day, Mama was horrified. She had been one of Reverend Swaggart's followers for years. His downfall was the main subject my parents discussed at the dinner table for the next few days.

"If a man of the cloth can't control himself, who can?" Mama said as she dumped turnip greens onto my plate. "The news says that he pestered another prostitute three years ago that I didn't even know about!" She let out a long loud sigh and shook her head. I had never seen her look so disappointed. "Oh well. I guess with Reverend Swaggart being famous and having money, greedy prostitutes were bound to come out of the woodwork eventually and tempt him. Right, Clarence?"

Mama and I looked at Daddy at the same time. I couldn't wait to hear what he had to say about the horny preacher today. First he took a long drink from his glass of buttermilk and let out a mild belch. After he excused himself and wiped a ring of milk off his lips with a napkin, he started talking loud and fast with a dreamy-eyed look on his face. "Aw, shuck it! I don't know why everybody is making such a fuss! I bet there ain't a preacher alive that ain't itching to fool around with a prostitute. And I bet a lot of them already done it. They just didn't get caught. Some women jump at the chance to hop into bed with a man of God. Especially if the man is as good-looking and weak as Reverend Swaggart."

"Ugly men are just as weak," Mama said with a smirk.

"That's true. I know a whole lot of butt-ugly men with some real pretty women chasing after them. But, by nature, a handsome dude has a much harder time fending off a frisky woman. She can't resist a man's good looks so she hounds him until he backslides all the way into a bed with her. Humph! Y'all wouldn't believe all the hassles I went through with women when I was younger. And I didn't even have no money. But I was as cool as a ice cube and my looks made up for my shallow pockets. I had to beat the women off with a stick. Everybody that knew me called me Stagger Lee."

"Who is Stagger Lee?" I asked as I dismembered a fried chicken wing with both hands.

"Oh, he was way before your time. They even made a record about him years ago. He was a real ladies' man," Daddy said, eyeing Mama with caution.

"Stagger Lee was a pimp," Mama tossed in, glaring at Daddy.

"But I was not a pimp," Daddy went on. "I was just cool like that." He softened his voice and winked at Mama. "When I met you, Mildred, everything changed. I had eyes only for you on account of you were one of a kind. You worked on me like a tonic. You really got my attention with them big, high-shelf titties and that bubble booty."

Daddy's words pleased Mama, but she didn't like it when he said anything even slightly related to sex in my presence. "Now, Clarence, I've told you time and time again not to talk nasty in front of this child," she scolded.

"Oops," Daddy chuckled, covering his mouth with his hand.

"Now you behave," Mama added, glancing from Daddy to me. "I don't want Lola to grow up thinking that, uh, the activities of the flesh are that important to a man." She sniffed and raked her fingers through her thick brown hair. Her gray eyes lit up and a huge smile formed on her small round face. Next thing I knew, she leaned sideways in her chair and hauled off and kissed Daddy on the cheek. He put his fork down and wrapped his arms around her trim body.

"Y'all need to get a room," I teased.

"This is our room," Daddy shot back.

He was right. One night when they thought I was in bed, I accidentally saw them making love backed up against the kitchen wall. It happened more than once and in other rooms. They never caught me watching them and I never mentioned it. I eventually realized that my folks were only dull when they knew I was around. But when they were alone, or thought they were alone, they got just as buck wild as other grown people.

I was glad I had parents who were not shy about showing their affection.

Apparently, Daddy had more love to give than Mama knew about. And it was no wonder. He was one of the best-looking black men in town. He was not that tall or that well built, but his piercing black eyes, chocolate skin, and wavy black hair attracted a lot of attention. Even though he claimed Mama was "one of a kind," he felt the same way about other women.

Chapter 2

Lola

*T*WO MONTHS AFTER MY BIRTHDAY, DADDY STARTED
taking me with him whenever he wanted to get out of the
house without Mama making a fuss. The first few times
we went to the market to get some beer and to visit one of
his sick friends. The "sick friend" he visited the most was
a tall, beautiful, honey-colored woman named Shirelle
Odom who had a shoulder-length blond weave and a
shape that wouldn't quit. With her huge brown eyes and
heart-shaped face, she looked like a model. But she was a
hairdresser. She worked for Kandy's House of Beauty, a
beauty shop located in a nearby mini-mall that Mama and
I visited a couple of times a month. It was the best place
in town for females to catch up on the latest gossip.
Shirelle was quiet when Mama and I were on the premises, but her eyes lit up and she got real frisky when
Daddy came to give us a ride home. Her eyes lit up even

more when he visited her at her apartment with me in tow.

"Don't tell your mama about us going to Miss Shirelle's apartment, baby. If she asks you where we went, tell her we stopped off at the mall so you could visit Santa Claus and there was a real long line of other kids," Daddy told me one Friday evening on the way home. We had just visited the mysterious Shirelle for the third time in the same week and had stayed out longer than usual. That was because Daddy and Miss Shirelle had spent a couple of hours in her bedroom while I sat in the living room watching cartoons. "Your mama wouldn't understand these things."

"Why not?" I asked. "Miss Shirelle is such a real nice lady."

"Uh, it's a grown folks' situation, sugar. I know I can trust you . . ."

"Uh-huh. I won't tell if you don't want me to," I said with a scheme already forming in my head. I liked a lot of things—dolls, cute outfits; puzzles, and whatnot. I usually had to do a lot of pouting to get my folks to take me to the toy store. Daddy had just put a cow in front of me that I planned to milk dry. "Do you think Santa Claus is going to bring me a lot of toys next week?"

"Huh?" There was a puzzled look on Daddy's face. Then his eyes suddenly got big and he nodded. "Yeah, yeah! I'm sure Santa Claus will bring you a bunch of nice toys. But in case he forgets a few, I'll take you to Toys-R-Us or Kmart right after the holidays so you can pick out a few more things."

"Thanks!" I yelled. Not only did I have a huge pile of toys under the tree when I got up on Christmas morning, Daddy took me to Toys-R-Us and Kmart two days after New Year's Day to pick out a few more. It seemed like the more we visited Miss Shirelle, the more toys I got. He never said it, and I certainly didn't, but the toys were his way of bribing me to keep my mouth shut about him and Miss Shirelle. When Mama asked him why he had sud-denly begun to spend so much money on more toys for me, he told her that it was because he loved me so much and wanted to keep me happy. He reminded her that he was also spending a lot more money on more things for her too. Daddy had been coming home (not long after he had started seeing Shirelle) two or three times a week with gift-wrapped boxes and roses for Mama.

With her job as a teacher, her commitment to the church, and keeping me in line, Mama had a busy life. She didn't have time to keep up with Daddy's movements. As the months rolled by, he spent more and more time with Miss Shirelle. I didn't have to tell Mama any lies about where we'd been because she never asked.

It was not long before I knew more about my parents than I wanted to know. And it was Joan who told me.

"I know something about your daddy," she said in a taunting manner during our walk home from school one Monday afternoon, two weeks before Thanksgiving that year. "I bet you can't guess what it is."

"I don't know what you know about my daddy!" I boomed, pausing long enough to catch my breath. "If you know something, why don't you just tell me?"

"All right then." Joan sniffed. "Your daddy is screwing Shirelle."

"Screwing? What do you mean by that?" Other than what I'd learned from watching late night R-rated movies on television behind my parents' backs and from Joan and some of my other playmates, I knew very little about sex. I had no idea exactly what Daddy and Shirelle did when they went into her bedroom and closed the door.

"They're having intercourse," Joan reported.

"Huh?"

"They are doing the nasty. The *big* nasty: intercourse."

"Oh. People call the nasty 'intercourse' too?"

"People call sex a lot of different things. Everybody in the neighborhood knows about your father and Shirelle," Joan said with a smirk on her face. She was only a few weeks older than me, but she was already a seasoned instigator and way too interested in sex for a girl her age. Last month when she told me she'd been masturbating since she was six, she was surprised that I wasn't doing it and that I didn't even know what it was! When she told me, I was horrified at first. But when I pictured people "playing" with themselves, I laughed. Intercourse sounded even more ridiculous.

"My daddy and Miss Shirelle are . . . are doing *that*?"

"Yep! Having s-e-x. What you got to say about that?"

I refused to show how agitated I was. I hid my feelings well so most of the time people didn't know what I was thinking. I just shrugged and kept moving, admiring the Thanksgiving decorations on the houses and in the yards along the way. I had increased my speed so Joan had to skip to keep up with me.

"Lola, what's wrong with you, girl? Don't you have anything to say about what I just told you?" she asked, stumbling along in the cowboy boots that her stepfather had bought her for winning the citywide spelling bee last month.

"Well, I didn't know about Daddy and Shirelle doing the nasty and I know my mama don't know about it. She'd divorce Daddy so fast it would make your head spin. You need to stop listening to gossip and rumors."

Joan laughed. "Gossip? Rumors? Honey, your mother is the one that told my mother! I heard them talking about it in the beauty shop last Saturday when they thought I was in the restroom."

My jaw dropped and I almost tripped over a huge pumpkin that somebody had set in the middle of the sidewalk. The way Daddy hugged and kissed my mama all the time, why would he be having sex with Miss Shirelle? I wondered.

"He wouldn't do that! He loves Mama!" I hollered.

"Love? Pffft! Love is just another four letter word. My daddy loved my mother and she loved him. But that didn't stop him from screwing that cow he left Mama for. And, Mama said she had a boyfriend herself before she even found out about Daddy and his girlfriend. Don't you talk to me about no goddamn love, Lola Poole. Shit!" That was another thing about Joan; she liked to cuss.

From that day on, I began to look at my parents in a different way. I didn't ask Daddy if he was "screwing" Miss Shirelle and I certainly didn't ask Mama if what Joan had told me she'd overheard in the beauty shop was true. I didn't have to.

The week before Christmas, I came home from school one day and Daddy had moved his girlfriend into our house!

Chapter 3

Joan

EVERYBODY I KNEW WAS YIP-YAPPING ABOUT LOLA'S daddy moving his girlfriend into their house. Ooh wee! I always thought that some of my female relatives were off the chain! I had never heard about any woman doing something as crazy as moving into her married lover's house while the wife was still living under the same roof! Shivers went up my spine when I thought about what my mother would do to my stepfather if she found out he was even *thinking* about cheating on her. Actually doing it could have been fatal for him.

No matter where I went in my neighborhood, somebody was discussing what was going on with Lola's family. Yesterday, two ladies behind me in line at the corner market were discussing it. This evening it was the main topic at our dinner table. I was probably the only one who even noticed that the oxtail stew had stayed on the stove too long.

"I don't know what old man Poole's got between his legs for his wife to let him move that woman in with them," Elmo said. My mild-mannered stepfather was tall and lanky and he had small black eyes, a sharp nose, and tobacco-stained buckteeth. Despite the way he looked, Mama was madly in love with him and everybody else adored him too. Even though Elmo was in his fifties, Mama often treated him like one of her seven children. He liked to stir up a good pot of gossip as much as the rest of us. "I wouldn't have the nerve to bring another woman around my wife, let alone move her into the same house."

Mama gazed at Elmo with a smile on her face for a few seconds. Then she reacted to his last comment the way I expected. She didn't put a mean look on her face or raise her voice. She didn't have to. "Elmo, you ain't crazy. If you ever bring another woman around me, or if I ever catch you with one, I'm going to teach you a lesson you won't never forget," Mama warned. "If you don't be-lieve me, you just try it."

"Aw, Pearline, you know my mama didn't raise no fool." Elmo chuckled, placing his hand on top of Mama's. He knew Mama's history with her men and how she had roughed up a few for doing her wrong. Had I been a man looking for love, I would avoid women like my mother.

Mama was nice to everybody until they crossed her and that rarely happened. Everybody knew that she was one woman not to mess with. She was a severe, fairly full-figured woman with tight brown eyes, a strong jaw-line, and short curly black-and-gray hair that she kept neatly styled. She worked as a guard for a local women's detention facility with some very violent inmates. She even carried a gun and a can of mace on her job at all times. "If you see me fighting with a tiger, help the tiger," Mama often joked. She was the third of eight children in a rowdy family from the projects in Barstow, California. Her first husband, my father and the father of my six siblings, lived in Sacramento. Daddy was a bitter man because he had only one eye. He had lost his other one during a fight with Mama when she caught him in bed with another woman. I was four at the time.

Mama had left work early that day and picked me up from preschool because I had been coughing all morning and the teacher didn't want me to infect the other kids. I was with her when she walked into her bedroom and busted Daddy so I witnessed the whole thing. The woman leaped off the bed and wrapped herself in a sheet. Then she snatched her purse off the dresser and shot out of our house like a bat out of hell. She jumped into the station wagon she had had the nerve to park in our driveway. Daddy was in his undershirt, shorts and socks, but by the time Mama got through clawing him with fingernails so long and curled they looked like Fritos, he was completely naked. With me running along behind her, she chased him with an empty beer bottle from one room to another. She fell when she tripped over one of my building blocks. That gave him enough time to make it back to the bedroom and lock the door.

Mama kicked the door until it fell off the hinges. That's when she really lit into Daddy with that beer bottle, breaking it on his face, severely injuring his right eye. He told the doctor at the hospital that he had been drunk and had fallen onto some broken glass. But we all knew he'd told that lie because he was too afraid of Mama to sic the cops on her.

While Daddy was still in the hospital recovering, Mama and all of us kids stuffed his belongings into moving boxes and garbage bags. My brothers stacked everything on our front porch.

A couple of weeks later, Mama served Daddy with divorce papers. He sent some of his friends to get his stuff. I had always been his favorite child and I still adored him. I missed him a lot but like the rest of my family, I was on my mother's side because my father was the one who had broken up our family.

We didn't hear from him again until a year later when he sent Mama the announcement of his upcoming marriage to the same woman she had caught him with in her bed. He even called our answering machine and left a long rambling message bragging about it. That really upset Mama. She called him back and taunted him by saying that she had cheated on him first. I think she just made that up to get Daddy's goat. None of us ever saw any evidence that she'd cheated.

Chapter 4

Joan

*L*ATER THAT SAME YEAR, MAMA MARRIED A JAMAICAN man named Cyril MacIntosh. She had met him on the Caribbean cruise that she had booked to help her get over Daddy. As soon as Cyril got his green card and a job driving cabs in San Jose, he got downright arrogant. He started coming and going as he pleased and throwing his weight around like he was king of the world. That was his first mistake. His second mistake was alcohol. When he was under the influence, he got hostile and tried to boss Mama and me and my siblings around. I stopped counting his mistakes when he stopped helping Mama pay the bills because I knew then that his days were numbered. All of that caused a lot of tension in our house. The family wondered when and how severely Mama was going to maim her second husband. We didn't have to wait too long to find out.

Cyril eventually cooked his own goose until it was burned to a crisp. He came home drunk again one night a month after he'd received his green card. During dinner in front of me and the rest of the family, he told Mama that the only reason he'd married her was so he could get that priceless green card. He also informed her that he preferred Asian women and had already started a relationship with one. Mama surprised us all because she didn't chastise Cyril herself. In addition to a bunch of uncles and male cousins that didn't take anybody's mess, Mama had four ferocious brothers. She calmly got up from the table and went into the living room and called up her three-hundred-pound baby brother, Leon. He showed up at the house twenty minutes later. The Jamaican didn't have a chance. My uncle worked as a bouncer in one of the roughest nightclubs in town and had cracked quite a few skulls so cracking another one didn't even faze him. Uncle Leon gave Cyril the beating of his life. He left the house that night walking with a limp and bleeding from his head to his toes. He never even returned to get his belongings and we never heard from him again.

Mama wasted no time divorcing Cyril. Then she married Elmo Witherspoon, my current stepfather. He had been a mechanic for more than thirty years and he made good money. He was also a nice quiet man and he treated us all better than my own father had. Most important of all, Elmo knew his place and so far, he had not stepped out of line once. He did everything my mother told him to do. He had even cooked the oxtails we were enjoying now as we discussed Lola's family and Shirelle.

"Mildred Poole must have lost her mind," my cousin Too Sweet stated, chewing and talking at the same time. "There is no way in the world I'd let my husband get away with something like that."

"If you ever get a husband," my obnoxious thirteen-year-old brother James threw in, making me and the rest of my siblings snicker. "You're the only woman over forty I know that ain't never been married," he added with a smirk.

"Boy, behave yourself," Mama scolded, shaking a fork in my brother's face. "And how many times I done told you not to be using ignorant words like 'ain't' in front of me? I don't want nary one of my kids sounding uneducated." Mama glanced around the table with a look on her face that was threatening enough to make us all stop snickering at the same time. Turning to my cousin in the seat next to her she added, "We took Too Sweet in on account of she didn't have no place else to go and she needs to be loved, not picked on."

Too Sweet, whose real name was Flossie, was a few years younger than Mama and she had had several boyfriends over the years. But none of them had cared enough about her to marry her. And I couldn't figure out why. There were several other older, overweight, plain women like her in our neighborhood who were married. Too Sweet was the only child of my real father's deceased sister, Flora. Mama said that it was her attitude that kept her from getting and keeping a man. According to my uncle Myron, she was a displaced deadweight who had become a permanent thorn in our family's side. She had already lived with him and several other relatives before she landed on our doorstep four years ago. None of her blood relatives had been willing to take her in when she had to quit her job as a housekeeper in a cheap motel. She had a serious case of diabetes and had not worked in ten years. In addition to a disability check every month, she subscribed to magazines that appealed to other miserable people like her: true detective and romance publications were her favorites. Sharing my bedroom with my pitiful cousin and sleeping in a bed a few feet from hers was no picnic. But I had learned to live with it without complaining too much. There were times when I even thought she was amusing.

"I could get a husband if I really wanted one," Too Sweet insisted. "I am real particular when it comes to men. I ain't about to lick the bottom of no barrel or scrape a bone that some other woman done tossed out."

Even Elmo couldn't keep a straight face after hearing that. He started snickering along with me and the rest of my siblings. All it took for us to get quiet again was another threatening look from Mama.

Marguerite, my eldest sister, cleared her throat and added her two cents. "I thought we were talking about all that madness going on in the Pooles' house," she said. Everybody nodded and mumbled in agreement. "Shirelle has always been a hoity-toity type of woman; a straight up *Miss Ann* if ever there was one. You can tell just by the way she bats her eyelashes and swishes around town that she thinks her butt has a silver lining. I wonder how this mess is going to affect poor little Lola," she said in a nasty voice. Marguerite was twenty-two. She had a cute round face like the rest of us and a decent body, but she was very insecure. The first time a man paid her some serious attention, she took him and ran. She was engaged to marry a man who delivered packages for FedEx. Her biggest fear had once been that she'd end up like Too Sweet; old, alone, fat, single, and shuffled around from one relative's residence to another. Just because she had a man now, Marguerite thought she knew everything about relationships. "Poor little Lola. She might grow up thinking that it's okay for a husband to cheat on his wife so if her husband cheats, she'll let him get away with it. If I was her mama, I'd take that child and check into a motel until her daddy comes to his senses and sends Shirelle back where she belongs."

"Oh, Lola don't care," I offered, waving my hand. Even though I was the youngest member of the family, I often had a lot to say during our discussions. "She told me it was like she had two mothers now."

Chapter 5

Joan

*A*FTER I HAD FINISHED EATING DINNER AND HELPED MY sisters do the dishes, I went up to my room and finished my homework. That took only a few minutes since I'd done most of it right after I got home from school. Then I trotted over to Lola's house.

The Pooles' house was not nearly as big as ours. We had five bedrooms, they had three. Their front and back yards were so small, when Lola and I and some of the other neighborhood kids wanted to play ball or something, we usually went to the huge fenced-in yard behind my house or Myers Park in the next block.

When I knocked on the front door, Shirelle was the one who let me in. She had a fan in one hand and a bottle of beer in the other. As usual, she wore a lot of makeup and her hair looked like it had just been done.

"Hi, Shirelle!" I wasn't able to hide the excitement in my voice. Being in the presence of a woman that Too

Sweet called a "home-wrecking hussy" intrigued me. It took a bold female to rub her affair with a married man in his wife's face. I liked bold women because I planned to be one myself someday. Not the kind who would steal another woman's man, though. I wanted to be a woman who lived by my own rules as long as I didn't hurt too many people. Shirelle had even quit her job at the beauty shop and now here she was greeting visitors in another woman's house like she was a queen bee and the Pooles' house was her hive. "Is Lola home?"

"She's upstairs in her room," Shirelle told me in a stiff voice. She was already walking back toward the living room couch, strutting and looking like a peacock in a low-cut, short, tight, multicolored dress. "Go on up there, but don't you stay too long. She's got homework and chores to finish before she goes to bed."

I held my breath because I was tempted to remind *Miss Ann* that she wasn't Lola's mama. One thing I didn't do to a grown person's face was sass them. I did enough of that behind their backs. I could not wait to tell my family how uppity Shirelle was acting already. That woman had some kind of nerve. Even so, I still admired her boldness.

"Joan, did you wipe your feet?" Lola's mother yelled. I glanced in her direction. She, Shirelle, and Lola's daddy were all sitting on the same couch with him in the middle looking as smug as a pampered puppy.

"Yes, ma'am," I replied, moving toward the staircase as fast as I could. I didn't want to give them time to start asking me about what was going on in my house the way they usually did when I visited. There was too much to tell, but none of it was as juicy as what was going on in this house. I still couldn't understand how Lola's mother had allowed her daddy's girlfriend to move into her house!

I was glad Lola was in her room so we could talk in private. Another reason was because her room was a lot more comfortable to me than the other rooms in her gloomy house. She had pink frilly curtains at her windows and a cute twin bed with a bright pink comforter and a matching ruffled skirt. A Winnie-the-Pooh the size of a six-month-old baby lay on his back with his head against one of the pillows on the bed.

One of the few advantages Lola had over me was that she didn't have to share her room or her toys with siblings or other relatives. All of her dolls, even the ones she'd had for years, still looked brand new.

"Lola, has Shirelle started bossing you around yet?" was my first question. "She seems like the bossy type."

"Not really," she told me with a shrug. "She's a real good cook and she doesn't mind helping us clean the house."

"I guess she don't," I said with a smirk. "I wouldn't mind doing a little cooking and cleaning if some man moved me into his house and started taking care of me."

"What . . . ever." Lola rolled her eyes and dismissed my comment with a wave of her hand.

I sat down next to her on the bed. I didn't complain about her lumpy mattress the way I usually did when I visited. Unlike my family, her folks didn't believe in spending a lot of money on certain things. They had not bought new furniture since Lola and I were in kindergarten. And, they were the only people I knew who didn't even have cable TV or an answering machine! I knew for a fact that Lola and her mother frequently bought clothes from thrift shops, Goodwill, and the Salvation Army. But one thing I knew for sure was that a high-maintenance woman like Shirelle was not going to be shopping in a secondhand store. She wore more designer clothes than any other woman I knew. Her former co-workers told

Mama that half a dozen creditors used to call the beauty shop for Shirelle and harass her about her overdue credit card bills. She didn't have to worry about that now. According to the latest beauty shop gossip, Lola's daddy had paid them all off *and* added Shirelle as an authorized user on some of his accounts. If that woman didn't have it going on, I didn't know who did.

"Shirelle took me to Macy's yesterday to get a few new clothes," Lola told me with glee. "Mama even went with us."

"I'm not surprised. I'm just surprised that your mama hasn't taken you to better stores before now anyway. She and your daddy make decent money and I notice the sharp clothes and spiffy hats he wears. Not to mention that shiny black hog he drives. He's the only person I know who owns a Cadillac. No wonder he hooked a big fish like Shirelle."

Lola gave me a dry look. "I wish you and everybody else would stop talking about Shirelle. You should be tired of that subject by now."

"Not really," I admitted. "I've never known anybody else who had a mama, a daddy, and the daddy's girlfriend living in the same house. I can't get used to seeing all three of them sitting in the living room watching TV together," I said, looking toward the door. "Which lady does the nasty with your daddy the most? I'd really like to know." I ignored the exasperated look on Lola's face. I was too curious to care.

"Miss Shirelle sleeps in the spare bedroom," Lola snapped. She snatched the *TV Guide* off her nightstand and started flipping the pages.

"That's not what I asked you. I meant—"

Lola flung the *TV Guide* to the floor. "I know what you meant. If you really need to know, Miss Shirelle is the only woman Daddy has sex with these days."

My eyes got wide. That information shocked me so much, I had to rear back and rotate my neck before I could tune up my mouth to ask the next question. "Do you mean to tell me that your mama and daddy don't even do the wild thing anymore?"

"That's right. I heard them talking one day when they didn't know I was in the house. Mama has some kind of female condition and having sex is real painful for her. She said her doctor told her that the operation she needs to correct the problem could cause even more problems, including a stroke. That's the reason she allows Daddy to have a girlfriend."

"Hmmm. I'll bet your mama was just tired of having sex anyway. She's such a prim and proper lady; I can't even picture her humping a man and hollering up a storm and stuff." I gulped because I was a little nervous about what I was going to say next. "I bet your mama has never even had an orgasm."

Lola looked at me like I had suddenly sprouted a beard. "A what?"

"Never mind," I said with a deep sigh. "I keep forgetting you, uh, still got some catching up to do when it comes to sex. I know so much about that from watching the nasty movie cable channels on my brother's TV. I'll tell you about orgasms some other time because if I told you now, you'd probably freak out."

"Okay. What I don't know now won't hurt me, I guess." Lola hunched her shoulders and continued. "Maybe Mama was tired of having sex. I used to hear her complain about all that sweating and flopping around in the bed." I pressed my lips together to keep from laughing. I could tell that Lola wanted to laugh herself by the way her lips kept twitching. She cleared her throat and raked her fingers through her long hair and pushed it back off her face. "Another thing I like about having Shirelle living with us is, she speaks up for me when Daddy and Mama get on my case about something."

"Most women would be hella jealous of another woman living in her house, especially when she knows that woman is her husband's girlfriend. Your mama must be a f—" Lola didn't even let me get the word "fool" all the way out before she interrupted me.

"I don't care what you or anybody else thinks. Last week Mama told me she knew about Daddy and Miss Shirelle a long time ago. She said she would rather have him be with a woman she knows—a *clean* woman—than out in the streets with prostitutes where he could either catch some deadly disease, get killed, or arrested. This way, she can control his affair." Lola paused and gave me a serious look. "Besides, Miss Shirelle gets unemployment checks. She pays room and board so we have some extra money now. Last Saturday when Daddy and Mama wouldn't give me extra money to spend at the movies, Shirelle snuck behind their backs and gave me five dollars."

I looked at Lola and blinked. "Well, Miss Shirelle is just as big a fool as your mama, I guess. I thought the whole idea of having an affair with a married man was so he could take care of you. She's paying her way like she's a hotel guest."

"You know something, Joan? Sometimes you sound like a grown woman. I guess you being the youngest one in a house full of grown folks is really making you grow up fast."

"You can't talk. You living in a house with your parents and your father's girlfriend is going to make you grow up real fast too. What if I do sound grown? What's wrong with that?"

"Nothing, I guess. Now shut up and let's see what's on

TV." Lola grabbed the remote control off the nightstand and turned on the portable TV on the dresser facing her bed. We didn't mention Shirelle anymore that night. But I had a feeling the whole situation bothered Lola more than she wanted to admit.

Chapter 6

Lola

*A*LMOST EVERY PLACE I WENT, PEOPLE WERE TALKing about my family. I got sick of them asking me the same stupid questions over and over again.

"Lola, how is this Shirelle thing affecting you?" asked Lorna Beale, the woman who ran the candy store down the street from my house. "I'm sure you must be thoroughly confused by now."

"I don't care about Miss Shirelle living with us. I like her," I replied with a shrug as I handed her the money for the Tootsie Rolls I'd just purchased.

"Well, you just be strong and pray about it. I hope you don't end up in the same situation when you get married."

"I hope I don't either," I said firmly. "But if I do, I hope my husband picks a woman as nice and pretty as Shirelle." I can still picture the horrified look on Lorna's face when I said that. She never brought up the subject in my presence again.

People eventually stopped asking me my opinion because I always said something similar to what I'd said to Lorna that day. I didn't care about Daddy's girlfriend living with us. She had brought some excitement into our dull lives.

Even though Miss Shirelle had come between my parents and had people talking about them like dogs, it was hard for me not to like her. She was only thirty-three but she seemed even younger. She was eager to do things with me that my own mother didn't like to do. Miss Shirelle took me roller skating and skated along with me, which was nice. She also liked to watch cartoons as much as I did. Since I didn't know anybody seventeen or older who could take me to the R-rated movies, Shirelle took me—as long as it was not a movie that she thought was too gory or featured too much sex and violence. It was nice to be able to see the good movies at the same time as my friends instead of having to watch them at Joan's house when they came out on a cable channel or on their VCR—a necessary item we didn't own until Shirelle went out and purchased one. Most of my friends liked Shirelle as much as I did. When the snow-cone truck rolled into the neighborhood she treated every kid present at the time. That drove my popularity up several notches.

Unlike Mama, I could ask Shirelle about anything. Mama was squeamish about certain things. When I was six, I asked her where babies came from. She said we'd have that discussion when I turned twelve. Shirelle didn't feel that way. When I asked her the same question, she sat me down right away and told me everything there was to know. Most of it made no sense to me, but at least I knew something.

When I mentioned what Shirelle had told me to Joan, she laughed. Of course, she had already been exposed to sex. With six older siblings, how could she not? There was that masturbation thing she had told me about, and she had already let a couple of cute boys fondle her. Every time I turned around one of her sisters was pregnant or one of her brothers had made some girl pregnant.

After a while, even Joan liked Daddy's live-in girlfriend as much as I did. "That lady is so *fly*," she told me one Saturday afternoon after Shirelle had treated us to a pizza and a trip to the video arcade. "What do you call her?"

"I call her Shirelle," I responded. Since this woman had literally become my other mother, I eventually began to refer to her as "my other mother" during conversations with my friends. The first two months, she slept in our spare bedroom. After that, she moved into the bedroom with Daddy and Mama moved into the spare room!

Mama had a few allergies that had become more aggressive and bothersome over the years. She began to get sick from all the various medications she had to take. That eventually took its toll on her looks. She looked haggard and older than she was, even when she wore makeup. No matter how sick and old she looked, Daddy still kissed her and brought her flowers a couple of times a week. Now he was also bringing flowers to Shirelle.

Shirelle had a lot of relatives in the area, but they rarely came around. From the conversations I'd overheard between them and her, they were not too happy about her living arrangement. One grouchy female cousin named Johnnie Bea had called her "a whore and a damn fool" and tried to convince her that she deserved better. Shirelle ignored her comments, just like she did with everybody else.

The only other person in the Odom family that I could stand was Shirelle's niece, Mariel. Her parents had died in a car crash a year ago so she lived with family members. She and I were the same age but she attended a different school. When most of the other relatives came to our house, they rarely came inside. They would sit in their cars and Shirelle would go outside to talk to them. Other than a couple of her older sisters and an elderly aunt who came to the house once a week so Shirelle could do their hair for free, the only other one who visited regularly was Mariel. We liked some of the same things so I enjoyed her company. When Joan or any of the other kids I knew were not available to hang out with me, I called up Mariel. She'd drop whatever she was doing, hop on a bus, and be at my door in a flash.

"I don't care what people say about Aunt Shirelle living with y'all. Shoot! Your mama ain't complaining so I don't know why everybody else is," Mariel told me. Even though her grandmother didn't like me or my family, Mariel was a free spirit like Shirelle. She called me up and came to visit whenever she felt like it. Not only that, she looked like a younger version of Shirelle. Being that pretty, Mariel got a lot of attention from the boys. A lot more than me because I looked goofy with braces on my teeth and a limp ponytail. "Granny keeps saying I'm going to be a man-magnet like Aunt Shirelle and I tell her 'I hope so'," Mariel told me during a lunch at Wendy's one Saturday afternoon during our Easter vacation week from school.

"I hope I'll be one too someday," I said. I loved attention but it seemed like it was the one thing I couldn't get enough of.

I didn't have to worry about my relatives calling up or coming around to make a fuss about Shirelle living with us. Mama had only two sisters still living. The older one lived in Newark, New Jersey and we only heard from her on Christmas or when somebody she and Mama knew had died. I'd never met her. Mama's younger sister lived in New Mexico. I'd only met her one time when Daddy and I accompanied another family on a camping trip to Albuquerque when I was six. She and her husband and their four kids were members of some weird religious group that didn't vote, eat meat, watch TV, listen to the radio, drive cars, or use public transportation. They lived in a commune with a frizzy-haired preacher and his frumpy wife, and a bunch of other religious freaks.

Daddy rarely communicated with his brother in Anaheim. He had a few distant cousins in various parts of Oklahoma where he was from but he didn't keep in touch with them either. Since my family was so disconnected, I was determined to have a lot of kids when I got married. I promised myself that I would keep as many of them as close to me as possible.

At the same time, there were times I was almost glad I didn't have a lot of relatives underfoot like Joan. I didn't like the way her family members stayed all up in each other's business.

After Shirelle had been a resident in our house for a little over a year and a half, the busybodies finally stopped talking about it. But when she blabbed to the folks with the biggest mouths that she and Mama had switched beds two months after she'd moved in, the gossip resumed with a vengeance. A lady I didn't even know had the nerve to stop me on the street one day and ask me if it was true. I told that nosy heifer that it was true and that it was "no big deal" and went on about my business. But the busybodies didn't ease up on us. The talk got so bad Mama stopped going to church. I still went with Daddy every now and then but that didn't last long.

On Easter Sunday the following year, the whole congregation at First Baptist Church on Pike Street greeted me, Mama, Daddy, and Shirelle with horrified looks, gasps, and whispers.

The talk was also still going strong in other places.

"Lola, I thought your mama was a fool to let Shirelle move in, but now I think the bigger fool is that Shirelle," Joan's mother said one evening when I was visiting Joan so we could work on a volcano project for Miss Allen's science class on the kitchen table. It had been three weeks since my family and I attended that uncomfortable Easter Sunday service at church. "It's one thing to have that woman living in the same house, but ain't no way in the world I'd let another woman kick me out of my own bed so she can slide into it!"

"Thank you, Mama. I was wondering that same thing," Joan eased in. She turned to me and gave me a pitiful look. "Girl, I feel sorry for your mother."

"You don't have to feel sorry for my mother. Except when she's sick, she's happier than she's ever been. She's got something now called shingles and my other mother even has to help her take a bath and put on her clothes. Shirelle does almost all of the cooking and cleaning now since Mama gets so sick so much," I pointed out. "She even does my hair and helps me with my homework."

Joan and her mother looked at one another then at me. "Then how come your father won't divorce your mother and marry Shirelle?" Joan asked, in a tone of voice that was so sharp it made me angry. Had she not been my best friend, I probably would have punched her in the nose.

"Because, he loves Mama, that's why," I said, rotating my neck the way Shirelle did when she wanted to get a point across. "He tells Shirelle all the time that he will never divorce my mama for her, or any other woman. Besides, she is just as happy as Mama is so I don't know what all the fuss is about." I paused and sucked in some air. "It's all good," I added.

Joan blinked and shook her head. Her mother gave me a guarded look. But at least the conversation took a drastic detour. By now Elmo and Too Sweet had entered the kitchen and joined the conversation. Now the subject was a mysterious woman who had recently moved into the neighborhood. The rumor was that she was our mayor's mistress. That story had so much meat, Joan's family could really sink their teeth into it. I couldn't wait to go home. They barely noticed when I excused myself and slunk out the back door.

Chapter 7

Lola

MY OTHER MOTHER'S POSITION IN MY DADDY'S LIFE was not as secure as she and everybody else thought it was. Especially me. The way Daddy had always fawned all over Shirelle ever since I could remember, I didn't think he'd ever put *another* woman before her. I was wrong. I don't think anybody was as surprised as I was about what Daddy did next.

Two years after Shirelle moved in, Daddy began to come home from work later and later, two to three times a week. He would often disappear for hours at a time on weekends. He had stayed out all night twice in the same month. Somebody would repeatedly call the house and hang up when anybody other than Daddy answered the telephone. Shortly after each hang-up, he'd leave to "go get a six pack of beer," or to "visit a friend." He used the same excuses to get out of the house that he had used in the early part of his relationship with Shirelle. The only difference this time was he didn't take me along with him. By now a lot of people knew what a smooth operator Daddy was. Even I knew that, so Shirelle had to know it, too.

"Where have you been, Clarence?" she asked when he came home around eight a.m. one Saturday morning. He had left the house the evening before to go visit a sick friend.

"Uh, my car broke down on the way home." Daddy had his hat in his hand as he shuffled into the house with a sheepish look on his face. "I got stranded on the freeway and couldn't get nobody to stop and give me a hand. I sat there for hours before a highway patrolman showed up."

"Is that right? Well, tell me this; how come you didn't walk to a pay phone and contact Triple A like you did the last time?" Shirelle hollered.

"I did walk to a pay phone! It was three or four miles from where I broke down, so it took me a while," Daddy claimed, nodding his head and wiping sweat off his face with the back of his hand. "Lord have mercy, that damn phone was out of order. And my legs were aching way too much for me to drag around and look for another one so I went back to my car and sat there to wait on the highway patrolman." Daddy looked at me and Mama standing a few feet away near the living room couch. Mama had her arms folded and her jaw was twitching. It didn't take a mind reader to know what was on her mind. I was sure she was thinking that Shirelle was getting what she deserved. I stood there as quietly as I could, hoping they wouldn't make me leave the room. I looked from Daddy to Shirelle to Mama, wondering who was going to say what next.

"Clarence, is that lipstick on your collar?" Shirelle asked.

"Lipstick? Oh hell no! I had some red wine while I

was at my friend's house and some dripped on my shirt," Daddy answered with his eyes darting from side to side. He could not have looked guiltier if somebody had written the word on his face with a red Sharpie.

"Red wine my ass! I'm not stupid!" Shirelle shouted, wagging her finger in Daddy's face.

"I know you ain't stupid but I'm telling the truth this time," Daddy replied, brushing past her. "I'm fixing to go up to my room and get some rest. You can chew me out later." Before he reached the staircase, he stopped and turned around. "Wasn't you worried about me? I could have been robbed and lying in a ditch somewhere for all you knew."

"You keep messing with me and you will be lying in a ditch somewhere!" Shirelle warned. She stormed into the kitchen and a few seconds later I heard the back door slam.

Shirelle was a lot of things but she was not a fool. When she was seeing Daddy on the sly, she had to know that he had to lie to Mama to be with her. Now, she was in Mama's position, in more ways than one.

Mama looked at me and shrugged. The only way I could describe the look on her face was "smug." "Miss Thing ain't seen nothing yet," she muttered. To my surprise, Mama covered her mouth with her hand and let out a muffled laugh. She had never complained about Daddy's outrageous behavior and still didn't. One day I heard her tell somebody on the telephone that as long as he handed over his paycheck to her and always came home after his "dates" with other women; that was enough for her. Mama had female friends who felt the same way. My father was not the only married man in our circle acting like a fool. The list of other unfaithful husbands was long and their wives put up with it too. But because of the mean looks that Shirelle eventually began to give Daddy and the things she said to him when he stumbled into the house after one of his late nights, I knew she was getting fed up. She was not going to continue to tolerate his behavior the way Mama had.

Daddy slowed down for a couple of weeks. Then he started up again the following month. One Friday he had not come home from work by six p.m., the time he usually did when he wasn't fooling around.

"I guess Clarence is working late again or having a few beers with his buddies," Mama said to Shirelle as the three of us ate dinner that evening. "Or visiting a sick friend . . ."

"Oh, there's just no telling where he's at," Shirelle said with a disgusted look on her face. "He could be lying in a ditch somewhere."

"Humph! Things like that never happen to men like Clarence," Mama said, just before she bit into one of the fried chicken legs Shirelle had cooked.

Eight, nine, and ten o'clock came and went. Daddy still had not come home by eleven so we all finally went to bed. I woke up in the middle of the night when I heard him and Shirelle arguing in their bedroom, which was right next to mine. I couldn't hear everything, but I heard Daddy holler, "I'll behave! Give me another chance, baby!"

I heard what sounded like somebody getting slapped and then things got quiet. After about a minute, I heard bedsprings creaking and a lot of moaning. I assumed that whatever Daddy had done, Shirelle had forgiven him and was going to give him "another chance."

Two nights later, Daddy stayed out late again and when he got home, Shirelle fussed at him for a whole hour.

I was worried about her. She was no longer the fun-loving, happy-go-lucky woman I used to love to be around. She didn't even fix herself up the way she used to. She slouched around the house in her bathrobe and bare feet with a puppy dog expression on her face and a drink in her hand. And she only left the house to go get more liquor when she ran out.

A lot of times when Daddy was out and about, Shirelle usually stayed in her room. At night I could hear her crying. I felt so sorry for her. I felt sorry for Daddy, too. He was a mixed-up, tortured soul. I was convinced that something was wrong with him. Why else would he keep cheating on the women who loved him?

Mama didn't get involved in the arguments between Daddy and Shirelle. As a matter of fact, she was about as indifferent as she could be. She kept to herself and went on about her business like nothing was wrong. She went to work, spent time with her friends, and did the same things she had always done. She was probably a mixed-up, tortured soul too. Instead of acting like the lady of the house, like she still was in my book, she seemed more like a boarder.

Chapter 8

Lola

*A*BOUT NINE MONTHS LATER, THINGS TOOK A TURN FOR the worse. That was when Mama was diagnosed with a terminal blood disease. She had to quit teaching and she lost the ability to take care of herself. For the next three months, she was in and out of the hospital. But Daddy and my other mother agreed that we would take care of her at home as much as we could.

Just like she'd done when Mama had shingles, Shirelle had to help her bathe and dress herself. Assisting my mother eventually became a full-time job for Shirelle. She did it without complaining and with very little assistance from Daddy. I helped as much as I could. When Mama got so sick she had to start wearing diapers, Daddy started coming home late *again*—with more lipstick on his collar.

My other mother finally threw in the towel.

It happened on a Friday evening in October, the day

after Daddy's latest romp. He and I had gone to the supermarket to get items for the cake that Shirelle was going to bake for my upcoming party to celebrate my thirteenth birthday in a few days. When we returned home, Bertha Mays, a woman who lived at the end of the block, strolled out of the kitchen wiping her hands on the crisp plaid apron wrapped around her pear-shaped body. There was a wall-to-wall grin on her moon face. A hairnet covered most of her gray-and-black hair. "Clarence, you won't have to worry about a thing," she said with a snort. Then she gave Daddy a hopeless look and slapped her hands onto her hips.

There was a confused look on Daddy's face, not to mention mine. He looked at me and we shrugged at the same time. "What the hell is going on?" he asked with his eyebrows raised. "Bertha, where is Shirelle?"

"Gone," she replied with a casual sigh as she turned around and started shuffling back toward the kitchen.

"Oh? Well, where did she go to?" Daddy hollered as he and I followed Bertha. When we reached the kitchen, he glanced anxiously at the back door as if he expected Shirelle to walk in.

"That sister called me to come over here right after you and Lola left the house and told me she needed my help. Me, being the woman I am, I dropped what I was doing and got over here as fast as I could. As soon as I made it in the door, Shirelle told me to make myself comfortable. Next thing I knew, she ran upstairs and came back down with two suitcases," Bertha told us. She gently removed the grocery bags from Daddy's hands. "I'll put this stuff away."

"She had to tell you something about where she was going and why. I can't see her up and leaving with suitcases without saying nothing," Daddy said.

"She didn't say where she was going," Bertha replied

as she set the grocery bags down on the counter. "All she told me was that she'd been planning to take off for weeks. A few minutes after she came down with her suitcases, one of her brothers pulled up outside in a car with a loud muffler and honked his horn. Shirelle ran out of this house so fast it made my head spin."

I didn't know what to think about Bertha. For one thing, she was not that attractive. She was a dumpy woman with a rust-colored complexion, a meatball nose, and beady black eyes. She seemed nice enough, but she had two children I couldn't stand. Twenty-three-year-old Libby and her twin brother Marshall resembled their mother in every way. They were both snobs and bullies and a few other unpleasant things. No matter how nice and friendly I was when I was around Libby, she looked at me like I was next to nothing. The looks I got from Marshall made me even more uncomfortable. No matter what outfit he saw me in, the way he looked at me with his eyes glistening and his tongue sliding across his bottom lip, he made me feel naked.

Bertha's husband had divorced her five years ago. He'd left her a nice big house and from what Mama had told me, a substantial amount of money.

"Clarence, I told Shirelle that I'd look after your sweet wife from now on," Bertha chirped with a firm nod. "Mildred and I have been close friends for years so I know she'd do the same for me."

"That's mighty generous of you, but what about your job at the school?" Daddy asked, blinking his eyes fast and wringing his hands.

"Pffft!" Bertha waved her hand and shook her head. "I used to love teaching, but the kids in elementary school got too obnoxious and dangerous for me. I took my early retirement last week so I can come over here every day and do all I can for Mildred. You won't have to worry about paying me. I'm glad I can help out. And I'm more than willing to help you out with little Lola, too," she added, winking at me.

"I can't believe Shirelle took off without telling me!" Daddy yelled.

"Well, she did," Bertha assured him. "But like I just said, you don't have to worry about a thing. I got everything under control."

"Yeah . . . uh, I guess we'll make do until she brings her tail back here," Daddy said, his voice cracking. I had never seen such a stunned and confused look on his face before today. He looked down at me and bit his bottom lip. "Lola, you mind Bertha, you hear?"

"Uh-huh," I muttered.

Bertha came back to our house Saturday morning around eight. She made the cake for my birthday party which was supposed to take place that afternoon. But because Daddy was so upset about Shirelle leaving, he made me cancel my party. I didn't mind. I was as upset as he was, so the last thing I wanted to do was entertain a bunch of my friends. I did tell them all that they could come by and drop off my birthday presents though.

Shirelle didn't call and we didn't know where she had moved to. The next time I tried to get in touch with her niece, Mariel, which was a week after Shirelle had left; her grandmother told me in a very impatient tone of voice that Mariel couldn't come to the telephone. When I called her again a few days later, the number had been changed and unlisted. That saddened me a lot because Mariel had become very important to me. She was the one I leaned on when Joan was being punished for doing something stupid and couldn't leave the house, talk on the telephone, or spend time with me. It was obvious to me that

Shirelle had wanted to make a clean break from Daddy and me and that had included the end of my relationship with Mariel. For some reason, Daddy thought Shirelle would return sooner or later, but I knew she was gone for good.

Mail still came to our house for her and instead of giving it back to the mailman, Daddy put it in the kitchen drawer where we stored other odds and ends. He had also refused to get rid of the few clothes she'd left behind, and a treadmill in the garage that she'd rarely used. The longer Shirelle stayed away, the more dependent we became on Bertha. By the end of the third week, she had moved so much of her stuff into our house, people predicted Daddy would get jiggy with her next.

And they were right. Two weeks before Thanksgiving, I saw Daddy and Bertha practically going at it in the kitchen one evening when they thought I was in my room. He had her pinned against the wall and one of her thick legs was wrapped around his thigh. How a heavyset woman like her managed to lift one of her legs up that high was something I could not figure out—especially since she was always complaining about arthritis in her knees, pinched nerves in her legs, and gout in her feet. She had her arms wrapped around Daddy's waist and he held her head in place as they kissed. They were both wheezing and grunting like hogs. I decided not to tell Mama or anybody else what I'd seen. Since the rumors and gossip about Daddy and Bertha had already begun to circulate, it was just a matter of time before everybody knew what was going on in our house anyway.

Two days before Christmas, I went into Mama's bedroom to check on her. "Shut the door and come over here," she ordered. I was surprised to see her sitting up in bed and even more surprised that she had spoken in such a strong voice. For the past couple of weeks, it had been difficult for her to talk in her normal voice. Bertha had put a note pad and a pen on the nightstand for her to communicate when she was too weak to talk.

"You look and sound so much better, Mama," I said as I slowly made my way over to the bed. Her eyes looked brighter than they had since she got sick. Her smooth, copper-colored skin had a glow to it that I had never seen before. But the smell of sickness was all over the room. Despite the fact that Bertha changed Mama's bedding every day and bathed her, the stench of urine and vomit filled the room.

"I just wanted you to come close enough so I could get a hug and tell you to be a good girl," Mama rasped, now speaking in a very weak voice again. "Find yourself a good man and raise your kids the way I raised you."

"I will, Mama. I'll be glad when you can get up out of this bed and be happy and healthy again."

"I will be real soon, honey," Mama assured me as I leaned over the bed to hug her. She was too weak to hug me back. I held her for about two minutes and then she let out a hissing noise and went limp.

It took a few seconds for me to realize she had died in my arms.

We didn't celebrate Christmas that year. It was the day before Mama's funeral. A couple of hours before the service, Daddy went to the funeral home and took a Polaroid picture of Mama in her coffin, which was something a lot of people I knew did. I could never figure out why. Who would want their dead body to be photographed in a coffin? Mama had never liked to take pictures when she was alive. If she had been able, she would not have allowed it. For one thing, she had lost most of her hair so she wore a wig and her favorite yellow dress. She looked much better dead than she had looked the last few months of her life. She even looked younger. I was not the only one who noticed, but it looked like *me* lying in that coffin.

"I didn't realize how much you and your mother looked alike," a woman from the neighborhood said when she saw the picture. "If I didn't know any better, I'd swear that was you fixing to be buried."

Daddy put that picture in a photo album we'd had for years and I forgot all about it.

Chapter 9

Joan

I'D ONLY ATTENDED A FEW FUNERALS AND NOBODY HATED them as much as I did. All that crying and looking at the body of the guest of honor lying in a coffin was too much for me. Mama's parents died three months apart when I was five. Daddy's parents died two years later in the same month! I had worn the same black blouse and black skirt to all four funerals. Now here I was again in another dreary black outfit—this time it was a pantsuit—for Lola's mother's funeral.

I had no idea so many people had loved Lola's mother. Second Baptist Church with its dark green carpets and huge colored murals on every wall of Jesus in various poses, was packed with people boo-hooing up a storm. I was glad that it was a closed casket funeral, which was a first for me. I had seen Mildred a couple of weeks before she died and she'd looked so pitiful then I could barely stand to look at her without feeling nauseous. There was a large framed picture of her on top of her casket. That was the way I wanted to remember her.

Like at most funerals for black folks, several people including my mother and my stepfather, went up to the pulpit and said all kinds of nice things about Mildred. "She was the salt of the earth," somebody else said. "She changed my life," another one said. Clifford Bates, one of her former students, stood up and sang five songs that he had written himself. His long performance was agonizing to sit through because the boy couldn't sing worth a damn. People were clearing their throats and glancing at their watches the whole time that boy stood up there braying like a wounded donkey.

Dennis Rosenberg the handsome young Jewish physician who had cared for Mildred and was also one of her former students, was the only one who said something that really made me feel a little bit better about being where I was. "Let's honor Mildred's life, not her passing. She's in a much better place now," he said in his gravelly voice. I could tell that he was struggling to hold back his tears. His last sentence got to me and I started howling again.

Since Lola and I were best friends, her daddy allowed me to sit in the front pew with them. Bertha, who looked like a pilgrim in a drab black frock with a white collar, had also sat her big ass on the front pew with the immediate family. A lot of Mildred's former students, some of them grown with kids of their own, attended. So did most of the teachers and the principal she had worked with.

I kept my arm around Lola's shoulders the whole time. She had cried so much her eyes were red and swollen. But at least she wasn't wailing like a banshee the way almost everybody else was.

"It's almost over," I whispered to Lola as I patted her

shoulder. She turned to look at me, and somehow she managed to smile.

"Thanks for coming and thanks for sitting with us," she whispered back.

As soon as Reverend Tiggs closed the service, everybody stopped crying and started glancing toward the dining area in the back of the church. I was sure that they were wondering how soon they'd be able to get up and go back there to get a plate of food. I knew people who attended funerals mainly to eat.

The weeks following the funeral were just as gloomy. I did as much as I could to help Lola get through the trauma of losing her real mother. But no matter how much I tried to cheer her up, there were times when she was so depressed, I avoided her. When she got depressed, she depressed me. She didn't have to tell me but I had a feeling she wasn't just depressed about losing her mother. She was depressed about life in general and had been for a while. One of the main reasons was because she was lonely. She often complained about not having more relatives; ones she could visit and have a real relationship with. The ones she did have were just as odd as they could be, so she was never going to have a relationship with them. Once she had even talked about going to the Philippines when she grew up to try and locate the three children her oddball uncle had fathered with his Filipino wife just so she would have some blood relatives to associate with. I felt so sorry for my girl.

"I don't have anybody but my daddy now. I can't wait to grow up and get married so I can have a bunch of kids to keep me company," she told me. It had been three months since her mother's funeral and she was still depressed about it.

"You've got a long way to go before you get to that

point," I told her. "You haven't even had your first boy-friend."

Lola gave me a strange look. "Joan, you know how to talk to boys and you know I'm kind of shy around them. I'm thirteen now and it's time for me to start acting like a teenager."

"True. What's your point?"

"I hope you'll hook me up with some cool dudes one of these days so I can fool around with boys like some of the other girls we know."

"I'll do that and more." I grinned.

I didn't want to confess to Lola, but *I* had already started "fooling around" with boys. I had not had inter-course with one yet, but I'd done a few other things. The boys I got involved with were two to four years older than me. All I had to do to keep them happy was jack them off with my hand.

I knew a few girls who were into giving oral sex to boys, but I wasn't ready for that. I had a feeling that at the rate I was going, I'd be ready for it soon enough. In the meantime, I was real particular about what went into my mouth. One time a boy stuck his tongue in my mouth and I almost gagged. I didn't want to think about what would happen when, and if, I decided to let one stick his pecker in my mouth. It was bad enough that what I was doing with boys wasn't doing much for me.

By now, both of my two oldest sisters were married to men who had good jobs and good personalities. They lived like kings in big houses in nice neighborhoods and drove fancy vehicles. My only other sister Elaine was anxious to get married too and she had made it clear that she was also going to marry a man who had a lot to offer. I wanted a dude who would be nice and generous to me too.

It was no wonder that I eventually started working on

getting things from my male friends that benefited me in some way. I refused to continue giving hand jobs unless my boyfriends spent money on me. And the more they spent, the more hand jobs I was willing to do. Some people would have called me a prostitute, but I didn't think of myself that way. Neither did Lola.

"Tyrone Patterson gave you a gold chain and gold earrings just because you jacked him off?" she asked when I called her up to tell her what I'd done last night while I was babysitting for a lady across the street.

"Yep!" I wasn't allowed to date yet, so I had to do a lot of sneaking around. One day I even got busy with a boy behind a vacant building.

"Joan, you are so smart. There's no telling what you'll be able to get from your boyfriends when you decide to go all the way."

"Hah! I'm going to get all I can from them without doing any more than what I'm already doing. I make them feel good enough."

"Do they make you feel good?" Lola asked in a shy voice.

I didn't answer with a shy voice. "Nope! I do much better on my own with my fingers!" I paused and laughed for a few seconds. Then I got serious again. "I feel good when they spend money on me, but when I let them touch me, I don't feel anything." I had not been able to figure out what all the fuss was about when it came to getting down with somebody. I had not felt any of the rip-roaring pleasure I read and heard about all the time. Not even when I let boys play with my titties or finger my pussy. I couldn't wait to find out what intercourse was like. Even as eager as I was, I was not expecting much. Most of the boys I'd been with were clumsy, and had not had intercourse yet either. Jacking them off was a lot of work because of the way they humped and twitched. I didn't even want to think about how much whooping and hollering and humping they'd do when they got to have sex with a girl.

"I guess sex is not all it's cracked up to be after all, huh?" Lola asked shyly.

"Probably not. But we're going to find out soon enough."

"We who?"

"You and me. I'm going to bring you out of that shell you've been in all your life if it's the last thing I do." I sniffed and gave Lola a few seconds to let my words sink in. She stayed silent longer than I thought she would, so I decided to change the subject. "How are things at your house with that Bertha woman always breathing down your neck?"

"Daddy enjoys her company and she enjoys cooking and cleaning for us. I think she's just lonely and wants to keep busy. Her kids don't seem to care that much for her so she's probably just as depressed and lonely as I am. She's always telling me I seem more like a real daughter to her than her own daughter."

"What about her other folks?"

"Her only brother died in the war in Vietnam. Her parents are both deceased and she's got a few cousins scattered around Mississippi. But other than her children, Daddy and I are the only close family she has."

"As long as she treats you nice, you should treat her nice. If something happens to your daddy, she's probably the only adult you'll be able to count on."

Chapter 10

Lola

MAMA HAD BEEN GONE ONLY FOUR MONTHS WHEN
Daddy came into my bedroom one Sunday morning and
stood at the foot of my bed with a look on his face that
confused me. His eyes looked sad but there was a smile
on his face. I sat up and swung my legs to the side of my
bed. I had not slept too well the night before because of a
dream I'd had about Mama dying in my arms.

"Sugar, I need to talk to you," he began, clearing his
throat and glancing around the room. I was glad I kept
my room clean and neat. It was one of the few things
Daddy didn't have to fuss at me about.

"Good morning," I said, yawning and stretching my
arms so high above my head my armpits ached. I sniffed
and rubbed my eyes. I held my breath because I had a
feeling he had something serious to say to me. I couldn't
remember the last time he'd come into my room before I
got up. "How come you're wearing your blue suit?" Daddy

had only three suits; two black ones and a blue one. He wore the black ones to funerals. He only wore the blue one to weddings, parties, and on other happy occasions. He called it his "happy occasions suit."

"I'm wearing my blue suit because I'm taking you and Bertha out to brunch. And we ain't going to no Denny's or I-Hop this time. We're going to a restaurant in one of the fancy hotels in downtown San Jose. I want you to pick out something real nice to wear, like that yellow frock you wore when we went to the Masons' daughter's wedding last month. And wait until you see how nice Bertha looks in her pink two-piece suit! She says the restaurant we're going to is real nice."

"I can't wait to see the menu." We had not been to a real nice place for brunch since my tenth birthday. "So she's over here again already?" Bertha usually waited for us to get out of bed before she barged in.

Daddy cleared his throat again and blinked at me. "Well, sweet pea, after you went to bed last night she decided to stay the night . . ."

"Why?" I gasped.

"Baby, I miss your mama real bad. And you know I'm the kind of man who likes to be close to a woman as much as I can. Bertha's such a good woman, I like having her around. She keeps telling me that I need another wife." Daddy suddenly looked agitated. I got even more confused when that look disappeared and an even bigger smile suddenly crossed his face. "Baby, how would you like to have a new mama?" he asked, sitting down on the side of my bed next to me. His arm went around my shoulders.

"Who?" I asked dumbly. As far as I knew, Bertha was the only woman in his life at the time. I wasn't sure if I liked her enough for her to be my new mother. She was not nearly as pretty as my real mama. But she was real nice to me. Last month she had surprised me with a weekend trip to Disneyland.

Daddy's face stiffened. I held my breath because my heart was beating so hard. Then he blurted out the words that almost made me freeze. "Bertha asked me to marry her last night. I told her I would be happy to marry her and that we'd get married in church like she wanted to do the first time she got married. She's always wanted to be a June bride. Her jackass ex-husband married her in one of them fly-by-night chapels in Reno in the middle of December during a snowstorm! No woman deserves that kind of treatment."

I gulped. "Why do you want to marry a woman like Bertha?" I didn't mind her being in our house so much and I appreciated how nice she was to me, but having her living with us as my new mother was another story. I knew kids who had been in her class. A few of them had told me some unpleasant stories about her. But to be fair to Bertha and other teachers, I could think of a few nasty things to say about all of mine, all the way back to kindergarten. One of my biggest fears was that once Bertha became my stepmother, she'd start bossing me around. I was afraid that she'd eventually show a side of herself that she'd kept hidden so far. I knew enough about grown folks to know that some of them wore one face when they wanted something and then they put on another face after they got what they wanted.

"What do you mean by that?" Daddy asked, looking concerned.

"She's not as pretty as Mama or Shirelle."

Daddy laughed. "Looks ain't the only reason to marry somebody. Bertha is the kind of wife any man would be proud to have."

"Oh? Then why did her husband leave her?"

"That's a good question. You see, not all men know

what a good thing they have when they have it. I'm sure that if that scoundrel could, he'd come back to Bertha in a heartbeat."

I shrugged. "She's already over here every day anyway. Why do you need to marry her? You didn't marry Shirelle."

"Well, for one thing, I'd never divorce one woman to marry another one. Besides that, Shirelle was a different story. She was no more marriage material than a nanny goat. Once I really got to know her, I wouldn't have married her even if I'd been single. She was too worldly to make a man a good wife. She smoked, drank too much, and at times, she behaved like a child. Her roller skating and watching cartoons with you wasn't normal behavior for a grown woman. And she didn't like going to church. Bertha's got more religion in her little finger than Shirelle had in her whole body. Bertha would never live under the same roof with a man unless she was married to him."

I had no desire to put up a fight to keep Bertha in her own house. I knew that no matter what I said or how I felt about this new development, Daddy was going to marry her anyway. Once he got a notion in him, nothing could change his mind. I sighed with defeat because I knew it was time to give in. "So when you marry Bertha she'll move in with us completely then, huh?"

"Not exactly. We'll move in with her. Her house is so much bigger and nicer than ours. And it's paid for. She don't have to pay rent and deal with a lazy, cranky landlord the way we do now. She's got a nice nest egg and a pension so she'll help out a lot financially."

Daddy's last statement piqued my interest. The cost of living had gone up a lot in the past few years so money had become tight in our house. The thought of bringing Bertha into the mix so she could share our expenses didn't sound like a bad idea. "We'll live with her for free?"

"No, baby. Very few things in this world are free. I'll be helping Bertha pay the household bills, the upkeep and the taxes on the house, as well as everything else she and you will want. We need a new car and I know you'd like some new clothes and other knickknacks once we get settled. Bertha's got a big back and front yard for you and your little friends to play in." Daddy paused and looked around my room again. "And, your new room will be much nicer than this one," he said, making a sweeping gesture with his hand. He said something else that made my stomach knot up worse than ever before. "Bertha promised me that she'll treat you like her own child."

I swallowed hard. "What about her kids, Libby and Marshall?"

"Won't it be nice to finally have a brother and sister? You used to ask me and your mama for a sister or a brother all the time, remember?"

"I wanted a *baby* sister or brother so I could have somebody to play with," I wailed. "Libby and Marshall are too old for that."

"Well, Libby is engaged and will be moving out soon. She's about to marry one of the Starks boys. Jeffrey's a real nice young man and he works for the fire department. Won't it be nice to have a fireman in the family? I'm sure he'll take you for a ride on the fire truck one day." The last thing I wanted to do was ride around on a fire truck with a man who was crazy enough to want to marry a straight-up witch like Libby.

"What about Marshall?" I couldn't decide which one I liked the least, Libby or Marshall. One was just as disgusting as the other.

"Marshall just moved in with the young lady he's going to marry in a few weeks. Her name is June Frazier. She works as a hostess at the same Denny's I used to take you and your mama and Shirelle to for breakfast."

I hunched my shoulders and let out a tired breath. "I like Miss Bertha, but I don't like Libby and Marshall and I know they don't like me. Every time I see Marshall he gives me dirty looks." Marshall didn't just give me and the other girls my age dirty looks. Four years ago on Halloween, Joan and I went trick-or-treating. When we knocked on Bertha's door, Marshall answered. After he dropped some lollipops and miniature candy bars into our bags, he unzipped his pants and whipped out his dick and shook it at us. Joan and I laughed because we had never seen such a shriveled up hairless nub before and we told him so. He cussed at us, we cussed back at him and then we ran. We could still hear him cussing after we had crossed the street. I had gone out of my way to avoid that man ever since that night and now here was Daddy telling me he was going to be my new brother!

"Well, you won't have to deal with them two scalawags that much. They don't get along that well with their mother so I doubt if they'll be coming around that much anyway. In the meantime, I want you to treat Bertha the same way you treated your mama and Shirelle. Do you hear me?"

I nodded. "I will."

Chapter II

Lola

WHY AN OLD WOMAN LIKE BERTHA WANTED TO be a "June bride" was a mystery to me. I had endured a lot of changes in my life, but I didn't know how I was going to adjust to a new mother and two siblings I couldn't stand.

One thing that kept me from losing my mind was knowing that as long as Daddy and I remained in our own house, I didn't have to deal with Bertha's children that often. Marshall still gave me dirty looks every time I saw him and he talked to me like I had no feelings at all. "Lola, do you ever wash your neck?" he asked after a Sunday dinner at Bertha's house, something Daddy and I rarely participated in. We were all seated in the living room. June was only about two months away and the more I thought about it, the worse I felt about Daddy marrying Bertha. "I bet you don't even wash your hands after you use the toilet," Marshall added before I could answer.

This occasion was especially difficult because he and Libby had come to dinner at the same time.

"If you think her hands and neck are filthy, can you imagine how nasty she must be under her clothes," Libby said with a smirk. Marshall snickered.

"Now you two behave yourselves. You're both way too old to be talking such trash to little Lola," Bertha said quickly, giving me a reassuring look.

"Shut up, Mama. I wasn't talking to you anyway," Libby said casually. With that same smirk still on her face, she took a deep breath and gave her mother a critical look and said, "Now are you going to lend me that money like I asked? I don't want to miss out on another Macy's sale like I did last month."

I gave Daddy an exasperated look. It was the same kind of look I always gave to him when Libby and Marshall talked in a disrespectful manner to their mother; which was almost every time we were all together. They did that and asked her for money practically in the same breath.

I usually kept my thoughts to myself, but this time I couldn't control what came out of my mouth. "Libby, your mama just gave you a hundred dollars last week," I said, looking her in the eye. "I saw her do it."

Her mouth dropped open and her eyes got wide. She looked at me like she wanted to slap my face. "That's none of your business, Miss Smarty Pants." After she took a deep breath, she turned to Daddy. "Clarence, I hope you don't let this child get away with acting this grown too often." She turned back to me with such a severe scowl on her face, I thought she was in pain. "Lola, what Mama does with her money has nothing to do with you."

Bertha hoisted her hefty frame up off the couch and stumbled upstairs to her bedroom with Libby walking close behind her. A few seconds later, Marshall wobbled up out of his seat and waddled off in the same direction. I knew it was because he had come to borrow money from his mother again, too.

"Pssst," I said to Daddy. As soon as he looked at me I continued, speaking in a low voice. "I hope they don't start asking you for money."

"You don't have to worry about that," he told me as he scratched the side of his neck. "I know how to say no."

A few minutes later, Marshall and Libby returned to the living room at the same time grinning like Cheshire cats. Libby plopped down on the love seat. Marshall stopped a few feet in front of Daddy. "Clarence, my man. You think you can get to your bank by Tuesday to get me that grand you said I could borrow?" he asked, winking at Daddy.

"I'm sure . . . uh . . . I'll be able to do that," Daddy stammered, scratching his neck again. He quickly looked away when I looked at him.

The way Libby was looking at Daddy, I knew she was going to put the bite on him too sooner or later. It wasn't long before I found out that she had already done that. When Daddy and I went home an hour later, he confessed that he'd already been "lending" money to Libby and Marshall since last year.

I was horrified and disappointed. Somehow I managed to remain somewhat composed. "But at Bertha's house you told me you'd tell them no if they asked you for money," I said with my lips quivering. "All the while, you'd already started giving them money."

"I know, baby. I don't like to lie to you, but sometimes it's necessary. You see, I want to keep the peace between them and Bertha. She's a good woman and I want to do all I can to keep her happy so I have to be nice to her kids. Please go along with me," Daddy said in a weak and whiny voice. My father had always been a strong man, at least in my eyes. I never thought I'd see him looking and acting as meek as he was now.

I was sick of hearing about what a "good woman" Bertha was. She must not have been too good if she couldn't hold onto her husband and her kids treated her like crap. Despite my feelings of frustration, I had to admit to myself that she was a good woman, at least to Daddy and me. She spent so much time, money, and energy trying to please everybody; I wondered how her own kids had turned out to be so mean and nasty. I didn't spend too much time wondering about that though. All I cared about was what was in the Bertha thing for me.

By the time I got to know her better, I loved her almost as much as I had loved my real mother and my other mother. I promised myself that I would go out of my way not to cause her too many headaches. I was also prepared to go out of my way to be nice to Libby and Marshall, no matter how mean they were to me.

My feelings changed right after Daddy and I packed up what we wanted to keep and moved into Bertha's big house on a rainy Friday the first week in June. I had inherited the bedroom that Libby had occupied. But I didn't like her plain blond bedroom furniture or any of that old antique looking stuff in the rest of Bertha's house. The things Daddy couldn't sell from our old house, he donated to Goodwill. I was glad he had no trouble persuading Bertha to let me bring everything from my old room into my new room.

The following Saturday afternoon, when it had stopped raining and the sun was so bright and warm, Daddy married Bertha in Second Baptist Church with only a few close friends and relatives present. I was pleased when he told me they were not going on a honeymoon. "All that foolishness is for young people," he laughed. I couldn't understand why he thought honeymoons were for young newlyweds when he had eagerly agreed to let Bertha have a June wedding, something I had always associated with much younger brides.

They did agree to have a reception after the wedding, which was at Bertha's house. The same people who had attended the wedding came to the house right after the ceremony. I was glad that Joan and several members of her family were among the guests. With all the new changes in my life, I needed her support more than ever. But Libby and Marshall and their mates didn't show up until the reception was almost over. As soon as they walked in the door, they began to gobble up what was left of the food and alcohol until it was all gone. So far, Libby and Marshall had not said anything bad to or about me since our last dinner together. That changed when Libby found out Bertha had given all of her old bedroom furniture to Goodwill.

"Mama, I can't believe you got rid of my stuff! Have you lost your damn mind?" she shrieked, ignoring the horrified guests who were still in the house. "What in the world is wrong with you?" I had never heard any child scream at their mother in such a cold, vicious way—especially on her wedding day. Had I raised my voice to my mother on *any* day, she would have slapped my face.

"Libby, I've been telling you since you got married and moved out that if you wanted that stuff you needed to come get it or I was going to donate it to Goodwill," Bertha said, sounding more defensive than I'd ever heard her sound with one of her kids. "I wasn't going to wait forever for you to do that."

"Well, like I had told you before I moved out, I was going to put my old stuff in one of our spare bedrooms for when Jeffrey and I have houseguests! I'm going to a furniture store first thing Monday morning to pick out some new stuff to replace it and you're going to pay for it!" Libby hollered. I almost lost my cool when this "daughter from hell" actually wagged her finger in her mother's face. "And I'm going to pick out what I want, no matter what it costs!"

For the next five minutes, Libby yelled at her mother about a variety of things, including her having to wear a "cheap" dress to her senior prom because Bertha had gone to Vegas with some church friends and had forgotten to leave the money for her to get the dress she'd really wanted. Then Marshall, who was sloppy drunk by now, started babbling about how "disrespectable" Bertha was for moving Daddy and me into the house that their father had paid for. Guests began to leave in such a hurry you would have thought the house was on fire. Joan and I remained seated on the couch. Bertha stood by the front door, looking like she wanted to escape. Daddy walked over to her and put his arm around her shoulder.

Libby whirled around and looked at me. Her eyes were so dark and narrow, she looked like a snake. I was scared but I was not about to let her know that. "Listen here, Lola! You'd better not take any of your thug friends into *my* room! Do you hear me?" she yelled.

"You don't have to worry about that because I don't even know any thugs!" I yelled back.

"Uh, let's remember this is a happy occasion," Daddy said. Then he steered Bertha to the wing chair facing the couch and she eased down. He stood by the side of the chair, glaring from Libby to Marshall as the rest of us attempted to go on like it was still a "happy occasion." By now, the only guests other than family still present were Joan and elderly Mr. Fernandez from next door and his lady friend.

Jeffrey, the fireman Libby had married, came up to me and gave me a hug. "Don't you worry about your stepsister. She's had a few too many drinks," he said, giving me a warm smile. I liked Jeffrey. For a man with such a pleasant demeanor, who turned a lot of women's heads with his almond shaped eyes, Tootsie Roll brown skin, and sexy bald head; I couldn't understand why he had married a crude frump like Libby. She had the nerve to wear a purple *spandex* jumpsuit that day. She looked like a giant eggplant.

For Marshall to be just as mean, nasty, and homely as Libby; he had a nice spouse too. His cute half-black, half–Apache Indian wife, June, came up to me next. "Lola, you've got my telephone number. If you ever want to talk, just give me a call," she told me in a low voice, winking one of her small, slanted brown eyes. I interpreted the wink to mean that she had her own issues with Marshall and Libby. And, I was sure that Jeffrey realized by now what a fishwife he had on his hands.

"Thanks, June," I mumbled, anxious to leave the room.

I felt somewhat better by the time Joan and I fled to my new bedroom.

Chapter 12

Joan

*T*HERE WERE TIMES WHEN I WANTED TO SLAP SOME sense into Lola's head. For her to be almost as fly and smart as me, some days she acted like Princess Dumb and Scared. Other than me and a few hoochies from the Brewster Projects, she was the only other girl in our school I knew of who didn't take any crap from other kids. Here she was letting Libby talk all kinds of trash to and about her! I was glad that I only came in contact with Bertha's kids every now and then. I was getting tired of having to hold my tongue around them. I knew that sooner or later, I might not be able to, though. I prayed things wouldn't get that serious because if I ever lost my cookies and got in Libby's face, or Marshall's, they'd take it out on Lola. *She* had to be the one to get them off her back!

"Girl, you need to get a backbone and stop letting people walk all over you," I told her as soon as we got inside her new bedroom and shut the door. "If that bitch Libby had talked to me the way she just talked to you, I would have cussed her out! I don't care if she is older and bigger than me."

"She was mostly mad at her mama, not me," Lola said, looking so sad you would have thought she was at a wake instead of a wedding reception.

"But it was because of *you*."

Lola shook her head and gave me a hopeful look. "At least my in-laws are real nice to me. Libby's husband and Marshall's wife are two of the nicest people I know. And so is Bertha for that matter. Besides, as long as I still have Daddy, I am not going to worry about anybody else."

Three months after Lola's daddy married Bertha, he got sick and had only weeks or months to live. I couldn't believe one person could have as much rotten luck as Lola. It was bad enough she had lost her mama and become a member in a family of creeps, now she was about to lose her daddy.

I knew something was wrong even before I got the news because Lola rarely missed school. When she didn't show up in homeroom that morning in September, I assumed she was coming to school late, another thing she rarely did. She didn't attend first period science class so when it was over, I went to the pay telephone by our principal's office and dialed her number.

"Are you sick or something?" I asked when she answered on the first ring.

The last words I expected to hear shot out of her mouth like bullets. "My daddy told us last night that he has liver cancer," she said flatly. "He'd been looking bad for a while, but he kept telling us he was all right. Last week he finally admitted that he had been feeling weird for about a month. Bertha and I fussed at him so he finally went to the doctor last week and that's when he found out. He didn't tell us until last night after he'd fainted."

"Damn! Well, is it serious? Is he going to be okay?"

"According to his doctor, the cancer is so aggressive he could be gone before the end of this year."

I was devastated. Just hearing that Lola was about to go through another traumatic experience made my stomach churn. Not to mention us attending another funeral so soon after her mother's. "I'm so sorry to hear that. Your daddy is such a good man. He'll be missed by everybody."

A long moment of silence passed before Lola spoke again. "After he's gone, I won't have any family left. Daddy called around this morning until he tracked down that roving brother of his in Anaheim to let him know he was dying. The first thing my uncle said was 'we all got to go sometime.' He claims he's too sick himself to even come to the funeral when the time comes." Lola let out a heavy sigh. Then, to my surprise, she let out a laugh; not a real one, though. This one was so hollow and eerie, it made me shudder. Was she so overwhelmed with grief that she was losing her mind? I wondered.

"Lola, are you all right?" I asked. My own voice was cracking and if I didn't end this call soon, I was in danger of losing my mind.

"Don't worry about me. I'm fine." She snorted. "Anyway, my uncle said that he just might 'kick the bucket' before Daddy does anyway."

"What about your mother's people in New Mexico?"

Lola laughed again. This time it sounded normal. "Puh-leeze! I can forget about them. How many times do I have to tell you that? They only travel on some kind of old-time buggy with a mule pulling it. Even if they agreed to come for the funeral, it'd take them God knows how long to make it up here."

"I forgot all about their crazy religion. What about your aunt in Jersey?"

"Daddy called her up last night. She told him she had never had kids because she never wanted any and she was not going to raise me. He hadn't even asked her to take me in when he dies. Bertha told me she'd always be there for me. I've always had feelings for her because of the way she jumped in and took over taking care of mama after Shirelle took off. Bertha has been so good to Daddy and me, I care even more about her now."

"That's your grief making you say that," I mumbled. "If you ask me, that woman is a pig-in-a-poke. You don't know what she's really like inside."

"She's always been real nice to me—"

"Yeah, because she wanted to keep your father happy. Once he's gone, she won't have any reason to be nice to you."

"Maybe so, but now that I know I'm going to lose Daddy, it's in my best interest to stay on Bertha's good side. I have a feeling I'm going to need her more than she needs me . . ."

Despite the fact that this conversation was not pleasant and I couldn't wait for it to end, I decided to keep talking. If the news about Lola's father was affecting me in such a painful way; I couldn't imagine how it was affecting her. "I feel so sorry for you. You must have been bad to the bone in a past life for karma to be kicking your ass so hard and often."

I was glad to hear Lola chuckle again. "I feel the same way."

"Well, you know I'll always be there for you. Do you want me to come over after school today?"

"No, you don't have to do that. I think I'd like to be alone with Daddy as much as possible now. Thanks, girl. I don't know what I'd do without you."

I didn't like being in the same room with a real sick person, but after Clarence got too sick to be cared for at home and had to go spend his final days in the hospital, I went with Lola as often as I could to visit him. It was even harder to be around him than it had been to be around her mother when she got sick. For one thing, Mildred had lingered on for months and it had taken a long time for her to look like a real sick person. Clarence already looked like hell. Within weeks after his diagnosis, he had lost all of that wavy hair that the women had loved so much. His eyes had turned a bluish gray and he drooled so much, he had to wear a bib.

By the middle of November, he was so bad off I stopped going to see him. It was too depressing. I was sorry that I was not with Lola when he took his last breath two days after Thanksgiving. Later that night when she called me up to tell me about the last conversation she had had with him, I was glad I had not been present.

"Daddy told me how lucky we were to have Bertha in our lives and he made her promise him that she would always be there for me. She said she would, but she reminded him that she had 'one foot in the grave' already herself."

"Please don't tell me she's sick too!"

"Other than the usual ailments people her age complain about, she's fine."

"Well, you have only four more years to go before you finish school and can take care of yourself. Then you won't have to worry about having to deal with those asshole kids of hers. You can pack up and get the hell up out of that house. I'll help you pack!"

"There's one more thing," Lola said, her voice dropping almost to a whisper. "A few minutes before Daddy died, he made me promise I'd take care of Bertha as long as she lives."

"People say a lot of strange stuff when they're dying. Two days before my grandmother died, she was having conversations with people who had been dead for years. When some people get close to death, their brains go haywire. I'm sure Clarence didn't realize what he was saying. He doesn't expect you to give up a life of your own to take care of a woman who is not even your real mother. Especially since she's got grown kids. She's their responsibility."

Lola sucked on her teeth for a few seconds. "Do you honestly think they would take good care of her; if and when she needs it?"

"I wouldn't worry about it if I were you. But you did the right thing by promising your daddy you'd do what he asked you to do. Even though what he asked you to do is unfair and unreasonable."

"I know." Silence followed for a few seconds. It was a very awkward moment so I was glad when Lola initiated the end of the call. "I have to go now. I . . . I have to help Bertha make funeral arrangements."

"Don't forget what I just said. I'm sure your father was too delirious to realize what a crazy thing he was asking you to do. Be good to Bertha, don't do a bunch of stupid shit that'll upset her and all that. But you don't need to give up having a life of your own for her. You do know that, right?"

"I know that," Lola told me in a very weak voice.

Chapter 13

Lola

*D*ADDY HAD BEEN SO SICK LAST MONTH WE HAD not celebrated my fourteenth birthday. He was even sicker by Thanksgiving, so we didn't celebrate that either. Two days later he was gone.

Marshall and his wife were in the Caribbean on a cruise that they had planned and paid for a year ago. We had no idea how to reach them and even if we could, I knew they would not cancel the rest of their expensive vacation and come home for Daddy's funeral. Knowing how selfish Marshall was he probably would not have even done that for his own mother's funeral.

When I called up Libby to let her know about Daddy's passing, she wasted no time reminding me that she had already made plans to go to Vegas for five days to attend her best friend's bachelorette party and had purchased a non-refundable plane ticket. "Lola, I'm sorry to hear about your daddy and I'm sorry I can't attend his funeral. If I cancel my trip, I'll lose the money I spent on plane fare and the hotel."

"I understand," I muttered. I was glad she wouldn't be at the funeral. I didn't really want her to attend anyway. After the callous things she had said on the day Daddy and Bertha got married, there was no telling what she'd say at his funeral.

"Poor Clarence. He almost looked like a corpse the last time I saw him, so I am surprised he lasted as long as he did. It's a shame he didn't hang on as long as your mama did when she got sick." Libby sounded just as impatient and indifferent as she usually did when she talked to me.

My chest began to ache and my stomach felt even worse. I moved my tongue back and forth and swallowed hard but I could feel the lump rising in my throat. The pain of losing Mama was still tormenting me and now to hear somebody sounding so nonchalant about Daddy's death made me want to throw up. "I'm glad Daddy didn't hang on as long as my mother did. She suffered a lot."

"Oh well," Libby sighed. "First your mother died, now your daddy. People drop like flies around you, girl. I don't know how you can go on."

"I guess I'm stronger than I look," I said dryly.

"You must be!" I couldn't believe how cheerful Libby sounded. I assumed it was because she thought that with Daddy out of the picture now, she didn't have to pay back any of the money she had borrowed from him over the years. I was not about to let her off the hook.

I cleared my throat and spoke in a very firm tone of voice. One thing I didn't want to sound like right now was a weakling. "Libby, you can use some of the money you borrowed from Daddy and have some flowers sent to the church." I couldn't stop myself from adding, "Since he was so good to you, that's the least you can do for him—"

"I'll have Jeffrey take care of flowers," she huffed before I could even finish my sentence. "I'll pick up a sympathy card before I leave for Vegas."

"That's fine. By the way," I continued, still speaking in a firm tone of voice. "I don't know how much you borrowed from Daddy, but when you figure it out, you can give it all to me and I'll donate it to charity in his name."

I was not surprised to hear a loud gasp on Libby's end. "Well, once I figure out how much I borrowed from Clarence, I will settle it with Mama, *not you*, understand? You're just a child and you have no business even thinking about something that was between me and your daddy."

"Okay, Libby." I knew that there was not a chance in hell that she would give Bertha a plugged nickel of the money she owed Daddy. If anything, she would "borrow" more money from her mother instead.

Libby let out a mighty belch and, as usual, she didn't excuse herself. On top of everything else, she was about as well mannered and dainty as an ox. "You just need to worry about yourself and how lucky you are that my mother is willing to finish raising you. Do you hear me, little girl?"

"I hear you." The next thing I heard was the dial tone.

Not only was I stunned by the abrupt way Libby had hung up, I was hurt by her last words. Now that Daddy was gone, my future looked so bleak I didn't even want to think about it. With him no longer around to "protect" me, I was going to be at Libby and Marshall's mercy, like a lamb in a lion's den. I told myself that I would stand my ground with them as much as I could, no matter what the consequences were. Every time I thought about how soon

I'd be eighteen and able to be on my own, I also thought about the promise I'd made to Daddy that I would "take care of Bertha."

He was going to be buried in the same suit that he'd worn when he married Bertha; the blue one that he'd always referred to as his "happy occasions suit." A lot of people came to the funeral. I received dozens of hugs and well wishes from everybody and they were considerate enough not to mention the absence of my stepsiblings.

Libby sent a sympathy card that came from a Dollar Tree store. It was one of the no-frills, two-for-a-dollar kind. Jeffrey came to the funeral, accompanied by his parents and his two older brothers and their families. They had all sent flowers. People who had barely known my father sent flowers and impressive sympathy cards, even some of the people who had ridden on his bus over the years.

"Lola, I'm sorry about your daddy's passing," Jeffrey told me after everybody had moved to the dining area. "I didn't find out until it was too late just how sick he was. Had I known sooner, I would have spent more time getting to know him better. Now I want you to know that I'd like to get to know *you* better. You've got our telephone number and you know where I work, so feel free to get in touch with me if you need to. And, I'll be coming to the house more often."

"Thanks, Jeffrey."

"And, uh." Jeffrey paused and scratched the side of his head. "I . . . I know my wife can be kind of abrupt and grouchy at times, and I apologize for her absence, but she's a good woman in her own way. She's a bitch sometimes, but I still love her."

I gave Jeffrey a sympathetic look because with a wife like Libby, he deserved one. "I'm sure she is a good woman . . . in her own way."

"I meant what I just said about you calling me," Jeffrey told me with a big smile. I nodded and when he hugged me I started crying again. I had cried so much in the last few days, I thought I had run out of tears. He held me until I stopped crying.

Chapter 14

Lola

I WAS GLAD WHEN BERTHA AND I LEFT THE CHURCH and went home. But the house didn't feel the same without Daddy.

"Now it's just you and me," she said in a raspy voice as she gave me an unbelievably sad look. We were in the living room. She was half sitting, half lying on the plush beige couch with her bare feet elevated on a brown pleather hassock. The same white handkerchief was in her hand that she'd been using to dry her eyes and blow her nose with most of the day. I sat slumped in the matching love seat facing her. It was an awkward moment for me because I felt so out of place. Even though Bertha had a nicer house than my old one, I had never felt comfortable in it. The hardwood floors creaked and the window frames leaked. The walls in every room were baby-shit-colored yellow. And three of the four chairs at the kitchen table had at least one wobbly leg. There were more than three dozen different size framed pictures of Libby and Marshall at various ages on the walls in the living room and on each end table. As infants swaddled in white blankets, they looked like two little pigs. Even at that age, they had mean looks on their faces. There were just a few pictures of Bertha's other grim-faced Mississippi cousins, one of Daddy, Bertha and me taken at their wedding reception, and only one of Bertha in her cap and gown on the day she graduated college. There were no pictures of me or Daddy displayed anywhere else in the house except on top of the dresser in my bedroom. I had over two dozen pictures of me and my parents in a photo album that I kept in my dresser drawer. I cried every time I looked at those pictures because they represented a happy time in my life. It was hard to believe that my situation had become so bleak.

I sat up straighter on the love seat and gave Bertha a smile. "Daddy looked so peaceful," I managed, not knowing what else to say. I expected her to make a similar comment but she didn't. What she said made me feel even more awkward.

"Lola, I'm pleased as punch to know that you're going to take care of me in my old age, which is already nipping at my heels. Some mornings I feel so decrepit, I'm surprised I can still get out of bed on my own. I'm so blessed to have a daughter like you, praise the Lord."

I wanted to remind Bertha that I was her *stepdaughter*, but I just nodded. I didn't want to talk about the last conversation I'd had with Daddy. "I will take care of you, Bertha. Even after I get married and move out."

She changed her tone so fast it made my head spin. Now instead of sounding bereaved, she sounded harsh. "I don't think that's what Clarence meant!" Before I could respond she added, "I can't live on my own!"

I was flabbergasted and I didn't attempt to hide it.

"What do you mean? You're not crippled or disabled and you've lived by yourself before."

"I was younger then and didn't have half the ailments I have now . . ."

"Libby and Marshall will make sure you'll be all right," I said with my heart thumping. *"They are your real kids,"* I added with as much emphasis as I could without sounding harsh myself. I immediately regretted making that last comment. I, of all people, knew how indifferent Libby and Marshall were when it came to their mother.

"Yeah. And it's a damn shame that I have to keep reminding them of that," Bertha complained.

"Let's not worry about all that for now. It'll be four more years before I finish school and even longer before I get married."

"Well, just as long as you don't forget what you promised Clarence. A deathbed promise is nothing to take lightly."

My heart felt like it was trying to bust out of my chest. "I meant what I told Daddy. I will take care of you when and if you need it, Bertha. But I have a life, too." I was surprised at how firm I sounded. "Even though you can't really depend on Libby and Marshall now, I know that if you get real sick or hurt in an accident or something, they'll do whatever is necessary for you."

Bertha sniffed. She shook out her handkerchief, which was pretty moist by now, and dabbed at her eyes and nose some more. "Trying to get my kids to do for me is like pulling teeth with a pair of tweezers. Just before I got with your daddy, I had a hip replacement procedure. I had all kinds of complications so I was out of commission longer than I expected. The whole three weeks that I was laid up in the hospital, Libby only came to see me three times. Marshall came once. If Deacon Bonner and other folks from the church and the neighborhood hadn't been there for me, I would have had to call a cab or take a bus every time I needed to go to my doctor for follow-ups."

I was stunned. I stared at Bertha in slack-jawed amazement. "Did your kids even feed and bathe you when you got out of the hospital?" I asked.

"Believe it or not, they did. Libby gave me sponge baths and she and Marshall prepared the special meals I had to eat. It was one of the few times they showed me the consideration I deserve. At the end of the day, my kids are not as bad as some folks' kids."

"I . . . I know what you mean," I stammered. As much as I hated to admit, even to myself, there had been a *few* times when Libby and Marshall had been nice to me. A couple of months ago when I had missed the last bus of the day from the mall back to my neighborhood, I dialed Libby's number, but only because I hadn't been able to reach anybody else with a car. I'd had no choice but to call her house, hoping Jeffrey would answer. But she answered. When she told me he was at a ballgame with some of his buddies, she eagerly volunteered to come pick me up herself. It turned out to be a pleasant fifteen-minute ride. She asked me how I was doing in school, told me what a cute girl I had become, and she even treated me to a Whopper at Burger King.

And I could never forget how Marshall had saved me from a beating by Paco Lopez one day about three weeks ago. Paco was a major bully in our school. His homeboys were members of a ferocious Latino street gang. He had followed me home from school, threatening to beat me up because I had blabbed to his girlfriend that I'd seen him kissing another girl at the movies. I didn't want to think of what might have happened to me if Marshall had not been standing on Bertha's front porch when I galloped around the corner with Paco a few yards behind me. As soon as Marshall realized I was in trouble, he picked up one of the heavy ceramic flowerpots Bertha kept on the porch and threatened to use it on Paco's head. He took off running in the opposite direction and never bothered me again.

"Yeah. Libby and Marshall are not *all* bad," I said, forcing a smile. The words tasted bitter on my tongue.

"It's just that I never know when they are going to be-have the way they should. And, the way I've been feeling so crappy the past few months, I'll be going to the doctor even more often so I'll need somebody to go with me." Bertha paused to let her words sink in. "I know I can count on you to take off from school and ride with me in a cab or the bus." One thing I hated about some needy older people, especially extreme cases like Bertha, was the way they used their failing health as leverage to get their way. Mama had suffered for a long time, but she had never used her health to manipulate me.

"I'll do everything I can to make you feel better when and if you get sick," I said.

"I hope so. You can't let your daddy down by going back on the promise you made to him on his *deathbed*."

I was already so sick of hearing Bertha say the word "deathbed" I wanted to scream. The way she was acting about my last conversation with Daddy, you would have thought that I'd had a conversation with the same burning bush mentioned in the Old Testament. I didn't regret making that promise (at least not yet) but I regretted that Bertha had been present. I had a feeling that if I didn't "take care" of her to her satisfaction, she'd lay a guilt trip on me that would torment me for the rest of my life.

However, my main goal was myself. I'd figure out a way to make Bertha think she was my priority, but some-how I'd also do whatever I had to do to enjoy life.

Chapter 15

Joan

I COULDN'T IMAGINE LIFE WITHOUT LOLA AND I WAS SURE she felt the same way about me. I could depend on her most of the time. It was the times I couldn't depend on her that irritated me. Tonight was one of those times.

"What do you mean you can't go out tonight? I had this all set up and I went to a lot of trouble to do it!" I was on the extension in the upstairs hallway across from my bedroom but I kept my voice low. It was the day after New Year's Day, a little over two years since her father's passing. "Something tells me that Bertha Butt is the reason."

"Yeah, it is on account of Bertha," Lola groaned.

"Shit! Why don't you get in that battle-axe's fat face and tell her to get off your back?"

"Are you nuts? You know I don't sass grown people. I'm only sixteen."

"Who said anything about sassing?"

"Well, what do you call getting in an adult's face?"

"Look, as long as you stand up to a grown person in a nice way, it's not 'sassing'," I snarled. I could not for the life of me understand how Lola continued to let that old lady run all over her. I knew from experience that a young person had to be firm with old people. Sharing my bedroom with gassy, loud-snoring, meddlesome Too Sweet was no picnic. I kept her in her place because I refused to let her boss me around the way most of my other adult relatives did. As long as Mama and Elmo didn't get on my case about how messy I kept my side of the room, whenever my cousin complained about me being a slob, I claimed I had cramps. That way, when I did clean up, it was when I was good and ready (or when my parents made me). Too Sweet didn't like the shows we watched on the portable TV that my daddy had sent to me, but when she was in the room, she watched what I watched. All I had to do was remind her that it was *my* TV. Most important of all, when I wanted Lola or one of my other friends to spend the night with me, I pouted until Mama made Too Sweet sleep on the living room couch on those nights. If I could keep an old person under control, so could Lola. Why she couldn't stand up to a woman who wasn't even her real mother, was one thing I could not figure out.

"You always do this to me," I whined. "Danny Knight is between girlfriends and he was really looking forward to meeting you. You know a boy like him won't be on the market for too long. Besides, he's the one with the car and if he doesn't go out with us, me and Frankie won't have a ride."

"I know and I'm real sorry. See, Bertha slipped on some water on the kitchen floor a little while ago. She fell and hit her head on the edge of the stove. She's been dizzy ever since so she's afraid to be in the house alone tonight."

"Aw shuck it! That woman has been 'dizzy' since the day I met her. We'll only be gone for two or three hours, maybe not even that long."

"I know that too. But remember last month when Bertha was alone and she took some pills that were a year past the expiration date? She passed out while she was in the middle of frying some chicken. If Mr. Fernandez had not come over from next door to borrow some meal, the house might have burned down. Something real bad could have happened."

"That heifer! That manipulating old heifer! I've got news for you and her. Something real bad could happen to her with you in the house just as easy as it could with you gone. Since your daddy died, you've practically turned into a prisoner. These are your best years before you get married and tied down with a husband and a bunch of kids. You should be going out like the other kids having a good time, not catering to some neurotic old woman! Sometimes you act like an old woman yourself."

"Listen up, I just got an idea," Lola said in a gentle voice. I was surprised that she was still able to remain so calm after the way I'd just come down on her.

"Well, I'd like to hear it," I said gruffly. "And for your sake, it better be good. I knew I should have tried to hook up Karen Prichard with Danny instead of you."

"You told me you'd already tried to and he told you he didn't like tall girls like Karen."

"Oh yeah, I forgot. And Danny told me that you were the only one of my friends he wanted to hook up with so I'm stuck. Please don't let me down, girl. I really want to be with Frankie tonight. So what's this idea you have?"

"We can still go out after Bertha goes to bed. She

sleeps like a dead woman. But if that's too late, you can bring the boys over here and we can still have a good time watching TV and stuff."

"Pffft. I can't believe my ears. Y'all don't even have cable yet. What boy in his right mind would want to do something as lame as watching regular TV when he can be at the movie theater or some other cool place? And didn't you tell me Bertha keeps track of her booze? What dude can watch regular TV without a buzz? Even I can't do that."

"We won't know unless you ask them. And, if those boys want to have a few drinks, they can bring some beer. We do have a VCR and I just got a few new tapes so we can watch them and finish off the black-eyed peas and ham hocks left over from the New Year's Day dinner Bertha cooked yesterday. I don't know why you're making such a fuss. It'd probably be a lot cheaper for us to get together in my house than it'd be if we went out. Shoot!"

"Forget it. I've already eaten enough black-eyed peas and ham hocks in my own house."

"I don't know what else to do. I can't leave Bertha by herself tonight. I have to hang up now. I hear her coming."

Chapter 16

Joan

*W*HEN I CALLED UP FRANKIE AND TOLD HIM LOLA couldn't get out of the house, he blew up. He hollered so loud I had to hold the telephone away from my ear. "Either you want to be with me, or you want to keep dragging around with that lame-ass Lola Poole! This is the third time in three weeks that you've canceled plans with me because of her! And you can forget about me hooking up that silly bitch with one of my boys!"

"Frankie, I—" I didn't even get to finish my sentence. The only dude I had been hot for since sixth grade had just hung up on me! I was so shocked I held the phone in my hand and glared at it. Less than a minute later when I called Frankie right back, he didn't answer the cell phone that his grandmother had given to him for Christmas.

He was not the first boy I'd lost because of my loyalty to Lola. Last year Scotty Hopper dumped me because I'd canceled on him more than once so I could spend time with her. Now that she was an "orphan" she got even more depressed than usual and needed my shoulder to cry on.

A few weeks after Scotty had kicked me to the curb, Ron Elliot gave me the boot. All because I had canceled a date with him on the same night that Lola wanted me to spend some time with her. There were times when it felt like I'd made a promise to her that was as serious as the deathbed promise she'd made to her father! As much as I got on her case about letting Bertha Butt control her life, in a weird way, Lola was controlling mine.

I was so agitated because Frankie had hung up on me, I had to call up Lola and talk to her again. I decided it was time for me to practice some "tough love" with my girl. It had worked on Too Sweet, so I thought it'd probably work on Lola. For one thing, she was easier to manipulate than my cousin.

"You're still my home-girl and I love you to death, but I can't keep altering my plans for you. After tonight, don't expect me to miss out on a date because of you. Life is too short and too hard."

"You don't have any idea how much harder life is for me than it is for you."

"My life is no bed of roses, Lola. At least you have a bedroom to yourself and only one grown person breathing down your neck. My house is like a way station for displaced people, any day of the year. Cousin so and so sleeping on the living room couch, Aunt or Uncle so and so sleeping on a pallet in the kitchen, you name it. And if that's not bad enough, every time another one of my roaming relatives moves in for a few days or weeks or months, that means another grown person bossing me around. I know you miss your daddy, but I *rarely* get to see or talk to mine and he's still alive so we're pretty much in the same boat on that subject. Don't you dare try to make it sound like you're the only girl with problems."

"Some of us have more serious problems than other people. I wish I had *your* problems. There will always be a bunch of family members around for you if you need them, blood relatives at that. When Daddy died, I couldn't go to any of the few blood relatives I have left. If it hadn't been for Bertha, they'd have put me in a foster home or I would have ended up living on the street. You know the pimps are lying in wait for girls like me."

"So you keep telling me."

"So I'm going to keep on telling you."

"Please let's not even go there. You didn't end up in a foster home or on the street selling pussy for some pimp. All of that has nothing to do with what we're talking about now. I'm trying to tell you something."

"What are you trying to tell me then?"

"You know what I'm trying to tell you. Every single time you blow our plans it's on account of your stepmother. You'll never have any fun if you keep catering to that woman. And I'm not going to keep catering to you unless you start catering to me the way you used to."

"How many times do I have to remind you that 'that woman' helped raise me and she helped take care of my mother when she got sick *and* Daddy too when he got sick. I owe her."

"Wake up and get a grip on reality, Lola! You've paid your debt to Bertha a dozen times over if you ask me. Why did you ask me to hook you up with some dudes in the first place?"

"I've told you before, you know how to talk to boys better than I do. I really appreciate the way you look out for me. You have everything I want; healthy, loving parents, a bunch of brothers and sisters, and all kinds of other relatives. I wish you could understand why it's so important for me to be nice to Bertha. I need her. If I piss her off, or if she up and dies, where would that leave me? If I don't go to a foster home or the streets, do you think Libby or Marshall would be willing to take me in? Hell no! And, I would rather go to a foster home or the street than with them anyway. You think you have problems? Well, let me tell you something I never wanted to tell you." Lola paused. I couldn't decide if she was crying or just clearing her throat on her end. But something was going on with her.

I got tired of waiting for her to continue so I jumped in and asked, "Exactly what is it you never wanted to tell me?"

"Joan, I'd give anything in the world if I could trade places with you."

Lola's confession really touched me. I had to blink hard to hold back my tears. She had said similar things before but she, nor anybody else, had ever said anything as endearing to me as what she'd just said. "You would?" I croaked. It was hard to speak with the lump that had suddenly formed in my throat.

"Uh-huh. I hope you're not too mad at me about tonight. If you ever stop being my friend . . . well, just thinking about that is too painful. I don't even want to talk about it. You go on out with Frankie and don't worry about me. Take the bus to the movies. You can even borrow my bus pass."

Blinking didn't stop a tear from rolling down the side of my face. I had to sniff real hard to keep snot from oozing out of my nose and cough to clear my throat. After I'd taken a few deep breaths, I let out a sharp cackle. Then I said in the warmest voice I could manage, "Fuck Frankie. I'd rather come over and watch a couple of movies with you." I didn't have the nerve to tell Lola that Frankie had dumped me a few minutes ago. But because of what she'd just said, I decided I would continue to go out of my way to make life easier for a girl whose life was so miserable that she wanted to trade places with me.

Chapter 17

Lola

I WAS NOT SURPRISED WHEN JOAN TOLD ME SHE'D LOST her virginity to Walter Terrill in his bedroom last year the week before Christmas. The way she ran around with this and that boy, I was surprised it had not happened much sooner. She made me promise not to blab because a lot of people still thought she was Miss Goody Two-Shoes.

"Girl, we've been keeping secrets between us all our lives. You know you can tell me anything and I'll keep my mouth shut," I reminded her during one of our frequent telephone conversations.

"Good! And keep it that way!" Joan yelled. "Because I'm going to cook up a way for us to make some serious money so we can afford to buy stuff that'll help us attract the hottest boys. And my scheme will be a secret we'll have to take to our graves."

I had no idea that a few months later Joan would "cook up" a plan for us to join a lonely hearts club so we could scam a bunch of elderly men out of money by pretending to be her sexy older sister, Elaine. And I had no idea that years later she would drag me into an Internet dating fiasco (another secret to take to our graves . . .) that would change my life forever. In the meantime, I was more interested in losing my virginity first.

When she offered to introduce me to Michael Crockett; Walter's best friend, I jumped at the chance. I was seventeen now and tired of being one of the oldest virgins I knew. One thing I realized about boys was, a girl giving up her cherry to them didn't mean much. The day after I'd given mine up to Michael, he told everybody he knew that I was a lousy piece of tail. That was probably true but that didn't stop a lot of other boys from trying to get a piece of my tail.

I turned down a lot of dates, and not just because the boys only wanted to have sex with me. One of the main reasons was because Bertha had gotten even worse about me leaving her alone at night. About three weeks after my date with big mouth Michael, Stevie Watson invited me out one Friday night. He'd already had a clumsy experience with Bertha when he'd come to the house the first time a few days ago. This time he didn't come in. He blew the horn in his old Firebird and I ran out and jumped in.

Ten minutes after we had slid into a booth at Dino's Pizza Parlor, Bertha walked in with a glazed look on her face. I wanted to crawl under the table but she had already seen me and was walking in our direction. I was used to her doing or saying something peculiar, but this surprised me. I was so stunned, I couldn't move. My head felt like somebody had hit it with a sledgehammer.

"Ain't that your weird stepmother coming this way?" Stevie asked with an amused look on his sharp-featured face. "I wonder what she's doing here."

Bertha stopped in front of Stevie, but her eyes were on

me. "Lola, I called your cell telephone but you didn't answer," she whined, massaging her forehead. "I don't feel good. I was afraid I'd fall again and hit my head on something. What time will you be coming home?"

Instead of answering Bertha, I gave Stevie an apologetic look and asked, "Do you mind if we leave now?"

He gave me an incredulous look. "You want to leave before we get our pizza? What . . . why?" he protested.

"Let's get it to go. I really need to go home with my stepmother," I insisted.

No matter how calm Stevie sounded, I could tell from the way his jaw was twitching that he was angry. "Cool," he said, looking extremely exasperated. "I feel you. Uh, listen; our order should be ready in a couple of minutes. You get it and take it home. I'll catch you later." He and I rose and he quickly reached into his pocket and pulled out a few dollars and dropped them onto the table. "This'll cover the pizza and cab fare."

"Cab fare? Can't you give us a ride home?" I asked.

Stevie looked at Bertha again then back at me and shook his head. Then he looked at his watch. "I just remembered I told my uncle I'd help him move some stuff out of his garage." Just like that, another boy had dumped me in the same month. And this time it wasn't because I was a "lousy piece of tail" because Stevie and I had not had the chance to have sex. This time it was because of Bertha. When I saw him in school a few days later, he ignored me. A week later he had a new girlfriend.

I didn't go out with a boy again for two months. During that time, I was so bored I didn't know what to do. Joan was one of the most popular girls I knew so she went on a lot of dates. I had a hard time catching up with her outside of school. I had made a few new friends, but none of them were as much fun as Joan. The Walker twins, Lynette and Lynda, were so timid they didn't want to do anything fun, especially if it involved boys. Heather Strong was dating two boys at the same time so I could rarely catch up with her.

Not much had changed at home with Bertha and me. If anything; the situation had become even more bizarre. She constantly complained about her health, but she usually looked fine to me. It seemed like she felt down and out mainly on the nights I had dates. But when she really was sick, like now with shingles, she actually seemed happy about it. For one thing, when it was obvious that she had a health crisis, she didn't have to work too hard to get my sympathy and help.

"Oh my Lord. These shingles are going to have me out of commission for a long time. You might even have to take some time off from school!" she told me with a twinkle in her eye I couldn't ignore.

"I hope not. We're in the middle of our March finals. Maybe Libby can come over and look after you during the day," I said.

"She's got her hands full taking care of her needy, helpless husband. That man can't even boil water or fry an egg right! He'd starve to death if it wasn't for Libby."

Other than "taking care of" Jeffrey, Libby spent her time watching soap operas and game shows, shopping and visiting the casinos, hanging out with her friends, and getting her nails and hair done. Bertha was as aware of what her daughter was up to as I was, so I saw no reason to mention any of those things. It annoyed me when she defended and made excuses for her children. Whenever I said something against them, she always responded by saying something like, "My babies inherited their bad habits from their daddy so they can't help the way they are." How could I argue with a woman who believed some shit like that? I wondered how her "babies" would have turned out if she had not spoiled and catered to them so much. In addition to everything else I had to keep my wits about, I was making all kinds of mental notes that would help me develop a better life for myself once I got out on my own. One thing for sure, I was not going to spoil my children. And there was no way in the world I'd let a child of mine sass or disrespect me the way Libby and Marshall did Bertha. Had she raised her children the way I planned to raise mine, she would be a much happier person. That was one thing that I was sure of.

I arranged to take off at least two whole weeks of school that month so I could stay home and take care of Bertha because shingles was pretty serious. I recalled how Mama had suffered with it so I really felt sorry for Bertha. Especially since her case was way more severe than Mama's. She had an itchy red rash and blisters filled with pus from her face on down. Not only did a few neighbors and people from church come by to visit her and drop off chicken soup, Libby and Marshall came by every other day, but they didn't do much or stay long. They always made a beeline to the kitchen before they even looked in on Bertha propped up on the couch. After they raided the refrigerator and left a mess in the kitchen for me to clean up, they shuffled into the living room and complained about how nasty Bertha's gown was and how bad she looked. When Jeffrey came with them yesterday, he checked on Bertha immediately. "Lola, my aunt Eileen does home care nursing. I can arrange for her to come over and help out," he told me.

"Mama can't afford a home care nurse," Libby hollered, walking into the living room with a glass of wine in one hand and a Pop Tart in the other. "Lola ought to be glad to help. After all, had it not been for Mama, she would have ended up in a foster home."

Marshall's wife had recently kicked him out of the house and he had checked into a motel. He was so depressed and helpless when he came to visit I ended up tending to him too. I had to fix him highballs, prepare snacks for him, and help him do his laundry. I was glad when his wife let him come back home ten days after she'd kicked him out.

Two days after Marshall's last visit, Jeffrey came by after work that Friday around six p.m. As soon as he entered the house and saw the weary look on my face, he gave me a long hug. "Lola, you are too young to be tied down like this," he said, glancing over my shoulder to where Bertha lay on the couch snoring like a moose.

"I know, but what else can I do? I miss my friends at school and I'm getting bored being cooped up in this house," I said with a pout. "I haven't even been over to visit with Joan since last week. I only see her when she drops off my school assignments."

"Well, I'll tell you what. Why don't you call and see if Joan's at home now. If she is, invite her over," Jeffrey suggested. "We can have some Chinese take-out delivered and watch a couple of movies."

"What about Libby?" I asked with a tight look on my face.

"Libby's not my mother," Jeffrey snapped with a hot look on his face. The only time I ever saw him look anything but pleasant was when Libby was the subject. "She doesn't control me."

I used to wish I could marry a man like Daddy. Now I wished I could marry a man like Jeffrey.

I didn't want to use the telephone in the living room because I didn't want Bertha to wake up and hear my conversation. I called up Joan from the kitchen phone and invited her over. She didn't want to visit me. Instead, she insisted I come to her house. Since Jeffrey had offered to hang around for a couple more hours to spend time with Bertha, I jumped at the chance to take a break.

As much as I enjoyed spending time with Joan in her bedroom, my visit was going to be short. Five minutes after I plopped down on the side of her bed next to her, she started saying things to and about me that I didn't like.

"Lola, I hope you don't turn out to be a damn fool like your mama." Joan was not a mean girl. She was just the type who believed in saying whatever was on her mind; even if it was something unpleasant. Her harsh words sent shock waves all through my body.

"What's that supposed to mean?" I asked as I rubbed my chest and glared at her.

"You're as smart as I am so you should be able to find a husband who treats you better than your daddy treated your mama."

"Don't worry about me, Joan." I stopped rubbing my chest and sat up straighter. "You need to worry about yourself because you might end up worse off than my mama . . ."

"Pffft!" She rolled her eyes and waved her hand. "I don't think so. For one thing, I would beat the dog shit out of my husband if I found out he was cheating on me!"

"Why are we talking about *husbands* now in the first place? We're still teenagers and don't even have steady boyfriends."

"Well, we won't be teenagers too much longer. All I know is, we both deserve something better than both of our mothers settled for. I'm only going to get married one time. I would never marry three different men like Mama did."

"What if your husband dies? Then what?"

"That's different. That's the only reason I'd marry another man. I believe that once you get married, it should be for life—even if it's a bad marriage. I don't care how bad it is, it can be fixed."

I gave Joan a pensive look. "Those words might come back to haunt you some day," I warned.

"I doubt it."

"Anyway, I don't want to get married but once myself. I hope I meet a real cool dude when I'm around twenty-four or twenty-five. I don't want to get married too young. After I finish high school, I want to have fun for a few years before I settle down and start my family. And I'm telling you now; I am not going to marry an average man. I want a man who's got everything going for him: looks, a good job, a great body, and a real good personality. And, he has to be good in bed."

Joan looked amused for a few seconds and then a serious expression spread across her face. "As pretty and smart as you are, you shouldn't have any trouble finding a man like that." What she said next sent a chill up my spine. "But a dude with all that going for him could also be a serial killer." Her statement was so disturbing, I didn't even comment on it.

And it was the reason I left a few minutes later.

Jeffrey had put Bertha to bed by the time I got home and I didn't stay up much longer myself. I slept well that night and by the next morning, I had put Joan's ominous statement out of my mind. I wouldn't think about it again until sixteen years later when a serial killer entered my life and decided he wanted to kill me . . .